THE BOOK OF APEX:
VOLUME 2 OF APEX MAGAZINE

AN APEX PUBLICATIONS BOOK
LEXINGTON, KENTUCKY

Also Available:
The Book of Apex: Volume 1 of Apex Magazine
The Book of Apex: Volume 3 of Apex Magazine

THE BOOK OF APEX:
VOLUME 2 OF APEX MAGAZINE

EDITED BY
JASON SIZEMORE

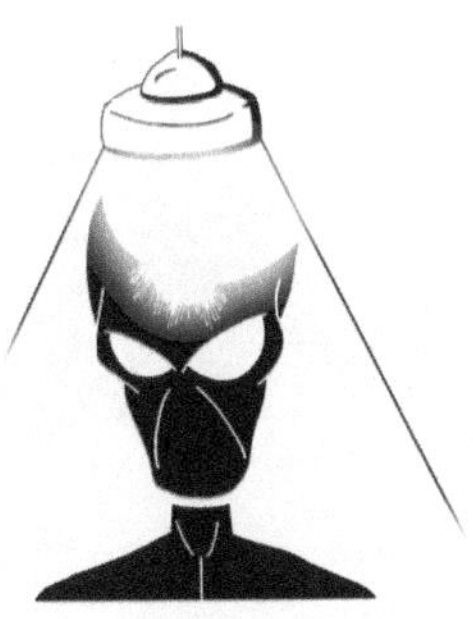

AN APEX PUBLICATIONS BOOK
LEXINGTON, KENTUCKY

The Book of Apex: Volume 2 of Apex Magazine

Cover design by Justin Stewart

Apex Publications, LLC
www.apexbookcompany.com

ISBN TPB: 978-0-9845535-7-0
Second Edition

For Glenn Lewis Gillette

TABLE OF CONTENTS

TABLE OF CONTENTS

SHE CALLED ME SWEETIE

Glenn Lewis Gillette

My throat clogging. My nose running. My eyes stinging with tears. I track down R in our game room. He's playing backgammon with O. He rolls his eyes, gaze panning up from the board to me. "What now?"

I want to cry, It's not fair! But I stick to the facts, the ones affecting the other boys in the room—The Rest, I call them. A few peek over at my sniveling. I wipe my nose with the back of my hand and stand straight to report: "Mrs. Ma'am says no more evenings with Mommy."

That gets them. Heads snap up or around from all the game boards. The clock over the mantel chimes twice for 7:30 p.m.—I should be sitting with Mommy! Laughing with Mommy! Reading to her!

R stands and towers over me. A couple sudden inches in the past months. Will that happen to me? Am I different enough to resist that?

"Tell us," he says.

The clock spits out more clicks, as I grab a breath.

"On, on—" Even more air. "On my way to Mommy's sitting room." Out of our wing of Gilchrist Manor into the Central Hall. Along the walkway at the top of the Grand Staircase. "Right by the Crimson Knight." Dumpy old suit of armor with a red crest on its helmet. "She stopped me. Mrs. Ma'am." Our teacher, 8 a.m. to 2 p.m. every day, when Mr. Sir took over in the gym. "She said…" I struggled to get the words right, though I can't do her voice like Y can. "Evening visits with Mommy have been cancelled for the time being. You will keep the afternoon schedule. Tell the others. Run along now." Run along now, like I was still five, like O2! I hated her for that, in that moment but, of course, that hadn't lasted as I returned to our part of the Manor. Mrs. Ma'am treats each of us too nicely to stay mad at her.

"Just like that?" R says.

I look up at him, and the words rocket up from my soul again. This time, I don't cut them off. I don't care what The Rest think, including R.

"It's not fair! When you come out of Mommy's chute, there's supposed to be just one of you, now and ever. Nobody else like you. Nobody!"

Only I hadn't come out of Mommy. None of us had. R knows that because I told him otherwise in the secrecy of the belfry, but none of The Rest realizes.

I know lots The Rest don't because I explore. The Rest don't seem to like that…except maybe A—I'll find out for sure next year when he turns eight, the age I started sneaking around and crawling through the heating ductwork and watching. I know our home like the back of my hand. Or R's. Or A's. Or G's, for that matter.

I've discovered that we get born in the clinic room over the tool room, next to the Manor's five-car garage. From hiding, I watched Y, C, and every one since, come down their chutes. Same day each year, August 6th. Only it's a different woman each time, and Mommy shows up when the baby's all clean and wrapped up. She smiles and cries and coos and gives the baby his name. From that start, she's treated us all the same—until G went to live with her this afternoon.

R gazes at me and smiles his patient smile, though something skitters in his eyes, excited, scared. "Let's go talk about this." Get me out of the room if I'm going to talk like that, but he needs to spill something too. He sets a hand on my shoulder, then turns to The Rest. With G gone, R is the oldest in our wing: in charge.

Eight other boys stare at him, identical faces, ages three to eleven. Three more, younger, sleep in the next room while we monitor with a radio.

R spreads a smile around, then shrugs. "I'll find out what's going on. Don't worry." He narrows his look, picking out G2 and L, each wearing sport coat and slacks, dress shirt and striped tie, and loafers. Just like me. "You were scheduled with Mommy this evening?"

They nod slowly.

"You know," R says, gently.

Tears bulge in their eyes. Just like me.

R looks back at O waiting at their backgammon board. "Later?" O nods.

R brushes past me, whispering, "Belfry," then marches out of the game room. I follow, avoiding all those gazes accusing me of ruining their lives.

Mommy calls me E. I came to the Manor third, a year after R, two years after G.

R heads toward the belfry above the Central Hall, expecting me to follow along, as if he'd found it and showed me, instead of the other way around. Overlapping planks, unpainted on this side, form the sides. No windows, though shutters on the outside pretend. It can be breezy up there, and at night, it's lit only by a battery-run light I snitched, but it's secret. Already sitting, R grins while I clamber to my perch, higher than his, under the slant of the roof's wooden underside.

"Me first," he says. "I'm glad you're back early so I can tell you sooner." He spots my teary glare. "Not why you're back early, dummy. We'll handle that after."

"Yeah," I grunt. My hour alone with Mommy, the focus of my week, every week, has been tossed away, rumpled and crushed, and he gets to go first as if a single year older makes him boss over me... which, of course, it does. Still, the poem I'd written for this evening—three stanzas with a refrain between, just like Mommy suggested—weeps in my pocket, unread.

Twice a week, I go visit Mommy. Just me. Just her. None of the others. Tuesday at 3 p.m. instead of fencing and Friday at 7:30 p.m. for dessert. Oh, the others get their times with her, I know, but it's not like when I'm there.

She calls me Sweetie. And she laughs with me and she listens to me. I recite. I read aloud from a fuzzy brown book she keeps in her sitting room.

And I read poems I make up. The others don't do that, I'm sure, because the first one surprised her. She'd had me read a poem, something about counting ways. I'd never seen words laid out that way, but she sat beside me and ran her fingers along, reading so softly that sometimes I couldn't hear... just to show me how. I caught on fast—she said so, and called me My only sweetie. So I wrote a few lines, like those, but different, and read them to her at my next visit. She smiled so large and hugged me so hard, so I kept writing poems and she kept smiling and hugging—until today when G went to live with her.

"—listening to me?" R declares.

I jerk so bad I have to clutch at a wall to keep from falling. Nails from a fake shutter scratch my hand. Hurts no more than I'm used to while exploring. "What?"

"The library," R says patiently." I finally realized that there's nothing there newer than twenty years ago. I didn't really notice it at first..."

Like he was boss of the library, when I was the one who'd shown it to him. Far end of Mommy's wing, back corner of the Manor, overlooking the formal garden, the overgrown experiment in micro-evolution, as R calls it. I came to it by heating plenum, long, dirty, dark, exciting—because I thought I'd crawled all the larger plenums and traced all the smaller ducts off the plenums by then, two years ago when I was ten—but Mrs. Ma'am had started me on geometry and drafting. Excited, I'd taken those tools and drawn the Manor from the inside-out as I knew it, hiding my drawings, not in my room, though it was supposed to be private, but in the belfry, because I knew it was private. And there, one early morning, I realized a gap in my exploring, a rectangle that no hall led to. But heating ducts go everywhere in a house—have to; it's a rule—and all I had to do was find where they'd thrown up a false wall. Whoever had hidden the library had been thorough, but I was more thorough. At the end of the hidden run, there it was, all those books. I could hardly wait to tell R.

We can all read. Mrs. Ma'am starts in early, lays down the basics, then guides the tutoring, six years' difference. I tutor L, for instance. Got me to read all the better for helping him pick it up. Works the same for other subjects: arithmetic, history, science, grammar, composition. About the only thing L and I have in common, though, those daily lessons. Not like A.

We do all study together for The Human Condition classes, reading Shakespeare's dramatizations of history as insights into people, alone and together. At least that's how Mrs. Ma'am puts it. On weekends, we act out his re-creations, playing all the parts, men and women, hags and children. Richard III, Romeo and Juliet, The Merchant of Venice. Love and hate. Service, ambition, and power. People stuff. We're people, too, Mrs. Ma'am says.

Only it's all the same books. Only those Mrs. Ma'am allows us. Lots of books actually, more than I ever got through. But there's stuff missing, R insists, ever since I showed him the belfry. The library had made us companions. The belfry made us friends. Still, I haven't shown him the hidden way to Mommy's bedroom… yet. I may never.

Mommy. Next Tuesday? Should I tell her then about how I found the library? Show her another way that I'm special? Probably ruin it for R, though. Adults stick together against the kids, that I know, but I don't care so much for R anymore—or G, for that matter—not since this afternoon.

"Listen to me!" R screams this time.

"I am!" I yell back because I wasn't really.

"What was I saying?"

I sag in defeat, and he starts again. R doesn't mind talking, which is one reason he likes the belfry, even when I'm not in it.

"I just didn't notice how old everything was," R says, "because with the fiction, it doesn't really matter—just having fiction, reading it, experiencing someone else's imagination! Well!" R stops, eyes glistening, breath coming fast. Then he glances with chagrin because he knows he's repeating himself. "Though I'm coming to see that Shakespeare might have used some fiction techniques in his re-creations." He watches for my reaction to that.

Who cares? I stare back, glum on the inside, probably the same on the outside.

R nods, shakes himself into sitting straighter, and announces, "Gregory Aloycious Penobscott."

"Huh? Who?"

"G," he says and holds up a finger. "R." A second finger, but pointed back at himself. "E." He jabs at me with that finger. Then he reels off the rest, spelling that name, counting off the letters. Then, grinning like a lopsided banana, he says, "Do you think Mommy intends to keep this up eleven more years?"

Again, I'm not sure what he means, but I suspect—suspect it means a flood of sameness that will overwhelm my chances for being different. "Keep what up?"

"Making more copies of him."

"Him?"

That slaps at his thinning patience, but he backtracks. "Someone— maybe Mommy—went through that library, removing every mention of its owner, its collector. Everything else but books gone, their front pages ripped out. No papers. No memos. Like someone wanted to erase him… or save every scrap of him in a special place somewhere else, I'm not sure which.

"When I finally realized this, just a week or so ago, I went through it with a fine-toothed comb."

"A what?"

"A metaphor. Comes from reading fiction," he brags. "I finally found something." He digs inside his shirt, into that secret pouch he's taken to wearing all the time.

He unfolds a letter and thrusts it at me. I look at the top, of course. "Dear Mr. Bryant." But R taps a finger toward the bottom. The printed signature reads "Gregory Aloycious Penobscott."

"That's us," R spouts. "We are him, each and every one of us. Mommy must've loved him very much."

"She loves us!"

"Not the same way. Man-woman thing. You'll understand soon." He squints suddenly, changes it into a frown, then sighs, though it sounds like, Ahh.

"What?" I'm dizzy from all his jumping to conclusions like they're stones in the stream behind the Manor, a stream that promises a way to the outside world through miles and miles of the forest that surrounds us.

"I figured it out."

"What?" My turn to declare.

"What's going on with G and Mommy—puberty."

Biology lessons had sneered at me while I struggled with them over the past year. We're engineers, all of us. Not doctors. Engineers! Doesn't Mrs. Ma'am realize that?

"You'll start puberty in three months. You'll get pubic hair in five. You'll grow—"

Burns me like an Indian rub on sunburn. "Will not!" I scream. "Just because we're clones does not mean—"

"Mommy doesn't call us clones. I do. At least, all the evidence, my books, your spying—"

"Recce," I correct him. Short for reconnaissance. I read outlaw books too, just not all of them, like he has, several times. Well, maybe just that series by Adam Hardy, but I know them by heart.

"I think Mrs. Ma'am is experimenting on us. Or maybe with us is more accurate. Using us as a means to deciding the old nature-versus-nurture question."

He's lost me, so I sputter and glance around for someplace else to sit, but there isn't any.

"Same genome. Same environment. So how could we be different from each other? 'Cause we are different, aren't we, E?"

I answer with another glare because he knows how important that is to me.

R sneers back, not happy about the G situation either, and nobody to take it out on but me. "You'll grow," he teases with the repetition, "three inches in the next year. Just like G did. Just like I did.

"Your penis—" he gestures in that direction "—does it ever get big and stiff?"

What a thing to ask! I shrug.

R persists. "Does it?"

I look away. "Sometimes."

"Well, it's called an erection, and it's going to do it more, a lot more even. Only you'll control it." He sniggers. "Or it'll control you."

My cheeks burn. I find the rafters of the belfry very interesting, anything till he quits talking about this.

"It's connected with what's going on here."

I snap back on that. "You knew this was going to happen?"

He puts out a hand. "Not exactly. It just makes sense. Mommy's a woman."

"She's Mommy!"

"But not our mommy. Not biologically. So it's okay."

I know the words he's using. I even understand the subject matter. But I just can't quite get it, what R means. I just can't make sense out of it, apply it to myself.

So I start to actually hate R, right then and there. Not sure why, but I do. Which is why I lie to him.

"Do you know the way to Mommy's room?" R asks.

"Sure," I crack. "We all do. Twice a week... before. "Before G went to live with her.

"No, not her sitting room, her bedroom."

That sickens me. R sickens me. The belfry sickens me. I hold it off long enough to tell him, "Mommy doesn't have a bedroom! I don't know where it is."

Then I fling myself at the ladder, ride its rails down, the rungs flashing by an inch away, and hit the bottom too hard—but I like that. I stagger away, limping.

R calls after me. The ladder rattles with his steps. I swerve toward the nearest vent for the return-air plenum. Flick and flick and it opens. I bend, thrust, then wriggle, escaping where he can no longer go because he's gotten too big. Him and his stiff penis.

I drop into a cul-de-sac on the third floor, out of sight of anybody who might be wandering Mommy's wing of the Manor. Three ways into Mommy's bedroom. A door from her sitting room, hidden behind a bookcase. A servant's access up a tightly wound staircase. A nondescript, locked door in the big hall, twenty paces past the archway into her sitting room. I pull out a key to that door, a key I copied from the housekeeper's master ring that always hangs in the pantry downstairs at night. That tool room next to the garage makes life so much easier.

No sneaking around. I trot to the door, but unlock it quietly and slip into…

Mommy's room spreads out before me. Frills and lace. Thick carpet and blond wood. Mommy and G.

Mommy… I've never seen her like this. So… I think the word is demure. She sits in a frilly robe at the foot of her four-poster bed, her ankles crossed, her knees clasped and positioned to one side, her hands clasped to her chest, and her full, smiling attention on G.

He poses in the middle of the room with his back to me, also in a robe, only thick and dark green and tied tightly around him. One hand holds the fuzzy brown book—the one I read from! Only I read to Mommy from that book. The other hand weaves through the air in time to his words.

So he can read poetry. Did Mommy teach him too? Aww, Mommy!

But can he write poetry? Can he create as Romeo did beneath that balcony?

"Smiles, tears, of all my life—and, if God choose," he says. "I shall but love thee better after death."

Mommy claps, a light patting of her fingers. "Nice," she says huskily, as she stands. With a shrug, her robe falls open, then off. She stands naked! Gorgeous! Ugly! I'm not sure which. She sets her feet apart, her legs braced as they come together in an odd patch of dark… hair? Her gaze wanders over his head, shoulders, chest, then lower… and lower. "You're ready again? Wonderful! So like my Gregory, only more so."

She lays her hands on her hips and spreads her fingers over them and tucks her elbows back. Her—breasts, bulbous and pouting, point straight at G. "Come to me," she says, "my sweet G. "

G flings open his robe and darts forward. His robe crumples to the floor. He grabs her. She catches him. They tumble onto the bed. Her legs bounce up, then wrap around him. And he—he starts pumping his hips, pumping against her.

Then I know! He's pumping his stiff penis into her again and again. And she likes it!

I should run away, but no, spiky curiosity whips that impulse away. Mommy moans and G picks up his pace. Embarrassment pricks me: be gone! But I have something to show Mommy, something that will stop all this, put things back until I can win her for me alone. I have something, but what?

The poem, yearning in my pocket. I scrabble after it, then rip its pliant stiffness loose. Thrusting it forward, I step toward the bed.

Unheeding, engrossed, G slows his pumping and bends his head down from Mommy's neck to suck on something. She opens her eyes wide and rocks her head and—notices me. She smiles while G works.

"Which one are you?" she says absently.

"E."

She lifts a hand in slow greeting, then flips it over and waves me away. "You'll get your turn," she exults, then closes her eyes again as she runs a fingernail up G's rippling back, leaving a welt.

The floor wobbles. The door jam brushes my shoulder.

Unsteady—me? Or the world around me? I edge back, slip out to the hallway, and—I give way to my fear and horror and sadness and hatred and—and I run. Along the hall, down the servant's stair.

A stiff penis he has and I don't—yet. Why couldn't she have waited? I am the same boy as G was. I will be the same man as he is now. If she'd just waited for me, her only sweetie, she'd've gotten the same thing—and more: she would've had me, the only E, the only me.

But no, she hasn't waited. And when G uses up his stiff penis— how long can it last—there will be R. His penis can get stiff already when he wants it to. Not like me. I can't—yet. Then, following me, The Rest, year after year—G, O, R, Y, and so on—The Rest will get their stiff penises, and Mommy will get them.

The Rest crowd in on me, crushing me like a wave of maggots. I hate them all!

A step wiggles under my foot, tripping me. I crash into a wall. Crying, gasping, nose clogging and running, I stare around, kitchen through one door, summer room through another, more steps going down.

Where to go? I can't forget what I've seen, G pumping, Mommy moaning. There is only one way to forget that—stop it from happening again. I race down those steps, then wind through the basement to her wing's furnace. We're all good at engineering; we breeze through Mr. Sir's workshops, machines, electricity, fuels. All the Manor's furnaces burn natural gas, electronic ignition, no pilot lights. A few whacks with a hammer will bypass their safeguards and make an explosion inevitable. And I know where to get that hammer.

Make us all the same again? All the same?

No!

I head toward our wing. The Rest huddle there, including R by now, many sleeping, the rest playing those silly games of ours. They have no idea what Mommy and G are doing. Well, maybe R does, but he can't guess what I'm up to. He doesn't explore; he doesn't know the basement; and furnaces exist only in Mr. Sir's textbooks. Along the way, I pick up a monkey wrench left behind by the regular maintenance crew. Oh, they never see us, but I watch them, learn from them. Too bad A will never get that chance.

What did Richard III say? Shall I be plain? I wish the bastards dead. And he made it happen. I can, too.

Staring at our furnace, I think about ignition. Wait on a thermostat to spark the explosion? Chance it'll come before I can rescue Mommy? No. I reach for those wires, going to rip them out, but hold off. I like electricity, pure, primitive, powerful. I just need to control its flow, delay that ignition till I'm done with my doing. On a shelf, a discarded doorbell push and extra 18-gauge wire give that to me. I add them to the thermostat circuit. Now for a timer. I fill a bucket with water, set it on a lever over a fulcrum, and tape the doorbell to the other end. Add a brick to give it weight, then punch a small hole in the bucket. In time, the brick will lie on the doorbell, heavier and heavier, until—

Grinning, I scoot back through the basement, pausing only to whack those furnaces with the monkey wrench and let loose their gases too, then climb that narrow stairway. I let up then to catch my breath, looking forward to leading Mommy down to the garage so she can drive us away. She holds my hand and flinches only slightly as the Manor erupts behind us. She says, At least I've got you, sweetie, and that's all I need.

But I can hardly wake her, sprawled in her bed, sheet tugged over her chest. G snores on the other side, hard asleep and covering any sounds I make, going through Mommy's closet for traveling clothes. Enough to handle the summer night's chill. I'll get by, dressed as I am, though I lost my tie somewhere down below. I'm sure we can buy more clothes and anything else we need.

"Mommy!" I call again quietly, this time right into her ear. No answer. So I put a thumb to her left eyeball and press hard once. "Mommy!"

She lurches awake. Her eyes bobble, then track me down. "You again. "Not happy to see me.

"Come away with me." A romantic phrase. I pray it works.

Mommy frowns, then glances over to check on G. He doesn't stir.

I'll never sleep that solidly again, now that I know why not. She turns the frown on me.

Desperate, I quote, "But soft! What light through yonder window breaks? It is the East, and Juliet is the sun!"

Now she smiles. I've won her! But she doesn't get out of bed. Instead, she says, "Silly E. You're not ready yet." She lifts that same hand, waves it with the same dismissal! "You'll get your chance, believe me." She leers right at me. "I look forward to it." And she rolls over, bare back a pale wall of rejection.

A bed post wavers. The drape above her flaps. I tip over but catch myself with a hand on the sheet where she'd lain. Her damp sheet. Damp with what? I jerk away, overcorrect, and stagger back, hitting the open closet door. Her clothes hang there. Her words come back to me: "At least I've got you, sweetie. "No, not her words, mine. My pretend words, my hopeful words, when this woman was still Mommy and I was still her sweetie.

Who needs her anyway?

Not me. Not E. The last clone left walking. Just me and the stream, leading me to the outside world, through a forest blurred with night.

As R said, same genome, same environment, how can we be different? Geometry talks about intersections where two lines cross. Genome crosses environment. Otherwise identical lines make unique intersections each time. Perhaps it depends on how well the particular genome listens to the environment. I, for instance, learned specific things from Mommy, poetry for one, obsession for another. Neither worked out. In the end, it's just me and the universe, one on one. No matter how many other times Mommy, Mrs. Ma'am, and Mr. Sir tried, I'm the one who counts.

An explosion slashes through the dark, floods the forest with tangerine light, then another catches up, then one more. In a moment, it drains away, leaving me alone—at last.

What should I call myself? Richard? Ah, yes, Richard, Richard Gregory.

Remember that name—you'll see it again.

...That Has Such People in It

Jennifer Pelland

When you voluntarily walked underground, you had no idea how long you'd be there.

People said you were crazy for doing it, but you'd been called crazy, and worse, for years.

Besides, the government said they were doing it for a good reason. When the aliens intercepted our Voyager 1 probe and told us they were on their way to Earth to evaluate us for membership in their confederation, the planet collectively decided to put its best foot forward. If the aliens knew just how many humans were poor, or homeless, or uneducated, or just flat-out broken, Earth's membership application might be denied.

And that meant sweeping people like you under the rug, at least for a little while.

So you got in the very short voluntary line to drive out to live in a massive warren of old underground bunkers left over from Cold War days. It had to beat living on the street, begging for change and leftovers, and scrounging cigarette butts from the trash to get whatever nicotine buzz was left in them. All the voices in your head were in agreement—they wanted a bed, and three square meals a day, and a roof over that head of yours that they lived in.

It wasn't bad underground. Sure, you didn't get to see the sun, and they wouldn't bring you any alcohol or cigarettes, but it was clean, and dry, and warm, and your clothes weren't stiff and itchy. And a doctor brought you pills every day that made the voices in your head quiet down enough that your voice was now always the one in charge.

The rest of the planet commended you for your sacrifice. Told you the aliens were sure to share all sorts of marvelous technology with us, and that you'd get to see it soon enough. That Earth would finally eliminate poverty, disease, pollution, illiteracy, and all sorts of ills, so long as you stayed down there and didn't queer the deal.

You carved out a little corner for yourself, near one of the Plexiglas-covered televisions, and invited two aging hookers and a toothless junkie to share it with you. It was more of a home and a family than you'd ever had. It was almost nice.

And then the people who didn't come willingly joined you underground.

Then it wasn't so nice anymore.

The new people rioted from the moment they were forced off of the busses. They mobbed the food delivery trucks, taking their share and yours, and threw it at the cameras, the televisions, the doors, the trucks, each other. They ran through the bunkers, tearing up mattresses and screaming that they'd burn the place down if they could only start a fire.

You scraped as much food from the walls as you could and ran to your little corner to ride it out. But you found a group of people in it, praying to a god that they claimed had deserted them, and you screamed at them to leave. They only prayed louder, and you ran, looking for some new place to hide.

No more food trucks came that day. Or the next.

On the televisions, bland faces lectured people to remain calm, told you that they really wanted to feed you, but it was too dangerous to send anyone in when you were all acting so badly. You were exhorted to stop fighting the inevitable, told you were only hurting yourselves and your fellow shut-ins.

Without your pills, the voices in your head got louder, and you and all those voices begged everyone to please just calm down, please just let things go back to how they were, please let the food and medicine come back. As the hours passed, you weren't the only one begging.

As the days passed, the begging got louder than the rioting.

Soon, the begging won out.

On the fourth day, the food trucks came back, bringing the doctors with them. The televisions told you to form orderly lines and behave like civilized people or they would go away again.

It worked. Four days without food had broken them. Apparently, few of them had the experience with hunger that you had. You queued up, took your daily ration of food and pills, and were deliriously happy to have both.

You reclaimed your little corner from the Jesus freaks, who believed the aliens were the anti-Christ and bemoaned the fact that they'd missed the rapture, and you waited.

You all waited.

And whenever anyone got impatient with the wait, the food went away again.

It was a perfect system for keeping you quiet.

No children waited with you, though. They'd all been left aboveground. And every baby born down here was taken away the moment it was born. It was for the best, you were told. Children needed sunlight, and schools, and families who were doing well for themselves. If you were only better about using the free condoms, you wouldn't have to worry about giving up your babies, so really, you had no one to blame but yourselves. They promised to reunite families when everyone was aboveground, provided, of course, that it wouldn't be too traumatic for the children. You listened to the wails of a new mother lamenting the loss of her baby and wondered why they didn't worry about how traumatic it was for you.

Every so often, you'd get news about how well the aliens' visits were going, along with vague news on the television screens of the incredible changes going on aboveground. And sometimes, you'd even get to see some of this miraculous new technology with your own eyes, like the day that doctor held a device up to your head that took the voices away. You were so grateful, until night came, and you realized that you were lonely without them. And there was the night that the blue glow spread throughout the bunker that restored everyone's health. Your limp was gone, the junkie's teeth grew back, and the prostitutes no longer looked twenty years older than they actually were. And as best as everyone could tell, the process sterilized everyone at the same time, because there were no more new pregnancies after that night.

And after that night, no one came down to visit from aboveground again. The food trucks were replaced by delivery machines that drove themselves. Mechanical doctors tended to you on the few occasions where anyone needed tending anymore. Little robots started carting away the trash and fixing the plumbing. You were completely cut off.

Any day now, they kept telling you. They just needed to keep you out of sight a little longer. You understood, didn't you?

You didn't understand, so you began to ask questions of the faces on the televisions. Sometimes, they even answered.

When you asked how bunkers could possibly hide you from species clever enough to travel across the stars, they pointed out just how deep below ground you were. When you asked how they'd managed to hide all the starving people in Africa, they said the aliens were only bothered by starvation in wealthy nations. When you asked what the aliens thought about all the petty wars that had been raging at the time they arrived, they said the aliens valued differences of opinion. When you asked what they were waiting for before bringing you up to join them, they said they were just erring on the side of caution.

Above your heads, humanity luxuriated in their shiny new world without being troubled by the sight of those like you.

Only those like you weren't exactly "like you" anymore.

They'd made you all healthy, all sane. They'd taken care of the mental and physical shortcomings that had slowed so many of you down. They'd fed you well. They'd even expanded your lifespan. You couldn't remember the last time someone had died down here.

You were placid on the outside. You had to be if you wanted to be fed. Even a simple fistfight between two people resulted in days without food for everyone and bland reassurances from the televisions that this was being done for your own safety. But on the inside, you roiled. You all roiled. And you were careful not to let it show. You were acutely aware of just how easy it would be for the people aboveground to stop sending food trucks down and let you rot down here. You would not give them that satisfaction.

It took nearly fifteen years, but surprisingly, they really did letting you all out. They said they'd been waiting until they had places in their new society for you. Nobody believed them. You very nearly didn't come out at all, afraid this would be some sort of trap, but the prostitutes dragged you out, and you blinked in the sunlight, wondering if your eyes would ever adjust.

The hoverbusses took you to cities you couldn't begin to recognize. New Ion. Friendship Pass. Osmium City. You stared at the gleaming towers, wandering streets that were perfectly clean and ordered, straining to find a glimmer of humanity in the form of a piece of garbage or an unpleasant smell.

There was none.

They gave you an apartment, stocked with clothes and food and furniture. They gave you a case worker, who signed you up for classes to orient you to this miraculous future. She had the same bland smile as the faces on the televisions underground had. She had the same bland smile that everyone aboveground seemed to have.

You didn't understand why everyone was so happy.

Earth was perfect now, they told you. We had clean, renewable fuels. We had enough food for everyone. All diseases and deformities could be cured. We had a real space program, with colonies on the Moon, Mars, and Ganymede. Everyone who wanted a job could have one, and anyone who didn't want one didn't need one. There were no more wars. We had flying cars, for Pete's sake! What was there to be unhappy about?

There was everything to be unhappy about. You missed the rough edges. You missed the stench, the disease, you even missed the hunger. How were you supposed to know you were alive unless you had to struggle for it? You tried throwing trash around the apartment, but little robots cleaned it up. You took a shit in the corner and pissed all over the walls, but the apartment absorbed it, odors and all. You tried to find a dark alley to skulk in somewhere, but there were none. You even took a flying car out of the city and tried sleeping in the cold woods for a night, but you woke up to find that a heated tent had been erected around you in your sleep.

You weren't even free to get hypothermia in this new world.

You weren't free, period.

Only no one but you seemed to care.

Scratch that—only those of you who'd been underground cared.

And the people aboveground knew this. They had to. Why else would they work so hard to keep the undergrounders apart? They made it easy for you to contact anyone but them, and when you complained, they'd tell you'd never successfully integrate into this new society if you spent too much time socializing with your friends from the bunkers. But whenever you managed a chance encounter with one of your old co-captives, you noticed that none of them were smiling, either.

Your case worker said this was a golden age. That humanity had been saved from its baser instincts. That everyone on the planet would be taken care of. That you, of all people, deserved to revel in the luxury this new world provided. She booked you spa treatments and massages, set up appointments with the brightest experts so you could learn how this new world worked, arranged invitations to extravagant dinner parties with stars from both before your captivity and after. You ignored all of them, except for one—the party where one of your new alien "friends" would be present.

Maybe they'd give you some answers.

You cornered the creature as soon as it arrived. It was hard to look at—the light seemed to bend around it in ways that made your eyes hurt—but its voice was crystal clear. You asked it what the hell its plans for Earth were, why it was making humans so damned complacent, and how it hadn't realized how many of you had been locked away for so long just to make things look prettier.

"Not all tests are obvious," it said. "And as such, it's not always obvious when one has failed. Everything comes with a price. You have already paid yours. They shall soon pay theirs."

You stood there, stunned, as it slid away.

And then you smiled.

The very next day, you booked a massage. You bought a fancy outfit and went to see what this atmospheric ballet craze was all about. And you started taking those orientation classes your case worker had set up for you. At one, you saw one of your old prostitute friends, and you and she shared a secret smile.

So, you weren't the only one who knew.

Your case worker was thrilled with your progress. She asked what had changed your mind, and you shrugged and smiled and said nothing. The alien's message hadn't been for her, it had been for you and the others like you.

Those classes had never been more important.

Because if this was all going to be yours soon, then you'd better know how it all worked.

Pimp My Airship

Maurice Broaddus

Who Stole the Soul?

"Citizens of the Universe, do not attempt to adjust your electro-transmitter, there is nothing wrong. We have taken control to bring you this special bulletin."

"Aw, hell nah." Hubert "Sleepy" Nixon paused mid-keystroke on the pianoforte. A system of pipes ran from the back of the instrument to the ceiling, steam billowing in mild tufts from the joints. The low, arrhythmic notes slowly faded into a dull echo as he turned to the gleaming carapace of the electro-transmitter with a countenance of mild exasperation.

A phlegmatic gentleman by nature, some mistook Sleepy's somnambulant demeanor for muddle-mindedness. Given nuanced consideration, this was rather true after a fashion. Sleepy reached for his pipe, tamped the side to even the spread of chiba leaves, lit them and inhaled. Holding the smoke in his lungs for the span of three heartbeats, he exhaled a thick cloud of noxious vapor. Only then was he prepared to amble his considerable girth toward the faded tapestry that concealed the descending spiral stairway. Wide-shouldered and bulbous framed as he was, each step creaked under his weight as he slowly made his way into the subterranean hollow. The basement smelled of a privy pit.

"That's right, today's mathematics is knowledge. Let me break it down for you: know the ledge." A glass-fronted cabinet contained a rotating cylinder that gyrated up and down. A series of antennae lined the top of the device, electricity arcing between them, the charges climbing the spires like tendrils of ivy. Pipes splayed like pleats of a fan, groaned and gurgled as the home kine burned. In the undercity, Fortune—as much as the government allowed—favored a neighborhood possessing a single kine or two, much less a home laying claim to its own. The voice emanated from the darkened corner of the chamber and belonged to the spindly-framed gentleman behind the strange apparatus. Barely seated on the many-times-patched ottoman, was (120 Degrees of) Knowledge Allah.

Knowledge Allah's strong handsome face was eroded by despair. His distant eyes had stared into the abyss of anger and hate for too long. A gold band pulled back his thick braids giving them the appearance of interlocked fingers. His thick cravat was tucked into his vest. The difficulty of Knowledge Allah was that one had to decipher the code of his thought language before he began to make any sense. Such a task rarely proved simple while under the effects of the chiba.

"You don't know who you are," Knowledge Allah's self-secure voice rang with steel. "Take on your true name. Arm. Leg. Leg. Arm. Head. You are the original man. You are gods. Yet you sit there, blind, deaf, and dumb to your potential.

"Few realize who they are and those that do—and seek to wake the people from their neglected truth—are incarcerated by this grafted government. The Star Child, leader of the F8, is due to be executed in a few days, but none of you could be bothered. The time for revolution is at hand, brothers and sisters. The time is at hand. We only await a sign.

"I exist between time outside time. In the between places. I am the voice of truth in these troubled times."

The clockwork gears ground to a gentle halt as the spindles of the machine wound down. The electric arcs sputtered and the entire apparatus darkened. Knowledge Allah stooped from behind the glass cabinet, daubing his sweaty brow with a handkerchief, a smirk of zealotry on his face.

"What the fuck man?" Sleepy asked, his insistent steps catching up to him as he found himself winded. He eased himself into the nearest chair. Knowledge Allah poured him some brandy from a nearby decanter before pouring a glass of water for himself.

"Are the mysteries I strive to illuminate too deep for you, my brother?" Knowledge Allah clinked Sleepy's glass with his own then downed his water. He often regaled Sleepy with the idea of forming a band, being the front man to the capacious Sleepy's music with the hopes of using their act to spread his message. Like many of their ideas, it collected dust due to inaction.

"The only mystery is my need to get high." Sleepy ran his pick through his blond-streaked Afro, his beard barely tamed by a comb.

His nose was too flat and too broad for his face, as if he'd been punched with an iron. His teeth, likewise, were too small for his mouth. Against skin like burnished onyx, a silver stud protruded from his chin. He puffed out another cloud. "Mystery solved."

"They set snares that have been prepared for you. Snares meant to lead you from your path of righteousness. You've let them cave you."

"They who?" Sleepy asked, forgetting his oft-repeated lesson of not asking Knowledge Allah questions. The answers were rarely of any use. However, Sleepy couldn't help but think there was an undercurrent of derision to Knowledge Allah's tones, as if the other man stared down the thin beak of a nose at him.

"Your so-called grafted government's behind it," Knowledge Allah continued. "The next phase is to destroy us. You think it stopped with Tuskegee?" The Tuskegee Institute. One of the few schools allowed in the undercities. The name sent a chill along the spine at the memory of the experiments done in the name of science. "No, they just got slicker. We don't have poppy fields. We don't have dirigibles. We do have wills sapped by opiate clouds."

"Sounds like we don't have shit," Sleepy said. "Speaking of, I thought we agreed on no more broadcasts until we got our act together?"

"The truth cannot go unvoiced."

"Shit." Sleepy pronounced the word as if it possessed three syllables. "You one of them long-winded niggas who just like to hear themselves talk."

"Look at how quickly you let their hate speech drip from your own lips, betraying your own. Don't get caught up in the game of the 85. We need to—"

"Blah, blah, blah, nigga. Blah. I hear you talking. What I don't hear is a plan. You got all this 'righteous knowledge' ...what we going to do?"

"I'm going to free the Star Child." Knowledge Allah stood up for maximum dramatic effect. "You driving?"

Sleepy remained seated, as the implications of the words reverberated in his mind; their import required a few moments to digest. Knowledge Allah beamed, obviously quite pleased with himself, and wrapped his great coat around him and nodded topside. Sleepy fastened a cape around his long, blue eight-button coat, the image of a flabby martinet.

Smoke stacks belched poisonous clouds. The oppressive sky, grey as prison issue uniforms, cloaked their furtive entry onto the streets. The air, redolent with a ferrous rock, was heavy with the stink of coal and sweat. He had bathed for an hour and a half to scrub off any trace of soot from him. Even the poor clung to their dignity. In the shadows of the steam trams of the overcity, a Hansom whisked by, held aloft by rusty trellises. Neither man dreamed of catching a cab in Atlantis, especially at night. A police trawler slowed as it neared them. Other denizens scurried away like rats caught in the light, quick to return to the burrow openings they called home. The pair held their ground, hard eyes unblinking at the passing vehicle. Sleepy spat a black-tinged wad of phlegm. Once out of eye line, Sleepy opened his garage door.

The metal gleamed even in the wan moonlight, polished to a glassy sheen every day. Twin brass tubes formed the body of the car, curving down on both ends stitched together by copper rivets. Headlamps, jutting cans, burned to life. The suspension bounced and lurched in a frenzy of steam belches, jolting them up and down. The bemused pair enjoyed the weight of stares from their neighbors. The 24"rims, whirring fans, continuously shuttered like deployed armor. With a roar, the car took off, spumes of steam left in its wake.

"Fear of a Black Planet"

The slow and winding White River neatly carved the undercity in half as the Victorian architecture of the overcity known as Indianapolis gave way to the more dilapidated homes in the undercity the natives dubbed Atlantis. Billboards of smiling brown faces endorsing opiate use sat next to adverts of money changers offering promises of quick loans. Both preyed on desperation and ignorance. America shone as the most prosperous colony in service to the Albion Empire. With its plantation farms and free labor force, America was the dirty sweatshop engine that propelled the Empire. Even the upper crust of the American social strata were held in tacit contempt by the Albion proper, unwilling to acknowledge how they kept their hands clean. The force of her colonialist spirit had long ago reduced the issue of slavery to a low simmer and the much talked about threat of an American Civil War never came to pass. With the rise of the automata, however, the economics of the unseemly endeavor proved too deleterious and the slaves were released.

Those of an African bloodline, no matter how much or little ran in their veins, were relegated to a state of vague emancipation. Not living in the massive, industrial overcities, but dismissed to ghettos—pacified by legalized, free-flowing drugs—a terra incognita somehow lost between the cartographer's calipers. Or they were imprisoned.

Viceroy George II, who pandered without shame to the interests of the Empire, currently governed the land. Though high born and privileged, he was no nobleman, but rather a spoiled bloodline of nine generations of insular breeding.

The buildings crumbled into screes of pebbles along rotted sidewalks under an air of imminent decay. Gas lamps produced forlorn shadows from the steeped darkness. Old men huddled in puddles of light, drinking brandy and smoking cigars blunted with opium by wan moonlight. Their garrulous conversation of the most impolitic kind filled the night with the bluster of oafs. A twinge of jealousy at not being able to join in fluttered in Sleepy's chest.

Knowledge Allah directed him to a two-story brick, Queen Anne home guarded by a wrought-iron fence. The house stood out from the rest of the neighborhood's squalor as if someone had staked a claim to retake this spot. Drab green with fine terra-cotta ornaments and lacy spindles, its conical-roofed turret had fish scale slate shingles. Stained glass sat atop curtained bay windows.

"Whose place is this?" Sleepy asked.

"An inventor's."

"He down with The Cause?"

"Do you even know what cause you serve?"

"I was just asking."

"You assume a lot. The Cause is more than attitude, affect, and wardrobe. You need to be open to the mysteries life offers," Knowledge Allah said.

"Like what?"

"Like the inventor."

Knowledge Allah rapped on the large obsidian knocker. The door swung open. A poor simulacrum of a person greeted them with the smooth manner of a well-rehearsed marionette. Its inner workings whirred—pistoning brass and steel gears—over the gentle hum of whatever powered it. Its face—dull, unpainted metal—held no expression and little attempt at humanity. Wondrous and intricate, a flawless design, it projected a knowing discomfort of the other. Sleepy suddenly grew terrified of the mind of its designer. With a mime's gesticulations, it offered to take their hat and coats and escorted them. Twin lanterns burned in empty spaces as optical receptors, a mechanical stare masking its inner workings. Its disjointed consciousness lacked imagination, the ability to create story, the power to question its being or its place in the greater scheme of things. It moved without the gift of ancestors and the weight of history, at best it held the illusion of electric dreaming against the cold void of blackness.

Sleepy envied its uncomplicated existence.

The double door entry opened into the foyer of the opulent home. An elegant curved staircase separated the living and dining rooms on the right from the library on the left. Walls, alight with whale-oil-filled lamps created an erudite glow within. A lone settee perched alongside a fireplace on the opposite side of the room. A deck of cards sat on a piece of silk atop a table. Sleepy cut the deck at random and saw a card inscribed with the number XVI over the picture of a tower struck by lightning. The building's top section had dislodged from the rest of it; two men were falling from the crumbling edifice. Filled with sudden disquiet, Sleepy set the deck down.

The automaton paused, like a bellboy awaiting a gratuity.

"One nation under a groove," Knowledge Allah said.

A bank of books parted to reveal a maw of shadows. The automaton withdrew, closing the library door behind it. The civilized façade of the pews of books gave way to the vaulted chamber of the laboratory. Rows of work-benches lined with test tubes, flasks, and beakers gurgling over Bunsen burners. Though a langorous whir of fans vented the air, the room roiled with the cloying smell of steam and coal, hot metal and ozone. A skirling of flutes emanated from a boiler, groaned under the strain of power and settling. A lithe figure bent over a metal frame of eight jutting arms spinning from a central mass, a mechanical arachnid contraption. Sleepy expected rolled up sleeves, moleskin trousers, and a grimy leather apron.

Instead, beneath a cap, goggled and draped in a lab coat, the figure welded a few more joints, testing the articulation as the work progressed, lit to a haunting blue hue behind the jet of the torch.

Once the goggles had been raised, the inventor took a step backward and nodded. Sleepy realized he regarded a woman. A green velvet jacket beneath the lab coat, with no décolletage or hint of femininity; the inventor held the bearing of a strict governess. She admired her handiwork and snugged her gloves. Her face retained an aqua tint in the dim electric glow. Wrinkles filigreed the corners of her eyes, belying the youthfulness of her face. A product of miscegenation, she radiated the afterglow of light-skinned privilege, despite her secretive life ferreted away in her laboratory. Upon noticing them, she stepped to Knowledge Allah and the two clasped hands.

"You're a lady of odd enthusiasms, "Sleepy proclaimed. He managed to hold his affable leer awaiting an introduction.

"I don't have time for social niceties." She ignored his proffered hand.

"Cooking stuff up in the lab," Knowledge Allah said.

"Just like 'Yacuub,' good sir."

Unabashedly vital, her high cheekbones framed an Aquiline nose against her sallow complexion, tea with too much milk; just light enough to be on the fringe of polite society. With a rigidity of face and a hardness in her hazel eyes, she possessed a noblewoman's airs. She probably had an A-level education, which meant her parents had money or connections. The mirth of aristocracy barely masked an anarchist streak.Her terrible impertinence of dressing like a man covered a repressed gaity to her Victorian effect. She polished her spectacles in a handkerchief.

"Bout time we got some ladies representing," Sleepy said.

"He rises in my estimation. Deaconess Blues." She shook his hand.

"It's nice to see not all of us had to struggle."

"Do not talk to me about struggle while you thoughtlessly squander what money you manage to scrimp together on instruments and automobiles worth more than your hovel." Her wan smile soured to a grim line. "My mother had been a governess, a high rank for Negroes, though she tried to program me with how it was unbecoming for a lady to fill her head with designs and equations. Though no mother would phrase it as such, she wanted me to be vapid and colorless. I had other ideas."

Though now he whiled away his days as a coal shoveler rather than as an artist or poet, Sleepy never fancied himself an anarchist by any stretch. Not like her who decided that she, if not the rest of society, was past the male supremacy's notions of womanhood. Her body and mind were hers to do with as she would.

Sleepy pulled a hair from his chin, closing his eyes at the fresh sting of pain; a nervous habit, anxious to remind himself that he could still feel. He didn't know who he was; a man out of place, a crowd of one. Jamaican born, but England-educated—through C-levels, the bare minimum for a citizen, appropriate to his station—and America employed; a one man Triangle trade. His father was a man of dreams and ideas. And causes. Sleepy joined the struggle in his youth and paved the way for the F8 through civil disobedience. "Life ought to be lived outside of yourself," he often preached. But Sleepy's passion for music provided release from his miserable existence, imbued with anger and vitality of the dwellers of the undercity; not the staid tones enjoyed by the ranks of nobles. Sleepy tapped percussive melodies lost in the rhythms of his thoughts.

"Am I boring you?" Deaconess Blues asked.

"Nah, I'm just waiting to hear the deal."

"All in good time."

"Funkin' Lesson"

Deaconess Blues led them back to the library where her automaton had spread out the accoutrements of high tea. A silver teapot poured a heady brew, the aroma-filled the room. A tray of crumpets and other delicate pastries lay before them, as the blank-faced automaton attended to etiquette in Deaconess Blues' fragile dance of civility. Going through the motions of refined breeding, protocol—appearances were paramount—despite being excluded from upper society.

"Are we all that's left of the F8?" Sleepy asked. He stifled a rheumy cough, slipping a trail of grey sputum into his napkin.

"I do not know, sir. We compartmentalize ourselves so that no one person knows too much about our organization." Deaconess Blues tilted her head with a glimmer of maternal concern. "You look troubled."

"I just don't know what we're doing and..." Sleepy paused. "What's the point?"

"Has it ever struck you that we aren't as ahead technologically as we should be?"

"Knowledge and the reflection of knowledge equals wisdom," Knowledge Allah said. "Knowledge and wisdom equals understanding."

"Then if you knowledge my wisdom, you will understand what I'm saying." Deaconess Blues said. He nodded as if they shared the same gibberish wavelength. "Knowledge is built on the back of itself. Those who come along later stand on the shoulders of those before them. That great capitalist machine called slavery robbed mother Africa of generations of scientists, artists, and creative minds. Think of where we'd be without that holocaust. "

"We'd have flying cars," Sleepy said "and show tunes. "

"We have show tunes."

"We'd have had them sooner, you feel me? What? A black man

can't enjoy show tunes."

"He isn't ready. He still needs verbal milk," Knowledge Allah said.

"Then this meeting is premature. I am...resources. Not propaganda."

"Time is of the essence. The Cause demanded this level of meeting."

"My job is to oppose the state," Deaconess Blues scowled. "I care about the liberation of my people."

"Your people? You a high yella, bougie dilettante." Sleepy shifted, uncomfortable with how defensive he sounded. Deaconess Blues remained unflustered. Strains of classical music reverberated from the large horns encircling the room, surrounding them with sound. With another dollop of chiba, the pungent sting of burnt weed sent his mind adrift among the clouds and made him much more receptive to high flung ideas.

An obviously delicate eater, Deaconess Blues drew a long sip then set her cup back onto its dish. "I'm black like you. I resist. I seek to end the chains and the extermination of all oppression."

"You don't talk like a scientist."

"I am an anarchist, insurrectionist, and a scientist. A scientist searching for knowledge and proof. For truth and meaning."

"You're a scientist of God," Knowledge Allah chimed in with a tone of deference.

Sleepy raised an eyebrow. He wondered if Deaconess Blues was one of the alchemist-spirit riders whispered about, those who combined science and the ancient ways.

"With the revolutions in engineering and science and industry, we have yet to see any in our social systems. We might as well dress up the automata in minstrel outfits and paint them with bright white eyes and red bulbous lips for how we are seen." Deaconess Blues poured herself another cup of tea. She stirred in milk and sugar as her words settled in their ears, their eyes anxious on her, though she was unhurried. "We've been promised universal enlightenment, an end to war, and a rationalist utopian... as long as everyone knows their place.

"We are at the intersection of class and race, class and sexuality, and class and gender. Any class reduction will face critical resistance. We have sold our souls in the service of commerce. We toil in the embrace of the machine and become a concubine of industry. So we rage against the machine and we must take extraordinary steps to defend ourselves. There must develop solidarity among our people, a swell of anti-colonial resistance."

"I feel you. I'm angry and I know y'all are angry, too. So what're we going to do about it?" Sleepy asked, not one for the intellectual stuff. "Civil disobedience?"

"I've no interest in begging for scraps from our presumed master's table."

"Let me lay it on you like this: blood for blood," Knowledge Allah said.

"Now we're talking," Sleepy said, stirred from his settling ennui.

"And you know that." Knowledge Allah outstretched his hand that was received with blitheness by Sleepy, as if he'd finally earned a spot at the table.

"You'd be happy with any militant action," Deaconess Blues sniffed.

"Blowing shit up is a plan," Sleepy said.

"I understand your anger and how you may think of blowing shit up—given your coarse leanings—as revolutionary. But it is the beginning of a plan, not one unto itself. There must be a greater vision. There must be a catalyst for change."

"Niggas are in a state of emergency. Got to start wilding out."

"You are a ruin to language," she said with the exacting manner of a spinster aunt.

Sleepy chafed against her civilizing influence. The discussion, though somewhat diverting, left him with the sensation of being out of his depth. Maybe it was Deaconess Blues' subtle condescension. Or perhaps it was the disconnection between the lofty ideas of the Cause and the practical reality of the people. Sleepy's views boiled down to pragmatism: the theory of struggle was great only insofar as someone actually was helped. It wasn't farther argument he wanted, but action. "You rebel in your way, I rebel in mine."

"I dream of different but similar worlds. I dream of one where we're free, not under the heel of Albion. There is something profoundly unwell in their sense of entitlement." Deaconess Blues shook her head as if the very act of reflection was wasted effort. Her stiff, stately bearing was the picture of restraint. "Eating their blood sausages and tripe, their raspberry tarts."

"The Inventor has a plan, "Knowledge Allah said as if reading his reluctance.

"Oh?"

"The plan is the paragon of simplicity. The local penitentiary..."

"The Ave?" Sleepy asked.

"The Allisonville Correctional Facility is a wretched place. Its serpentine bowels, and those of its ilk, incarcerate a third of our people. Little better than slave pens with us little better than beasts."

"Including Star Child and the rest of the F8."

"The Star Child is a powerful symbol of the struggle. Imprisoned for speaking of a better way. Of revolution."

"But the Ave is..."

"Impregnable? No, its design bears the fruit of the very hubris of its designers. Think of it: a lone spire, defying the heavens like the tower of Babel. All the guards, knights of the realm, gathered there more as symbol than actual need. Were it to come crashing down, our brothers and sisters would be free."

"Oops upside their head," Knowledge Allah said.

"Wouldn't they be trapped?"

"Don't you see? The same underground shafts that entomb them now also protect them. All we would need is a group of folks to shepherd them to safety."

"And something to bring down the tower itself."

Deaconess Blues stood up and strode to the coat rack. Donning a hat and gloves—though Sleepy distrusted the cock of her hat—she announced, "Come on. We need to be armed with a bop gun."

"Bop Gun (Endangered Species)"

"Citizens of the Universe, do not attempt to adjust your electro-transmitter, there is nothing wrong. We have taken control to bring you this special bulletin. "The attenuated pulse of Knowledge Allah's voice echoed along the airwaves. "The Albion Empire bloated itself on its own myth—a proud, corpulent pustule of wealth—spreading across the land, a decadent cancer of corporate greed and industrial indulgence all in the name of national pride.

"Washington aristocrats with vested interest in our eternal domination, governing to their interests not ours. The Empire is a corrupt federal leviathan, swollen and lazy, and we are the cheap table legs propping it up. Revolution is inevitable. We are the First Cause. In our tiers of rage, we call for direct action. We resist constituted powers through property damage. We impede the flow of goods and capital, using their system against them and making the cost of perpetuating domination prohibitive. And it is time to co-opt their instrument of military guarantor to break out the F8. There's a party at the crossroads.

Watch the skies. Freedom or Death.

"I exist between time outside time. In the between places. I am the voice of truth in these troubled times."

Escaped the low ceiling of the undercity. No sunlight, only the arc of electricity from the tram. A city of shadows consuming their bodies as grist to drive the Empire forward. The trio rode in silence following the banks' scenic greenway to the summer homes of the overcity. They quickly left the shadows of Atlantis to the sprawling suburbs of greater Indianapolis, careful to avoid the constabularies who might pull them over or otherwise detain them for not being where they were supposed to be. Deaconess Blues' fair skin granted her passage to casual observers. Soon they reached an immense pole barn structure on property ringed with barbed wire. A mad grin danced on her face as she activated the lock controls via a sequence of numbers punched into an electro-chirographer pad. Gears winched and the doors trembled before parting. Inside the makeshift hanger was an airship.

From the first day the sight of a bird in flight fired his fancy, man dreamt to one day take to the clouds; to conquer the air as easily as he conquered the land and the sea. Unlike the massive warships of Lockheed or Sir Halliburton, this one did not bristle with armaments. No mighty bombs would drop on unseen enemies or innocent school buildings, nor would the blood-soaked dreams of nation-states be enforced by it. A ridged watermelon with a hull of black with a red underbelly, gas filled tubes ran along the outside of the ship and burned to life to ring the ship in a brackish green. A gold ankh, like an uplifted key, emblazoned its side.

"Where did you get it?"

"I am not a lady of unlimited resources…"

"You stole it."

"We wrested it from the control of the military industrial complex who deemed this model a failure and relegated it to a barely guarded warehouse," Knowledge Allah said.

"Why didn't you say so?"

"Haven't you understood yet? We proceed on a need to know basis. You didn't need to know."

"One man's failure is another person's treasure. "Deaconess Blues climbed a scaffold. "Coming inside?"

The decks of the cabin divided into small rooms, tiny tombs in the greater sarcophagus, connected by tiny ladders Sleepy had little hope of navigating. A network of cables, ropes, and pipes ran throughout like capillaries. Pressure hissed from the valves of the Malcolm-Little engines. Mahogany bedecked the main cabin and retained the reek of stale cigar smoke. A luxurious box, a den of sorts, formed the sanctum sanctorum of noble breeding. A decanter of pear wine sat in the middle of a table spread with finger foods, as another blank-faced automaton whirred out of their way.

Knowledge Allah reclined on a bench, a gentleman of leisure. Deaconess Blues stood before an array of membrane discs and tuning forks, lost behind the steady cadence of whirs and clicks. A wave of nausea swept over Sleepy as he imagined himself squeezing into the small window seat, staring out over the sea of land.

"Wisdom is water. I'm about solar facts. God is the sun. It's all about the elements," Knowledge Allah said, a brutal curl to his lips.

"You and your outlandish expressions," Deaconess Blues remarked with admirable dispatch. "Your peculiar phraseology never tires." She moved about the cabin, examining the controls with considered elegance.

"The sundial speaks. We prepare to ride as Afronauts."

"So how does this all play out?" Sleepy asked. "We become the villains they assume us to be?"

"One man's villain is another person's Star Child. Do you know how we're seen? Human chimpanzees. Immature, in need of constant guidance. Emotional, not rational. Unreasonable and easily excited. Without religion, only superstition and fanciful mythologies." She nodded to Knowledge Allah. "Criminals with no respect for private property. Filthy. Excessively sexual. We are niggers left to fester and shamble in the undercities."

"Us and the Irish." Uncomfortable in the awkward pause left by his attempt at humor, Sleepy pulled another hair from his chin and examined the kinky strand against his fingertip.

"Their blue-eyed, blond-haired Jesus used to keep us in our place. We are but noble aborigines. Such is the result of their gradations of mankind. Here I am, too black for their tastes, too white for yours, trapped by their index of nigrescence." Deaconess Blues manned a station, the controls warming the dirigible to a full-throated bluster, pulsing with steam. Baffles and stanchions, ballasts and air ducts pumped furiously. "Where is our justice?"

"Justice? There is no justice, there is Just Us," Knowledge Allah said.

"Aluminum and iron oxide are elements of the fabric doping. This zeppelin ought to be filled with helium or another inert gas. However, as our purposes are of a more combustible nature, I've filled our little dirigible with hydrogen. I wouldn't advise any more of your chiba indulgences." Her stiff upper lip set to grim resolve, she remained unruffled by the chaos springing up about her.

"I ain't down with no suicide run," Sleepy said. "This brother don't go out like that."

"Yet our best trained, best educated, best equipped, best prepared troops refuse to fight!" Knowledge Allah recited with an evangelical fervor and a sneer of contempt. "Matter of fact, it's safe to say that they would rather switch than fight!"

"Who's going to fight for The Cause if our best keep taking themselves out?"

"An arm, a leg perhaps. But not the Head," Knowledge Allah said.

"I am not one to shrink from such deviltry. Besides, it's not suicide. We are meant to be among the stars, signals from the heavens, showing others the way home." Deaconess Blues stepped from her perch to meet Sleepy eye-to-eye. "Nor are we asking you to come."

"What?" Sleepy's sated gaze fixed on her.

"We accepted you because we saw your potential. Ancient tribes had truth-tellers and history keepers and story tellers. You are like one of those ancient griots. We give you the space to tell stories. Our story."

"Vainglorious," Knowledge Allah echoed.

"I detest long good-byes," Deaconess Blues said.

Sleepy glanced from one to the other, tasked and dismissed. His lips parted to protest, but no sound escaped. He backed out toward the rear of the deck, ignoring his sense of relief while wanting to feign the injured party. As if he was deemed unworthy to partake in his own struggle.

"You smell that?" Deaconess Blues called out, her skin like luminescent butter. A static charge hung in the air. "The air smells like freedom."

"Freedom or death," Knowledge Allah said.

"We fly into glory."

"Black Steel in the Hour of Chaos"

"Citizens of the Universe, do not attempt to adjust your electro-transmitter, there is nothing wrong. We have taken control to bring you this special bulletin."

Sleepy raced along the back roads desperate to beat the landing of the mother ship. A great shadow filled the sky, the pride of the empire.

Clouds blackened into banks of ominous dark swirls by the endless entropy of Night. The wind howled. The gleaming overcities and jutting spires must look so different from up above, Sleepy imagined. Air raid lights filled the sky, spotlights on the stage of the night sky. The dirigible, their Bop Gun, moved with implacable grace, an airborne whale, strident and regal.

"My message is simple. Tonight the Star Child... all of us will be free. By any means necessary. Freedom or death.

"I exist between time outside time. In the between places. I am the voice of truth in these troubled times."

By the time Sleepy pulled up, a throng of people had gathered, held in check by too few constabularies. The Ave's tower, impregnable and arrogant, saluted them. Slowly, the ovoid silhouette of the Bop Gun came into full view. The crowd burst into a roar of applause and cheers. As if in response, the behemoth canted forward in a sharp downward arc. Sleepy stared, filled with profound apprehension. The crowd became a pantomime of motion and fury and panic. Knowledge Allah stood before the grand bay window. Backlit, his grand gestures were perfectly visible to the spectators as the ship careened earthward.

He raised a clenched fist. "Vainglorious," Sleepy whispered.

Everything happened at once, a series of images broken into shards of memory one tried to forget. The roar of the crowd, an exhalation of panic. An explosion. A billowy fire cloud, a phoenix springing toward the heavens. The smell of India rubber burning. Shrapnel of stone. A body, encircled in flames, stumbled two steps then collapsed. Fiery scraps blew about in the night breeze. The injured structure suddenly unable to bear its own weight, the tower collapsed. The terrible crash, thunder flattening the ear-drums. Smoke and flame, thick and choking, burning the lungs with each inhalation.

"Revolution"

Watching the skeleton of the Bop Gun continue to burn—its tattered shell buckled upon itself—Sleepy waited, carried along by the undertow of the crowd. The constabularies, with their thick night sticks and steel-riveted riot shields, cordoned off the scene. Fear glazed their faces. He spied no one immediately fleeing and prayed that the prisoners had been moved. He feared that they remained trapped beneath the ground, escaping slaves caught in a cave in. Soon, among the wreckage and destruction, black bodies scrambled from the underground, a stream of ants fleeing their hill. Some of the constabularies fired at the escaping prisoners. Something stirred inside Sleepy. The caustic smoke stung his eyes, his vision little more than watery blurs. Soot-tinged spittle dropped to the ground.

The voices rose into a chorus. Knowledge Allah. Deaconess Blues. His father. Lost in the din was his voice. Sleepy felt the anger. The urge to join the fight. To retaliate. Blinking through a haze of pain, he ground his heel into the desiccated earth and punched the nearest guard, a tacit signal to the crowd to surge forward. The horde spilled in every direction, blind fury, pent up aggression in search of a target. A mob of chaos, arms swinging blindly, clubs battering senselessly. Sirens sounded. Bodies clambered through barbed wire. In the ensuing mêlée, Sleepy was arrested. To the chants of "let him go," the constabularies clapped him in irons, his expression more frustrated than fearful. At the precinct house, the questions came fast and furious. "Who were involved in the organizing?" "How did he get involved?" "How many were there?" "Who were the leaders?"

Sleepy fought his revolutions his own way. And raised a single fist.

KENNY 149

Brad Becraft

The mud looked up at him and grumbled, "Who the hell are you?"

The musty smell of the grass and ground clogged his nostrils as he strained for a single, clean breath and dug his fingers deep into the dirt. His eyelids quivered and strained to open while he felt himself mixing into the ground as blood and flesh sought refuge in the soil of the battlefield.

The whispered sizzle of a particle beam was followed by a smell like burning aftershave. Somewhere in the smoke, amid the staccato of clanking metal, something screamed an unrecognizable sound.

The mud drawled with a slow, familiar twang, "I'll ask again ol' buddy. Who the hell are you?" It always spoke with his voice.

"Trauma induced disassociation," one of the Docs had explained.

It used to bother him, a long time ago; but since it never had anything new to talk about, he mostly learned to ignore it.

The air suddenly went silent, but for the constant thrum of his heartbeat rushing inside his ears. He peered through matted, bloody eyelids and surveyed the smoking field around him. Billows of grey and brown crawled like carrion creatures along the piles of unmoving bodies and he realized that again he was the last. Like so many times before, it was just him and the mud.

A mortar exploded somewhere to his left. His body rocked and he grimaced in unexpected pain. The extras hadn't kicked in yet. He shivered.

"Hey!" the mud protested. "Do I come and mess your house like that?!"

The cool of the earth pressed against his stomach, and he probed with his fingers. They encountered an opening just abovehis navel and the sticky, wet warmth of his own blood covered his hand. The sensation sparked memory and the memory spilled into his thought.

"It's a synthetic coagulant, Private," Major Ghunda explained, as she withdrew the needle from his arm. "We're going to include it with your weekly anti-rejection therapy for a while. We're very excited about it and you're so lucky to pilot its use."

"So what does it do?" he asked her.

"And call me Kenny, Doc. All the docs do."

She smiled and patted his hand. "It responds to trauma much faster than your human coagulating agents. If you are wounded, Kenny, this material will immediately begin forming a silicone coagulate at the injury site and slow the fluid flow."

"Well, I guess that would be useful." He shrugged.

She smiled again and shook her head. "I think you'll appreciate it, although I hope you don't have any use for it soon. Now let's go over your latest test results. The latest transplants seem to be doing nicely."

Her face faded from his consciousness and he absently pressed a palm against his stomach. Blood still trickled along the seam where his stomach had been ripped open by the fragments of the biod unit that had been standing in front of him just moments earlier. He could feel the rupture in his skin begin to seal over with a fresh silicone coating.

Bubbling and tiny popping sounds came from beneath his vest as the gel bled into the perforations of his chest and allowed him to take a full breath. He sucked air in grateful relief and tried to roll over.

A chorus of pain sang out from his legs and hips at the movement. He collapsed back into the earth, face first.

"I don't know who you are," the mud grumbled, "but you're makin' a mess. How long you gonna be here?"

He breathed in a lungful of dirt and coughed violently. The mud on his tongue was tinted with the metallic taste of blood and perspiration. His brain whirled with the continued pain until, finally, the extras began to work and his arms and legs grew numb. His consciousness slipped into a foggy grey haze, while the here and now became interspersed with more memories.

"The titanium hip joint is obsolete." Captain Quarterstock sneered and waved his hands. "How long you been active anyway, Corporal? I can't find your service date."

Whenever one of the docs asked him that, Kenny grinned and replied, "I've lived a while Cap'n. And just call me Kenny, all the Docs do."

"Kenny, huh? Well Kenny, we're doing some extra upgrades this time around. Not just repair and redeploy. We're replacing that old hip of yours with the latest in carbon composites. A nano-fiber structure grown on a matrix of bone tissue we cultivated from human donors. Hell, we're even using the same materials in the new AI biod artillery units. Just like all your organ replacements. God couldn't have designed it better."

It was a bold statement which had seemed a bit blasphemous to Kenny's Lutheran, mid-western, Kansas brain at the time. But since the Luminari invasion, there was no Kansas and only a few Lutherans. And since Kenny wasn't one to generally question the Docs, he let the blasphemy pass without comment.

Another mortar explosion rocked his thoughts back to the present. He grimaced and gingerly ran his hand along his side and down to his damaged hip. Sure enough the metal joint was still in one piece. But the organic femur, shattered and useless now, felt like a bag of marbles as he placed his palm against it.

"Hey!" The mud seemed genuinely concerned now. "You all right? Do I know you?"

He groaned and squeezed the sub-dermal contact between his fingers that would activate the beacon. He closed his eyes and recalled the first time he'd completed that motion.

"Suppose my hands were hurt, Doc?" he asked the tall, lanky female surgeon whose name he could never remember.

"How would the beacon work?"

"That's why the auxiliary unit is in your neck, Kenny, right here." She reached behind his head and pressed a bump at the base of his skull. His skin tingled as her fingers brushed his neck. She jumped back in surprise and looked at him through narrowed eyes.

"How long have you been active anyway, Kenny?"

He grinned. "Aw, I've lived a while."

She ignored his grin and stared intently at the data pad in her hands, and her eyebrows squirmed anxiously. "No, really," she insisted, "how long have you been active? Your medical records don't show your service initiation date. There's nothing here until after the second Bio-gain campaign."

He scratched his head and shrugged. "I don't know about that, but I came in the Corps when the Luminari first invaded."

Her eyes widened. "But you'd have to be...."

"I was just a kid. Mom and Dad and the rest of the town were taken in the first Collection. Missed me, though. I was shootin' cats out in the scrapyard across Turner's Creek. The platoon of Marines that found me took me in and kinda adopted me. They taught me all about soldiering and showed me how to stay alive. I guess I never really enlisted. The Corps just sorta joined me."

Her lips pursed, as her gaze scanned up and down his body. "That's amazing, Kenny."

"I don't think it's so amazing." He shook his head. "Anyway, it's been a long war and all of them guys are dead and dust. When can I get back to my unit? They'll be needing me back."

She stepped forward and brushed his leg with her hip. "You're probably one of the few who've seen the entire war first hand. Not like the soldiers here now. They're just overpaid mechanics that send out others to do their killing for them."

"Well, ma'am, I have done some fighting. I been in over a hundred skirmishes and even fought in the counteroffensive to retake Washington. But don't get down on the Docs, ma'am. I mean, without them we wouldn't have a chance in this war. Why, I wouldn't even be here. I'd be dead a hundred and seven times over."

"Well, Kenny, One Oh Seven, you deserve a medal!" She tossed the data pad aside and smiled. "But since the Service doesn't give out medals anymore, maybe we can reward you a better way." She squeezed his thigh and moved closer.

The memory scattered as the ground began to hum beneath him. A Luminari Chariot entered the sector and began to clear away the battlefield debris, alien and Terran alike. Kenny slowly reached to his belt for a plasma grenade, holding his breath as the humming grew louder and louder. He released the safety and clutched the trigger until it felt like the Chariot was almost on top of him, then he tossed the grenade in the direction of the approaching sound. He heard it clank against metal and a flash and pop followed, as the plasma sparked and fried the electronic components of anything within a three meter radius. The Chariot groaned as its wheels ground to a halt, then turned silent.

He lay back and tried to recapture the memory of the tall, lanky female surgeon. He wished he could remember her name, but it eluded him completely. It was too long ago and one name among a million crowded into his memory. He'd seen too many of the Docs to recall each and every one. And nobody ever stayed around long. The Luminari took care of that. Only the mud had been with him through all the years—wherever he went, it was there.

"I recognize you now," the mud muttered. "Long time no see, buddy. Not in the best shape today are we?"

He felt up and down his body, trying to find some wound or injury his extras had missed and stopped when he reached the side of his face. A large section of the right skull was absent and he felt the soft tissue of his brain along with thin strands of wire and plastic exposed and open to the elements. He touched one of the wires and his vision was immediately filled with sparkles and lightning flashes of impossible colors. He moaned in surprise and fear until, finally, the light show faded.

He took a slow cleansing breath and tried to lie still, remembering once more. "I don't like this," Captain Yueng growled. "No, Kenny, I don't like putting this thing in you." Captain Yueng was the oldest Doc he'd met in his service with the Corps. His sharp nose and deep set eyes were framed by a webbed collage of wrinkles with flashes of white in his thick, otherwise jet black hair. He never smiled, but Kenny liked him the best of all the Docs.

"Well, you know me, Doc," he answered and shrugged. "Kenny One Twenty-Nine, just servin' my country. Don't you think it'll work?"

"Oh, I know it will. The trigger is when your biometrics indicate serious trauma. The low energy EM pulse will block your pain receptors."

"That seems like it'd be handy in the field. I know lots of times when I get downed it hurts a lot."

"I know son, and I can only imagine how bad it is sometimes. "Yueng furrowed his brow and patted Kenny on the shoulder." But that pain is there by design. It lets you know when to stop and take care of business."

"I ain't sure what you mean, Doc. Takin' care of business means winnin' this war, don't it? Seems like anything that helps us do that is a good thing. Y'know things ain't goin' so great for us. They need guys like me up there."

Yueng frowned. "I know and we're doing all we can to help, but what we're doing...what we've done. I don't...it seems like an awful price to pay."

Kenny liked Yueng but didn't always understand him. "Well, Doc, I don't know what you mean. I watched lots of friends pay a bigger price. I watched it until they ain't nobody left hardly but me. Seems like I been blessed somehow and it don't seem right to give up. I gotta get back to the line in three days, so if you're gonna do it...." He shrugged, as the Captain eased him back onto the cot.

Now as he lay motionless on the ground and his body was embraced in a cocoon of numbness, he began to understand what Yueng had meant. He felt like he could just leap up from the ground and run off to the medical pod.

"Well, why donchya do it?" the mud asked.

But Kenny One Forty-Nine knew better. If he moved or lifted his head, he could twist open his stomach again, or cause bone fragments to erupt through his thigh, or spill his brains onto the ground. No, he would lie there and either die or get picked up by the clean-up crew.

He relaxed and waited for what seemed like hours until, finally, he heard an excited voice approaching.

"Here, over here! The transponder's from this one!"

"Okay, I see him," another voice followed. "Let's hurry and get it and get out of here. We've only got a few hours before we have to fall back to the pulse shelters."

"I know that. Here, secure its spine and we can turn it over."

He felt the steady, practiced hands grip him. "Unit designate: K-NE V149. Multiple fragment entries, but the seals are all holding. P and R are stable. I…wait…oh shit. That's not good."

"What?"

"Look at this, Corbin. His head is half blown off. Can we fix that?"

"I don't know. He's still functioning, isn't he?"

"Yeah. Biometic log indicates salvageable. I… Damn!"

"What is it?"

"Look at the service stamp on this hip joint. The date is over a hundred years old!"

"You're shittin' me."

"No, really. According to this, this old timer was in service back when human soldiers were still fighting! How is that possible?"

"Wow! Hey… You don't think he's…?"

"Let me do a deep tissue scan. Hmmm. I'll be damned! He's human! Human with over seventy percent bio-gain grafts!"

"What is a human doing with that much tech in him? And why is he out here?"

"I don't know, but it…I mean…he is."

"What should we do? I mean there's not what, a few thousand humans left alive? Oh man, somebody's gonna get their ass handed for this, and we don't have time for this. The closest pulse shelter is thirty klicks away. This has to be some mistake."

The mud laughed. "You're a wonder ain't you boy! Them tech-heads can't get their heads out of their waste ducts long enough to know what to do about you."

"It's no mistake," Corbin growled. "We've got to get him back to Evac Station. Let them sort out the record keeping. Then we can get to the shelter."

"Hey, soldier!" Kenny felt synthetic hands pat gently against his chest. "Can you hear me?"

He started to nod and lift his hand, but felt those same hands binding him firmly. Instead he muttered a weak, "Yeah."

"Can you tell us your name soldier?"

"Kenny,"he answered, "Kenny…One-Fifty, now I guess."

"Well, Kenny One-Fifty, I'm Corbin and this is Dotson. We're going to get you back to the base and get you all fixed up. Then you're getting evacuated to the last shuttle off of Earth."

"Off…Earth?"Kenny muttered.

"Yeah. Earth is being evacuated," Corbin answered. "The humans have fallen back to Proxima Terra and in about five hours they're going to nuke every Luminari base on this planet."

"Yeah,"Dotson added. "You're lucky you were injured so badly. Otherwise we might not have recognized you for human. We have to evac you with the rest of your people. We bios can handle the radiation, but it would kill you."

"Lucky," Kenny One-Fifty muttered, as he felt himself being lifted.

"Right," Corbin said, "the fight's moved off-world and the humans are taking it all the way to the Luminari home world. Now, let's get you to the evac station as quick as we can. Then it's off to Proxima Terra and Station Big Horn. You've been in the service a long time, soldier. I bet you got lots of buddies waiting up there for you."

"No." Kenny's voice crackled and was barely a whisper. "No buddies, no more, just me and the mud."

The mud looked up and whispered, "I'll miss ya, bud."

Advertising at the End of the World

Keffy R.M. Kehrli

Five years after her husband died, two years after she moved to a cabin in Montana, and six months after the world ended, Marie opened her curtains to discover her front garden overrun with roving, stumbling advertisements. Marie hadn't seen one since she'd sold her condo and moved out to her isolated cabin. She shuddered.

There were at least twenty of the ads, and for all it seemed they were doing their damndest to step lightly, her red and yellow tulips were completely trampled. Marie had stubbornly continued to cultivate those flowers despite the certainty that she ought to be using the gardening space, and the captured rainwater, to grow food. Not that it mattered what she'd been growing there. It was all mud now.

The ad nearest her window looked quite a bit like a tall, lanky teenager. It moved like one as well, and might have fooled her except that its forehead was stuck in price scrolling mode. Faintly glowing red letters crawled across its forehead from right to left.

TOILET PAPER...2 FOR 1 SALE...RECYCLED...

Marie could only recognize the daffodil bed by memory. She snapped the curtains shut.

She wrapped a floral print terrycloth robe around herself and hustled from her sparsely furnished bedroom into the kitchen. She was relieved to see the fences she'd put up to keep the deer out of her vegetable garden, while never quite successful, had at least managed to keep her vegetables safe from the ads.

That, of course, would not bring back her flowers.

She glowered at the ads through her kitchen window and filled a glass from the pitcher of well water she kept by the sink. She fumbled open the Tuesday box on her medication canister. Like most mornings, she was thankful that she had filled her prescriptions prior to the end; otherwise she would have none by now.

She would have to go to the garden, and although the advertisements were designed to be perfectly harmless, Marie found she was frightened by the way they lurched over the ground. She suspected this was due to the uncomfortable way their silent progress reminded her of zombie films.

Robert would have been fascinated. A year or so before his death, an advertisement had come up to their door. In those days, the ads had acted more like people than those that now plagued her gardens, and it had stood obediently on the front step until they'd opened the door.

Marie had argued that it was better to leave the door shut, because if an advertisement left without delivering its pitch, it would learn not to come back to the house. The way she figured it, and the way several of her favorite independent video bloggers figured it, listening to the ads was like feeding a stray cat.

Robert did not seem to be overly concerned that they would never get rid of the ads. "Don't be ridiculous," he said. "They'll last maybe another few years at the most, and then the companies will all move onto something that costs less. Right now, they're cheaper than sending employees door-to-door." He opened the door, despite Marie's protestations.

"Hello," the advertisement said, hands clasped before it. "I was wondering if you had a few moments to talk about your retirement?"

Marie just shook her head and turned back into the house. She busied herself with embroidery, although she still kept an eye on Robert to be sure he wasn't buying anything. No matter how clever her Robert thought the ads were, she did not want to encourage the companies to make more of them.

After a few minutes of animated conversation, the ad left and Robert came into the dining room. He asked, "Have you ever wondered how sentient they are?"

Marie shook her head. She didn't like the ads, and the best emotion she could muster toward them was similar to the way she felt about mosquitoes. Other people thought they served a purpose; she didn't, and it was not worth the argument.

It became apparent that Robert was actually waiting for her

answer, and he sat down heavily in one of the other dining room chairs. Marie finished a particularly difficult stitch. "They aren't. They just recognize patterns."

"Yes, but so do we," Robert said. He put both hands on the table and sat up straighter. "How close are they to sentience? They're so much more sophisticated than a recorded ad. They're art."

A few more stitches. Marie laughed. "Art? They're advertisements, not art. It can't be art if it's just meant to sell things."

Robert had looked thoughtful. He'd leaned over the table slowly, put his chin in his hands and looked at her. "And yet you like Mucha prints, and those were all selling something," He'd said.

If Robert were still alive, and the world had not ended, Marie supposed he would have gone out the front door and immersed himself in a sea of advertising conversation. As it was, she faced the corporate-orphaned menace alone with an old broom and her largest hammer.

She had hoped they would simply wander off on their own, but after watching through the window for a few hours, she determined they knew where she was. Marie suspected her RF chip was still broadcasting her ID number. She and Robert had bought them before they truly understood how much advertising money had subsidized the price.

She stood on the threshold of the home she'd purchased with her retirement and the last of Robert's life insurance pay-off, ready to defend it against even the most pernicious of sales pitches.

Marie hefted the hammer over her head and held the broom out like a lance. At least thirty ads were in the front garden now, and more stumbled up the gravel road to her home.

"Get off my property!" Her voice only shook a little.

The ads turned to face her. They were designed to understand when they were told to leave. This was meant to limit the annoyance factor. Even in the best of times, the command had rarely worked. Forehead screens changed from flesh colors to scrolling text. The subtlety had gone out of advertising entirely. She wondered if that was a function of being away from human contact for months on end, or if she was just surrounded by a crowd of defectives.

"Go away!"

The ads crowded in closer, becoming an ocean of words and prices and mark-downs, factory blow-outs and Email addresses for the next get-rich-quick scheme, male enhancement drug names, tag lines for movie sequels that shouldn't exist, and cash advance loan shark promises.

"Marie…it's been so long."

At the corner of her cabin, just behind her favorite rhododendron, she saw a figure she recognized immediately and might have known by voice alone.

Robert.

Robert as he'd looked when they'd first met, back in the twentieth century, when they had both been younger and he had been alive. He — it, the ad, wore a very simple black two-piece suit, and held a hat under its arm. It looked like the suit Robert had worn to their wedding, but the shoes were different, as though the advertisement had not fully accessed the public files on their marriage.

Through the first three years after his death, Marie had never grown used to the way the ads shifted to Robert's form. Now the image spread out like ripples on a pool, the skin of the ads universally deepening almost to a shade of olive, hair lengthening and straightening and taking on that blue-black sheen she'd fallen in love with.

The forward press of ads stopped just outside of her reach, processing the shift from advertising bot to facsimile of her husband. The ads stopped broadcasting on their foreheads, all except for the broken one, which was now fidgeting from one foot to the other in a way that would have tricked Marie into thinking it was actually human if the sale on toilet paper hadn't been scrolling from one temple to the other.

They were all malfunctioning.

"Have you been waiting?" one of the Ad-Roberts in front of Marie said. She poked it in the chest with her broom handle, and it didn't seem to mind.

Another ad said, "Have you missed me?"

"Lonely out here," said a third.

Marie picked up her hammer and slowly, careful to avoid tripping on the door frame, backed into her house.

She shut the door.

The first time Marie had ever seen an ad take on the appearance of Robert had been only a few weeks after the funeral. She had opened the door one morning to find Robert standing just outside. There was a split second when she found herself wondering if she'd imagined the past few weeks. Then she realized she was looking at an ad. Marie thought about Robert rotting in the ground, dead and alone.

The ads were not meant to use the likenesses of the deceased. What they could do was almost as bad, but far less illegal—taking those likenesses and shifting them ever so slightly until the ad looked familiar, but not sufficiently to be recognized.

Whether it was an act or not, the ad looked just as surprised as she was. Its eyes opened wide as it accessed her file and, for an instant, it looked like Robert had when he realized he'd said something he shouldn't have. The ad opened its mouth as if to speak, but Marie hadn't wanted to know what it was about to say. She'd slammed the door shut.

It turned out later that the malfunction had been semi-common. Marie could have gotten in on a class action lawsuit but, instead, she'd packed up and sold the condo. She'd moved to the cabin shortly afterward, wanting a place that wouldn't remind her of Robert, who had always loved cities.

All the ads except for one shifted back to their default appearances after Marie returned indoors, but they didn't go away. She kept her shades down and tried to ignore the tromp-tromp-tromping noises of footsteps outside her house.

The gardens had seen better days.

The most curious thing was that no matter how content she had been with her hermit's life before, now the ads were outside her door she missed the sound of Robert's voice. She wished she could hear it again, as long as it wasn't a haphazard lead-in to a sales pitch.

Marie sat alone on these mornings, extremely alone, now she had the rustling sounds of the ads to remind her.

That was why, on one fine Wednesday afternoon in mid-April, Marie invited an advertisement in the guise of her dead husband inside for lunch.

They sat together at a white table with a blue checkered tablecloth and a plate of tiny sandwiches inside Marie's small kitchen. Ad-Robert had attempted to pull her chair out for her, but she would not allow it. She had placed her hammer under her seat before letting the ad in. Even though she didn't think it was dangerous, Marie thought it best to be prepared. Once they were seated, she poured mint tea for them both.

Marie had cultivated the mint herself, of course.

The ad that looked like Robert smiled dumbly at Marie, and the sunlight that filtered into the room lanced brightly across faintly silvered hair. When it smiled, crow's feet spread from the crinkled skin around its eyes. Try as the ad might, however, the months without upkeep had so eroded its ability to keep up with its reference recordings of Robert's inimitable gestures that the resulting attempt looked like a badly choreographed farce.

Marie sipped her tea, watching the ad in silence. It had asked her a leading question, as they'd walked through the front room: something about stock options, which would never draw Marie's interest, even if stocks or money had meaning anymore. Ads were designed not to speak again until the thread of conversation was taken up by a human. She looked out the kitchen window. Ads still filled the back yard. She wondered if they were sharing her location, like bees dancing to show each other the path to fresh flowers. The ads wandered back and forth through what was left of the pansies.

Marie sighed, and Ad-Robert cocked its head.

Either the conversation lag had been too much for its memory banks, or it parsed the sigh as an answer.

The ad asked, "I mean, I don't mean to pry, dear...but you have thought about retirement, haven't you?"

The ad sounded like Robert and, at the same time, sounded like the ad that had spoken to Robert six years before. Marie thought of the hammer under her chair and had to wait to respond because of the sudden thickness in her throat. "Of course I have." It wasn't exactly a lie, but at the same time, the question was moot.

Ad-Robert looked down at its tea but did not drink. It held the cup a few inches above the table and let it steam out into the air. "You ought to be buying biotech. I can help you find the right companies."

Marie said, "I'm sure they're not in business anymore."

The ad tried to do one of Robert's dismissive hand waves, but its wrist motors jerked and the effect was lost. The ad didn't seem to notice. "Of course they're still in business!" Its eyes focused on the space above Marie's left shoulder, as it tried to connect to the Net. Marie was fairly certain that, with the exception of any identification chips she may have, there had never been a wireless connection in a twenty mile radius.

Marie finished her cup of tea and maneuvered the conversation into a realm she cared for a bit more than imaginary finances. She poured more tea and dumped a spoonful of honey into it. "I've been thinking about planting corn soon, but it's hard to get to a flat patch of ground that isn't constantly underfoot these days." She'd heard rumors that some of the ads were able to carry on regular conversations if prompted properly. A few companies had discovered their ads had been held hostage by lonely people for weeks or months on end.

Ad-Robert didn't move, frozen with what would have been confusion if it had been human.

Marie waited, but the hope she had for a decent conversationalist faded when Ad-Robert only asked, "So, about your retirement?"

Marie had tried to look for survivors a week after the satellite television signals had gone out. She'd loaded up her old pickup truck with water, emergency bandages, and even a few fall vegetables to share with her neighbors.

One eye on the road and the other on the gas gauge, she made her way down the mountain, looking for turnoffs to the isolated cabins of her neighbors. She hadn't known them well before everything went to shit, but she figured now was a good time to make an exception. It was a beautiful, quiet day. She pulled onto the highway, and no cars passed her in either direction. All the cabins were empty. This confused Marie, since she hadn't taken the people who lived in them to be the sort who would run for civilization at the first sign of trouble. She supposed she had been wrong about them, for whatever that mattered. Marie filled the back of her pickup truck with canned and dried food from their pantries and tried to ignore the smells that emanated from their closed refrigerators.

She only made it halfway down into the valley before the wind shifted to come up out of the south. She gagged, slammed on the brakes of her truck and pulled over onto the shoulder. Even a few miles away, the collective stench of several hundred thousand bodies, rotting sour in the early September heat, was too much for her.

She couldn't imagine anyone living closer. Reluctantly, she had turned the truck around and headed back to her house.

Marie couldn't destroy the ads. She had trouble even thinking of it because, no matter how wrong their gestures, every ad looked too human.

The ad she kept indoors at least pretended to listen to her from time to time. She could almost ignore the outdoor ads, except for when she had to pass from her house to the well, from the well to the garden, or from the garden back to her house. She had given up on her makeshift pump system the second or third time the ads had trampled holes into the hose. She'd forgotten how hard it was to carry water from the well to the garden by hand, and it didn't help that the ads were always underfoot.

"Get out of the way," she said, exasperated, when the ads stumbled into her few well-worn paths. Even if the ads were not in her garden, it was hard to get enough water to the plants. Every trip with the bucket took twice as long as it should have.

In the evenings, she did not embroider as much as she used to. She was too tired, now, and too worried about whether or not she'd be able to keep her food crops alive and healthy enough to give her a harvest that would last the winter.

Marie grew used to the indoor ad's, "Good morning, sweetheart." It said the same thing every morning, as she passed from her bedroom into the kitchen. The ad always sat in the same chair at the table, in the same position, waiting for her to wake.

When it became apparent that Marie wasn't interested in the ad's sales pitch, it was confused for a long time. It sat and listened, nodding absently to her words in the way Robert had done just before he'd died, when she hadn't been able to tell if he'd understood or not.

She remembered how her own grandparents had spoken exclusively about the past in their old age. She'd still been studying for her math degree, and she hadn't had any time for those stories.

Marie told the ad about other things, about how to know when it was time to pick a pear, about the earth-poison smell of tomato vines and the acid-sharp taste of the fruit.

She was trying to explain the particular crumbling feel of good soil and the moist smell of fresh potato when Ad-Robert interrupted.

It was the only time the ad interrupted her. At all other times, it had been perfectly behaved.

"Have you ever considered your death?" it asked.

Robert had once asked her that. They'd been young, and it had been more a joke than anything else. Marie couldn't look at Ad-Robert when she answered, so she stared out the window at orange-tinged clouds that hung over the forested mountains around her home.

"Yes," she said.

She had been planning to go grocery shopping the day the world ended, after she'd weeded the gardens and picked some zucchini. But she'd turned on the news that morning to pick up the one local channel available from her satellite dish.

Biological agents. Super bug. Nobody on the channel or in any of the borrowed clips they showed could determine if they thought it was terrorism, or just freak random chance. It was a virus, then it was a bacterial infection that antibiotics couldn't touch. Masked and suited reporters questioned the sobbing, quarantined mothers of sick children. Scientists or doctors postulated that if the illness killed its victims so soon after infection, then it couldn't spread much farther.

The rebuttal was simple: there was no way to know how long it gestated, and how long it was contagious. The rebuttal sparked more panic, because the man giving it finished by pointing out that the entire human race could already be infected and not know it.

Marie had turned off the television and sat on her porch in the late summer sunlight for a few hours, and when she'd turned it back on, she hadn't gotten any reception.

A day later, the electricity had been cut off.

One morning when she walked into the kitchen for her medication, the ad did not greet her as it had for the past month. Instead it sat, silent and dark, a life-sized doll made out of LCD and carbon. It no longer appeared to be anything like Robert. It was just a lifeless machine that had grown tired of masquerading as her husband.

She stared at it for a long time, expecting it to come to life with another skewed economics lecture. In case it had a sleep function, she prodded it with a wooden spoon, poking it resolutely in the stomach, the arm, the face. Nothing.

Marie sat down on the other side of the table, leaned far over it and stared at the ad. The face was not really human, but she traced the features with her fingertips, over the smooth hills and valleys that gave the ad a physical presence when it was on. The screen itself was cold to the touch, and she left little skin-oil smudges behind.

Down the neck and across the chest, she could see scratches and scrapes from tree branches and possibly animals. Places where she might have noticed pixels out if she'd looked at it more closely.

Marie sat back in her chair. When she had finished crying, she was left with the problem of disposing of the body. She felt foolish, too... Hadn't she meant originally to kill the stupid things?

The ad was lighter than she'd thought it would be. For all it was nearly the size and build of Robert, it was made of far lighter materials than flesh and bone. Marie was able to drag it with one hand under its left shoulder. She carried her lightweight shovel with her other hand, prodding or swatting any of the outdoor ads that got in her way.

They were still as obnoxious as ever, hovering, surrounding, circling Marie and the dead advertisement like sharks around a sinking boat. The air filled with pitches, slogans, prices.

"We don't have to pay until 2045!"

"I really think you'd like these perfumes, honey."

"Come and visit, the alcohol's free!"

Marie trudged along the thin dirt path that led from her little house, until dry pine needles crackled under her clogs and under the feet of the ads that followed her in a herd. When the ground went flat for a bit, she dragged the ad through a few feet of sparse sword fern.

She dug a shallow grave under a tamarack, and covered the ad with just enough dirt to hide it from view. She didn't think anything would dig it up, but she felt a little bad for not making the grave deeper when the other ads walked over the mound of dirt mixed with pine needles.

Marie wiped her face on the sleeve of her rosebud blouse, and then she took her sweet time walking back down the mountain, still ignoring the advertisements that seemed entirely unaware of the loss of one of their number.

Marie found the second dead advertisement a few days later, toppled over on the front walk-way to her house, scuffed from the feet of the other ads, as motionless and empty as the one that had died in her kitchen.

She thought very seriously about burying it with the other ad, but then she looked at the crowds of them that filled her yard and thought better of it. So Marie dragged the second advertisement out to her shed, and she propped it up between a rake and a hoe, leaving it for the dust to collect on. She realized she could have left it out among the other ads, but she didn't like the idea of her home being surrounded by forgotten bodies.

Every few days she found another, sometimes only toppled over as though its batteries had simply quit, and sometimes sitting tucked against the side of her house as though it had powered down.

She filled her shed with them, and started setting the others up as scarecrows, guarding her vegetables from the birds, though they did nothing to keep away the smaller animals and deer when they didn't move.

The month lengthens and becomes two months, then three, four, five. The ads still come, but there are fewer, and as time goes on, Marie finds that sometimes weeks pass between appearances. Now, when the ads arrive, they are very little danger to her gardens, and she is able to harvest what she needs without them getting in her way.

They come to her to die and sometimes, when it has been a long time between visits, she lets the ads inside, and she listens to them while she serves sandwiches and tea she has made from what she can grow on the plot of land behind her house. The ads that make it to her mountain are moving slower and slower, and Marie is not surprised. She is moving slower these days, too, though she is not sure if that is the weather, leaning in toward winter, working cold into the ragged edges of her joints, or what is left to her now the pills have run out.

Every so often, the ads look like Robert. Sometimes they look like her friends; sometimes they look like her mother. Sometimes they look like nobody she has ever known, and sometimes they look like she imagines her children would have if she and Robert had ever cared to try.

Maybe when the winter is done, she thinks, she will climb down from her mountain to see what is left. The smell of the dead in the city will have gone by then, and there may be other survivors on other hills, looking for her. She holds the slightest of hopes that there are fewer ads because they have found others, and not just because they were never meant to last for so long, lost and alone in a dead world.

FUNGAL GARDENS

Ekaterina Sedia

The phone call from Johnny came late that night, after nine, when I'd already decided that the dinner was a bust and was sadly finishing the entire pan of chimichangas.

"David," he said, and I immediately knew that he was not alone. Otherwise, he would've called me one of his affectionate nicknames— for a man of his profession and gruff disposition, Johnny was surprisingly mushy sometimes. "Sorry I'm late, but there's this…body here. I might actually need your expertise."

Surprise at my usefulness was obvious in his voice, but I decided not to get upset and instead forgive myself the chimichanga excess. One thing canceled the other, you see. "What can I do for you?" I said in my most professional tone and added, "Also, I ate your dinner."

"No problem," he said. "I grabbed a hotdog on the way. Listen, we have a possible homicide here, and it's just gross. But we don't know what or how. And also, there's a case like it in Arizona."

"And I would be useful how?" I was a biologist, teaching at a community college, not a junior detective or anything.

"We have some slides we need you to look at. Tissue slides."

I specialized in fungi, but really, most tissues were familiar to me. But so would they be to any pathologist, one of which they surely had at the morgue or otherwise available, and I pointed that out to Johnny.

"We need an expert," he said. "The morgue says that they've never seen anything like it. Can you come down to the precinct?"

Of course I could and I did, barely taking time to smooth down my hair, wipe the telltale sour cream from my face, and grab a leather jacket. It was not strictly necessary—it was warm outside, seeing how it was August, but this jacket smelled of familiar leather and old sweat, and was always comforting. I thought I'd need that.

It wasn't the first time I stopped by the precinct—while dating a cop, it was necessary. I wasn't sure how much Johnny ever told anyone about us; it was his style not to explain anything and hope that no one would notice. So I usually picked him up after work or before lunch and tried to be non-embarrassing.

Johnny waited for me outside, the pale strip of skin on his upper lip eerily resembling a smile—it was still lighter than the rest of his face after he shaved off the mustache he'd sported when we first met. Good riddance to that thing. A cigarette dangled, limp, and he slouched against the rod iron banister by the doorway, hands in pockets, looking more like a teenage malcontent than a proper detective.

My heart went out to him.

He glanced about him to make sure we were alone before giving me a quick hug. That was pretty good in such proximity to his place of work. "You have to see this,"he said, and pressed something large and white and cottony into my hand. It was a face mask.

"Something infectious?" I offered, as I followed him inside.

"Possibly."

We trotted down the linoleum corridor and weaved between the cubicles, to one of the back rooms where they had a makeshift lab set up. The pathologist, an old balding man named Cramer, and a few other men I'd never met before, sat around a long, chipped table, with two microscopes and a handful of slides strewn about. Their faces were featureless, hidden by the masks, and their troubled eyes above the white muzzles disturbed me more than anything else.

I put the mask on and looked through the eyepiece. At first, I only saw normal brain tissue—grey matter, little neuron bodies splayed like stars. Then I realized that there was something else: white filaments stretching between the cells, like some weird shadow axons connecting them, while the real axons were nowhere to be seen.

"Huh," I said out loud. "That's a fungus. "

"What kind?"

I looked up at Cramer who'd asked, anxiously, and shrugged. "Hard to say. Looks like a dikaryon to me, so likely a basidiomycete or an ascomycete. Cup fungus. The same group as a truffle."

"What is a truffle doing in his head?" Johnny muttered, and his lovely dark eyes looked at me, tortured, the white palimpsest of a former mustache twitching.

"Not a truffle, probably," I said. "More likely, some mold like a bread mold or some parasitic thing. I don't think any are parasitic on humans."

"Can you find out exactly what it is then?" a previously silent man I've never met before asked.

"I suppose I could do some DNA testing on it," I said. I could, and really, this was kind of interesting. You don't see a lot of people killed by a fungus in their brain. At least, I didn't. "Can I get a sample?"

"Only dead tissue," Cramer said. "CDC is on us. Even the slides have to be treated cautiously. CDC is saying it's an epidemic."

"It's not," Johnny interrupted, and the rest of them nodded. "They just have to overreact. Boy who cried wolf, you know."

"There are similar cases?" I asked.

Johnny nodded. "We just heard that there was another case in Atlanta. One in Texas. One in India. One in Russia, two in China, two in Korea, one in Western Europe, one in the Philippines. Possibly in Ghana, but that one wasn't confirmed."

Even though I wasn't an epidemiologist, I finally understood the perplexed expressions of everyone here. It didn't make any sense—with an epidemic, one expected a localized cluster. Some connection between people. With no discernible pattern at all and just a few cases per continent, it didn't make any sense.

"I'll find out about the fungus," I promised. "I'll be careful."

With that, Cramer handed me a slide, and that was that. "I'm going home then," I said, and looked at Johnny. "Unless you need me for anything."

He shook his head, sorrowful. "No one needs anything right now. We should all go home. You mind driving?"

And that was how I ended up with the mystery fungus in my figurative lap. The labs in community colleges were not exactly state of the art, but neither was their security, so I smuggled my slides in and made sure that no other faculty members were interested in using the thermocycler. I figured I'd amplify some standard sequences with Neurospora markers to see if the ascomycete databases turned up this particular sequence. Because if that didn't work, I would have to bother someone better off in terms of lab equipment...although it could be a good excuse to go see Alan.

I chastised myself for managing to drag the poor undeserving Alan into my tawdry schemes. And really, I owed it to everyone involved to keep my love life uncomplicated and straightforward, and I had decided a few months ago that Alan was a mere friend, a good friend, with whom

I had daily chat sessions. Nothing unusual there. Plenty of people did that; but I would be the first to admit that the fact that my scientific interests lately boiled down to excuses to see Alan was, at the very least, problematic.

I dug through the freezer, looking for primers which I surely had and Taq polymerase that I possibly had, and promised myself to talk to Alan as soon as the thermocycler was up and running. The whole process was way too close to magic for my taste—you never knew when the temperamental apparatus would decide not to work, and I considered sacrificing small animals to the unknown, but hopefully amenable to bribery, gods of the PCR and molecular biology.

Thankfully, I found the polymerase and the primers and all the buffers, and loaded the machine. I had a computer in the lab—an old, embarrassingly outdated, PC which ground and whined every time I attempted to run AIM and internet browser at the same time, as if it were the greatest indignity ever inflicted on machine kind. It sat squatly, like a plastic toad, on the chipped bench of which I claimed only half (the colleague to whom the other half belonged was thankfully not as interested in research as he used to be a few years back).

The thermocycler was doing its mysterious thing, and I said a stupid little prayer for my controls to work at the very least. Then I logged on.

Alan worked in an IT department of a bigger and better university barely fifty miles away. I'd met him when they'd had a conference on fungal ecology, and Alan had shown up repeatedly to fix people's laptops that wouldn't interface with projectors or to help with other technical crap a roomful of academics couldn't deal with. I offered to buy him lunch out of gratitude and the fact that his jeans fitted surprisingly well for an IT guy. We have talked daily ever since, and I've meticulously hidden it from Johnny, even though I wasn't doing anything untoward.

Alan pinged me immediately—I didn't even have to pretend to ignore him.

"Hi," he said. "A friend of mine died."

"Who?" I messaged back, thinking about the body in the morgue not a mile from me. A body with its brain removed and sliced and infected by an ascomycete. An ascomycete whose DNA was hopefully being amplified at this very lab.

"No one you'd know," he replied. "A friend in Kenya. They think it's some brain infection."

Even better. "I didn't realize you had a Kenyan connection."

"I traveled a few times. My grandparents came from there."

"Sorry to hear about your friend." I wondered if I should tell him. "Johnny says there've been a few cases like that all over the world."

A long pause. Finally, he typed, "Do they know what's causing it?"

"No. There was a dead man at the police station yesterday. I'm helping out with some work."

"I'm sure they have CDC cracking on that too."

He didn't have to be dismissive. Sure, I was small potatoes, but someone cared enough to find out what I thought. I held my whining back because the man had just lost a friend. "I'm sure I'm not humanity's only hope," I typed with unnecessarily forceful keystrokes. "But the more people are working on it, the better."

"Sorry," Alan said. "You want to get together soon?"

By now, I'm certain that Alan had no romantic or sexual interest in me. And yet my heart sped up.

"Sure."

There were things that remained unsaid between Alan and me; for example, Johnny and the fact he's a cop, and what was I doing and all that. Alan disliked Johnny on general principle, I think—he confessed his mistrust of the cops almost as soon as we'd met. We ran an interesting continuum of GLBT activism—I was always signing petitions and organizing things at the college, while Johnny, if not exactly closeted, preferred not to mention words like GLBT.

On the third hand, Alan seemed to be used to several different kinds of oppression so that neither one stood out as particularly deserving of anger. I supposed that when you catch enough shit, every new offense becomes just one more thing. Early on, he told me as much. "You're white," he said. "You expect to be treated well. When people don't, you get outraged and run to the nearest pride parade. It must be nice to have only one thing to ever be annoyed about."

"Not as nice as having nothing to be annoyed about," I parried, but took his point. Between the three of us, we presented a nearly comprehensive picture of neuroses and coping strategies. Neuroses were mostly mine and strategies mostly Alan's, with Johnny partaking as little as possible of either.

Alan's IM screen timed out, then he came back on. "Sorry. On the phone with another friend. It's weird but it seems that someone I know is also dead. In Denver."

"What happened?"

"They don't know. Dropped dead in front of his computer."

I swallowed hard. Johnny had said they'd found the fungal corpse (this is what I'd started calling him) in front of the computer, too. Then again, if I were to drop dead, the likelihood would be that I would go in the same way—I was spending too much time in front of the monitor. It was becoming a cliché, like death in front of the TV. "Was he online a lot?"

"Yes. Isn't everyone?"

"LOL," I typed, obligatorily. And immediately added, "Sorry about your friend."

"We gamed together sometimes," Alan said. "Isn't it sad how virtual friends become your actual friends? I swear, between you and my gaming group, that's most of my social life."

I felt flattered that he included me.

Alan logged off soon after, and I played spider solitaire until the thermocycler did its dirty business and spat out some DNA. Fortunately, it worked—the control shone nice and brightly, but the sample wasn't even there. I cursed and called the bio-tech supplier to get primers for every fungal group known to humankind. Afterward, I checked online to see if Alan was back on (he wasn't), and headed home soon after.

Johnny got home early too—I was barely starting on dinner. I decided to make pork loins with sweet potatoes and mango relish, and Johnny sniffed the air suspiciously. "Fruit?"

"Some," I said, and chopped mangoes. This place had an all-right kitchen, with a vaulted window and spacious slate counter tops, but I wished for a bigger stove and a breakfast nook. Perhaps we could remodel some day, if Johnny overcame his distaste for any sort of domestic tasks. And gourmet food.

"Don't make it too fancy, okay?" he said.

"Okay. "

He lingered in the kitchen, two steps behind me, and I could see the frown on his forehead out of the corner of my eye.

"What's up?" I said. "Any word from CDC?"

He shook his head. "They think it's fungal meningitis. Crypto-something."

"Cryptococcus." The word hung uncomfortably. For a gay man of his age, Johnny was so naïve—it's like he'd never heard of cryptococcal meningitis. "But it mostly affects immuno-compromised people."

"That's what the CDC said."

"Only it's not—Cryptococcus is usually a yeast, and these grew into filaments."

Johnny shrugged. "Can't help you there."

"I'm getting basidiomycete primers tomorrow," I said. And added when I saw his blank look, "Crypto is a basidiomycete."

"There was another case today," he said. "In Denver."

"How did he die?"

"Collapsed in front of his computer. The weird thing though…that guy in Denver had ants crawling all over him, and there was broken glass. When he fell, it looks like he broke his ant farm."

"Ant farm?" What was he, five?

Johnny nodded. "The guy last night…he had one, too. Do you think…"

"Ants and humans don't share any fungal parasites. There are some fungi that parasitize ants, like Cordyceps, but it's an ascomycete. The sample isn't."

I peeled sweet potatoes and talked, trying to cover up the sensation of quiet dread that was starting to stir in my stomach. If you're a kid, you get this sensation in the dark, walking to the bathroom in the middle of the night, that pure maddening fear that makes you forget your dignity and run and leap into bed, irrational fear turning into no less irrational triumph at having escaped and made it under the blanket. As an adult, I had nowhere to run and no way to overcome the fear but by talking. I felt Johnny's irritation with my chattiness growing, like a billowing steam cloud very close behind my back, but I couldn't help it.

"David," he said, after I babbled about ascomycetes for a good five minutes. "I have no idea what the hell you're talking about, but it smells delicious. I'm going to hit the shower and I'll see you in a little bit, all right?"

I felt perverse as I said, without turning, just imagining his hunched over back receding toward the living room, "Alan knew this guy, I think."

"You spoke to Alan." He stopped. "When?"

"Today." I really never meant to use Alan to make Johnny jealous, but I always did nonetheless. "He said a friend of his died in Denver, collapsed in front of the computer. I think it's the same guy."

"Could be." Johnny sounded thoughtful rather than pissed off or upset. "Can you ask him the guy's name, and if that's the right guy, ask Alan what the dead man had wanted with an ant farm."

"What happened to the ants?"

"In the criminology lab," Johnny said. "they're testing them for pathogens."

I was certain that they wouldn't find anything, but kept quiet.

Johnny resumed his tired trek to the bathroom, and I was left with my cooking and my guilt. And a great excuse to call Alan and meet him for coffee—why, Johnny had practically encouraged me to.

I got hold of Alan first thing in the morning. "Did your friend have an ant farm?" I messaged.

"Larry? Yeah, he did." The right guy then. "Spoke about it a lot. Weird that you asked."

"Why?" I asked, warming up to my new role as an interrogator.

"Last time we spoke, he kept asking me to get an ant farm. He said, these are not some stupid regular ants—these are leaf cutter ants, and he could mail me a starter colony because he just got some flying ones. He said he would mail them to me if I wanted. And the mushrooms they grow—you know, for food. It is kinda neat. Ever heard of it?"

I did. Leaf-cutter ants and their fungal gardens had always fascinated me—the fungi more than the ants, because those were the ones not found anywhere else but the ants' burrows. Talk about mutualism! I just wasn't sure they would make great pets.

"But why?"

"Dunno." Alan fell silent for a few minutes, and I was starting to worry. When he came back, he only said, "He liked the way they mulched those leaves, and the fungal gardens."

And then he logged off abruptly. I waited around, hoping he would come back and it was a computer malfunction and not a virtual slammed door. He never returned, and I started another round of PCR—thank God for overnight primers.

Things nagged on my mind—the deaths, of course, but also this subdued strangeness and the interplay of the fungal groups. What I had at first thought to be an ascomycete was likely to be a basidiomycete, the group that included edible mushrooms and Cryptococcus and some disease-causing fungi, and— I stopped abruptly, my mind searching for tentative connections where there weren't any. Molds that leaf-cutter ants grew were also basidiomycetes, only they were edible, not parasitic.

The phone rang, startling me. It was Johnny, of course—who else would call me at the lab during the summer break? College was such a ghost town then, it was difficult to believe that it was packed with young bodies for most of the year, and I was just a pale, pudgy apparition among their exuberant, fleshy youth. Now, however, I was fully present, solid, and flinching at the sound of the ringing phone. I picked up.

"Interesting thing," he said. He often started mid-sentence. "CDC says it's not crypto—you were right. They don't know what it is. Sequences don't match anything in the database."

Scooped by the CDC—not surprising, they of course have better equipment and more people who are better at this stuff. "They're sure."

"Yeah. Apparently, there was another body. Some shut-in, he must've died days ago. He never came out, just played his online games. Neighbors complained about the smell. Anyway, he was in bad shape to begin with, but the weird thing was, there was something like a black horn growing out of his head. They sent a bio-hazard team and sealed the area, because they think it's the mushroom, or whatever you call it."

"Fungal fruiting body," I mumbled, trying not to be too alienating. "You sure it looks like a horn?"

"Sure, but I can Email you some pictures." He paused, humming to himself. "You know, it's so strange to be working with CDC. They really get on those cases quick, and I like that they keep us in the loop."

"They can't arrest people. Or do all the legwork. They need you."

"I suppose." He heaved a sigh. "Listen, I'll be home early. I'll make dinner."

Well, that was new. "Thanks. I'll work a little later then."

"Have you spoken to Alan?"

"Briefly, on IM. He said his friend in Denver was really into ants. I'll look into it."

"Thanks."

As soon as we hung up, I collapsed onto my stupid metal chair with the twisty leg that didn't quite work properly, and clasped my head in my hands. There was something awfully familiar about all this, and the black horn…I logged into my Email and shuddered when I saw the pictures Johnny had sent: the man's face was carefully blotted out, but the blue and purple streaks on his balding scalp spoke of decomposition, and there was an ugly protuberance emerging from the back of his skull. A long thin black horn stretched upward, like a leech doing a tail stand. I had to remind myself that I was looking at the actual picture of an actual dead person, so fascinated I was with the alien structure.

I shifted my attention to the background—behind the swollen purple head with no face, there silvered a rectangle of the computer monitor opened to a blank page. And to the right of the head, there was a dark angle streaked with white, and it took me a second to realize that I was looking at a fish tank filled with earth, and the white streaks were mere reflected light from the monitor. An ant farm, with the possibility of a close look.

I opened the picture and zoomed in—high resolution photography made everyone a blade runner—and stared at the twisty, creviced mass of the soil. There were darker specks of underground tunnels, as one would expect in an ant farm, and I moved the cursor around, looking for any hint of anything unusual. In the very corner, I finally found something: thin threads of yellow and blue, coalescing into a lace-like pattern, fuzzing upward. Mold, I thought, good old fashioned ant food. That looked nothing like the black horn growing out of the dead man's head.

I sighed and opened the browser. I knew now what I was looking for, only I still had no clue as to what it meant. I Googled "Cordyceps" and Emailed the images to Johnny.

Cordyceps was a parasitic fungus, infecting ants and other insects. It would take over their minds, make them behave in a strange manner—like climb to the very top of a tree, where the fungus would produce a fruiting body, a tiny slender horn, that would then disseminate its spores from the highest point possible. The horn that looked just like the one in Johnny's picture.

There were two problems with that: first, Cordyceps was an ascomycete, and I'd already ruled out this possibility. Second, humans were not insects, and no fungus ever jumped host from insect to a human. Also, there didn't seem to be an explanation for involvement of computers or ant farms.

The thermocycler beeped, helpfully letting me know that it was done. I slapped the tube contents onto a gel to run it. While the gel was doing its thing, I called Alan.

It took him a while to answer.

"I need to talk to you," I said.

His voice came slow, dreamy. "I can't. I need to set up the farm."

"What farm?" I asked, chilling inside.

"An ant farm, stupid," he said, and breathed his usual affectionate laugh. "Larry was right—it's awesome."

There wasn't anything particularly great about the one in the dead man's apartment. It was just a drab ant farm with some colorful mold, and by now I had no doubt it was dangerous. "Listen to me,"I said slowly, my mouth suddenly dry and my heart too sluggish to pump thick corn-syrup-like blood. "Don't touch those ants and the mold, okay? I think they might be killing those people."

His laughter came distant now, as if through a layer of cotton wool. "They're fine, really. Larry told me all about them."

"Larry's dead," I said.

There was the pause and the peculiar silence that let you know when someone had hung up on you. I put the receiver down and drew in a deep breath.

I felt light and empty and transparent as the things that had been happening to other people, in my proximity but not actually inside my sphere of concern, suddenly became personal and mattered to the point of heart palpitations and sick stomach and sweat on my palms. I didn't like the feeling one bit.

Now it was my turn to call home and apologize for being late; I would've found a perverse pleasure in it if I weren't so rattled. Thankfully, Johnny didn't pick up. I left a message, hoping that my voice was steady enough. "Johnny,"I started. "I need to go see Alan. I think he got some of these ants. They grow this fungus, this mold—and it's a basidiomycete." (A quick shine with a UV lamp at my gel confirmed it—basidiomycete primers did their thing and there were fluorescent smudges of DNA all over the gel. "Yes, sure enough. See, those are leaf-cutter ants, and they grow a basidiomycete that they eat. But this one seems to be different—its fruiting body looks like an ascomycete, a parasitic fungus. I think it's a fusion organism of some sort." I caught myself then, and unplugged the gel—it would be fine 'til tomorrow. "Anyway. I worry about Alan, and I'll go see him, all right? Don't worry—I won't go inside and I'll call the police if anything seems amiss. Love you."

Alan lived about forty miles north, in Elizabeth. I used to live there once, many years ago, and I still had a warm regard for the city, no matter how ugly-polluted-industrialized-gentrified it grew by the day. I'd never been to Alan's place even though his address was in my Rolodex—I mailed him a book once, more of an excuse, the card in the pile of other cards a potential promise. I took it with me and, guided by recollection rather than useless GPS, drove along Elmora Street, looking for Vine that would take me to Dehart. The store fronts were just as I remembered them, Portuguese bakeries and bodegas, only older and with fraying awnings. I had no time to grieve for them, and I finally found the street and then the house, and rang the doorbell with a sense of dark foreboding.

There was no answer, and I knocked, and then banged on the door. The hallway, barely visible through the gauzy shade on the glass door, remained dark and dusty and empty. I rang the doorbell again.

Just as I was about to call the police, I heard footsteps. An old woman came to the door, dragging a foot and glaring at me from in between her hunched shoulders wrapped in a cabbage rose shawl.

"Looking for Alan," I said, as soon as she opened the door.

She waved her desiccated arm to point me up the stairs. "Third floor," she said. "Loft. He's probably playing his game again. He always wears headphones and cannot hear a thing."

Somewhat relieved, I thanked her and rushed up the stairs, taking three steps at a time. First I would have to flush those ants down the toilet...no, too dangerous. I needed to get Alan out of there and then call the hazmat team. That made sense.

Alan's apartment was located at the top storey, which was smaller than the other two—it was practically a turret or a garret crowning the old house. I knew places like this; I always loved them for their open floor plan and surprising nooks and crannies. But now was not a good time to consider architecture, and I knocked. Alan didn't answer, but the door squealed open the moment I applied some force to it.

The windows were tiny and the loft was dimly lit by fading daylight. No lights were on, and the nearest window was all but blocked off by a sizable jade tree in a clay pot. "Alan?" I called.

There was no answer except for faint, distant clacking, and I squinted into the dusk, past the raised platform with an undone bed on it and a tiny kitchen adjacent, separated only by half a drywall, and to the opposite end where another window was hidden behind drawn curtains and the milky light of a large flat monitor beckoned me.

"Alan?"

Nothing but the keystrokes, and—despite my promises to Johnny and myself—I didn't turn and call the cops, I, instead, took a cautious step toward the computer.

Alan did not turn even when I was barely a foot behind him. The accursed ant farm sat next to him on the table, and Alan's IM window was open.

"These ants are great," he typed. "You have to get them. I have some extras."

"Alan?" I called without much hope of him ever hearing me.

He continued to type with stiff fingers, dead like those of a marionette. I fought the familiar quiet terror that had been twisting my stomach into knots and suddenly remembered danger. I started to back away—I remembered that the ants took those who were infected by Cordyceps as far from their anthills as possible. I was supposed to be smarter than an ant; then again, if they didn't get infected by casual contact...I remembered the black horn, the spore-producing fruiting body. It was only when it bloomed out of the wretched head of an unfortunate insect and shed spores that it became dangerous. I hoped it worked the same here.

Then another window popped up, and he typed the same text, intent, oblivious to everything but the tapping of the keys. Then another. I was about to pull him off, to warn people on the receiving end of his messages that they didn't need ant farms, when a video-chat window popped up. As if moved by an invisible force that filled him like a hand filling an empty glove, he picked up the ant farm and held it up, to the blinking eye of the small camera on top of the monitor. In the chat window, a pale pair of hands and a fish tank with ants appeared. It was very quiet as two men held their ant farms, as if the fish tanks were talking to each other.

Of course not. It was the ants—and the dark, damp room span before me as if a fissure opened before my feet. Of course, of course—the ants took over gamers, geeks, and others who spent time online so that they could persuade others to get more ants, and then ants made them facilitate communications between colonies. Ants took advantage of technology.

Very carefully, I pried the tank out of Alan's fingers. He didn't look at me, his hands still curled, fingers twitching as if struggling against imaginary weight. I rested the tank on the table, and grabbed Alan's elbow. He felt rigid beneath my fingers, as if rigor mortis were already setting in.

"Come on," I muttered, and dragged him to his feet.

He swayed but stood, empty. Cordyceps took control of ants' brains; the fungus that they'd made (and by then I had no doubt that the mold in the tank was some unholy union of a parasitic ascomycete and a mild-mannered edible basidiomycete ants have been cultivating for millennia, created by ants) was likely to influence human behavior in a manner conducive to ants' designs—spread them around and then let them talk to each other by video, so that they could teach each other how to grow the terrible fungus.

I almost laughed out loud at the absurd marriage of hive minds, ant colony and the internet, as I maneuvered Alan, stiff and light like a dead cat, toward the door of his apartment. Was he contagious? I hoped not. I hoped that there was some anti-fungal that would clear Alan's poor infected geeky brain right out. I also hoped that I wasn't messing up too badly.

I propped Alan against the wall as I dialed 911. They apparently got the CDC memo—as soon as I mentioned a fungal infection in the brain, I was transferred and a very calm, very kind voice told be not to take Alan outside but to wait inside the apartment.

Now that he was away from the ants, he seems to have lost the animating essence that moved him, and I let him collapse onto his bed. He sat, slumped, hands dangling between his knees, unresponsive to the world. If the fungus was still sending signals to his brain, he was unable to obey them. "I'm sorry," I whispered. "I tried to warn you. I'm sure they can fix you." I wasn't. More disturbingly, I was getting a little light-headed from all the exertion and excitement. I tried to breathe deeper, all the while wishing I had a paper bag. Then I thought about the spores and held my breath.

There were sirens outside, and voices, and then the day caught up with me and I watched the darkness slowly fold over me, like a midnight-dark steamroller.

I woke up in a hospital bed, a blue corrugated curtain blocking the view of the rest of the room, but I knew someone was there. A chair squealed and I looked up to see Johnny leaning forward in his chair.

"Don't move," he said. "You're on the IV drip for the fungus."

"They sure it'll work?"

He smiled. "Pretty sure. You know you're crazy to have gone in there. You should've just called the cops."

I sensed his anxiety, thick in the air like the smell of sweat. "I would've done the same for you," I answered the question he didn't ask. "It was just so awful to think of someone all alone, and no one there to help. Like that man with a mushroom growing out of his head, you know?"

Johnny nodded. "Yeah. It was noble of you."

I listened for traces of sarcasm but couldn't find any. "I saw him showing the ants to the camera while someone else did the same. The ants, they talk via video-chat"

Johnny raised his eyebrows. "You saw that?"

I nodded. "See, it's a good thing I went inside. I'm sure that this fungus both feeds the ants and helps them spread by infecting people and making them do the ants' bidding."

Johnny shrugged. "Weird," he said. "Thank you for doing the work. CDC got some genes of this thing but they had no idea what it is or where it came from or what it does."

I thumbed at the IV line. "Am I infected for sure?"

"They're not sure—you crashed pretty badly. Feel a need to act like an ant?"

I smiled at the joke. "Not at all. I feel like squashing them all, really."

Johnny managed a smile. "Then you'll be all right."

"What about...."

"He should be all right too. They think that fungus doesn't have any immunities, so the meds should work." He paused a while. "Anything else you need to tell me?"

"I told you everything I know."

"Not about the fungus. About—" he thrust his chin in the direction of the curtain behind which Alan presumably lay in an identical bed.

I closed my eyes and smiled. It was nice to see him return to normalcy so quickly—on the one hand, there were intelligent ants and their weaponized fungus. On the other, Johnny was jealous, and it made me feel comforted, as if nothing was too bad when there were people who found energy to be jealous. As long as our little relationships mattered to us, there wasn't going to be the end of the world.

"Well?"

I shook my head, the hospital pillowcase whispering starched and parchment-thin with every movement. "No," I said. "Nothing at all."

Ghost Technology from the Sun

Paul Jessup

Master told us that the Earth was hollow, and that we lived on the inside of it, clinging to the top of the crust. Below us was another world, a world inside the world, a glowing bright sun of a place. What Master called the summerlands. That is where the dead live, he said. That is how we can talk to them, he said. They send us signals across the air, and the mediums pick them up and drink them in.

And when the words came in, we had to speak them. We cannot deny the dead our voices—the dead would be angry if we did. And nobody wanted the angry dead to fly their zeppelins up from the sun and attack us crust dwellers.

That wouldn't do anyone any good.

Master knew this because he is an ambassador to the land of the dead. At night he walked through the door of the dead, and it beamed his body down above us, into the summer sun inside of the earth. That is where he talked to them, worked out trade between our two peoples.

The dead have a lot to offer the living.

He came back with schematics.

Ways of building circuit boards.

Ghost technology from the sun.

I remember when Ma first drank in the voices of the dead and talked with the tongue of paper and fire. We'd only been here a week or so and I was frightened of what was going to happen, having heard stories of horror from different members of the God's Foot Spiritualists. I kicked and screamed, refusing to go with her into the lodge, refusing to let her destroy herself for religion.

Eventually I gave in.

They took us into the Dead Man's Tongue. This was a lodge built for dead drinking. It had no windows and was covered in paintings of ghosts and the summerlands. It was lit entirely by the Master's halo, blue light bouncing off of the walls and illuminating the circle of faces in an eerie chilled light.

I remember clearly the shadow chanting and the fingers moving and the feet pounding out that rhythm. Ra-tat-tat. Ra-tat-tat. A hum of sounds: ah-m-m-m-ah. Ah-m-m-m-ah. The air thickened, and we could hear a clear barrage of whispers. Like everything started whispering around us, the trees, the lodge, the stars and the sun. Everything had a voice, and everything spoke in hushed tones.

Mother rolled her eyes back in her head, the marble white of her corneas reflecting the cities in the sun. Her mouth opened wide and out came fire and words and long streams of paper snakes. She danced and spat and spoke, she revealed her breasts and screamed. The chosen in-scribers jotted down everything she said into small red-and-black note-books.

It is said that past the gardens and into the woods there is a hidden library filled with small red-and-black notebooks. It is said that the Master goes there every night and reads them. Over and over again. Never sleeping.

"The dead don't sleep," he once told Ma. "And neither should I."

The Master was handsome.
The Master was tall.
The Master was a bone setter and an electrician.
We called him 'he who walks among the dead.'
When I turn fourteen I want to marry the Master.

I practiced writing my name and his in a small red notebook. I would run the names together, combine them into new shapes and new words. I hoped that the truth in ink would become the truth in flesh.

I wandered through the garden at night, in hopes I could see him as he returned from the hidden library. I always tried to strike up some sort of conversation with him, flirting with him a little. He acted non-chalant, but I could feel something there—a spark, a chemical connec-tion. A magnetic pull from his eyes to my heart.

I am scared for the Master when he beams down into the undersun. The cave made so much noise. The screams of the dead, wailing as he walked between dimensions. I was afraid that he would never return.

And then where would we be?

Lost and haunted by the dead.

With no one to lead us.

I was so lonely in God's Foot, being the only child there and with no one to play with. Most of the people in our commune were women, and they were all pregnant with the Master's kin. He called these women the Blessed, and he said that they carried the weight of Angels inside of them.

Last week I noticed my ma's belly was full and shaped like the moon below us, and I asked her if she was Blessed. She said she was, and she said that in a year or two I could become Blessed as well. That made me so happy I bounced around for the rest of the day. I made extra certain that the Master noticed me, and tried to look my best every time I went out to play.

I wore my blue dress and tied gold ribbons in my hair. He saw me twice, and both times he mentioned how pretty I was and how happy he was for me to be here, living amongst such fine folk. Just hearing the deep rumble in his voice made me feel so happy.

Imagine that! Me! Blessed!

What a wonderful day that would be.

The garden was pretty at night.

So blue and full of shadows.

Master said the sun had two sides, one blue and one yellow. It span beneath us, and that is why we have night and day. And all those stars and clouds—those were voices of the dead, moving through the ether for us to bring into our bodies and interpret.

We used the séance in order to drink in the words.

Our bodies became balls of light.

The words etched into our skin.

Last night I saw a rabbit in the garden.

I shooed him away, but he just smiled at me.

With a mouthful of human teeth.

One day the Master came out of the Door to the Dead with a roll of ancient looking blueprints. He unrolled them and told everyone to begin work on this right away. This would be out greatest achievement. By the end of that week the whole village was lit up with electricity, and we called him the light bringer. Some of the people even compared him to Prometheus or Hermes, stealing the light of wisdom and bringing it down to us poor mortal folk.

I remember the first night we had all those lights up, strung between the trees in paper lanterns. They glowed and hummed and I remember touching the wires, feeling the electricity sharp and alive inside of them. Master says that this was just the beginning.

He was working on something bigger, better.

Earlier today the dead came into me and made me paint them. The canvas was stretched out beneath me and dyed brown with tea. I felt a surge of power in my head and the whispers of the dead in my ears. The air became thick, heavy. Like a wet blanket around my skin.

Then my hands moved and I couldn't stop it. At first I was scared, my body taken over by an outsider. I tried to keep the dead out; I did not want to drink it in. My hands moved anyway, my thoughts and motions no longer mine. My whole body felt numb around me, completely unresponsive to my thoughts.

I stopped fighting it and just went with the flow. It was what the Master called the rivers of our soul, which the dead ride like boatmen. They taint the water inside of us with their fingers as they ride, and we drink in this taint and become the words they speak.

I saw the summerlands as I painted.

I saw the golden sphere within the earth below us.

I saw all of the dead looking at me, their flesh rotting, their teeth grinning. I wanted to scream. The summerlands was no paradise. Not at all. It was all dark and dank architecture and filled with the bones of the dead. They wanted to pull me down, yank on the river of my soul and push it into the summerlands.

When I came too I looked down and saw my painting.

Red, red.

A crow in red.

And that rabbit. With teeth. And his bride in white right next to him, frightened and with a veil of the dead across her eyes.

And there, in the middle of it all, was a sun.

Smiling, hungry.

Wanting to eat me whole.

When I was done I ran outside and threw up in the bushes. The Master came by and I was so embarrassed, and I knew he wouldn't want to marry me now. No one ever would. How could he love me when I smelled of vomit?

The Master praised my painting. He hung it in the Dead Man's Tongue with all of the others. He said that I had been possessed by Uk-Olak-Ken, the dead god of Atlantis. Gods die too, he said, and they also go and live in the summerlands of the afterlife just like the rest of us mortals.

He said that this painting was very special, and no one had ever been possessed by Uk-Olak-Ken before. He told me he had a secret job for me. One that no one else could ever know about. Not even Ma.

I made dolls out of the corn husks in the garden. The dolls were very tall, about as tall as I am, and I dressed them up in my clothes and took them outside and danced with them. Sometimes I pretended they were real and they were my friends.

Some nights I could hear them whispering after the séance, and I wondered if the dead voices were trapped within them. As if they were possessed somehow. I meant to tell the Master or Ma about it, but during the daylight hours I forgot.

There was so much work to do on the farm, and everyone had to help out. Even those who were Blessed.

I once lined up all of the corn dolls in the garden and dressed them in red and black dresses. I called them the army of corn, and made them ready for war against the trees around them. Out of the corner of my eye I saw something brown and furry dart between the rampion.

I stood and walked toward it, following it.

The air felt thick with dreams and whispers. Like it did during a séance. I heard the screams and howls come from the door to the dead and realized that the Master must be descending again. Going down and above us, into that sun in the center of the world.

I saw a furry puff of a tail peek out from between the cabbages, and two brown ears slicked back onto a mangy skull. "Rabbit," I said, as I walked towards it. "Rabbit, what are you doing in our garden? This is our food. "

The rabbit turned his head and smiled at me with a mouthful of human teeth. "Get on my tail," he said.

"No, never. Go."

He hopped closer to me, the grin widening into a threat. "Come on.

Follow me to the Door of the Dead."

I stepped backwards, frightened.

"Who are you?"

He hopped closer, and then stood up. His back uncoiled and he grew as tall as I am, standing on his hind legs like a human. His eyes were dark and troubled, and the center of them looked like suns stuck into his hollow head. "I am the keeper of doorways."

I stepped back and pointed at my dolls." They are armed," I said, "with the voices of the dead."

They whispered then, the sound filling the air with the smell of turpentine and rotten eggs.

The rabbit hopped backwards.

"Ah, then. I guess I'll be getting on. But I will return. You are far too pretty to leave be, and I need a wife sooner than soon."

And then he shrank down and hopped off, leaving the dust of his footprints across the garden.

The Master brought us all together before a séance one night with an announcement. He had brought new schematics from the land of the dead, and we will have new ghost technology in order to build and use. He laid out the plans on the grass and started pointing out different things that would need to be done.

"This will be," he said, "an amplifier to the voices of the dead. No longer will they whisper in the void between our worlds. This will take the ether between us and the summerlands and thicken it—making them louder and more audible to us."

The people cheered.

The Master is taking us into a new era of enlightenment. Humanity will evolve now—faster and more sure, toward the shores of the dead. No longer will we be separate, and travel between the worlds will be as easy as riding on a train.

I was possessed by Uk-Olak-Ken again. He came into my skull and ate away at my mind, forcing the rivers of my soul to overflow and flood. I screamed in angst and my mother said I bit her on her leg. She showed me the rings of broken skin my teeth had made, like red moons on her flesh.

I painted the walls of my room in the lodge while in the trance, red crows all over it and rabbit brides. I painted a large sun, grinning and hungry. I painted rivers of black slime and castles crumbling on the moonside of the sun. I painted the hollow earth, and a bridge that moved between it.

And I painted the zeppelins.

The skullish dead riding in them, ready to war with us breathing meatsacks. Their eyes glittered in my paintings, all hollow and holy and wanting to feed on us.

The painting frightened me.

Master said it was a good sign. A great omen. Uk-Olak-Ken had blessed us with this message. It meant that the dead will come to us soon, come and take us to the summerlands where we will be happy and no longer dependant on this crust of a world.

I felt sick and queasy, as I realized Master was wrong. This was a warning. The dead were preparing for war. They wanted to destroy us. They were jealous of our flesh and lives and they wanted to take our skin and wear it, steal our beating hearts and use them to pump the blood of life into their own dead bodies.

I slept in the garden after that incident.

I couldn't stay in the same room with that painting ever again.

There was a large gathering and ceremony before the Master switched on the newly built amplifier. The celebration started with prayers to the dead and an offering to the doors between worlds. Then it moved to a séance, with fourteen people all becoming possessed and two whole red-and-black notebooks filled with the mad sayings of the dead.

He then went forward and turned the machine on. It looked like a vivisected robot, all metallic intestines and beating artificial hearts. On top of it stood a brain molded in copper with black rubber tubes and a spine of bronze spouting out from it. The spine curved up and into the air, and shook and hummed when the machine was switched on.

It vibrated and sang while people celebrated. We danced to the music of the amplifier that night, the voices of the dead a chorus around us. The air felt thicker, wetter. A hot moisture dripping onto our bodies. We all felt possessed, and every one of us could hear the voices now, so loud and so clear.

And the smell.

The air smelled of sweetness and ripeness.

The next day my ma was outside, lying on the ground in a mud puddle near the back of our house. The mosquitoes hung like a biting buzzing veil around us, hungry in the sticky air. My ma's belly was round and sticking out of the mud like a moon stuck in the center of the void below us. I wondered if there was a world inside of her stomach with people like us clinging to the crust, and another world in the center with the voices of the dead.

Ma had mud all over her face.

Her eyes looked so tired.

All around us the voices of the dead carried on in conversation, forcing us to speak a little louder if only to be heard. "Marybeth dear," Ma said to me, "why did you sleep in the garden last night? I missed you."

I shrugged.

"That painting. It scares me. All those faces, dead faces, looking at us with such hatred." She waved her arms in the mud, making mud angels. Her face looked elsewhere, toward the ether. So murky, this air, I thought, so thick and deadly. "I can't sleep at night with you gone. Come and sleep with us, dear. Or the Master will think something's wrong with you."

I sat down in front of her, the mud staining my blue dress. Tonight, I thought, I will take the ribbons out of my hair. I don't want to wed the Master anymore. "Maybe there is something wrong with me. This air is suffocating."

Ma laughed. It was a strange and deadly sound.

"I don't feel pregnant. Isn't that weird? It's like what's inside of me is a ghost. Like my stomach is haunted, or even that an insect is living in there, getting larger with time. And I feel like this whole place is a dream, and the dead are the ones that are really alive."

Ma then rolled around in the mud, thickly coating her stomach. It looked like a brown and sticky circle of flesh, hidden under the dark shadows of her dress. I wanted to reach out and touch it, to feel the ghost beating under her skin.

It's so hard to breathe.

The air is so fluid.

Like trying to breathe underwater.

And the voices get louder and louder every day.

They sound like shouting snowflakes in a blizzard of sound.

The Master changed. I don't know if anyone else noticed it, but he started glowing brighter. So bright that the daylight gave way to his glow.

And his skin peeled and cracked. Beneath the holes in his skin more light throbbed and glowed, even stronger and more radiant than before.

He called himself Xansu.

Lord of the Lights.

And he would talk to people in half-heard whispers. I saw bits of paper stuck under his fingernails, and I saw him at the library more and more. He must be constantly reading those notebooks.

He stopped going to the séances.

And the séances became more violent, more disturbing. Almost everyone became possessed, and they attacked each other, the ghosts burning holes in their eyes and poisoning their soul rivers with rot and plague. Yesterday Erica blinded her husband. Ripped out his eyes with her own fingers.

The dead made her do it.

The dead make us do everything.

Their presence is overwhelming.

Master came by to visit me while I played in the garden one night before I went to sleep. He looked at my corn dolls and smiled. Their voices were louder now, I realized. They were practically screaming in the language of the dead.

The Master's body glowed as he approached me, sending away the light of the moon with his own disturbing blue illumination. He held his arms out to me. The closer he got, the more disgusting he looked. His face had holes in it, and his eyes were falling out. His hair was un-kempt and flaking off with patches of his scalp, and I wanted to scream at the sight of him.

Instead, I stayed silent.

"Hello, my child."

I nodded.

"I have a secret job for you."

I moved a little away from him. The corn dolls hissed at the Master as he moved, trying to send him away. Their voices clattered out in-sults, as they tried to move their corn-husk bodies to get close enough to attack him.

"Don't you want to know what it is?"

I stumbled back.

Still covered in sweat. This heat was unbearable even at night. No reprieve from the thickness of air. "No, it's okay. You can tell me tomorrow."

The Master smiled.

"Tomorrow might be too late," he said. "I need you to summon Uk-Olak-Ken. I need to talk to him."

I shook my head. "Why can't I do it during the séance tomorrow?"

The Master moved closer to me, his body gliding across the ground. "Too many people. I need to ask him secret stuff. Only stuff I need to know. Something is being hinted at in the notebooks. Something dark and terrible. I need to talk to him and learn what."

I looked at my corn dolls. I only wished I could give them life, let them move and protect me. "I don't want to. Have someone else act as your human puppet."

He grinned, and then clapped ash he chanted under his breath. My mind swam and my body felt moist. I rolled in the rivers of my soul, falling over the earth and up below us into the undersun. I could see the curvature of the crust above me, and Uk-Olak-Ken taking over my body.

I fought and tried to swim up through my mind and back into my flesh. I did not want to be trapped in the cellar mind anymore. I wanted to be out and stopping him. The Master was doing dangerous things, and we are going to pay for them soon enough.

I crawled against the currents, and fought against the rebellion in my mind. I forced that Uk-Olak-Ken back into the sun, forced him out of my body and back into the ether and the dank cities of the dead.

When I came too I realized I was sweating, naked.

A light was flowing out of the Master. It flew into my body in streams of fire. I started to cry as I realized what was going on. The light of him span inside of my stomach, weaving against the walls of my womb.

When he looked down he realized it was me in my body and no longer Uk-Olak-Ken. "My child," he said as my stomach span inside of me, "you are one of the Blessed now. You carry my seed, and the weight of Angels inside of you."

I wiped my tears away with my hands.

"Did you get the information?"

He nodded.

"Thank you, my child."

Good, I thought. Maybe you will do something to stop this, stop all of this. We are in danger of being eaten by the dead, our bodies used as costumes for them to parade around in and pretend to be alive.

He walked away, and I felt sick to my stomach, and certainly not blessed.

The next day I decided to wander through the woods and find the library. It took me a few hours, but I eventually found the ruins of an old Catholic church, and inside of it, notebook upon notebook scattered among the pews. The walls of the church looked like old bones, bleached and full of holes.

The notebooks were mostly arranged by importance and relevance. Most of them had pages bookmarked, and some were impossible to read due to water damage. I flipped through a few of them at bookmarked pages, and started to find an unsettling pattern.

Every bookmarked page mentioned a war of the dead. It mentioned fire from the sun, and the destruction of the crust dwellers. It mentioned war machines of unbelievable power, and of ways to travel between the lands of the living and the dead.

I felt something slick move in my stomach.

He'd known all along.

And was going to do nothing.

It wasn't long before my stomach extended.

Fast, I thought, whatever it is, it grew fast.

I knew what Ma meant—it felt haunted. More of a ghost inside of me than a child growing.

A night or two later I saw the rabbit again. He walked up to my corn doll army, staring at them as he went. When he saw me he stood upright, his teeth shimmering in a grin beneath the moon. "Marybeth," he said, "will you get on my tail and join me?"

I had nothing else to lose.

"Where are we going to go?"

His grin deepened, wide and wider still. "Someplace you need to see. The Door to the Dead."

I climbed onto his tail.

"Let's go then," I said. "And when we get there, if you still want me to, I'll marry you."

The rabbit turned his head almost fully around, his mouth full of human teeth. "I would and still might. But what grows in you is dark and deadly, and I will not raise it. Not I, not ever."

He turned his head and got on all fours, his body shooting out and darting with me on his tail toward the cave known as the Door to the Dead.

Above us I saw the light of red crows, dancing under the moon.

The cave was empty. The door was a chalk drawing, and the sounds of screams and horrible noises came from a cage full of geese that the Master poked with a red hot poker. Rabbit showed me these tricks, how he deceived the people. In the corner of the cave was a series of diagrams and maps. All these schematics, all this hollow earth — he did not get this from the dead at all.

He came up with it himself.

Using us to get information about the dead with his séances, never once putting himself in any danger.

I saw rituals described in other pages, tales of sacrifices and stones that make you immortal. I realized then what the Master was doing — that each of us would be used to make him live forever. Even if he meant to bring the dead here and put us in danger.

I looked at Rabbit.

"Thank you," I said.

He held my hand in his paw.

"I love you. Come back to me when you are free from this burden. I will marry you, and we will live together in perfect harmony, far away from this dead world."

Outside of the cave I heard the red crows cawing, and the voices of the dead getting louder and louder still. It was so thick in the air, and it corrupted our thoughts and poisoned our soul rivers. Outside the moon became bright and turned into the sun, and the sun became bigger and bigger, like it was coming right toward us.

And I could see cities on the surface of the sun.

Bright, brilliant cities of light.

I held the rabbits paw in my hand.

So soft, so comforting.

"It may be too late," I said.

He nodded and then I jumped on his tail. Back to God's Foot we flew, fast and with the trees blurring around us.

In the sky above we saw the Zeppelins of the dead, flying from the sun cities to us crust dwellers. The voices around us floated in the air, angry, yelling. Wanting their light back. Wanting the stones of immortality back.

I searched for my ma when I got back, the rabbit following me, making certain I would be okay. The air made me feel like I drowning, the water of it entering our lungs and corrupting our breaths. We could not talk, not over the voices of the dead being amplified in the world around us.

My head was filled with so many thoughts.

So few of them were my own.

Rabbit helped keep me calm.

Helped keep me sane.

The creature inside of my stomach swam through me, licking my blood and grating against my bones. I wanted to flush it out of my system, to destroy it if possible. I was afraid to give birth, fearing that it might rip me apart as it crawled out.

I found the body of my mother with the others. Her stomach a mess, her ribcage poking out from her flesh. They were all stacked there, back behind the Dead Man's Tongue. They had all died in childbirth, their bodies being destroyed by whatever lived inside of them.

I saw the shadows of giants as they slouched about town, and heard the voice of the Master screaming and singing songs to them. The Master seemed to be almost completely light now, his skin discarded on the ground at his feet.

I wanted to tear this thing from my stomach.

I did not want to die like that.

I turned and looked at the stack of bodies. Standing next to them, all in a row were my corn husk dolls. The dolls turned and looked at me, and spoke in unison.

"They are here," the dolls said.

"The dead have come."

A Poor Man's Roses

Alethea Kontis

At first, she sang to remember. It was a way to pass the long, dark time, a way to drown out the buzz in her head when the earth shook and the bunker rattled, a way to live outside the bars of her cage, to be a woman who smoked and drank, flirted and pined, flipped her pin curls and married a man for his car. Eventually, Patsy Cline became Kerri's reason for living. In five years, she hadn't found a better one.

"Good morning," said Stella. It was the only clue Kerri ever had to the time of day, or the notion that days passed at all. Stella opened the cage hatch and slid the food through. "I have a surprise for you today." She smiled. "You'll like it."

Let's see…what would she like? Kerri would have welcomed a hot poker in the eye, an asteroid hitting the earth, or the blast from that damned super volcano the world had been holding its collective breath about for the past decade. It would be ironic, Kerri mused, if all three suddenly happened at once. About as ironic as someone surviving cancer just to live out the rest of her days in a prison.

"You're using your head-voice again," said Stella.

"Sorry." Kerri often forgot when she was speaking aloud, and when she wasn't. Stella seemed to be able to carry on the conversation regardless. "Surprise?" Beside her cardboard poultry and marbleized peas was a box. Kerri mentally dumped in that box all the bitterness she tried not to heap on Stella. The Bastard never had been able to make more than cereal and burnt toast, and his AI wasn't much better. Every time Kerri was tempted to advise Stella on how to make a palatable gravy, she asked herself why. Herself never had a decent answer.

Kerri lifted the box up to the laboratory light that slanted through the bars. "Animal crackers," she read…aloud? Stella smiled, so she guessed she must have. Then again, Stella was understanding more and more these days, whether Kerri spoke or not.

Surprise. Once upon a time the gesture would have meant something. Now, Kerri only felt empathy for the two-dimensional zoo creatures imprisoned by the lines drawn on their own cages.

"Aren't they wonderful? Dr. Petrakis brought them back on his last trip."

Kerri couldn't stop herself bursting into laughter; nor did she want to. Laughter told her she was still alive, and each guffaw brought her this much closer to insanity. *Oh, blessed insanity, why hast thou forsaken me?*

As if The Bastard actually gave her a second thought. "Doctor" Petrakis indeed. In this backwater life at the end of the world, you were whoever you pretended to be. There were no background checks anymore, and no point. No one begrudged another man his delusions of grandeur.

Fine. The Bastard could be a doctor; Kerri would be Patsy Cline. She put her fingers to her lips and took a long drag on an imaginary cigarette. "Wonderful," she said. "*Cra-zy,*" she crooned. Perhaps insanity was closer than she'd thought. Thank God. Oops, no, wait, God left in the last exodus, too. For Mars. Or Europa. Kerri had forgotten which. Patsy was better company in the dark than God ever had been. All those Sunday vows broken on Monday. Every day was Monday now.

"They'll make a nice treat after today's session," said Stella. "Did you drink enough water this morning?" It was a rhetorical question. If Kerri didn't drink her minimum water requirement, the alarm would pierce her skull until she did. She ran her fingers down the needle tracks in her arm to the shunt in her wrist, connecting the dots into imaginary constellations, her map to a galaxy far, far away. That one could be a rose. Or a rabbit. Or a crashed airplane.

Kerri shrugged. "Sure."

"Fantastic!" Stella slid her knuckles across the doorplate so the scanner could register the microchip in her ring. Stella's response to anything was always followed with an imaginary "Whoopee!" Kerri couldn't fault the programmers; one could only laugh at comments like "The toilet is broken!" and "Guess we'll try another vein!" and "Looks like the world is ending now!"

Kerri felt the bolt pull back, a hum in her blood, before the door snapped open with a bone-scraping buzz of the same quality as her dehydration alarm, only briefer. Kerri counted down the thirteen steps to the purple chair. Sometimes she made it in seventeen. Sometimes she made it in nine. She was always walking, always after midnight.

"Let's strap you in," said Stella.

Whoopee!

It always surprised her how warn Stella's hands were. Kerri looked forward to the slight shock, the mass of long, dark hair bent over the tubes and dials that was so much like hers—dark like her daughter's might have been. Kerri closed her eyes and felt her essence flow out of those tubes like silken ribbons. It was Patsy Cline who kept her here, not Stella, not this android who might-have-sort-of-not-really resembled the daughter Kerri almost-maybe-never had. A daughter who played prison warden and stuck her like a pincushion and… She would *not* think about what perversions The Bastard did to Stella beyond that door at the top of those stairs.

That door at the top of the stairs squealed open. Kerri remembered the last time The Bastard had come to visit, so long ago; she still fell to pieces every time she saw him. Now, after all this time, he wanted to see how she liked her little gift. He wanted her to thank him.

Thirty-five thousand angels screamed in the hinges and cried in his shadow as he walked down, heavy step by heavy step. Kerri kept her eyes closed. She imagined seven chins, sausage fingers, a gluttonous stomach rolling over his waistband to hide his severely inadequate manhood. She saw the blackness inside him, the inkblots in his eyes that gave proof to the Elder God who had eaten his pirate soul. His cologne triggered her gag reflex. Stella squeezed her hand. Whoopee.

Ribbons, not blood. Red silk. A poor man's roses. A ball gown and a crown on her head; all ways about here belonged to her, and off with his head. Pins and needles. The straps bit into her thighs. She had lost enough weight for Stella to tighten them a notch.

"Hello, wife," said the voice that made her wish she had electrocuted herself a long time ago. Nanomeds be damned. Would that the cancer had taken her. "How's my golden blood today?"

Kerri opened her eyes and denied the angel she saw: wheat-blond hair, eyes as blue as the sky was, once. That flat stomach that did not have her spear thrust through it mocked her, teased her, tortured her. She wished she could take her own share of his worthless, mortal blood and watch it spread out on the floor, seep around the bolts and through the cracks, down into the worthless soil of this wretched world that the universe had balled up and tossed in the waste bin. The Bastard and this planet deserved each other. *Why are you here?* Her head-voice cried. *Why are you still alive? Why haven't you crossed the wrong person or been hit by a meteor? Why haven't you dropped dead from the evil inside you? Why hasn't the earth opened up and swallowed you piece by dark piece?* Stella looked sad. The bunker trembled as Kerri's heart cried gold coins into her husband's leather pockets. Aftershock. Or premonition. Or both. Nanomeds were magical things. They made the recipient slightly more than human…and any enterprising harvester slightly less so.

His eyes had cried for her once, one solitary tear, the first day he'd strapped her into that chair, the first time—she had thought—he'd sold his soul to the devil, and the first time he'd sold her superblood on the black market to those vampires. He had made her believe it was her idea, made her think that this selfless gesture was for him, for their future, made her believe he'd loved her even half as much as she'd loved him. He had played her from the beginning, even before he'd bent down on one knee and asked her the question she would always regret answering. He was all lies. He was a mosaic, made up of exotic, multi-colored pieces of lies.

But that tear haunted her, that tear shed from those eyes that had looked at her in a moment of sadness. It was easier for her to live this unlife, to survive this pain, if she believed he was truly evil, that he had never had a soul, that he had never loved her. He wasn't a good enough actor to pull off actual emotion. What then, what was that damned tear?

"Have you ever been lonely? Have you ever been blue?" Kerri sang aloud, more for Stella than for herself this time. She wished her heart really was broken beyond repair and not fertile ground for more torture. Her mind continued its escape. Ribbons, not blood, poured out of her. Garters, not straps around her thighs. The toughest decision she'd make today would be which shoes to wear. Then again, not really. Red shoes went with everything.

And then the pain stopped. The blood stopped flowing. The straps fell away, along with her fantasies, and she was naked before him. "Surprise," he said. "Go, if you want to go. I wonder which of us will be the happier."

This time Kerri stopped herself from laughing. Always the head games with him. Always the gifts, absolving him of all wrong-doing. Even the way he had phrased the sentence—if she left, it wouldn't be his fault. Nothing was ever his fault. And now he gave her freedom? From underground cage to doomed planet. How magnanimous of him. Five years, blissful and blameless.

Kerri's head pounded. The glasses on the table shook as another contraction seized the planet sick with ague and ready to spew forth her boiling crimson insides. She could feel the nanos already replenishing the bits of her that she'd lost. She could feel the earth around her and the pressurized chaos it yearned to release. She could feel Stella beside her, feel Stella's love for The Bastard. But AIs couldn't love, so the love Kerri must have been feeling was her own. It made her want to vomit. She'd been so wrong, for so long.

The Bastard pulled the shunt from her. He collected the tubing, leaving Kerri to awkwardly bandage the hole in her numb arm with a stray scrap of rag. Not that she needed it; the nanos would heal that too, soon enough. "Stella and I are leaving," he said. "It's not safe here. Roger Garrison's offered us a place on his ship."

It had never been safe on this planet. The Bastard would only be leaving if he had gotten a better offer somewhere else, on someone else's dime. Kerri looked at the blood bag Stella held, not even half full.

"Oh, don't worry," he said, as if she would. "I've been injecting Stella with your blood all this time; the nanos have finally taken hold and started to replicate. I'll still have something to fall back on."

Worry? Why would she let herself worry? The feelings she shared with Stella suddenly made sense. Kerri braced herself on the IV pole and stood shakily before him. His height made her feel small. He didn't deserve a goodbye. He didn't deserve to hear her speak. He didn't deserve to watch her walk away. But he did deserve something.

Kerri slid the IV pole over to Stella—she didn't even have to use her head-voice. The nanos read Kerri's thoughts and transmitted them to the AI receptacle now pumping with her blood, her heart, her desires. With all the strength Kerri didn't have, Stella took the pole, broke it in half, and stabbed The Bastard in the heart.

Whoopee.

My blood, my daughter. You fool. He slid to the floor. She felt taller. *Now you know what heartache is.* She waited for the light in the blackness of his eyes to dim, just to be sure.

Kerri made her way up the stairs without a backward glance; Stella followed. Upstairs, she changed into some of Stella's clothes and packed a bag. She did not vomit in the drawers of Stella's extensive lingerie. She was proud of herself for that.

It was dark outside, and the air smelled like brimstone. She waited until they had walked at least half a mile before she sent her message to the wind. The nanos released the magnetic field she had been using to keep the bunker in one piece. With a rush the earth shivered again and imploded, crushing the bunker like a tin can, cleansing the evil that had been done there with elemental fire, and burying whatever love she'd once known in a coffin of black glass.

Now that she didn't have to hold that anymore, power flooded through her. The Bastard had never known her true potential, and before now Kerri had been too afraid to unleash it. He had only known the submissive wimp she'd been. He would never meet the woman she'd become. She was proud of that.

But while her blood could protect her, it could not save the world. Nor would it ever truly heal her. The pain would fade. Her strength would return. She would live, and she would not sail this next ship alone. That was enough. "Where is Roger Garrison's hold?" she asked Stella. "It's time to go." Time to move on, just like Patsy would have.

Stella took the duffel bag from her and pointed east. "This way. Not far," she said, her dark hair clouding around her alabaster face, making her look like an angel. There was a drop of blood on her cheek. His blood. Kerri wiped him away.

"Thank you, Mother."

Kerri picked at the rag on her arm and pulled off the makeshift bandage. She wanted nothing on her body that reminded her of him. She was in no danger of bleeding to death; the hole where the shunt had been had already begun to scab over. It was shaped like a tear. She tossed back her hair and started walking, following her angel across Hell. Walking, always walking, today, tomorrow, and forever.

To Dream of Stars: An Astronomer's Lament

Peter M. Ball

The first time he sees the Royal Observatory he is three days shy of his twelfth birthday. It's spring, a clear night, the stars unveiling themselves in small groups as the sky overhead grows dark.

The tower rises from the hills, dominating the uneven horizon, a crooked silhouette against the twilight. The glowing dome at the tip points at the emerging stars, the length of the tower twisted like the four-joined finger of a great and alien hand. He feels the strangeness of the building, a discordant note casting echoes in the chambers of his heart, but the otherness calls to him regardless. John Flamsteed is promised to God in both body and spirit, but he knows his heart and mind now belong to that tower forever.

"Eyes off it," his father orders, cuffing the boy across the back of the head, and John falls forward, clinging to the horse's mane to keep himself in the saddle. The older Flamsteed rides on, glaring at the observatory. "It's evil," his father says, "and dangerous yet. You will not look at it. You will not even think of it, or the creatures that dwell within. Do you understand?"

John Flamsteed nods, used to obedience without understanding. His father sees evil where other men see nothing, though perhaps this once John can see the hint of corruption his father fears. He averts his gaze, but the tower remains. It looms on the fringe of his vision, a constant threat. The sight of it pulls at his heart, luring him as though he's been hooked on a silvery strand of twine wrapped around the tower's domed tip.

They have three days of business in town, just long enough for John to hear the stories. He absorbs them, one by one, the details coalescing as he weaves rumour and folk-tale together. There are those that tell him the yellow texture of the tower comes from tiles made of dragon bone, that its twisting mass is held upright by prayer and dark magic. The accusations of magic perturb him, an affront to both God and reason, but he listens and nods and asks again when the moment presents itself. There are folk-tales aplenty to hear, but none to satisfy his thirst for comprehension.

On their final night in town, his birthday, John Flamsteed skulks out of the room he shares with his father. The moon is a thumbnail sliver overhead, a sliver so brief its presence barely registers against the scattered wash of stars. John Flamsteed stumbles through the unfamiliar streets, toes catching the rough cut cobblestones, tripping his way into the open fields and the hills beyond. The air smells fresh and clean, but the aftertaste is sour. He climbs the unfamiliar slopes, his young body straining against the rough terrain hidden by darkness.

The Observatory serves as a compass, allowing him to orient himself against the empty darkness the tower casts against the endless stars. Eventually John stands at the base, staring up at a tower tall enough to brush against sky. John Flamsteed examines the pale shingles, stands close enough that he can reach out and touch their worn exterior with the tips of his young fingers. They feel like the smoothed edge of a predator's incisor, noble, deadly and beautiful in a single moment.

He thinks of the stories the townsfolk tell about children raised to the Astronomers Royal, kidnapped and replaced by changelings, stripped of their humanity by the Astronomer's training. In the lonely light of the thumbnail moon, John Flamsteed makes a promise. He will return here, one day, free from the shackles of his father's assumptions. He will give himself over to the stars and the Others, all in the name of God and his country. Damn the impossibilities, he will enter the tower and join the ranks of the Astronomers Royal.

All he can see is the long teeth, clusters of bone-yellow fangs that shine as they jut away from her gums. His eyes are closed but the image stays with him, echoing through his head as he waits for the first teasing bite. He can feel the length of her tongue, the cat-lick rasp of it as she works her way along his thigh. The image of those teeth growing larger and stronger as the tongue works up his leg, the damp warmth of her breath sliding over him. He wonders what it will feel like, that first piercing bite. What will happen when she starts ripping and rending his flesh while he's trapped beneath her bulk.

The Other begins her work. There is no hint of teeth in their interaction. No teasing bites or sharp incisors against his skin, but the quiet menace of their arrangement lingers. It is difficult to forget those teeth, even for one such as him, trained and equipped to handle the intricacies of the exchange.

She raps his forehead with a six-knuckled hand, uses the brief flash of pain to focus his attention. He forces his eyes open and meets her gaze, staring into her gold-flecked pupils that have seen more than he can imagine. He ignores the quiet menace of her grin. This is, after all, what he longed for as a boy. It would not do to fail the public trust after all he has done to earn it.

"Focus," she hisses. Her voice is awkward to listen to, a croak full of slant inflections and awkward syntax. "You are not here. Your thoughts on the moment must be here. Very important. Focus."

She lowers her head and the tongue works its way across the plump line of his stomach, leaving a trail of sticky fluid in its wake. He forces himself to focus, to keep his eyes on her. He lets the image of her teeth dissolve.

"It's important," she says, murmuring, the tongue working at the fold of his belly button. "Must be present. Must be here. To lose focus would be bad, very bad. Very bad for both of us."

And Flamsteed swallows, just once, acutely aware of the way his Adam's apple bobs and dances with the gesture. He focuses on the moment, on the rasp of the tongue and the needle pricking as she suckles, the pain that starts boiling through his chest. He focuses on the long teeth and the tongue built for sucking marrow, the tongue that coils around him like a serpent as the Other explores his body. He keeps his focus and he watches her, gives himself over to the moment.

"Good," the Other says. "Good. All is well. Now stay with me. Stay with me. Stay with me through the pain."

He learns the danger of ambition early. There is a stray moment as they rode home; his father asks about the future and Flamsteed answers honestly.

"I wish to become an astronomer," he says, and the statement is followed by the stinging pain of a backhanded blow, the whistle of the wind as he tumbles into the dirt.

"Foolishness," his father says. "It is an insult that you consider such a thing."

And perhaps it is. John Flamsteed curses his own inattention, the foolishness of revealing himself so soon. It's easier than acknowledging the foolhardy desire, that he wishes for something that cannot be earned, that can only be bequeathed by the Other taking a child at birth. His lip drips blood as he climbs back into the saddle, dark spots staining the cracked leather. His father's dark eyes are on him, blazing with the angry flame of the Almighty, and John subsumes the pain with practiced ease. He will not seethe in front of his father, will not allow himself to be distracted by thoughts of the tower.

He looks forward with due attention, keen eyes tracing the winding road leading him to a future filled with grain and trade and the secrets of malt. His father lectures him through the endless hours it takes to reach home: on the evils of the tower, on the devilry of the outsiders who journey there, on the taint that lingers over those who live in its shadow. As always, the lecture revolves around the same words: "Better we had destroyed the place when his Majesty fell in the war. Better that the heavens had remained the palace of God alone."

And through it all John Flamsteed nods, dabbing his bloody lip until the dried crust forms. He probes the small wound with his tongue, feels the tiny spark of pain that exists beneath the chrysalis of hardened blood. He can endure this, if it is necessary. John Flamsteed defines himself by his ability to endure, to survive the rigors of life as his father's successor.

And that night, as he slumbers, he dreams of the tower. The Royal Observatory, the stars above it, the quiet thrum of its walls when he placed a palm on its surface. He wakes an hour before dawn, sweating and heavy under the covers of his bed. One hand is raised to press the wound on his lip, to let the pain burn beneath the fleshy pad of his fingertip.

The sharp nails pierce his flesh, digging in below the surface, drawing out a feeling that's almost pain, right on the edge of it, a sharp bite that reminds him of stabbing his finger with the nib of his finest pen. John Flamsteed remains still, his breathing shallow, trying not to disturb his lover's concentration. He feels the fluid seeping into the membranes of his skin, spreading out like an ink-splotch on wet paper.

Something in the back of his mind, some scrap of his brain that struggles to retain a semblance of the ordinary, tells him that he should be panicking. It's a voice he's learned to ignore many lovers ago, a voice that's subsumed in the name of duty. Flamsteed lies back, soaks into the hard mattress. He sighs, unsure if it's prompted by pain or contentment.

"Turn," she orders. This one's voice vibrates like a mosquito's wing, high-pitched and delicate. He rolls over and feels sharp fingernails walking the length of his back, each step another needle-prick. There is a faint stirring of real pain now, down beneath the layers of muscle; a dull ache in the hollows of his bones, the first real register of his body protesting the intrusion.

"Still," she says, caressing the nape of his neck. One finger lingers on the hollow, the point where cranium and spine connect, the same place a hunter strikes when he wants to kill a rabbit. Flamsteed knows better than to tense, knows the pain it will earn him if he attempts to resist penetration. His body stiffens anyway, an ancient reflex he thought conquered years ago. He wonders if it's a sign of age, this inability to control his base reactions. It is only a matter of time before his role is assumed by a younger man, before his wrinkled flesh will refuse to obey him or absorb the rigors required by his duties.

"Now," she says. His neck is stiff when she penetrates, the crisp point of her nail cutting through the taut sinew. The pain that washes through him is magnificent, a sweeping agony that leaves him with the coppery taste of blood in his mouth. Something drips from his nose, making it hard to breathe. He grits his teeth and draws breath through them, waiting the pain out. The nail is removed, a swift withdrawal accompanied by the wet suck of flesh drawing closed.

A moment later he is numb, the pain driven out by a sweep of frostbite that leaves him shuddering. The universe resolves around him, points of pale light superimposed over the walls of the room, silver-white spots that gradually congeal into familiar constellations.

For a few brief moments, he can feel the universe spreading through his capillaries. He runs his fingers across his ebony skin, tracing the pull of the stars as they rotate around him. He understands, for the first time, the way they pull against the universe, each star determined to draw everything in and shine, alone, as a perfect centre. Once he orients himself, it's possible to make out familiar constellations and old discoveries, the faint glow of 12 Monocerotis and 24 Tauri, the powder-bright dot of 3 Cassiopeia more distinct than he's ever seen her.

He wishes for a sheaf of paper, some means of annotating the exact locations while he has them in such close proximity. By the time he inks a quill they are gone, fading away until his wrinkled flesh is as pale as the moon against the midnight sheets.

"Done," she says. She brushes her nails against one another, sets them tinkling like crystal chimes as she rises. "Your reward, Astronomer, for all you have discovered."

Flamsteed simply nods, weary. He wants to say something, to thank her, but the words do not come.

His father's house runs on strict cycles: six days for business, one day for faith. John forfeit's sleep to his ambition, embracing the freedom to watch the heavens while his father slumbers. He begins his career without details or training, no numbers or names or theories to build on. Life in father's household has no room for stars, no books beyond the accounting ledger and the Bible on the shelf.

Flamsteed builds his first star chart from the night sky visible through the bedroom window, a square frame surrounding three-hundred-and-twenty-nine sparkling dots of light, each memorized and catalogued without the help of paper. Travel with his father becomes a curious pleasure after this, allowing him to study the night through unfamiliar portals, quilting the celestial maps together like the scraps used in a patchwork. His understanding grows as the years pass, each patch constructed from the safety of a new bed, each memory as square and neat as a window frame. He tells no-one what he's doing. The stars he studies for himself alone.

He encounters his first book on astronomy at fourteen, its yellowing pages full of crudely sketched constellations, archaic and constructed without the benefit of the Other's machines. John is fascinated by the childish depictions of the sky, the graceful waltz of the heavens superimposed on straight lines. He closes his eyes and transposes the dots of ink to the sky, tracing their patterns on the canvas of his mind for later study.

He reads for an hour, savouring the experience, the elder Flamsteed discussing business in a nearby parlour, too engrossed in the deal to register John's absence. John commits the pages to memory, as easy as breathing, aligns them with the patchwork he's built over the years.

He acquires his first true book on astronomy three years later, each page pristine and carefully choreographed, the work of the Royal Observatory and the Astronomers whose ranks he still dreams of joining. Flamsteed hides it under his bed, stores it in a small crate still touched with the sour scent of old grain, the book wrapped in waxed paper to protect it from mildew.

It is not long before it's joined by other tomes, by telescopes and star charts he constructs in the night.

They have bypassed the formalities, the flagellation that leaves red welts spiraling across his back like the distorted arms of a newborn galaxy, his limbs crisscrossed with cuts and red lines of inflamed flesh. Flamsteed grits his teeth against the pain, against the soft suckle of her lower appendages. She is pulling herself forward on long and muscular tentacles, each looping grasp giving her new purchase, dragging her bulk through the viscous liquid until she can settle it over Flamsteed's torso.

Tears are permitted in this encounter; discreet trails of saltwater flowing over his craggy cheeks until they merge with the viscid muck of the pool. The salt burns at his raw skin, painfully warm against the cool weight of the sea-green slough covering his body. She moves easily through the thick liquid, reaching out with one of her lower appendages to trace the line of his tears. Flamsteed doesn't flinch from the bone-hooked tip of her tentacle, doesn't shudder as she runs it across his softened flesh.

He rakes the squamous bulk of her body with his fingers, acutely aware of the futility of penetrating her scales with his blunted, human nails. One hand working its way down the double-boned ridge of her spine, the second caressing the open expanse of her torso. She thrums beneath his touch, a dull echo deep beneath the cavernous mass of her chest, extremities writhing in a politely simulated act of pleasure. Flamsteed rakes again but cannot break the thick flesh. She will be disappointed, he knows that. He remembers her from her last visit.

They proceed, politely, playing out the exchange that's expected of them. Flamsteed chides himself for the lack of foresight, for making contact without preparing the required prosthetics, for limiting himself to merely human physical abilities. He has reduced the exchange to simple choreography for the first time in a decade. They will replace him now, dubbing him too old. The thought terrifies him more than he can say.

Flamsteeds nocturnal studies manifest in exhaustion, prompting others to regard him as sickly for the remainder his childhood. His father deems him too weak for college, igniting furious arguments with his son.

Flamsteed clings to his dreams. Letters are written in secret, the necessary books acquired by friends and smuggled into the house. By the time he is permitted to walk into Cambridge Halls, twenty-three and handsome despite his nocturnal pallor, he possessed more knowledge than many who propose to instruct him in the ways of the stars.

He petitions the Queen and the Royal Observatory every year after graduation, his letters echoing the sentiments of a hundred other astronomers who have studied and dreamed as he has. There is a call, a hunger, pervading the Empire, for the secrets of the conquering Others and the Astronomers who serve them.

At thirty, John Flamsteed is the first man to be accepted into the ranks of the Astronomers Royal, his petitions supported by a catalogue of undiscovered stars that's unmatched by any within or without the Royal Observatory. He is first full-grown human to be initiated, the first Astronomer raised outside with an understanding of humanity.

He meets his first Other in the Astronomer's tower, deemed ready after three years of training and preparation. The Other looms over him, her pale face like a narrow sliver of moon, silver stars shining from the empty canals of her eyes.

They taught him the rituals needed to control his instincts in the face of the unknown, but he feels fear despite the training, the dry taste in his mouth and the chill running through his trembling legs. There is something primal there, a quiet voice screaming for him to flee. It takes courage to stand at the ready, to stare into the endless void of those eyes.

He takes comfort in the void, the gaze that resembles his beloved stars.

Most Astronomers fail in this moment, unable to sublimate their fear. It is death to fail, he knows this, and Flamsteed forces himself to stay, to remain steady as the luminous hand strokes his clenched jaw. The air is thick with humidity, the Other's wildflower scent mixing with the flickering taint of tallow. He forces himself to breath normally, to ignore the lightning-sharp tingle that accompanied the Other's presence. He holds firm as she caresses his face, leans in to study him like a prize horse, forcing his mouth open to check his teeth.

There is no offering in this first encounter, no contact beyond the gentle touch of her fingers, but the solemnity of the moment digs deep into Flamsteed's chest. This, John Flamsteed is sure, lies at the very heart of the evil his father saw in the Observatory; this moment when man may brush against the divine without seeing God behind it.

There is an afterglow with this breed, an ambient luminescence that projects the path of her stellar journey across the domed ceiling. John considers the unfamiliar stars, watching a new sky spread out, magnified by the complex array of curved lenses and glass arrays built into the dome.

There is a beauty to its endless tranquility, to the stars that twinkle in the boundless regions of space, and in their absence are spaces that even the Others do not visit. Even after all these years, after all the homage and services he's performed, this sight awakens the same quiet awe within him.

The Others tell the Astronomers that the darkness was infinite, stretching on forever in an eternity of empty space. It is only in this room that Flamsteed can comprehend what that may mean. He thinks about the endless, the subtle thrill of pleasure with every new quasar that is found. Thirty years in the observatory and there is still no end to it, no point in the eternal distance that could be the end of a long journey.

And for the first time he wonders if the Others truly do come from stars, all of them connected as the Others claim.

Or whether the gaps in their knowledge speak of some other truth entirely.

John Flamsteed delights in charting unfamiliar stars, studying them and recording them in the neat ledgers that line the walls of his cell. Innumerable ledgers, leather-bound and hand-crafted, their pages filled with neat script and a careful record of what has been found. The legacy of three-dozen years of Astronomy in the name of the Queen, so many years of research and still so much to find.

He is forty-five when he meets the first Astronomer to train as he has trained, another outsider named Edmund Halley whose brilliance has given him access to the tower just as John earned his own place among the Astronomer's Royal. Flamsteed is forty-seven when he first hears the name Terra Optimus whispered in the halls, forty-eight before he realizes that the dissidents have sympathizers amongst the ranks of the Astronomers. John Flamsteed struggles to comprehend the logic behind such a group, to comprehend a world without the Others and their gifts of the stars and the Observatory; it seems tantamount to madness.

Yet he contemplates the possibilities late at night, ignoring the insistent tug of sleep just as he's done since childhood. He fills his journals with sketches in addition to the charts and the stars, recording notes about all the Others he's encountered. Every night he considers the question, what if, conceiving of ways to continue his work if he was suddenly bereft of the Observatory and the Others and the gifts they have offered him.

Later still, in the moments before sleep, he offers up silent prayers that his plans are never needed.

He finds Edmund Halley waiting for him in the main Observatory, the younger man paging through Flamsteed's journal. There is something about Halley that Flamsteed finds disagreeable, an unfamiliar cockiness that seems unseemly, even here. The sight of him touching the annotated pages of the journal fills Flamsteed with fear. He fights the itching need to slap the leather covers closed on Halley's fingers.

"Halley," Flamsteed says, the deep croak of his voice causing the younger astronomer to start. Despite his five years of service in the tower, Edmund Halley is not yet ready for anything. It isn't a good sign; the ability to react, to adapt without surprise, is vital to the astronomer.

"John," Halley says nervously, one hand scratching the back of his head. He shuffles across the room, right hand extended, thin lips drawn into a tight, controlled smile. Flamsteed takes the offered hand, shaking it with disdain, his skin crawling as he makes contact. As though Halley were one of the Others, Flamsteed thinks. As if he were just as alien as they.

"I've been reading your journals," Halley says. "Impressive work, I must say. You're to be commended on your diligence."

There is no passion in Flamsteed's cold stare, just a quiet distaste that the conversation has lasted this long. Halley refuses to wither beneath John's gaze when Flamsteed doesn't respond.

"Well, yes," Halley says. "Impressive; a work of genius, if you'd prefer. There has been talk, among the younger astronomers. Some rumbles about distributing your notes."

"For the good of the Empire?" Flamsteed says.

Halley smiles and nods, ignoring the dangerous tone. "Yes, for the good of the Empire. Quite right."

It is a cool day, even behind the insulated stone of the Astronomers' tower. John Flamsteed blinks in the momentary silence.

"No," he says.

"John." Halley looks around, as though preparing to share a secret. "John, this is important. This isn't about us, the astronomers. Your journal represents the most significant catalogue of Other forms known, details beyond the dreaming of any Astronomer half your age. We need this information, urgently."

John Flamsteed's anger is a quiet spark, smouldering with urgency. "No," he says firmly, leaving no room for discussion.

"John," Halley says, but he stops when he hears the hint of a growl in Flamsteed's voice.

He is permitted to meet Her Majesty when he is fifty-three, escorted via carriage to the aging cathedral that has become her throne room. There is a silence beneath the hammer of the horse hooves, an empty space that leaves John Flamsteed alone with his thoughts.

He watches the great building through the window of the carriage. It was God's place, once, but the cathedral now houses the stuff of stars. It is the home of Her Majesty, first among the Other-kin, the great lady who brought the Other to England and awarded the Astronomers her tower. As the carriage thunders into town, the great cathedral looming in the forefront of his vision, John Flamsteed is surprised to find himself weeping.

Her Majesty is a leviathan of pale flesh, her vast bulk expanding to spill over the arms of her throne. She does not speak, but her presence weighs against Flamsteed's mind like the roar of the ocean. You are the Astronomer Flamsteed.

"Yes."

You are the first of a new breed, the first willing to sacrifice in exchange for knowledge. It is a great thing, Lord Astronomer, a step forward for your people.

Flamsteed stands in the ancient church and stares.

There were concerns about your appointment, about your ability to survive the rigours required of the post. Was it worth it, Lord Astronomer? The sacrifices you have made?

Flamsteed can feel his stomach boiling, the nausea rising up like steam escaping a kettle. He keeps his mind calm, contemplating Her Majesty's question in secluded pockets of thought, places he has learned to keep hidden from the mental prying of the Other. It occurs to him, for the first time, that he does not wish to know the answer to this.

"It is a difficult question, Majesty. You ask me for conjecture when you have rewarded the Order for their pursuit of proof."

The mound of flesh boils, folds in on itself as Her Majesty rolls forward. Flamsteed watches as a great eye forms amid the flesh, a violet orb shot with a fistful of stars.

We ask for opinion, Lord Astronomer, nothing more. Indulge us, we command you. Give us your answer.

His scars ache, a hundred niggling bites of pain that stretch out across his skin, the cost of too many nights in the open chambers that look up into the stars. There is a hollow feeling that accompanies the pain, an emptiness that spreads through his limbs like the endless dark of the night sky.

"You gave us the stars, Majesty. Is there any price that is not worth that?"

Her Majesty's great eye stares at him, an open window to the universe. Flamsteed stares back and wonders which of the multitude of lights she descended from.

She towers over him, her body composed of insect limbs and chitin skin that gleams in the candlelight, her faceted eyes studying him with detached interest. It is a new breed of Other, the first unfamiliar genus he's seen in years.

John Flamsteed holds his breath as her needle-sharp proboscis penetrates the flesh below his nipple. There is pain, there is almost always pain when dealing with the other, but he expected the heavy appendage to gash flesh like a knife-blade rather than sting like a mosquito bite. He waits with apprehension, breath burning in his lungs, offering a quiet prayer that this time the narrow length will find the space between his ribs. He watches her burrow through the flesh and the layers of muscle, searching for the fleshy sack of his right lung. He cannot breathe until the lung is penetrated, cannot draw breath until she is ready to breathe with him, but penetration takes time and he can already see the star-filled sky of his childhood encroaching on the fringes of his vision, narrowing his perception to a single tunnel that shrinks until there is nothing more than the faceted eyes that keep staring.

The penetration occurs, a popping sensation that leaves him deflated and lethargic. He starts heaving his chest, trying to swallow air, but all he can feel is the quiet pull of her proboscis, the sucking sensation as she breathes in the air of his lungs. He forces himself to concentrate, forces his body to recognize that he isn't choking, but the empty sensation in his chest will not be ignored. He struggles, just a little, enough to give her pleasure. He forces himself to remember the stricture, the litany that all Astronomers are taught before they are paired with their first Other: we are the servants of the universe, sacrificing ourselves for the gift of the stars; we exist for her pleasure, for our knowledge relies upon their pleasure; we do not ask, do not question, in this moment we belong to her, always to her, and we are their lovers. This is the price we pay to keep our people safe. This is the cost of learning about the darkness.

Flamsteed forces himself to ignore the unspoken advice at the end of the litany, the careful implication that every Other is female. To consider them anything else is unthinkable, even among men who touch the unthinkable day after day.

She reaches the moment of pleasure, quiet moans vibrating along the needle that penetrates him, the black heat of her climax filling the air with the fetid stench of rotting eggs. Flamsteed twists beneath her, pinned on the delicate needle that penetrates him, holding his tongue while he waits for the moment of release.

Flamsteed is dead fifteen years when the Observatory falls. It is the beginning of the revolt, the end of Her Majesty's rule. The yellow-tiled stone ruptures with the force of a dozen explosions, each carefully placed at important junctures that will bring the great tower low. The long finger of stone bends, twisting as it falls. The stones warp and crumble under their own weight, bearing the crystalline tip of the great tower down until it shatters against the earth. There is a slow inevitability to its fall, like a breath long-held suddenly free to be exhaled. The tremor of its impact roars through Greenwich town, shattering windows and kicking up dust. Flamsteed does not live to see it, but it is his notes that make this possible.

They say it was Halley who fired the first shot, setting taper to the fuse that brought the tower down. They say it was Newton who waged the great war, who brought weapons and worse to the rebels who fought to take Her Majesty down. They say little enough of John Flamsteed, remembering him for less, but the Astronomers Royal continues even after the fall of the Others. We chart courses for the ships we discover and negotiate treaties with those who come after. We prepare Britannia for the other worlds, for the depths of space and beyond. We use Flamsteed's work to determine from where the next attack will come. He studied them and understood, charting their strengths and desires, treating them like the stars he so loved. We say it was

Flamsteed that provided the means of Her Majesty's death, for all that it was Halley who put plan into action.

On the anniversary of his death we lie flowers on Flamsteed's tombstone; white lilies resting against a yellow stone taken from the tower he loved.

We mourn him and revere. We promise we shall not forget.

Benjamin Schneider's Little Greys

Nir Yaniv

Translated from Hebrew by Lavie Tidhar

When Benjamin Schneider came to my clinic and complained of mysterious coils on his left wrist, I wasn't overly surprised. The term "hypochondriac" may have become overused years ago, but Benjamin nevertheless lived and acted as its perfect archetype. He had been that way ever since he was a child. I remember the first time he came to me, when I was still a minor family GP at the National Health clinic in town. He was about fourteen, short for his age, thin, curly and bespectacled, and a thorn was stuck, mortifyingly, in his behind. His mother, Mrs. Romina Schneider, did not spare him her wrath—"Every time, something strange has to happen to you!" she said—and the embarrassed child gritted his teeth and gave me a pleading look. His mother, too, gave me a look—the kind an older woman gives a younger woman she doesn't trust, doesn't want to trust, but is forced to, if only by the vagaries of the National Health Service. I don't remember how I got her away from the room—one of the nurses helped me, perhaps— but five minutes later the thorn was removed, to the relief of everyone concerned. Benjamin's grateful gaze was something I could never forget—if only because, for years afterwards, I received it from him, on average, about once a week.

The week after the thorn incident, for instance, he grazed the back of his neck on barbed wire—I had no idea how—and came to me to clean up the wound. I asked him if they didn't have iodine at home, and he shrugged and didn't reply. In fact, he never talked about himself, beyond—more or less—the medical reasons for his current visit. Every week he visited me, with one reason or another, as he grew up from a boy to a teen and then a man, still thin, still curly and bespectacled. When I opened my own clinic twelve years later, Benjamin was my first client.

His medical problems were always a little odd. He was bruised in unlikely places—his right ear, for instance; suffered diseases like an arthritis that had the same symptoms as gum disease, didn't respond to medicine, and disappeared after a week; and indeed always healed miraculously and returned to me to verify the fact and perhaps discover some new ailments in the process. It is possible other doctors would have ridiculed him and his various ills, and certainly my cooperation with it and with him, but I couldn't bring myself to be so cruel to him.

The coils, however, despite our long history together, were something new. I had sent him for an X-ray several days before, at his insistence. He brought the prints back to the clinic in the brown paper folder of the National Health, searched through them for a minute or two, and then found what he was looking for. I spread the print over the white fluorescent board designed for that purpose and examined it, not expecting to find anything out of the ordinary, or at least of the ordinary as considered in the case of Benjamin Schneider. But, to my surprise, something was there. Two greyish coils, half-transparent, testifying that whatever they were made of was not solid enough to completely block the X-rays. And there was something else that was odd in the picture, but to begin with I couldn't figure out what it was.

"Does it hurt?" I asked. He shook his head. His arthritis had already disappeared. I examined the wrist myself, but externally it was not possible to discern anything out of the ordinary. I told him I had to think about it, and to come back to me in a few days. I looked at him, worried he might be upset by that, but he just nodded and left, satisfied, to all appearances, that his fate was in good hands. How little did you know, Benjamin. How little did we know.

I had quite a lot of work to do in the office that day, so I took the print home with me afterwards. I didn't have a fluorescent board at home, so I hung the print before a desk lamp. I looked at it all through dinner, and for a change didn't wait in vain for the phone to ring. The coils were odd, but there was also something familiar about them, and these were two separate things, the strangeness and the familiarity.

After a while I lost my concentration and watched a little TV. One of the channels was showing a horror B-movie, and I watched it disinterestedly as my mind floated here and there on its own without my being fully conscious of it. It's a way as good as any of dealing with problems, but this time the solution came not from that, but rather from the tiny part of me that was actually watching the television. One of the monsters there was sawing through the arm of another monster, and I noticed immediately the cheap special effect—the saw and the hand about to be cut were two separate images filmed at different times and joined artificially. It was easy to see that the saw didn't really touch the arm. And it was the same phenomenon that I could see in Benjamin's X -ray—the coils looked like an artificial addition to the picture.

There was something calming about this, of course. Incidents like this are not common, but sometimes, despite all precautionary measures, they happen. A foreign object finds its way between the camera and the subject, the result being spread in all its glory before my reading lamp. If Benjamin still needed it, I would send him for a repeat scan, and if not, all to the better.

And still the coils seemed familiar.

On his next visit I explained all this to him, apart from the strange feeling I had about the coils, and he seemed pretty happy. Another problem occupied him by now. He had something in his eyes. That's how he put it, and I couldn't get a better explanation out of him. I examined his eyes and could see nothing out of the ordinary, apart from a redness that could have been caused by a thousand and one things, most of them not worthy of attention. But when I examined his right eye through an ophthalmoscope I saw it: a tiny grey circle, barely seen against the redness of the cornea.

There was one in his left eye too.

They both seemed familiar, just like the coils. They also seemed, as hard as it was for me to believe when watching something that was real and not a scan, unconnected. If the coils in his arm seemed like foreign bodies that had entered by mistake into the field of vision of the X-ray camera, then the circles in his eyes seemed like foreign bodies that had entered by mistake into the field of vision of reality.

I think I managed to hide the shock I felt. I gave Benjamin eye drops, closed the clinic early, and went home to rest. And watch TV. And think.

In the morning I arrived at the clinic two hours before opening time and dismantled the ophthalmoscope. I examined all the parts through a magnifying glass, but found nothing to explain the little grey circles that were similar to the little grey coils that were similar to nothing I knew even though my brain insisted otherwise.

I didn't know how to reassemble the device and decided to just buy another. I had money, after all, and besides, it was tax-deductible. I spent the rest of the time before my first patient's appearance in thoughts of this nature, which were relaxing in their simplicity and mundanity but which led me nevertheless, in one way or another, to the mystery of Benjamin's grey parts; thoughts that were only halted with the appearance of the patient himself.

"Benjamin," I said, surprised. He never came to me two days in a row. "Is everything all right?"

Usually, he would merely point at the source of pain or discomfort, speaking as little as possible, and let me complete the diagnosis on my own. Not today. "I have a crop circle," he said.

"Excuse me?"

"A crop circle. You know. Like the ones aliens make."

"Benjamin—" I said, but he had already launched into an explanation that was exceptional both in its length and its content. Crop circles are giant circles, and sometimes more complex shapes, that are formed in wheat or corn fields by the pressing down of the stalks. All kinds of attributes are ascribed to them, and stories are told of strange things that have happened to the stalks. There are people who believe that they are proof of the existence of aliens. The rest of the world, of course, assumes it's merely a practical joke.

"Fine," I said. "I don't really believe in aliens either, but let's get back to you, Benjamin."

He looked at me. "I have a crop circle," he said again. "On my tummy."

I stared at him, thinking about whether I needed to send him to see a psychiatrist. Then I had him lie down on the examination table, turned on the strongest lamp, and opened his shirt. I asked him to point to the place where the circle was, and he did.

Despite everything, I needed all my willpower not to laugh.

"Benjamin," I said, "that's your navel. Your belly button."

"It's a crop circle. Look at the hairs there, see what happened to them."

"It's only natural that the hairs around..." I said, and then I saw.

They were bent. Or stood, erect, in unnatural angles. Circles within circles, around the navel. But more than that—they were grey.

I passed my hand over his stomach, touching them. I wasn't sure I was touching them all. It seemed to me that some passed through my palm, as if they were air. As if I was air. It was not a pleasant feeling. Under my hand, Benjamin shuddered. I felt a kind of electric current, something passing between us through my spread fingers, touching-not-touching his crop circle. Many things were suddenly clear. Many things. Little clues, grazed necks, strange illnesses, illogical pains. Aliens.

"What do you think?" he said. "Am I going to be all right?"

I looked at him, straight into his eyes. They were grey. There were strange geometries behind his eyes, and I thought I understood them. I didn't say anything. His eyes grew large. Only after a moment I realised he was afraid. And only a little after that I realised he was afraid of me.

"You too, Dr. Katz," he said. "You too!" And he passed out.

I climbed on the chair, and from there onto the table, and stood there, high, looking at the thin, silent man who had spent the majority of his life with imaginary diseases that were, at the end, quite real. Maybe he was in love with his diseases. Maybe he was in love with me. It didn't matter. Not now, with the aliens controlling him—and me. I gritted my teeth and jumped, head first, into the crop circle, into his navel.

He still comes to visit me every week. Right after they released him from the hospital, he came to see me. How nice of him. Maybe he's still in love with me, even after I jumped into him. They told me the doctors managed to recover his digestive system. My head, though…

He comes to visit me every week, and the little greys are in his eyes, on his hands, forming and growing, growing and spreading, all over his body. I have no mirror here, and I can't look at my body, but I think it's the same with me. I think I hope it is so. It's hard to be sure, with a head like mine.

I think I see the world in black and white, or grey. Apart from Benjamin, no one would understand, of course. I know exactly what the medical thinking is. I know exactly what the people who surround me would think of anything I would say. I know what I would have thought. I'm well-behaved, but that doesn't help. Only Benjamin, only Benjamin can help me. He and the little greys, the growing greys, the great big greys. Now, when I see the look in his grey eyes, when I imagine the touch of his hands, the coils in his wrists, beyond the reinforced glass window separating us, beyond the jacket enfolding me, I know that he loves me.

I love him too.

But most of all I love the greys.

AFTER THE FIRE

Aliette de Bodard

In her dreams, Jiaotan saw Father: hands outstretched, the flesh of the fingers fraying away to reveal the yellowed, tapered shape of bones, the deep-set eyes bulging in their sockets, pleading, begging her to take him away.

"You're dead," she whispered. "Rest in peace, with the Ancestors—watch over us from Heaven."

But the Ancestors were bones and dried sinews, shambling upright from the wreck of their graves—anger shining in the hollows of their eye sockets as they walked past the devastated gardens, the withered trees, the dried-out waterfalls and rivers. And clouds marched across Heaven, a billowing mass of sickly grey spreading to cut the path of The Red Carp as it rose away from Earth…

Jiaotan woke up with a start, instinctively bending over to cough out the fluid that blocked her lungs. But something held her, pressed against her as tightly as the embrace of Earth.

Where… She tried to pull herself upright—to breathe—but she was still held. She couldn't—

Father…

"Shun Jiaotan," a voice said with the cultured accents of the Court, loud enough to cover the frantic beating of her heart. "Stand by for awakening procedure."

Something shifted, and she was upright, the fluid choking her. A cough wrung her body, spraying the obstruction out of her lungs. She inhaled in huge gulps while the light around her slowly grew, the stale air searing her throat.

Where…

But she remembered. All the dreams—the grinning skulls and the withered flesh on brittle bones, the forests coated in liquid metal, the wind that bore the rank smell of carrion…

When the hibernation couch released her, Jiaotan stumbled out on her knees and bent over, racked by coughing fits, feeling as though she was going to spit everything out, lungs and liver and stomach. But the only thing that came out was more of the hibernation fluid, a grey ooze that spread across the pristine metal surface of the ship's quarters.

It took her a while to stand, and a while longer for the images to stop hovering in front of her face—for Father's burnt face to disappear, back among the dead where it belonged.

"Shun Jiaotan," the voice said again, echoing under the metal ceiling. "The Red Carp has need of you. Go to the navigation room."

A quick glance around her confirmed that all the other sleepers were still in their couches; the ship around her was silent. What had happened?

But she knew better than to ask. The only way to communicate with the ship's Mind would be to jack in physically, and that could only be done by the engineers and the pilots, those with the proper implants and authorizations.

Why had they woken her up, then? What need had they for a poet, brought on the Exodus only as a favour to her sister?

Her sister.

Sukuang—she was the engineer, she was the one who truly mattered—the one they'd wake up if there was a problem.

Something was wrong. Jiaotan pulled herself to the door, sliding it open with a touch of her hand, and moved into the corridor, trying to ignore the growing hollow in her stomach.

Everything was deserted; everything gleamed with the coldness of metal. The light, reflected on a thousand surfaces, danced and coalesced into ten thousand patterns, ten thousand forms that might have been drawings or characters—the beginning of sentences hovering on the edge of significance, always dissolving before Jiaotan could focus on them. And there came no other noise but her own laboured breathing as her lungs struggled to re-accustom themselves to a normal atmosphere. She hadn't realised, before the Exodus, how huge The Red Carp was; going upwards, she passed row upon row of hibernation rooms, from the scholars to the officials, from the officials to the lower ranks of the Court—and further up was the highest room, where the Emperor, the Son of Heaven, the holder of the Divine Mandate, slept in his own couch. A little lower than this would be the navigation room, a reminder that the pilots of the Exodus were almost—yet not—as powerful as the Emperor.

Jiaotan walked through the corridors, seeing everything merge and blur into an endless dream of metal.

There was a wind, blowing through the ship—not the cold one between the stars, but a hot and rancid one, with a smell like spoiled butter, like curdled cheese left too long in the sun. The metal quivered and danced, became the red of flames which swept up, and Second Cousin Yu's skin crinkled and blackened like charred paper, and her eyes popped like chestnuts in the Fire's wake...

Something swam out of the darkness in which she walked: a picture against a red background—a fierce, dark face with a beard and eyes like black beads. Batons, crossed in front of silk robes.

A guardian deity, and his twin by his side, pale-skinned, his two straight swords drawn against threats. The doors they protected were tight metal panes, cold and reassuring.

Jiaotan laid a hand against the doors, feeling the coolness travel up her arm—into her heart. If she closed her eyes, she knew, she'd see Father again, or perhaps Aunt Qin or one of the other concubines: all the dead she couldn't forget, an endless chain of ghosts stretching back to the wreck of Earth. Blood, stronger than mountains, more enduring than jade or cinnabar.

Why had they woken her up? It should have been Sukuang at the door, not her.

"I'm here," Jiaotan said aloud. "Now would you tell me what you want?" She moved her hand to the control panel, long enough for the ship's Mind to recognise her. The doors parted like the leaves of a book, and she entered the navigation room.

Inside, it was cool and dark and silent. The air smelled of ginseng and pine essence—not quite enough to mask the staleness of the recycling.

This was ridiculous. She couldn't possibly fix whatever was wrong. Couldn't the ship's Mind tell the difference between Jiaotan and her sister?

Something shifted in the shadows—the sound of breathing coming in small, ragged gasps. Someone? Impossible. All the colonists slept in their hibernation couches; all the pilots were in their berths, augmenting the ship's computing capacity with their own minds. There should have been no one—

"Jiaotan?" a voice asked.

Sukuang. But she didn't have her usual confidence; her voice sounded empty, and a little startled, as if she'd been doing something that Jiaotan had interrupted—something reprehensible.

Cautiously, Jiaotan approached. The hollow feeling in her stomach, if anything, grew larger.

Sukuang sat on her knees at the foot of the pilots' wall. Above her, bulges in the metal marked the crew members' berths. The metal was translucent, letting her see the crew, resting as snug in there as in a hibernation couch. Their faces were pale against the grey fluid, their eyes bruised; their mouths were set in troubled grimaces. One of the control panels—that of the second-in-command—blinked dark blue, the sign of a problem.

"I should have known they'd wake you up," Sukuang said, as Jiaotan approached.

"I—" Jiaotan stopped, seeing what Sukuang had spread on the ground.

A letter on white paper, stamped with the seal of the Courts of Hell, filled with scrawled, disorderly characters—and a welding knife, carefully set aside from the writing brush.

That wasn't good. You only wrote to the dead Ancestors for one reason, and that was to apologise for the shame you would be bringing on the family.

Such as the shame of not living on.

"Aren't you supposed to be fixing the ship?" she asked slowly. All that Sukuang had to do was pick up the welding knife and open her own throat; and there'd be nothing Jiaotan could do—and nothing the ship could do either. It had been programmed to take care of itself and the passengers in the hibernation couches, but it couldn't act outside of that.

No wonder the ship had awakened Jiaotan.

Sukuang raised bruised eyes towards her. "I can't."

"What do you mean?" Jiaotan asked. "You're the best engineer we have. That's why the ship picked you."

Sukuang shook her head. "I'm capable of repairing the damage. But what's the point?"

"The point?" Jiaotan knelt by Sukuang's side, carefully, and laid a hand on her arm. "We're the only ones left. The hope of rebirth for the whole world. When we reach the colony—"

"We destroyed Earth, Jiaotan."

Jiaotan tried to ignore the images of the Fire, sweeping through the steppes and the grasslands, racing up towards the launch rail in the instant before the ship took off in a blaze of light. "The alchemists did," she said. "Whoever made the White Fire did."

"We all did." Sukuang sucked in a breath, went on, her voice shaking. "The alchemists, the engineers, the soldiers. Every one of us with our little experiments, every one of us reporting on what worked and what didn't, building the sum of knowledge that they used to make the Fire. Do you really think we deserved to be carried away?"

"The Emperor ordered us to board the ship. Would you go against that?"

Sukuang's hands clenched. "There are higher powers than the Emperor."

"Not many."

"Enough," Sukuang said. "Please, Jiaotan. Just leave me be."

"I can't. You know I can't. "Sukuang's presence had made the Exodus bearable—the knowledge that the Shun lineage wasn't reduced to Jiaotan alone, to a mediocre poet unable to pass the state examinations; that in the vastness of the ship, in the strangeness of their new home, they could still watch out for each other as they'd done when they were children.

"And you know I can't ignore it anymore, either." Sukuang was silent, her lips compressed—she couldn't ignore Jiaotan without being rude, but neither did she agree.

Jiaotan tried something else. "We're the only ones left. Father's flesh, Mother's blood. If we die, then the last trace of them will vanish."

Sukuang's eyes were as dark as scorched meat, her pupils dilated by grief. "I know what we've done, Jiaotan. I still see them—they're in my dreams, in my waking days. Father and Mother and Aunt Qin, and the rest of them."

All those we left behind, Jiaotan thought, shivering. But it didn't matter; it shouldn't matter. The dead were dead, and the future belonged to the living. It had to.

"Sukuang," she said, "I share your grief. I understand." Truly, she did. She saw them, too: all the ones they couldn't save, all those the Emperor had been forced to abandon as they flew away, all those the Fire had taken. "But to commit suicide...." She paused, looking for a suitable quote to paraphrase, and finally settled on Grand Historian Sima Qian. "Some deaths are weightier than Mount Tai, some lighter than a swan's down. Your death will achieve nothing."

"You're wrong," Sukuang said, but her gaze strayed to the dark blue light, still blinking in the shadows, and wouldn't come back to

Jiaotan. "It would atone for what we've done."

Jiaotan took a deep breath and called on the Classics, which Sukuang would know by heart, just like her. "A person's virtue is seen through the whole of their lives, not the manner of their death. It is seen by the benefits of their acts. You know this."

"I used to, once."

"You can't bring them back," Jiaotan said. "You can't change the past. And death is no atonement; it's just a way to preserve your dignity."

"That's not what I'm doing. It's different, Jiaotan. You know it is." Her voice shook.

Jiaotan said nothing. There was no need to.

At length, Sukuang said, "You're right. I've been selfish, Jiaotan. And arrogant." Her smile was devoid of any joy. "And I have a ship to repair."

She rose and laid her hand against the faulty berth. The wall softened, flowed up her wrist, her arm; the gleaming metal coated her skin and her clothes, burrowing into her body to connect her implants to the ship's Mind.

"It's going to be a while," she said. "You might as well make yourself comfortable."

Jiaotan propped herself up against the farthest wall, watching her sister. Nothing happened that she could see. Sukuang did not move, though the metal of the ship shifted from time to time, changing colours like a living being.

Her mind drifted into the land of dreams. The metal flowed upwards, covering Sukuang as it had covered the trees and the flowers, choking them to death…

She and Sukuang ran on the dry earth behind the wall of the Fire, which grew more and more distant as it swept away from them. The trees were shining masses coated with the melted metal of skyscrapers, the mountains sterile rocks with the corpses of acid-eaten forests; underfoot were ashes—and bones, crackling like corn in the frying pan, their pale fragments billowing in the air, small and sharp.

The only light came from a figure dressed in white—a woman with an androgynous face who gathered bones in her hands with the plodding method of the desperate. She smiled bleakly when they came nearer, holding out her soot-stained hands. "See my children," she cried, and her voice was the quivering wail of oboes at funerals. "They are one with the universe, and the universe is no more."

And tears ran down her cheeks, evaporating in the roiling heat, and the Fire ate at her skin and at her bones until her light had become that of the flames and her voice was overwhelmed by the screams of billions.

See my children…

Jiaotan woke up with a start, in the dark, the afterimages of the Fire imprinted on her retinas and the woman's grinning skull superimposed on the navigation room. The woman—Guanyin, Bodhisattva of Mercy—she, too, taken by the Fire, eaten away to nothing.

Jiaotan's heart beat in her chest with the frantic desperation of a caged hummingbird. They hadn't done this—not any of this, it wasn't their fault, they couldn't have done anything…

But, deep where it mattered, she knew it for a lie; a flimsy, unacceptable excuse.

The light above the berth blinked red, the colour of good fortune and things gone right—slow and steady, the anchor for her flailing sanity. The ship's metal flowed away from Sukuang, revealing once more the green of her clothes, the pale colour of her skin, the exhaustion in her eyes.

Jiaotan stood up, trying to calm the frantic beat of her heart.

"It's done," Sukuang said. "We'll have a safe journey."

Jiaotan forced a smile she didn't feel and held out her hand to Sukuang. "Come. Let's go back to sleep, then. With luck, they won't wake us up before we reach the planet."

"No," Sukuang said. "I guess they won't." She sucked in a breath, her gaze shifting down to the welding knife.

The hollow feeling returned in the pit of Jiaotan's stomach, sharp and cold. "Sukuang. Think of the others…"

Sukuang raised her gaze again—eyes filled with such a desperate need that Jiaotan knew, with absolute certainty, that she couldn't stop her sister, that she didn't have the right to.

Sukuang's hand moved towards the knife; the outstretched fingers hovered over the handle for an agonisingly long while. At length, and with a visible effort, she withdrew. "You're right," she said tonelessly. "Let's go back."

She didn't speak again until they'd walked back to her own hibernation couch—close to the navigation room, along with the ship's engineers and the few remaining alchemists—until Jiaotan had wedged her into the couch and the cycle of hibernation had started.

"Sleep well, sister," Sukuang whispered then, as the couch swung shut.

Jiaotan laid her hand against the outer panel of the couch and caught a distorted reflection of herself in the metal: dishevelled and pale, her eyes bruised and haunted, her skin the colour of things that no longer saw the sun, and ten thousand ghosts on her back, bowing her shoulders and spine.

"Sleep well," she whispered in return, though she knew the truth, as did Sukuang: that in sleep there was no oblivion. The weight of their transgression would never be erased. The dead were with them, carried in their minds and in their hearts—and, as the Fire had eaten those left behind, they in turn would gnaw at the sleepers, every hour, every day, tearing away at the will to live, at the fabric and sanity of their beings, until nothing was left.

Red lights hummed on the control panel and from inside came a sound like rushing water: the hibernation fluid, filling the couch, flowing into Sukuang's nostrils and lungs like water into a drowning man.

Drowning, Jiaotan thought. All of us, floundering in our couches, carrying our grief and guilt and madness between the stars, all the ghosts that we won't ever exorcise dragging us down; a slow, lingering death instead of the Fire. Drowning.

She thought of the desperate hunger in Sukuang's eyes, and she wondered how many among them would ever come up for air.

OVERCLOCKING

James L. Sutter

They're waiting for him when he comes out of the tank. Whether plainclothes or just another pair of clockers, he can't quite tell, but the way they avoid looking in his direction tips him off in a heartbeat. When Ari Marvel walks by, you look.

They start drifting idly in his direction, and that clinches things. Reaching down into the lining of his pocket, Ari palms the whole batch and trails his hand over the edge of the bridge railing. The brittle grey modsticks crumble with ease, and by the time the two have dropped their cover and made the sting he's moved smoothly into position, hands against the brick and legs spread wide. The pigs don't even thank him for being so efficient. The patdown's rougher than necessary, but after a minute they throw their hoods back up and move off down the street.

Ari runs his hands through his faded blue-green spikes, then takes the stairs down to the tube. A beginner might have lingered at the railing and thought about all the time and money now floating down the culvert, but Ari doesn't look back. Necessary expenditures. Expected losses.

It's just business, baby.

Back at the pad, Maggie's waiting by the door. She looks like hell: hair in ratty dreads, shirt stained with god-knows-what. Crust in her eyes.

"Hey, Ari," she says.

Ari slides his keycard into the lock, checking first to see if the hair he put over the swipestripe has been moved. Still there. It doesn't mean that nobody's been there, of course—just that if they have been, they're good enough that there's no point in worrying about it. You win some, you lose some.

Inside, it looks like he's won. Maggie plops down on the couch, worrying a hangnail that's started to bleed. Her foot taps on the coffee table.

"Hey," she says again. He drops his coat onto the chair and moves into the kitchen to get a soda. She picks up the remote and begins flipping rapidly through the channels, then turns the set off again. Eventually he leaves the can on the counter and comes back into the living room, sitting down on the coffee table across from her and taking her hands.

"Maggie, look at me." She does—or, at least, as well as she's able to at this point.

"I'm only going to say this once. You're welcome to crash here, but you're not getting a fix. I won't have that in my house. You understand?"

She nods—those wide doe eyes the color of egg yolk—then goes back to gnawing at her thumb. He stands and leaves her there, entering the bedroom and closing the door. Once it's locked, he jimmies loose the bottom drawer of the dresser and flips a wad of sweaty bills into the crudely carved hollow. Then he drops fully clothed onto the mattress and covers his eyes with his forearm, blocking out the ruddy afternoon light that still filters in through heavy curtains. Out in the apartment, he can hear her moving about restlessly.

He's doing it again. It doesn't matter that he knows how it'll end, that he knows how it has ended more than once. It's simply a given: she'll show up. He'll let her in. Things will proceed accordingly. He bears down with his arm until the muted red of his eyelids turns to black, and then to stars.

The worst of it is that even through the filth, he can still see her. Inside the shell of those dreads, her hair is still gold verging on white, so fine as to be almost intangible. Behind the bruises and bags, her eyes would still crinkle upward if she smiled. And if he opened his arms, she might still flow into them like water, sparkling and warm and full of life.

Ari is not a stupid man, but Maggie is an exception.

Eyes clenched tight, Ari curls up on his side and falls asleep.

Any idiot with a fifth-grade education can get into it. If X is the price you pay for the product and Y is the cash you get from the girl-boys and junkies down on Madison, how many hits do you have to sell to earn one for yourself? Simple algebra.

The problem is that so few people get beyond that phase. Buy the goods from a lifer like Mickey or C.T., sell enough to pay for the rest, then get blasted in an alley or flophouse and hope the pigs don't raid until you come down. That's the killer, right there—as soon as you stick that junk in your head, your profit margin drops immediately to zero. Do not pass Go.

Ari knew better. Where small-time boys like C.T. were just middlemen, Ari cut straight from the source code. Where Mickey would drop his stash and run at the sight of a pig, Ari tied his shoe and made the product disappear, only to have it back in his pocket by the time they rounded the corner. It was an art and a science, but always—always—a business.

It's eight o'clock and she looks better, if one corpse can look better than another. Head back and mouth wide, snores threaten to shake apart her tiny frame. Setting his gear down, Ari gently takes the hand trailing onto the carpet and lays it across her chest, scrawny and thin as a prepubescent boy's. She doesn't even stir. He moves past her into the bedroom.

Slipping on a pair of thick glasses he'd never be caught dead in on the street, he unfolds the laptop and sets up shop. With the software loading, he spools up the burner and busts out a package of generic modsticks. Cheap, easy, and infinitely upgradable, whatever's on sale at the pharmacy is usually fine. Tonight it's anti-flu mods. He checks the make and model, then logs into the company's network remotely and anonymously, sliding past the firewalls and into the secure servers.

Back in the day, this would have been an all-night affair, chugging coffee and stayawakes as crack after crack failed to breach the infrastructure. Now it's down to a simple login—as long as he never shifts stuff around, the nanoceutical corporations never notice him. A ghost among giants.

Once the modstick's code downloads, he begins the real work: slicing and fusing lines, carefully reprogramming to remove certain safety features and incorporate his own. It's more than just tripping the right biochemical switches—there are the secondary effects, the sweet afterglow that gives his mods the edge over everyone else's. For a minute, he forgets about the business and lets himself be carried away by the beauty of it, the purity. Just code. No junkies. No pigs. No cash. Just code.

He inserts the first stick and cues the burner.

Cutting was everything. Amidst all the bullshit, the simple act of cutting was the one part of school that Ari truly enjoyed, and it showed. Time and again the teachers would hold up his latest creations and ask why he couldn't apply the same level of commitment to, say, physics or history. How was he supposed to explain it to them? They might appreciate his code, but that didn't mean they understood it. When one of them uploaded a bioexe, they saw expediency. Function. Utility. They never saw it in the way that he made it. Codecutting was art. Efficiency wasn't enough—it had to be elegant.

He'd been nicked jacking the editing software from the educational consoles, but that was only to be expected. He wasn't a hacker like the petty script kiddies that filled the labs, joyriding across systems and leaving their graffiti everywhere. For him, hacking was a means to an end, and once he'd hidden the backups he handed over the software and did his time in juvie like a man. At eighteen the smear was wiped from his record, and Ari "Marvel" Magnusson was free from the stigma of youthful indiscretion.

God bless America.

It's not like he was doing anything immoral. The store-bought nanoceuticals already ripped you apart and reformatted you according to their programming, he just removed limitations and changed objectives. Of course, it was the voluntary serotonin reuptake inhibitors that paid the bills—the happy sticks. Like all mods, bliss hacks were a temporary fix—once the programs ran their course, half a million years of cell memory took over again. But use often enough and the body forgot exactly where it left its natural set point, leaving you with a full-on case of the jones. By themselves, the hacks were harmless—as long as you had another mod headed your way, you could keep going indefinitely, and plenty of rich folks did just that. The problem was always the cash. Maybe you started out buying top-grade stuff, but once the need got its claws into you, you started to take what you could get, and sooner or later someone slipped you some bad code. The results could be seen in doorways up and down Madison or Seventh, when they hadn't been rounded into a public health van and whisked away to finish festering in a nice quarantine somewhere.

The whole thing was beyond stupid. Ari never touched the stuff.

She's cooking when he wakes up. From the doorway to the bedroom he can smell the eggs blackening, hear them growing crumbly and bitter on the Teflon coating.

She smiles, a little shakily, but her eyes are clear and steady. The dreads are clean, and she's found another shirt somewhere. He drops his coat and wanders into the kitchen. To his surprise, the eggs don't look as bad as they could—as they would have, once upon a time. A pepper lies minced on the cutting board, waiting to be sacrificed to the flames.

"Hey, Ari," she says, and the smile makes her face a little rounder. She looks like she wants to say something else, but before she can he moves forward and wraps her up from behind. Her head nestles into the gap between his collarbone and neck, and their breathing slows into unison, eyes closed. Her hair smells like his shampoo.

He reaches out and turns the burner down.

"Thanks," she whispers.

His first sale had him sweating bullets. What the hell was a nineteen-year-old suburban kid doing out on Madison after dark, lurking in the shadows with the crazies and the whores? The worst were the genuine clockers—leather-clad punks covered in piercings that street superstition said messed with the pigs' alloy scans. If they had known that the 'burb rat was trying to clock, not a mark there to make a purchase, they probably would have handed him his ass in a second, but the sweat on his forehead must have convinced them he wasn't serious competition. Honestly, Ari didn't think he belonged there either, but cutting equipment kept getting more expensive, and delivering pizza wasn't going to do the trick.

He'd only been there half an hour when he spotted his mark—a kid his own age, in slacks and a sweater, looking even less appropriate than Ari. Sensing a kindred spirit, the boy hustled over.

"Hey," he whispered, "you holding?"

Ari leaned back against the rail and did his best to play it cool, hoping the damp patches in his armpits weren't showing.

"Hell no, man," he spat. "I'm a paperboy. What you need?"

The kid thrust a fistful of notes in his direction, whispering the laughable street name of a sexual performance mod. What a lack of imagination these kids had. Ari snatched the bills.

"Get out of here," he growled. "You think I do that trash?" He shoved past the boy, hard enough to knock him over. From the mud, the kid started to protest, only to realize partway through his tirade that his right hand now held a tiny grey stick. Down the street, Ari allowed himself a quick smile. He turned the corner.

A stinking mass rose up and slammed him against the wall before he could cry out. Pinned by his shoulders, all Ari could see were yellow teeth and eyes. As his breath returned, so did his focus, enough to make out the pustule-covered face an inch from his own.

"Whatcha think you're doing, boy?" The old black man pinning Ari to the wall twitched with rage and withdrawal. "You think this is fun?"

Ari shook himself, and little flecks of the man's arm came off on his shirt. He fought the urge to vomit.

"Please," he gasped. "It's not like that. I don't do that."

The old man pressed harder against him. "Oh, really?" he asked, sliding his diseased cheek against Ari's, letting him feel its oozing warmth. "You think that kid out there deserves to end up like this?"

"No, please, no, I—" This time Ari did retch. "I don't do that, I'm a good cutter, clean, I wouldn't let that happen, I-oh-please-I-god…" Tears began to leak down Ari's face. With a final shake, the old man let him drop, and Ari stumbled forward and past, sprinting to the end of the alley before turning back. The old man sat where he'd collapsed, blood oozing from open sores where his hands had held the soft fabric of Ari's shirt. He put his head down on his knees and wept like a baby.

Ari turned and ran.

She's not there when he gets home, but he can smell the remains of breakfast in the sink. Setting his coat down on the couch, it takes him almost an entire breath to notice that the door to the bedroom is open. Dishes clatter as his hip slams into the corner of the counter, but he doesn't feel it, scrambling across the linoleum toward the doorway.

She's on the floor next to the computer chair, limbs twisted at strange angles by contracted muscles. He drops to his knees and puts an ear to her chest, listening for any flutter, but her skin is already cool and the drool on her cheek is a dry white trail. Her eyes are closed, face taut with a pleasure beyond bearing.

"Maggie…"

He wants to scream, to cry, to explain, but realizes as he opens his mouth that he has nothing to say. Instead he kneels over her bird-thin frame and cradles her head in his hands, rubbing swollen eyes through clean hair and breathing it in with each shuddering breath, as above them the computer hums softly with lines of sloppy code.

They're there by the bridge again, still thinking that a jacket and dyed hair can cover up the way they carry themselves, years of pride and academy training. Ari leans back against the rail and casually scratches his groin as they approach through the crowd, feeling the modsticks in his pocket, ready to be palmed, rubbed, and dropped.

Choreographed, all of it. Just a flick of his wrist, and he's free to walk away. Every day, the same dance.

He leaves the sticks where they are and moves his hand away.

Up against the wall, the pig jerks in surprise at the shapes in Ari's pocket, then slams Ari's face against the concrete and reaches for his cuffs. A voice in the background calls it in to the station. From his place on the sidewalk, Ari stares past the railing at the gurgling water in the culvert, endlessly carrying away the grime of the city. He smiles.

It's just business, baby.

59 **BEADS**

Rochita Loenen-Ruiz

Air limousines floated by like ghosts in a night filled with a jangle of sounds. A mad juxtaposition of chords, wailing voices and crooned-out tunes mangled by the sound of honking horns, curses and the cries of the desperate filled the dark streets. Cordoba's End, home to migrants and refugees.

After their parents succumbed to the rot, Pyn and Sienna wandered the streets of Cordoba. Together, they trekked the back side of the posh quarter. Ecstasy street, Ilona's Oord, Sonatina's Point, the words tasted as exotic and beautiful as the places themselves.

"You think we'll ever be rich enough to live on High End?" Sienna asked.

"I don't know," Pyn said.

"We could join one of the lotteries and win a prize," Sienna said. "I'd wear a long white dress and violets. We could go to the fair, and I would push a trundle cart with my dolly in it."

Pyn snorted.

"You ever heard of anyone from Cordoba's End winning a lottery?" Pyn asked.

She pretended not to hear Sienna's sniff, pretended not to see the tears trickling down her young sister's cheeks.

"Come on, Sien. Time to go."

It wasn't fair, Pyn often thought. It wasn't fair of Mama to die and leave Pyn to take care of her younger sister. Mama should have stayed alive; instead, she'd chosen to yield to the rot. Pyn didn't mind scrounging for herself, but it hurt her to see the bloom on Sienna's cheeks give way to grey grey haggardness that made her look older than her ten years.

Summer brought searing heat. Dust and flies abounded, and Sienna's skin broke out in sores that heralded the onset of rot.

"It must have been something I ate," Sienna said with a wan smile.

Pyn nodded, but it was hard for her to ignore the circles under Sienna's eyes, and when she laid her hand on Sienna's forehead, the low burn frightened her.

"You'll be all right," Pyn whispered. "Hang in there, Sien. You'll be all right."

She held Sienna's hand, promising her chocolates, and lollipops, and a thousand other things she knew she could never give. She sang bits of remembered lullabies and when Sienna finally fell asleep, Pyn sat staring at her sister knowing she didn't have much time.

Out in the street, the harsh glow of sun reminded Pyn that the recycle hounds wouldn't be about until sundown at least.

"Take good care of your sister," her mother's voice came back to haunt her. There was only one thing left to do now. Squaring her shoulders, Pyn set off for Farrier Corso's cubby.

A low building with polished black walls housed the cubbies of agents to Procurers and Healing Masters alike. Farrier was a legend in Cordoba's End. She'd once been owned, but luck had been on her side and her former owner had given her freedom. Farrier's story had captured Pyn's imagination. If she could find an owner just like Farrier had, she would still have a chance at a good life with her sister.

"Are you sure this is what you want?" Farrier Corso's question jolted Pyn out of her reverie.

Pyn stared at the older woman, wondering whether it was the built -ins that kept Farrier looking young.

"Sien's all I've got," she said. "I can't let her die."

"Healing takes time," Farrier said. "There's no guarantee she'll ever be wholly restored to who she was. Rot's a cruel thing."

"But a Healing Master can help her, right?"

Farrier nodded.

"She's got youth on her side, and a skilled healer may be able to restore her. But treatment comes at a high price, Pyn."

"I just want her to get well," Pyn said.

"Do you have the credits?" Farrier asked.

"I can get them," Pyn replied.

"I'd help you if I could," Farrier said. "But my own funds are limited."

"I..."Pyn paused and stared at Farrier. "Can you wire Sebastian for me?"

"You'll be one of the owned," Farrier said. "Sebastian won't extend credit without you signing a contract with him."

"You found a way out," Pyn said.

"I was lucky. Not all owners are so generous. Many of those who were bought along with me wound up on the scrap heap. It's a truth you'll have to face, Pyn."

Pyn bit her lip.

"Sien's only ten," she said. "If I can get her cured, she can have a better life than this."

Pyn waited as the older woman drew up the papers. She set her finger to the seal, and listened to the hum of the join boxes talking to one another. Farrier nodded as the boxes confirmed Pyn's identity and the order was taken—one for speedy pick up.

Thinking of the order floating away in the ether, Pyn wondered if she was doing the right thing. She steeled herself. If Sien died, what point was left in living?

Farrier handed her a seal.

"Pick up when payment is confirmed," she said.

"I'll have the credit," Pyn promised.

Tears blurred Pyn's vision as she left the building. Memories of Mama on her deathbed came back to haunt her. Mama's face wracked with pain, the endless retching, and the pus that seemed to ooze from every pore of her body.

"Mama, let me call the Healing Masters," Pyn had begged.

"No," Mama said.

"They can make you better, Mama. They'll make the pain go away."

"At what price?"

"There's no price too great, Ma."

"I can't do it," Mama had said. "Let me go, Pyn. You're a big girl now. You take care of Sienna."

"I'm fifteen, Mama. Please don't leave us."

But Mama hadn't listened to her pleadings. Pyn curled her hands into fists. Mama would say it was Sienna's fate to die, but Pyn would be damned if she let her little sister rot to death.

Ahead of her, the streetlight turned red. An air limousine floated past her, and a dilapidated land jeep screeched to a halt. She felt as if everyone on the street knew what she'd done.

Sien would be better, she consoled herself. Sien would get well and she'd live a fairytale life.

In her mind, she was already talking to Sienna.

You won't have to scavenge for food any longer she said. You'll be okay, Sien. And if the Virgin smiles on us, we'll be together again.

So what if Sienna didn't remember Pyn?

She shook her head. Even if Sienna forgot, Pyn would always remember.

She swiped at the tears pouring down her cheeks and hastened her steps.

"Everything will be all right," she whispered. "Everything will be all right."

Hotel Usurpia simmered in the noonday heat. Light prisms cast rainbows of color over the entire street. Here was where the city's top procurer touched base. Pyn stopped and fingered the card in her pocket.

Sebastian had come to Cordoba's End one afternoon when Mama was still alive. He'd seen Pyn dancing on the street podium and, afterward, slipped the card into her hand. Mama turned white with fury when she saw the procurer, but he slipped away without answering her curses.

"He's a parasite," Mama said. "Feeds off others to enrich his own pockets. I don't want you listening to his lies."

Pyn had kept the card secret from Mama. Now, she stopped and stared at the tall building, willing her heart to stop pounding. Her finger brushed over the embossed ribbons and the lone dancer printed onto the face of Sebastian's card.

"Talent and energy," he'd said to her. "If ever you decide to leave Cordoba's End, come to me."

Of course, there was a price attached. Pyn didn't need Mama to tell her that. She'd hidden the card away because it was the best thing anyone had ever said to her. Talent, he'd said, and he'd told her she could be one of the best.

She bit her lip, tasting dust and sweat. She was suddenly unsure. What if he'd forgotten all about her? Two years had gone by. Surely there were other talents on the planet. Despair gripped her heart. Since Mama's death, there hadn't been much time for dancing. Nevertheless, she didn't dare back down now. There was only one chance left for Sien. The best she could do was try. If Sebastian had forgotten about her, surely there were others who would welcome a new girl into their fleet.

She took a deep breath and squared her shoulders.

"All or nothing," she whispered. "Godson help me."

Nobody stopped her. Not the guards standing outside the carved crystallite doors, not the bright watch eye. She walked past them, conscious of the dust clinging to the hem of her tattered skirt, smelling her own fear and uncertainty.

"So you finally made it here," Sebastian Uraro said.

Since she'd last seen him, his hair had turned silver-grey. He had grown a neat beard, and his skin changed color as he spoke.

"It's a perk," Sebastian said, when Pyn didn't speak. "The latest innovation. I wanted to try it out. Do you like it?"

"It's different," Pyn said. She felt conscious of the layer of dust on her dusky skin, and she crossed her arms slightly.

"Farrier sent me your message," Sebastian said.

"I need help," Pyn stammered out. "It's my little sister. She's ill. I need to get her to the Healing Masters. She's all I've got."

She came to a halt, realizing her words sounded like a demand rather than a plea for help.

Sebastian snapped his fingers, and his skin returned to its own milky color.

"I remember you," he said. "You danced when I was in Cordoba's End. Your mother was quite upset. Does she know you're here?"

Pyn shook her head.

Understanding dawned on Sebastian's face.

"Gone, is she?"

Pyn lifted her chin, determined not to cry.

"It's just me and Sienna," she said. "If you can't help me, I'll find someone else who will."

"Not so rash, young Pyn. I'll take on your contract and provide the credits, on one condition."

"Name it," Pyn said.

Pyn genuflected in front of the altar. The enhancements around her waist affected her balance. She had yet to get used to the awkwardness in her knees and her elbows where connectors had been installed.

True to his word, Sebastian had arranged for Sienna's pick up. Pyn had been to visit her younger sister at the Healing Ward, but Sien was in a coma and the Healing Masters said there was no waking her until the process of rejuvenation was done.

She sat at Sienna's bedside, holding her sister's hand until the ward sisters shooed her out and her beeper told her it was time to head back to where Sebastian waited with the Renovation Experts.

"It'll hurt," Sebastian said. "But without built-ins, there's no shaping or wielding energy. Collectors won't pay top money for a Dollygirl who can't give or take a feed. It's what makes you valuable—not your ability to dance, but your ability to project energy in waves the owners can feed on.

"A Dollygirl who can't project energy is useless. Remember that, Pyn."

He feeds off the misery of others, Mama's voice echoed in her head. Pyn gritted her teeth.

"I'll do it," she had said.

She had endured the awful sculpting of muscle and bone, borne the rearranging of the contours of her body to allow room for feeds to tap into her system. All through recovery, she had reminded herself that the renovations were only a means toward her goal of saving Sienna.

Pyn dipped her finger into the holy water and made the sign of the cross. The sun shone off the stone face of the grieving Godson.

"Godson, forgive me," she whispered. "I don't mind the renovations. But if you're listening, keep me from the recycling heap."

She touched the silver band on her wrist. Even if she wanted to, escape was not an option. She'd seen what happened to one of the girls who'd tried to escape after signing contracts. By the time the recycling hounds were done, even rejuvenation couldn't save her from the scrap heap. If Pyn ran, there would be no mercy for her, and there would be no future for Sienna. She took a deep breath. It was time to head back to Hotel Usurpia.

A line of limousines hung static in the air when she reached the hotel.

"Just on time," Sebastian said when she went in.

Pyn shuffled into a ballerina costume. She pulled on long white gloves, tied ribbons in her hair, and tied on her shoes. As she connected the feed to her built-in, she looked around for her partner.

Korian was a mute from Ayudan. Sebastian had taken Korian because his body type was a perfect match for Pyn's. Their feeds were attuned, as were their bodies.

When they'd performed for Sebastian for the first time, he'd clapped his hands and wept with joy.

"It's just as I envisioned it," he said.

Pyn smiled, giving lie to the pain she'd experienced when she'd joined with Korian. Music seared through her veins like electric fire, and she pulled loose from the feeds.

"I can't," she cried.

You have to, Korian signed. It's this or the scrap heap.

She read the fear in his eyes, and guilt coursed through her. She couldn't jeopardize his life, and neither could she give up on the hope of seeing Sienna again. She'd gotten up from the floor and pushed herself past the pain into a zone where the burning was almost pleasure.

Sebastian's voice summoned Pyn back to present.

"Connoisseurs and collectors, girls and boys. That means good owners and good money. Don't let me down."

Pyn maneuvered herself into the line, thankful for Korian's hand under her arm. Even if he couldn't speak, his touch communicated assurance and comfort. She pressed her hands together. She would do whatever it took to escape the scrap heap. No matter what they did to her, she'd still be in the same world as her sister.

"Ssst..." Sebastian's hiss brought the line to attention.

One by one the air limousines disgorged their owners.

Here were the Originals. Descendants of the first settlers, there was something about them that wasn't quite human. The sleek males in their long silver coats, and the females in their Basque-like skirts floated onto the tarmac. Sparks glinted from their feet as they glided onto the purple carpet spread along the length of the lobby and down the front steps of the hotel.

Pyn made her bows, keeping her face still and void of emotion. She was a Dollygirl now. A commodity to be bought or traded as her master wished. If she performed well, her value would go up. If she were lucky, she would find an owner who would eventually give her freedom instead of sending her to the scrap heap.

One of the females paused in front of Pyn. Her eyes were pale and heavy-lidded, the skin of her face pulled so taut there was only a bump where her nose should have been. She brushed her finger over Pyn's nose, and Pyn controlled the shiver of fear that ran down her spine as she met the woman's considering gaze.

"You're new, hnn," the female's voice sounded flutelike. "Have you got enough amps on you, I wonder."

Her fingers felt cold against the curve of Pyn's cheek.

"Warm," the female said. She shuddered and her eyes opened and shut quickly. "So much passion for one so young."

Down the line, one of the men had stopped in front of a Dollyboy named Anjo. There was no hiding the avidity and the excitement in the eyes of the Originals. Their voices rose and filled the hall with cooing and compliments.

"What a fine fleet of girls and boys, Sebastian," one of the females crooned.

"Lovely, lovely," a male said. "I might be tempted to add one more to my collection."

Pyn watched from the corner of her eye as Sebastian bowed and smiled.

"You haven't seen them in action yet," he said. "My fleet has pre-pared a show. After you've seen it, you'll remember why it's well worth your time and your money when you come to Sebastian Uraro."

In the backroom, Pyn and Korian, shrugged out of their costumes. Strands of filament joined them to each other—an almost invisible line feed connected to the built-ins in their elbows and their ankles. Except for the gossamer threads floating about them, they were both naked.

Pyn knew the dance well. The renovations created the appearance of delicate grace and hid the effort behind the movements. Tiny holes along her ribcage opened up to the jacks allowing music to flow through her system. The feeds tapped into the energy produced by the dance, enhancing emissions. She'd practiced with Korian for months, going through the steps of coupling and disengaging until the slightest touch produced a constant surge of energy issuing from their combined strength.

Onstage, the light turned blue. Music fluted in through the walls of the auditorium. Pyn couldn't see the audience, but she knew they were there. She felt Korian's hand on her back, and she closed her eyes.

Her nerves shivered as music fed into her system. She felt the trace of Korian's movements and allowed her body to follow in the patterns of the dance.

There was a brief moment of static when her hands pressed against Korian's hands. Pyn opened her mouth to his kiss, felt the bloom of en-ergy, heard the oohs and aahs from those watching as light rose up and dissolved into an illusion of birds and fire. She was on fire, fountains burst into sparks of flame around them.

A curse on your soul.

She brushed away the echo of her mother's voice.

This is for Sien, she reminded herself. Her body opened up, flowered under Korian's touch, their limbs entwined, coupled and separated, and the air reverberated with rainbows of color and light.

She heard gasps and shrieks as the assembled audience fed on the rays of ecstasy induced by their coupling.

The pale-eyed female bought them.

"Sandusy's a good owner," Sebastian said. "She's always taken good care of her property, so you two should be in good hands."

Pyn was in no doubt about the profit to Sebastian himself. Sandusy had offered not only a large amount of credits, but she'd also offered Sebastian a large holding on the edge of the Siargao region.

"Better me than anyone else," Sandusy said after negotiations were done. "I would've taken only you, but Sebastian insisted I take the boy as well."

Pyn didn't know what to say to that. She cast a glance at Korian. He was staring straight ahead, his face void of emotion.

The flat line that was Sandusy's lips twitched slightly.

"I take care of what is mine," she said.

For a brief moment, Pyn felt a twinge of rebellion. If not for Sienna, she'd still be free. She suppressed the thought. She'd made her choice. With the signing of the contract, her future was sealed and Sienna's ensured.

Fifty-nine beads. Pyn kissed her prayer necklace. Each bead on the necklace represented performances and alterations she'd undergone since Sandusy had bought her. She'd stopped counting years in service when the number of renovations she'd undergone exceeded them. With Sienna still in process, Pyn wasn't sure if there was such a thing as redemption. At least, she wasn't sure if there was redemption as far as her soul was concerned.

Still, she kept on saying the prayers.

She kept on praying because no matter if she no longer believed in miracles and all the religious crap preached on the streets, she had to hold onto the hope that everything she'd gone through hadn't been in vain.

She kissed the statue of the Godson and dropped the beads into her pocket.

Sandusy was giving a feast to celebrate her retirement from public office, and her acquisitions were expected to be at their best.

She'd sent Pyn for renovations.

"You don't have to, if you think it's too much," Sandusy had said.

Pyn had wanted to say no, but her pride wouldn't let her.

"If Korian can do it, so can I," she said.

"You don't have to prove yourself to me," Sandusy said.

"I'm not doing it for you," Pyn said.

"If I set you free, would you stay with me?" Sandusy asked.

Pyn didn't know what to say to that. A Dollygirl staying with an Original after ownership had ended was something she'd never heard of.

"I'll take the alteration," was all she said. She pretended not to hear Sandusy's sigh. Her owner favored her, she knew that, but she didn't understand what else Sandusy expected of her.

She'd taken the alteration, ignoring the signs that her body was no longer as young or as quick to heal as it used to be.

"Maybe you shouldn't perform," Sandusy said.

"I can perform," Pyn insisted. "I won't give you an excuse to send me to the scrap heap."

She regretted the words when she saw the way Sandusy's eyes refracted.

"I'm sorry," she said.

But Sandusy was already turning away.

"I'll be waiting in the practice room," was all her owner said.

Pyn's elbows and ankles hummed and sent waves of pain through her body. She hugged herself and waited for the spasms to pass. The intensity of her body's reaction told her what she'd refused to admit. The constant upgrades were taking their toll.

She straightened up, holding onto the wall for support.

Korian would be waiting for her. They'd been practicing with the newest feeds all week. Mangled music sent rivers of pain tumbling through Pyn's veins. The new routines were torture, and Sandusy wasn't satisfied with anything less than perfection. Micro-sized boosters upped the production of their energy. Every move sent fresh burn through Pyn's body, but the waves of color—the release of evoked emotion was stronger than any they'd ever produced before.

Pyn stopped, her breath coming in short gasps. Sandusy might just decide to gift them with freedom. She could feel it in her bones. She hugged herself and whispered a prayer to the Godson.

Through the open door, she could see the sun shining on the smooth green curve of the front lawn. An air limousine swooped down and hovered above the gleaming driveway. Sandusy's valets rushed out to welcome the new arrivals.

Whoever they are, they're early, Pyn thought.

Then her thoughts ground to a stop. Sienna, her eyes gleaming with excitement, hair shining black under the light of the reflectors, descended from the limousine. Beside her, a woman wearing the badge of a state keeper twisted her hands in nervousness.

"Sienna," Pyn whispered.

She watched as Sienna moved on past her.

"We shouldn't be here," the woman said.

"I want to see the Dollygirls," Sienna replied.

"We'll have to wait for Sandusy," the woman said. "That's what the letter said. Wait for Sandusy."

Sienna's laughter tinkled, as she skipped alongside the keeper. Pyn fought the urge to reach out her hand and touch her sister.

"Here, that won't do at all," the woman said. "Sandusy won't be pleased."

"Sebastian said something about a surprise," Sienna said.

"Well, Sebastian isn't here yet."

Pyn's breath came in shallow gasps. She watched her sister walk carelessly over the smooth floor.

"Sienna," she whispered.

Tears pooled at the edges of her eyes and trickled down her cheeks, as she stared at her sister. Sienna's skin was smooth and unblemished, her limbs were strong and firm, and she moved with a supple grace that told Pyn her younger sister had never gone through renovations.

"Sienna," her voice rose slightly.

She waited expectantly as Sienna turned.

"It's me," Pyn whispered.

She watched as Sienna came toward her. Saw the look of wonder cross her younger sister's face.

"You're a Dollygirl," Sienna said.

Pyn smiled and nodded, waiting as Sienna reached out her hands. Her fingers felt cool as they traced the rigid landscape of Pyn's forehead. Pyn winced as Sienna's fingers probed the connectors recently installed along the line of her brow. But she stood still, allowing her sister to explore the ridges of her cheeks where new software nestled under sculpted tissue.

"Do you remember?" Pyn heard the tremble in her voice. "Do you remember Cordoba's End? Sonatina's Point? Ecastasy Street? Sisters?"

"Sisters?" Pyn saw the confusion in Sienna's gaze. "I don't under-stand."

"Sisters," Pyn insisted. "Don't you remember? You said you'd wear a white dress with violets..."

Sienna shook her head.

"I don't have a sister," she said.

"It's the rejuvenation," Pyn said quickly. "They said this would happen. But you'll remember. I'll help you." But Sienna was backing away, shaking her head in denial.

"Sien."

Desperate to keep her sister from leaving, Pyn forgot about the surgeon's admonitions to be careful. She stepped forward, felt the full weight of her body come down on her left foot, heard the crack as new bone gave way under unexpected pressure. As if from far away, she heard the skittering of beads as the prayer necklace fell out of her pocket and hit the hard stone floor.

WONDROUS DAYS

Genevieve Valentine

W e should make a map," she says. "Just to keep track of things."
I keep my mouth shut, try not to look at her.

We live in a sooty half-dawn that never wakes. Nights are so dark
it's better not to think about it. (The nights had only just begun to get
dark at all; for a while it was just as bright as the day, from all the fires
eating through the dry forest, and we walked until we dropped just to
keep ahead of the smoke.)

Sleeping is the worst. You don't know if you've been asleep for ten
hours or ten minutes. I'm never rested—the darkness and the smoke
have swallowed everything—and there's nothing to go on, and whenever I open my eyes everything's still pointless, and she's already
awake.

"It's morning," she says, or, "It's afternoon," like she knows any
better than I do what time it is, and she's looking away from me and
out at the wreckage.

Maybe that's why she wanted to make a map; just to pretend that
there was something better coming, that we'd meet someone who
would need it.

The real map of the new world is tacked to a wall in the Darkroad
Project wing of the Ames Research Center. It's already yellowing;
NASA's acid-free paper can't hold up against the atmosphere.

The map is stuck with little green pins where explosions are most likely to affect the tectonic plates. There are circles drawn in black and red, in
orange and purple and green. The map key names them: twenty years, ten
years, five years, one. The black circles are widest, and marked Xibalba.

The papers posted around it are from algorithms that have been run on the Pleiades supercomputer. They're printed thickly with core temperatures, trade winds, a Refractive Index to gauge the best chances to preserve the ice caps. There's a list of temperate vegetation six pages long, Latin names and English names side by side.

There are smaller maps, anonymous close-ups of deserts and forests and plains and islands. Beneath each map there are pages of notes on maximum water levels, likely periods of drought, natural shelters; each one has a tacked-up list of flora and fauna marked with Xs, or E for Edible.

It's a drastic future, carefully planned, waiting patiently for its day.

She looked like she had been ready for something. She had hiking boots that laced up her calves, and a backpack big enough to live from. My canvas sneakers lasted less than a week; I had to wrap them with drawstrings from my jacket until we found a corpse with my shoe size.

She never said what she had been doing in the forest. She hardly ever talked. I talked; when we met I talked about what had happened, about where my girlfriend was. ("Dead," she said.) I talked about where we should go to look for others.

There were none. Just corpses with my shoe size.

After we'd walked where I wanted for ten days, she said, "I think we should try another way. "It was the longest speech she'd made, and the way she said it sounded like the whole thing was my fault.

"Like you know where to go," I said, but we headed another way.

That was when she started the map; like wherever I'd been going didn't matter.

She kept a book in her cargo pocket where she made hash marks for the dead. She had a page for women, a page for men. Sometimes there was no telling from the parts who it had been to start with; those hash marks had a page of their own.

"You should give up," I said.

She knelt, turned the body over.

(Eventually you stop throwing up when you see corpses; your body holds onto whatever nutrients you can get.)

We found a deer. Most of the meat had turned, but maggots had kept part of the loin clean enough to eat.

She cut off what she could with the knife in her pocket, and she found a cave deep enough to block the wind, and after she had twisted grass so it would burn, I used my lighter to start the fire.

Weird what you're good for, when circumstances change.

In the morning she's sitting at the mouth of the cave, looking out at the boggy forest. She doesn't like to be near me; when we've got tree cover she sleeps out of reach; when we're in caves she sleeps as far away as the walls allow.

(Cave living. Shit. Sometimes you wish you had died.)

After a second I realize she's looking at the sky; maybe she could navigate just by the stars, back when there had been stars.

Something turns over in my stomach. Hunger, maybe.

Point Zero, an activist group of historians and academics, had held a rally in New York to protest The Darkroad Project's access to Pleiades. They carried signs that read 13 TO ZERO; SCIENCE NOT SUPERSTITION; THE MAYANS WOULD BE ASHAMED.

"The Mayan Solstice is just resetting a clock!" one guy shouted into the cameras. "We're wasting taxpayer money on an astronomy lab that only generates scare tactics! Mindless superstition like this is catching!"

Point Zero vaulted to Public Enemy Number One. The Pope declared the intervening year a gift, and bid his congregation, "Use these wondrous days to make peace before the End Times, when Jesus calls His faithful children to Heaven." Superstition about 2012 spread faster than the media could track it, and Point Zero's rationalism looked like a losing fighter until twelve of them took over the NSA's Sequoia computer.

(They'd had an insider on the development team, which the NSA never admitted.)

They hacked C-SPAN, announced the takeover, activated the nuclear grid, and held the Svalbard Seed Vault hostage.

"We have no wish to harm Norway or any other country," they broadcasted, "but we are willing to take drastic measures to force humanity to confront its own future and to work for the planet's survival."

Norway provided boats for evacuees. (The Wildlife Federation sent in their own boat teams to rescue the reindeer, bears, and foxes that had been forgotten in the crisis.)

The Point Zero faction also demanded the dismantling of the Darkroad Project at the Ames Research Center, and the public acknowledgement of any quakeproof cities being constructed.

The manifesto they disseminated talked about "the fetishization of disaster as religious experience" and "the inevitable emergence of suspicion as commodity."

It named the Darkroad Project "an underreporting think tank whose members should be using their intelligence to educate the world about astronomic research, rather than burying their disaster-scenario findings under government hush money. "

"Unless this 2012 Doomsday theory is debunked publicly," the manifesto concluded, "we will protest the waste of international resources in any way necessary to make it clear that we are serious about our goal, and ensure that we eliminate the rising and dangerous power of mass delusion in the hands of the under-informed."

The manifesto was roundly decried as sensationalist.

Construction on several subterranean cities came quietly to a halt.

(No one could tell what Point Zero might already know; no one knew what Sequoia could do in the hands of the right people.)

I was driving across the mountain when it hit.

The earth snapped once from side to side, like a wet dog shaking off the rain, and my car flew into the rock face sideways because the road had spat it out.

(I was lucky. The others must have been spat out the other side, down the rock face.)

When I finally came around, I broke out of the car and limped back onto the road, and I couldn't even recognize where I was; the mountain had crumbled to dust around me, and I was standing in the center of a world I didn't know. It was like a pile of puzzle pieces snapped together by a careless kid; everything looked unfinished, forced together with gaps between them, so two halves of a tree were suddenly standing a mile apart.

Everything was colorless and dim, so I thought it must have been almost night, and I dragged my way back to the car to sleep until it was morning. (I didn't know yet that there were no more mornings.)

I go ahead of her with a walking stick, in case of animals or sinkholes. Whenever I look back, she's frowning off to one side, making notes on her cheap road map (my cheap road map, the most useful thing I'd offered).

Finally she says, "We should go back to the cave tonight. The ground is too soft here to sleep on."

Her profile is sharp and bright against the grimy day, and I feel like

I've faded to nothing, like she's the only living thing left.

I watched her fall asleep near the cave mouth (where there was still enough light to see). She had her book tented on her chest, her head turned away.

I slid the book out of her fingers (her fingers were cold, she was too close to the cave mouth), and tucked it into the inner pocket of my jacket.

(She trusted me only because she had to, because otherwise there was nothing left. Let her ask for it back; find out what it's worth.)

After the manifesto came out, the Ames was publicly cleared out; the governor insisted it was for the safety of employees, not as a concession to Point Zero.

The Nobel Mathematics Committee issued a statement disowning the "Point Zero extremists, who turn a legitimate standpoint into a terrorist platform."

The board members of the mainstream Point Zero held a vote and had a very long discussion. Zeropointzero.org went offline.

Reset13.org popped up the next day, its homepage dotted with strings of 13s and 0s and a palatable explanation of b'ak'tuns and k'atuns. It had a comic strip featuring a pair of sarcastic Mayans who cracked jokes about resetting a long-form clock.

Their members list grew.

A week after the taking of Sequoia, there were only those twelve members of Point Zero left, and they were surrounded by police, locked into a little operating room with a world at their fingertips.

She doesn't mention the book. All day I walk in front of her, tense and waiting, ready for a fight that never comes.

I had figured she'd be better than this, somehow. (Better than what? My mind is muddy; I breathe through the coat of grime on my lungs, put one foot in front of the other, grind my walking stick into the ground so I don't fall through.)

Behind me she breathes a steady in-and-out, like she's drilling slowly through my skull.

We don't start fires at night. You find cover and you huddle in and hope not to freeze. At first it was awful, but now I don't really even shiver any more; my body's bracing itself for a very long winter.

She hunkers down into her coat, and I try to make out the line of her profile against the crawling night, until it gets too dark and I give up. I can't see a thing at night since the fires stopped.

(Strange, the things you miss.)

"Why were you sky watching, before? What were you looking for?"

After too long she says, "What makes you think I was looking for something?"

Bullshit. She'd been looking for something since the day I staggered through the woods delirious from hunger and half-sick from my own smell, and she appeared out of nowhere to take me back to the hollow trunk where she had made shelter from the grimy light.

"Don't lie to me," I say. I hardly recognize my own voice, like the dark distorted it.

But I had listened to the news back when Point Zero was protesting. I knew that if you looked up at the night sky you saw Xibalba Be, the Dark Road that the Mayans had seen, the biggest clock humanity could set by. Someone from the think tank had gone on the news and explained the galactic alignment with a computer graphic. The planets had already lined up like a string of beads; nobody knew if anything would happen before they split, but you had to think that something could.

I wait for her to call me a liar; to ask about her book. I count to ten. To ten. To ten. She's so quiet I can hardly hear her breathing.

I keep my eyes squeezed shut (you get vertigo at night trying to look around with no light anywhere), but there are little white flecks in my vision, a tiny constellation of angry stars.

It's the dark that does you in. It's the dark that slides over you worse than the ash or the wind, because you know that all the ways to keep back the dark are gone, that when your lighter is gone there will be no more fire without flint and sticks and admitting that there's no hope for anything better.

The dark swallows up the new geography that's been shaken out over the old one, swallows up everything but you (she's sleeping next to you, propped up against the cave wall, but the cave is so small you could reach out and slide your hand into her pocket), and you wake from nothing and know that the dark has pooled like oil in your ears and your nostrils, and even with your eyes squeezed shut you know it's stained your vision until you can't see, that you're walking in circles as the ground under you is crumbling, that with the next step you're going to fall, and then you wake and open your eyes, gasping, your hands scraping at the roof of your mouth to claw the darkness out, and she's leaning over you, marking on your body with pencil where she'll carve away the good meat, and when you scream at her the darkness slides into your stomach, and you wake to the sooty sky and her silhouette already standing outside the cave, untouched and impenetrable, and as you sit up something coils around your lungs and squeezes tight.

Point Zero knew they had been abandoned; they knew that whatever happened, their lives were over, and it was only left to decide how they would go out.

They didn't want to damage the seed vault, no matter what. They never had. Of all the doomsday propositions Point Zero dismissed, the swift extinction of nature was not one. (They cheered when they heard that the animals were being evacuated from Svalbard.)

Resolute, they wrote a new broadcast, where they would announce additional targets; they'd force oil fields to stop production, they'd frighten the world into a worldwide cease-fire. They would sit in the Ops Room with Sequoia and slowly starve out, to buy enough time for the world to come to its senses.

"These wondrous days you're waiting for don't come from prayer, but from deed," they wrote. "They are the provenance of those who care enough to make sacrifices for a better world. We are your caretakers; we will craft these days for all of you."

(Hunger was setting in; they were getting evangelical.)

They didn't know about the room in the basement of the Ames with maps tacked to it, with pinpoints and predictions from the Darkroad Project about how a new world could be carved from the old one.

Point Zero didn't know there were plans that had already been made.

The next day is dark and heavy, heavier than yesterday; I can't breathe (she had stuffed soot down my lungs overnight) and with every step I can feel her staring at my back like she knows something I don't—

I turn on her.

"Is this about your fucking book?"

She doesn't say anything, just gives me that hard, closed-off look

I'm getting pretty sick of.

"If you want it back," I snap, "you can ask for it."

"Why did you take it?" she asks, like there's an answer, and all I can think of is, "It's a stupid thing to carry," I say, which is the truth but it isn't an answer.

But she doesn't question me, just says, "You can't do that," so calm it stings, and I sink an inch into the mud and I hate her for pushing me like this I hate her and my hand flies at her and as she ducks I scream, "I'll do what the fuck I want to you!"

She staggers a few paces back. Then she looks at me for a long time, and I feel like I've sunk into the ground up to my knees. I make fists at my sides.

Finally she says, "I'd like it back."

The last fucking thing I need from her is that tone, that tone like she's disappointed in me, like I'm the one who's not making sense.

I yank the book out of my jacket and throw it on the ground at my feet. It hits the mud with a wet thwack, hovers for a second before it starts to sink.

She never looks at the book; never looks away from me.

I step on it as I turn around, just for the satisfaction of forcing it down, and then I keep walking.

Eventually, I hear her footsteps behind me. When I look back at her later, there's no mud on her; she's finally wised up about that worthless thing.

There's no need for it. Not like the past is going to change.

After the second broadcast from Point Zero that stated their intentions and put a dozen cities under the gun, there were stampedes from the cities into the countryside. There were cease-fires in war zones as countries pulled their troops back to handle the home fronts. Churches were overrun with congregations hoping to make amends before Point Zero pushed the button.

No one was thinking any more about an empty Research Center; it was nominally under guard, but since Point Zero had ignored it, so had the police. All five members of the Darkroad Project slipped in through a side door without even being seen.

As world governments argued about how to protect against the threat posed by Sequoia's nuclear grid, as Point Zero's broadcast was picked up by news stations with panicking anchors, as people rioted over canned food in grocery stores, the Darkroad Project stood at the control console of Pleiades and executed the program they had been working on for two years.

Xibalba.exe ran flawlessly; they knew as soon as the earthquake hit and the room buckled.

(They were too close to a fault line to expect to survive; but a true scientist must accept the risks of the experiment.)

We walk for hours. We walk until the dark is almost on us; I want to see how long she'll keep up. (Every step; I have to stop myself from looking over my shoulder.)

The dark rolls in from all around us (the dust hides everything), but she doesn't stop, and I can't—I can't show any weakness, not after all this. I keep walking. Soot has coated my nostrils, and the whole world smells like char, and the darkness is sliding over me.

"It's getting dark," I say, "we should stop," and my voice is small in the dark.

She says, "If you're tired."

Fuck her. I keep walking.

My legs are numb; I feel like I can hardly walk, like I'm falling asleep from the bottom up, and my walking stick isn't helping. I let it fall; I need my hands for balance, and I swing them out a little away from my sides, my hands fisted. I won't stop until she stops.

Behind me, she says, "I voted yes, you know."

Her voice is far away, and it pushes me deeper into the ground. I turn—I try to turn, but I'm thigh-deep in mud, and I realize her voice is far away because she hasn't followed me. She's been paying attention to the lay of the land.

"Get me out of here," I say.

She says, "I voted yes. It was a two-two split until I voted. I thought it would be worth it to suffer for a while, until everything could be set right. We thought it would be worth it, to start over."

The mud is slimy against my stomach.

"I was willing to die," she said. "Then I made it out, and I was willing to help anyone I found. I helped you."

I realize she's speaking in past tense; that she's done helping me.

I try to step back out of the sinkhole, but the mud is slick and heavy, and it pulls me off-balance, and I sink deeper. I take a breath, trying to calm down. You can't fight sinkholes, you have to spread your arms or something to slow yourself down; I remember this from a movie, I can get out of here.

"Point Zero was right," she says, and her voice is angled toward the sky. "The threat would have been better. We gave too much credit to people."

I choke out, "Fuck, I'm sorry," in a tone that cuts the roof of my mouth.

It falls quiet. The inky dark has made my other senses sharper; I can hear the mud sucking at my clothes, my pulse pounding in my ears. Far off, I hear an owl.

"I'm sorry, too," she says, and I hear leaves crunching under her feet as she steps back.

I scream; I kick wildly, I dig into the mud to try to swim out, but it's too slick and I'm in too deep and the oily blackness swallows me; when I scream, I choke on it.

"The new world has to be better than the old one," she says. "That's my project now."

I can hardly hear her. The darkness has slid into my nose and my ears, leaking past my squeezed-shut eyes, and I know the next time I open my mouth I'll swallow clay and it will be over.

"Next time," she says, not unkindly, "I'll know better what kind of person to look for," and there are two footsteps before the mud closes over me.

(Strange what you're good for, when circumstances change.)

WHITE CHRISTMAS

James F. Reilly

1

"We should probably stop, no?" Margot pointed at the glowing sign of a general store up ahead. "I feel funny just showing up empty handed."

Billy shook his head and squinted into the swirling snow. "It's only another couple of miles, babe. I just want to get the hell out of this shit. Besides, we're not showing up empty handed. We come bearing the gift of booze, remember?"

Margot laughed. "I meant food, dummy. I don't want to look like a freeloader."

"If I know my sister-in-law, dinner's already on the table waiting for us." Billy rolled his head from side to side, eliciting a few audible snaps and pops from his neck, and then let out a deep sigh. "And, if I know my brother, he's probably bitching about how I'm always late." Billy placed a hand on her knee and gave it a gentle squeeze. "We'll come back out in the morning and get some stuff. You can cook dinner tomorrow night."

"Oh, I can, huh?" Margot punched him in the arm. "You are such a man."

"I'll take that as a compliment," Billy said, craning his neck over the steering wheel. "Christ, it's really coming down."

"Maybe just milk and eggs," Margot said softly. Billy said nothing. He just stared ahead into the churning white vortex, his face illuminated by the red taillights of the truck in front of them.

Margot stared into the windswept parking lot of the store as they passed. There were at least a dozen cars in front of the building, and six more at the gas pumps. A few of them had Christmas trees tied to their roofs, crushed under the weight of several inches of snow. Margot had a tingling feeling in her stomach as she watched the store slowly recede behind a glowing veil of white.

"Is it always like this?" she asked.

"What, the snow?" Billy shrugged. "Sure. Sometimes, I guess." He took his eyes off the road for a second and smiled reassuringly. "Trust me, you're gonna love it. Skiing, sledding, roasting chestnuts—all that good shit. This is a New England Christmas…a real Christmas."

"What? You don't think we have real Christmases in Georgia?"

"No offense," Billy said, "but backyard barbecues and pool parties aren't my idea of a real Christmas. It's like those people who go to the fucking Bahamas for the holidays. To me, that's like celebrating the fourth of July in Antarctica. It's…it's sacrilege! You can't have a real Christmas without snow. Period."

"Jesus was born in a desert."

"Yeah, and how did that work out for him?" Billy replied.

"Okay. First, you're going to hell for that, and, second, I disagree." Margot crossed her arms in front of her and leaned her head against the cold glass of the passenger window. "I happen to think Christmas is about surrounding yourself with the people you love, whether it be in the mountains or under a palm tree."

"And that's why you're with me." Billy squeezed her knee again and Margot pushed his hand away. "Oh, come on, babe. You know I'm just playing. This is our first Christmas together. I just want it to be special, you know?"

"I know. And I appreciate it."

"And I'll tell you what. Next year we'll go down to Georgia and have a lame-ass southern fried Christmas with your family."

Margot grabbed Billy's earlobe and crushed it between her thumb and index finger.

"Owww! Fuck! Owww!" Billy whined. "Truce, truce!"

"Not until you admit you're a dick," Margot said, squeezing harder.

"Fine! I'm a dick, I'm a dick! Jeeeesus! You're gonna get us killed!"

Margot jerked her hand away and retreated back to her side of the car. She milked the silence between them until the crunch of the snow beneath the wheels and the monotonous swipe-and-thud of the windshield wipers was more than she could bear. Finally she sighed, "Mind if I turn on the radio?"

"Knock yourself out," Billy said with a laugh. "I gotta warn you, though; once you get past Bretton Woods the pickin's are pretty slim."

Margot hit the auto-tune button on the radio. John Cougar Mellencamp's "Hurt So Good" gave way to Elton John's "Tiny Dancer" and then Young MC's "Bust a Move."

"Christ, what decade are these people living in?" she asked.

"I told you," Billy said. "Slim pickin's. Just put in a CD."

Margot opened the glove box and groaned. "Ewww. All of your CD's suck."

"So now I'm a dick with bad taste in music? Why is it you're with me, again?"

"Apparently so you can show me the true meaning of Christmas," Margot quipped. "Otherwise, I can't think of a single reason."

"Okay, well, so long as we're clear on that."

The radio jumped through a couple of channels of static, a warbling old country song, and a Spanish talk show before Margot turned it off and fell back into her seat. "Okay, New Hampshire radio officially sucks," she proclaimed.

"Well, not if you grew up in the 80s," Billy said.

"Or you've been in a coma since then," Margot replied.

"Touché."

The road ahead divided and Billy veered toward the right fork. The Camry bounced as it crossed the tracks of the truck in front and then fishtailed as he turned onto the road and started up a steep incline. Margot grabbed his shoulder and let out a faint squeal.

"Trust me," Billy said. "I've been driving in this stuff for nearly fifteen years." He peeled her hand off of his shoulder, rested it on his lap. "I'm a professional."

"Uh-huh," Margot said. She felt the tingling in her stomach again. She squeezed Billy's thigh.

The road curved sharply, and the car slid again as Billy took yet another sudden turn, this time up a narrow road hardly wider than the Camry. Gone was the yellow pall of the street lamps; beyond the swirling snow now lay nothing but inky blackness.

"The secret," Billy said, "is to steer into the skid."

"Okay, how much fucking farther, Billy? I'm seriously freaking out, now." Margot tugged on the shoulder belt until she felt it lock into place.

"Relax. "Billy laughed.

The car lunged forward up one final incline before coming to a stop a few feet from the bumper of a snow covered Land Rover. He shut off the headlights and, once Margot's eyes had adjusted, she could see two shafts of warm, sparkling light emanating from the windows of a small chalet at the top of the hill.

Billy smiled and gave her a peck on the cheek. "We're already here."

2

Dinner was waiting on the table just as Billy had expected—a small pre-cooked Chicken, a bowl of mashed potatoes, baby carrots, and a salad. Billy could sense his brother, Rob's, displeasure at their late arrival, but they both loosened up after a couple of glasses of wine. They ate quickly and Rob's wife, Linda, took Margot up to the loft to show her their room while the couple's daughters, eight-year-old Maxie and five-year-old Quinn, rushed back to their handheld video games in the living room.

"This snow's something, huh?" Rob asked. "Must've been a bitch to drive in."

Billy shrugged and poured himself another glass of wine, and then slid the bottle down the table to his brother. "I've seen worse. Didn't get too bad until we got up past Concord. It's the wind, mostly. I didn't want to get Margot worried, but, man, it was like a whiteout once we hit the mountains."

"This her first snow?" Billy asked.

"Her first real snow. I mean, she's lived in Manhattan for a couple of years, now, so she's seen the stuff, but nothing like this."

"Yeah." Rob took a sip of his wine. "She's a good girl. Mom would have liked her."

"Yeah, she is." Billy smiled. "She's a lot like her, you know? I mean, not in a Freudian way or anything; just her attitude. She's a tough chick. Has a mouth like a sailor sometimes." He laughed.

"So how's it lookin'," Rob asked.

"How's what…? The relationship?" Billy shrugged. "I don't know, I mean, it's good. It's great, actually. But it's only been nine months, so…"

Rob smiled. "You'll marry her," he said. "I can tell."

"Oh, and how's that?" Billy asked.

"I just can, is all," Rob grinned. "I see it in the way you look at each other. I got a gift for that sort of thing, you know?"

Billy finished the rest of his wine. Rob slid the bottle back to him. As he poured himself another, Margot walked into the kitchen and rested her hands on his shoulders. She kissed Billy on the top of his head; her long, curly hair, still damp from the shower, draped over his face. It smelled of lilac and citrus. Billy leaned his head back and gave her a kiss. Her lips were soft and inviting and, in that moment, he knew his brother was right. This was the girl he would marry.

"Am I interrupting boy talk?" She asked.

Billy sighed. "Well, my brother was asking me if we could swap women tonight, and I told him you'd be up for it."

"Oh really?" Margot asked. "Sounds kinky!"

"Count me in." Linda shuffled into the kitchen, wearing a pink robe and matching slippers. She had a towel draped around her neck and three different bottles of shampoo and conditioner tucked under her arm. "God knows, I could use a change."

"That's nice," Rob said. "Real class acts, the lot of ya." He swigged down the rest of his wine and washed his glass out in the sink. "I'm gonna go get some firewood."

Rob left the kitchen and returned a couple of minutes later in a bulky, white, down jacket and white knit hat. Billy burst out laughing, and that set off Margot and Linda.

"What?" Rob asked, his arms hanging stiffly by his side.

"Need a hand, Michelin Man?" Billy asked.

"Yeah, real funny," Rob said. "We'll see who's laughing on the slopes."

"I'm pretty sure it'll still be me, Frosty," Billy said.

Rob flipped him off as he cracked open the back door and slipped on his gloves. A sudden strong gust shook the house and blew the door wide open. Rob took a step back as an avalanche of snow poured into the kitchen. "Woah!" He laughed, and tried to close the door. "Will you look at this?"

"Oh my God." Linda grabbed a broom from the closet and handed it to Rob. "There's got to be two feet out there already!"

"It's just a drift," Rob grumbled, as he swept the snow over the threshold.

"Still, you said we were only going to get a few inches!" Linda looked panicked. "If I knew it was going to be this bad…I mean, shit, the roads…we only picked up a few things from the store. I knew we should have gone to Stop & Shop! We don't have any milk or bread or…"

"Linda, it's fine," Rob barked. "I'll hit the grocery store first thing in the morning, just like I said I would. The Land Rover will roll right over this shit. Believe me, we'll be fine."

Margot's fingers dug into Billy's shoulders. "I told you we should have stopped," she whispered.

"Babe, relax," Billy said. He got up and slipped on his leather coat. "Rob, let's go get that firewood."

His brother heaved a sigh, leaned the broom up against the wall, and threw up his hands as he stepped over the drift and out the door. Billy followed, slamming the door behind him. Rob had already been swallowed up by the squall.

"For fuck's sake, wait up, Rob!" Billy took two steps forward and sank into a thigh-deep drift. He pulled himself free and followed his brother's tracks around to the front of the chalet. Rob stood at the top of the stairs that led down into the sunken driveway. The light from the chalet windows cut a swath through the night, making the snow that danced around them look like a luminescent swarm of fluttering moths.

Billy looked down into the driveway. The Land Rover was buried up to its headlights, with huge, windswept domes of snow on its hood and roof. Billy's Camry was completely covered, reduced to a smooth white mound.

Billy turned to his brother. "What are you thinking?"

Rob stood silently for a moment, his eyes shimmering, his face caked with snow and rivulets of snot and frozen tears.

"What am I thinking, little brother?" He asked, his voice nearly lost to the wind. "I'm thinking we're good and truly fucked."

3

The weatherman danced in front of a map of the northeast with a mixture of excitement and sheer panic. He pointed at New England—at least what little of it that could be seen beneath the massive animated cloud—and then ran his finger down the entire east coast, stopping at the Carolinas.

"Folks, I can safely say that this is something we've never seen before," he said breathlessly. "This massive system literally came out of nowhere and, in the past few hours, has absorbed several smaller systems riding the jet stream, forming a 'super storm' that is now blanketing the northeast. We're talking hurricane force winds, and snowfall at a rate of several inches per hour; in higher elevations, we could see as much as a foot or more an hour, with no sign of slowing ..."

"Yeah, tell us something we don't know," Billy muttered. He cradled Margot in his arms. She snored softly, long ago surrendering to the valium Linda had given her. Linda sat next to Billy, equally as doped, but working on her fifth glass of wine nonetheless. Maxie and

Quinn lay curled up on the floor beside Rob, who sat Indian style in front of the small television.

The weather-map had changed and now depicted the entire United States. The Great Lakes were obscured by a swirling mass of clouds the size of Texas, while two huge tropical storms book-ended Florida, one in the Atlantic, and one moving up toward the pan handle from the Gulf.

"This is unprecedented stuff, folks. Completely unprecedented. And they're no better off across the pond, where, we're told, much of northern and central Europe is experiencing blizzard conditions, with London reporting more than two feet of snow fall in the last three hours." The weatherman took a deep breath and shook his head and laughed. "This is...it's a little scary, is what it is." He looked at his watch and laughed again. "Here we are, thirty minutes away from December 21st 2012. I don't have to remind most of you what that date signifies. It's got to make you wonder, right? I mean..."

The camera panned violently and then cut back to the news desk. The anchors—a meticulously coiffed silver-haired man and an overly made-up middle-aged woman—stared slack-jawed at a commotion off camera. After a few seconds of silence, the male anchor regained his composure, looked into the camera, and smiled unconvincingly.

"Dan...Dan is obviously joking, folks," he said. The reporter paused, his smile wavering, as he held his finger to his ear. "We, here at WCTV, want...to...assure you that...okay, hold on a minute folks. We're getting some news out of...I can't make this out. Is somebody going to throw this on the prompt...?"

The image on the screen froze and flickered before giving way to color bars and a droning, high-pitched tone. Rob flipped through the stations and, after nothing but static, test patterns, or no picture at all, switched off the television.

"Satellite dish is probably buried," Rob said. "With that wind, I'm surprised we had reception as long as we did." He threw the remote onto the sofa and grabbed his beer off of the coffee table. "I'll get up there and clean it off in the morning."

"What if he's right?" Linda asked, her voice barely a whisper.

"What? What if who's right?" Rob asked.

Linda's eyelids fluttered and her head bobbed forward. "The fucking weatherman." She practically spat out the words. "What if this is it? I mean...you know...it?"

Rob sighed. "Jesus, Linda, you're half in the bag. Use your head, for Chrissake," he said. "That's all tinfoil-hat-wearing bullshit." He took a hearty swig from his beer and set the empty bottle back down. "A fucking Aztec fairy tale."

"Mayan," Billy said.

Rob waved his hands in the air. "Who gives a rat's ass? Mayan? Aztec? They could be fucking Oompa Loompas for all I care. It's a bunch of goddamn nonsense that I don't want to hear about. End of story."

Rob knelt down and scooped up the girls, one in each arm, and then carried them off to bed. Linda cursed him under her breath, and took another sip of wine. She looked at Billy and offered him a weak smile.

"I'm not stupid, you know," she said.

Billy nodded. "Yeah, I know."

"It's just…why the fuck not, you know? Why is it so impossible?" She reached for the bottle of wine, started to pour herself another glass, and spilt most of it on her wrist. "I mean…it's happened before…so… what makes us so fucking special, you know?"

Billy steadied the bottle for her.

"Thanks." She laughed. "I guess I'm just a little…I probably should go to bed."

"That sounds like a good idea," Billy said, setting down the bottle and wine glass for her. He helped her up from the couch and started to walk her toward her and Rob's bedroom.

"I'm okay, I'm okay." She tapped him on the wrist and pulled away. "I'll see you in the morning, Billy." Linda gave him a peck on the cheek. "We'll probably be laughing about this tomorrow."

Billy nodded and smiled, and wished he could believe it.

4

Margot awoke to cold blackness and throbbing inside her head, blissfully unaware of her surroundings until she sat up and her feet touched the frigid hardwood floor. With the realization came panic. She frantically patted the bed, hoping to find Billy sleeping next to her, but nothing lay beside her save for the sweater and damp jeans she'd worn on the ride up. She felt for the lamp on the night table and turned the switch, eliciting a loud click and nothing more. She turned the switch again, and again, the anxiety swelling within her.

"Billy?" she called.

There was no reply, just a distant penetrating whine, and a rhythmic, muffled crunch that came from below. Margot stood and fumbled through the darkness toward the dim light that bled in from beneath the door. She wrapped herself in her robe and stepped out into the loft. She could see Linda down in the living room, sitting on the couch and flanked on either side by her daughters. A Coleman propane lamp burned on the table in front of them; the source of the high-pitched drone Margot had heard from the bedroom. She hurried down the stairs and along the hall into the living room.

"Did we lose power?" Margot asked, her breath hanging in the air before her.

Linda nodded and offered Margot a tight, quivering smile. Rob sat on the ottoman, sweat-slicked and breathless, and cradling his head in his hands. His overstuffed jacket lay drying in front of the fireplace; a single log smoldered within it.

The front door was ajar and, through the gap, a pile of slush and snow spilled into the room. The two large windows above and on either side of the door, however, were grey and opaque.

"Where's Billy?" Margot asked.

Rob didn't look up. He just pointed at the door. She went to it, the snow crunching beneath her bare feet.

Beyond the door lay a long, ice-blue trench that ascended at least six feet before meeting a roiling dark sky. At the peak, Billy, caked in snow and a shovel hanging over his shoulder, stood screaming silently into the wind.

5

A box of Cheerios, six bagels, a small package of frozen chicken nuggets, five cans of Spaghetti-O's, and two bags of salt and vinegar potato chips. Those, along with the plate of leftovers from the night before, various sweeteners and condiments left behind by previous tenants, and an energy bar Rob had stashed into his overnight bag, were laid out on the kitchen table before them.

"That's it?" Billy asked.

"That's it," Rob said. "We figured we'd do groceries with you this morning. This was just...stuff from home. Stuff for the kids..." His voice trailed off and tears welled in his eyes.

Billy peered back into the living room. Linda was sleeping on the couch, and Maxie and Quinn were sitting in front of the fire bickering over whose turn it was with the Nintendo DS, and Margot was standing at the front door, holding her cell phone aloft trying to get a signal.

"So what the hell do we do, Rob?" Billy whispered.

Rob raked his hands down his face and sighed. "I'm gonna go for help," he said. "I've got my skis. I can bushwalk back down to the main road. I don't know; maybe it's not as bad as the mountain."

"No," Billy shook his head. "Fuck that. We should wait…"

"Wait for what, Billy?" Rob asked. "For help? You saw it out there. No one knows we're here. No one is coming. We've got, like, three logs left. After that, we'll have to start burning the fucking furniture. And this…" Rob motioned toward the table. "This won't last more than a few days. A week at most."

"At least wait for the weather to clear," Billy pleaded.

"We don't know when that will happen, Billy. It could get a lot worse before it gets better. I…can't take that chance. Not…not with the girls."

"Fine. Then I'll go," Billy said.

Rob laughed. "Don't be ridiculous."

"What? I'm younger, and I'm in better shape than you," Billy said.

"Younger, yes. Better shape?" Rob smirked. "That's debatable. Either way, I'm the better skier. It just makes more sense this way."

Billy sighed. His brother was right. He hadn't tackled anything more challenging than the bunny slope since he was a teenager. Skiing had always been Rob's forte.

"Look. It's only a few miles to the main road." Rob said. "I'll go; I'll see what I see and, if I don't find help, I'll turn right around. If I leave now, I can be back before nightfall."

Billy ground his fists into his eyes and groaned.

"Trust me, little brother. I've got to do this." Rob rested his beefy hands on Billy's shoulders. "C'mon. I want to show you something."

Billy followed Rob down the hall to his bedroom. They stepped inside, and Rob closed the door behind them. He moved to the other side of the bed and knelt behind it. When he resurfaced, he held a square plastic case, which he placed on the bed. He pulled a small key off of his key ring, opened the box, and turned it toward Billy.

"Jesus, Rob!"

"It's a beauty, ain't it?" Rob pulled the Khar 9mm out of its case and handed it to Billy. "Don't worry. It's not loaded."

"Yeah, famous last words," Billy muttered, as he took the weapon. It was surprisingly light, not that Billy had much experience with guns. "When did you get this? Fuck. Why did you get this?"

"It's not mine," Rob said. "It's Linda's."

Billy shot him a quizzical look. "Why the hell would Linda need a gun?"

"There was an incident a few months ago. Nothing major. Just some punks. Made off with her purse, and… well…it shook her up pretty good. We thought…" Rob waved his hands. "It's not important. I wanted you to know that it's here. You know; just in case."

"In case of what?" Billy asked, handing the gun back to him. "In case you don't come back?"

Rob shrugged. "I don't know, Billy. Just…just know it's here." Rob locked the gun back in the box and put the key in the nightstand drawer. "If push comes to shove, Linda will know what to do. Hell, she's a better shot than I am." Rob laughed and slipped the box back under the bed.

"All right," he said. "I'm going to get ready."

Rob stomped through the living room, his ski boots gouging the tile floor. Billy carried his brother's skis and poles and Maxie's Dora the Explorer backpack. Margot helped Rob slip into his coat, and Maxie handed him his gloves. Quinn held his hat. Linda was still in the bedroom, crying hysterically, as she had been ever since Rob had told her he was going.

Rob knelt and pulled the girls toward him, squeezing them hard.

"Daddy, you're crushing me," Maxie said.

"Me too," Quinn cried.

"I'm sorry, guys." Rob planted a kiss on both their heads. "Daddy just loves you both so much. You know that, right?"

The girls nodded in unison, and Rob smiled. "Now I've got to go, and I might be gone a while, but I'll be back."

"You promise?" Maxie asked.

"I promise," he said. "Now you guys behave, okay?"

"We will daddy," Maxie said.

"Can you get us batteries for our Nintendo?" Quinn asked.

"I'll see what I can do, honey." Rob stood and looked to Billy, tears welling in his eyes. He pulled his hat down over his ears, strapped on his goggles, and grabbed the ski poles from Billy. "Okay, let's do this."

Billy nodded and opened the door. The sky had darkened considerably, and at least another foot of snow had fallen since they'd finished shoveling out the trench barely an hour earlier. Rob started through the door, and Margot grabbed his hand.

"Good luck," she said. She kissed him on the cheek.

"Watch out for them," Rob said. He nodded over his shoulder toward Billy and winked. "All of them."

Rob bounded up the steep incline, and Billy followed, laying out the skis when they reached the top. Rob planted his poles in the snow on either side of him, locked his boots into the bindings, and propelled himself forward a couple of feet.

Billy opened the backpack and pulled out the bundle of shredded fabric he'd made from a day-glo orange fleece he'd brought with him. "Tie one of these to a branch every so often," he shouted above the wind. "To mark your route. "

Rob laughed. "You're not nearly as dumb as you look, you know that?" He took the backpack and slung it over his shoulder.

"I threw that energy bar in there, too," Billy said. "Just in case."

"Yeah, just in case," Rob said. He pulled up his poles, grinned, and pushed himself forward. "Leave a light on for me," he shouted, as he vanished into the squall.

Billy waved, knowing then that it would be the last time he would see his brother.

6

On Christmas Eve, Margot decorated the fireplace with candles and some of the ornaments Linda and Rob had brought up with them. The girls' stockings were hung from the mantle, a single sleeve of fruit leather in each. Linda had left all the gifts in the Land Rover, so Margot had wrapped a couple of pieces of her own jewelry in the pages from a tattered copy of Life magazine and placed them on the mantle above each of their stockings.

Quinn wolfed down her dinner—a quarter can of Spaghetti-O's and half of a stale bagel. Maxie only ate a few bites, and set the rest down on the coffee table.

"Can I have it?" Quinn asked.

Maxie shrugged. She hadn't said a word since the night her father had left. Quinn happily finished off what was left in Maxie's bowl and then sat back on the couch.

Billy broke down another kitchen chair and threw the legs onto the fire.

"Did you talk to her?" Margot asked "What'd she say?"

Billy shook his head. "She didn't say anything."

Margot took him into the kitchen, out of earshot of the girls. "Linda hasn't eaten a thing in three days, Billy," she said. "She's hasn't even come out of her room."

"Can you blame her?" Billy snapped.

Margot saw anger in his eyes. She held his face in her hands. "Billy, I...I can't even imagine what she's feeling. What you're feeling. But those two little girls need their mother right now, and she needs to know that."

Billy closed his eyes and took a deep breath. "I'll see what I can do," he said.

As if on cue, Linda emerged from the darkness of the hallway, holding a small, flickering candle, her eyes were almost swollen shut and her face was smeared with mascara.

"Linda, I..." Margot started.

"I just thought I'd come get the girls," Linda said. "Give you two some time alone."

"Why don't we all sit in front of the fire for awhile?" Billy asked. "We've still got a bottle of wine left."

Linda's eyes drifted to the girls on the couch. "No, that's all right. Really. I...I'd like to be with my babies. You two should be alone."

"C'mon Linda, don't be silly," Billy said. "None of us should be..."

Linda ignored him. "Maxie. Quinn. Come with mommy ."

"But I wanna open presents," Quinn cried.

"You know we never open presents until Christmas Day," Linda said. "Now you two come along. Let's leave Uncle Billy and Auntie Margot be for a while."

Quinn pouted, as she shuffled past her. Maxie drifted by in silence.

"Can I get you anything?" Margot asked.

A weak smile crept across Linda's face. "No," she said. "They're all I need right now."

"Okay," Margot replied. "Well, just let me know if..."

Linda turned and shuffled up the hallway.

Billy put an arm around Margot's waist and walked her back into the living room. He sat on the couch and pulled her down next to him. She rested her head on his chest and listened to his stomach bubble and growl. He hadn't been eating either. He told her it was because he was trying to conserve food, but she knew better. He was as crushed by the loss of Rob as was Linda; he was just better at hiding it. Or at least he thought he was.

They sat in silence for awhile, staring at the fire, and then Margot sat up and slapped Billy on the thigh. "I know," she said. "Let's open presents."

"What? Now?" Billy asked. "No, c'mon. Let's just...let's wait until morning, okay?"

"I want to give you yours now," Margot persisted. She grabbed the flashlight from the end table and shone the light at Billy. "I promise, you'll love it."

He leaned his head back, threw up his hands, and smiled. "Fine," he said. "You've piqued my curiosity."

"Just give me a minute," she said. "And no peeking!"

Margot tiptoed up the hall, pausing outside Linda's room along the way. A dull light spilled out from under the door; from beyond the door, she heard a gentle rustling and a high-pitched snore. Margot smiled and padded up the stairs to the loft and into their room. She aimed the flashlight around until she found her suitcase; she then hoisted it onto the bed. She rummaged around inside until she found the black Victoria's Secret bag, and emptied the contents—a sexy-cute satin Santa skirt, matching red bra, and Santa hat—onto the bed.

Until a few minutes ago, sex had been the farthest thing from her mind but, as she'd lain with Billy on the couch, basking in his warmth and mesmerized by the lapping flames, she'd felt a strange urgency, an urgency unlike anything she'd ever felt before.

She needed him.

It wasn't entirely sexual. She needed to feel that closeness, that connection. She needed to get lost in it and let the feelings take her to another place somewhere far from the pain and the grief and the fear, if only for a few moments.

And she knew he needed it, too. Perhaps now more than ever.

Margot propped the flashlight up against the suitcase and stripped down to her panties. Her nipples stiffened the instant the chill air hit them, and the goose bumps followed. She wedged herself into the form-fitting skirt, and slipped into the bra. As she fumbled for the clasp, a whip-like crack shattered the stillness.

"Billy?" Margot cried.

She grabbed the flashlight, and ran out into the loft. She heard footfalls below, and rushed down the stairs into the hall.

"Jesus, Billy, what was that?"

Billy pounded on Linda's door. "It's locked," he shouted. "Goddamn it, Linda, open the door!"

There was another loud snap, followed by a muffled thud. Billy stepped back and kicked the door, splintering the jamb. He kicked it again. This time the hinges gave and the door fell inward.

Margot shone the flashlight into the room.

Quinn's body rested face down on the bed, arms by her side, a crimson soaked sheet draped over her head. Maxie lay across the threshold, her dark hair matted to her face; blood from a dime-sized hole in her forehead trickled into a slowly expanding pool beneath her. Linda stood in the corner, eyes shut, head hung to one side. She hummed softly and tugged at the front of her blood spattered nightgown with one hand. The pistol was in the other.

"Linda, please!" Billy shouted. "Give me the gun."

A manic smile spread across Linda's face, and her eyes snapped open.

"We're going to be a family again," she said.

And, with that, she put the gun barrel in her mouth and pulled the trigger.

7

Billy dragged Linda's body up the trench, rested it beside the girls, and began to dig three shallow graves in the ice. By the time he'd finished, nature had already claimed the bodies, coating them in two inches of fresh snow. He decided to leave them as they were, so planted the markers—three hastily assembled crosses fashioned from strips of fabric and the spindles from the back of a kitchen chair—in front of each smooth, white mound.

Margot clambered out of the trench and stood beside him. She grabbed his hand and bowed her head.

Billy wanted to say something—anything—but words eluded him. Instead, he found his attention drawn back toward the chalet. The snow had reached the upper windows, obscuring all but the peak and the chimney. The twenty-foot pines that dotted the property appeared to be reduced to the size of saplings. Only their tips poked through the icy crust.

In a matter of days, everything would be buried and, by then, they'd be out of food, out of firewood, just plain out of options.

Billy stared down at the shapeless mounds that formed before him, and wondered if Linda had had the right idea.

8

New Year's Eve came and went. There was no countdown, no midnight toast, only a long, desperate kiss as they clung to each other, naked beneath a pile of blankets, and watched the last of the cabinet doors go up in flames.

"I love you," Margot said, her sunken eyes glistening in the firelight.

"I love you, too," he said.

He caressed her sunken cheeks, kissed her again, and lifted her up onto him. Margot gasped softly in his ear as she wrapped her legs around his waist and took him inside of her, their bodies shuddering in unison as they made love one final time.

9

Margot died on January 5th.

Billy had gotten up early that day and, after a breakfast consisting of a handful of Cheerios and several cups of water spent the morning shoveling out the trench (which, at that point, had become more of a cave). At around 10:00 AM, he noticed that the sky had lightened and the snowing had slowed considerably. An hour later, it stopped altogether.

Billy threw down the shovel and scrambled up to the mouth of the trench, and what he saw caused him to drop to his knees.

Beyond a sea of rolling white hills and dwarfed pines, Mount Washington lay bathed in a shaft of golden sunlight, framed by the bluest sky Billy had ever seen. Shadows danced across the valley as the clouds raced eastward, leaving nothing but clear skies in their wake.

Billy howled and pumped his fists. He jumped back into the trench, sliding down on his backside, and threw open the door.

Margot lay amidst a pile of blankets, her hair draped over her face. He knelt down beside her and squeezed her shoulder.

"Margot, honey," he said. "You've got to see this."

She didn't move.

"Margot, wake up!" Billy shook her gently.

Her head lolled back, and her hair fell away from her face. Her eyes were half open and glazed; the side of her face was caked with a dry, greenish foam.

Billy pulled her toward him and, as he did, an empty prescription bottles rolled out of the blankets and into the puddle of acrid vomit and undigested pills that lay beneath her.

Linda's pills.

Somehow she had managed to take Margot with her.

10

After Billy had buried Margot, he went back into the chalet and gathered his things.

He knew he was going to die. He not only knew it; he accepted it.

But he'd made up his mind that he was not going to die here.

He rounded up the last of the food—the fruit leathers from the girls' stockings, a cup's worth of Cheerios, and three frozen chicken nuggets—and stuffed it into the pockets of his ski jacket along with the last two boxes of matches. He made a small fire, melted some snow in a pan, poured the water into three empty wine bottles, and packed the bottles, along with some extra clothes, into his overnight bag. The next morning, at first light, he slung the bag over his shoulder, slid Linda's pistol into his belt, and clambered out of the buried chalet for the last time.

He stood atop the roof, bathed in the early morning sunlight. He smiled and reveled in its warmth, amazed at how—despite everything—its mere presence offered hope. Snow crunching beneath his feet, he started down the hill, and then he saw movement out of the corner of his eye. A rabbit darted out from a hummock of snow and froze not more than twenty feet away. The rabbit's nose twitched, and then it bounded off in the opposite direction.

Billy stared at the valley before him; vast and white and immaculate. He didn't know what lay beyond it, if anything at all. What he did know was that, up until now, he'd gotten it all wrong.

He'd convinced himself it was the end of the world.

Now he realized it was only the beginning.

THE LADY OR THE TIGER

J.M. McDermott

Re-imagined from a tale by Frank Stockton, 1882

Many years ago, when I was a boy of only ten, I was in a terrible crash on the cliffs south of Io Town, where nights are a deep tundra freeze and afternoons are as hot as a summer on the long plains. Even now, I close my eyes and I can still see Sheila's face just before she was crushed under two thick layers of plasteel.

I had watched her half of the flyer cracking away from mine, and rolling on top of her.

And collapsing.

On top of her.

Her scream disappeared from the icy air so fast, the only way I knew it had been real was the echo of it, down the canyons, where a small avalanche threw rocks and snow down to the stream.

I tried to free her, but my brother, Jiri, stopped me because the freeze would preserve her until we could dig her out during the warm day, and we had to make our shelter before we froze to death. We had our survival to worry about. We could save her in the morning.

So that's what we did.

We were in our shelter. We were warm, and mostly safe enough. Jiri had told me to try to get some sleep.

I couldn't sleep because I was thinking about her. I tried to remember the songs she sang over me while I swam in the river, or the special way she had of preparing sandwiches for me, with the crusts cut off and the sauce on both sides. Then, all I could think of was the explosion, the fall, the screaming, and the crushing sound of the plasteel, and blood in the snow from when my brother had used flaming wreckage to burn the stumps shut at his lost fingers.

The only thing I could think of to take my mind off of Sheila, and the crash, was asking my brother about Guj Sarwar, the tiger on the back of the great and mighty lizard, Samarkand. When I was a boy, I didn't understand why it was the only other thing I could think about, like something was on the tip of my tongue.

And, Jiri knew everything there was to know about the wastes of the far west, the lizards, and the tigers. He was fifteen years old. Next year, he'd be driving cattle up the highway to Io Town in a flyer all by himself. I was only ten. I didn't even have my own computer terminal yet. I had to share his when he wasn't using it. Everything I knew about the wastes had been from the computer, and from Jiri.

"On the wastes, Simsa," said my brother, "you can't walk on the ground. The sand is all quicksand. It sucks you up and swallows you. You have to ride on the back of giant lizards as big as walking mountains. There're only twenty-five lizards. They have names."

"Are there plants on the wastes?"

"Of course there're plants, Simsa. There're plants everywhere; even out here on the high canyons, clover grows, and molds line the cliff walls. The lizards of the wastes eat the floating molds and large bushes that grow on top of the quicksand like forests of soap scum. The people keep their houses on the back ridges because the constant up-and-down of the head drives you nuts when the lizard's feeding. "

"How do they survive there?"

"People live in huts, on the lizards. They grow blood wheat. They mine for lizard flesh, but they have to be careful not to cut a vein, or the beast will bleed like crazy. They trade, like we do at the station."

It was sixty below freezing outside by now. The tent skin radiated enough heat to keep us warm. The dead grass and snow blowing around outside wouldn't penetrate past the magnets that held the flap shut.

My brother had wrapped his bloodied, burned hand in part of his shirt. He had lost two fingers in the crash, and had burned them mostly shut. The wound extended up his palm. It still bled a little, now and then. Jiri had gotten his smoke-smelling blood on the handles of our hot mugs of chocolate milk.

I leaned back. I closed my eyes. "What about the tigers?"

"There's only one tiger left. And, he's not really a tiger," he said. "Not really."

"At school, I heard Frankie say there was a lizard that had nothing but tigers."

"Frankie's so dumb; he wouldn't know which end of the battery to shove up his own ass."

I laughed. "That's what Frankie said to me about the tigers," I said. "He said there was a lizard with only tigers on it."

"Well, don't believe everything you hear. There's only one tiger left. One. He's not even really a tiger. He just has a tiger-like head. He lives on Samarkand, the biggest, oldest lizard in all the wastes. You know Samarkand because his legs are covered in scars. Nobody knows why. A scientist said the scars were from when Samarkand tried to walk out of the waste. Lizards don't leave the waste, though—not ever. They can't survive out of the quicksand. Their feet only work right in the wastes. "

The winds outside swelled. Sand splattered the side of the tent. Both of us grabbed for the edge of our tent. We waited until the gust passed. When it had, my brother lay his sleeping pad over the edge, right up against the heat.

"Simsa," he said. "Try to get some sleep. We'll have a million things to do in the morning."

"Where do you think Samarkand's scars came from?"

He rolled over onto his side. He looked at me, lying in the middle of our little tent. "I think he got in a fight with another lizard. And, I think he won. I think that's why there aren't any more lizards with scars. The other lizards give Samarkand a wide berth along the wastes. They see him walking over the horizon, they turn away." Then, because he was too tired to speak anymore, he said, "Go to sleep, Simsa."

I sat in the dark. I watched Jiri sweat, pressed against the heated tent skin, breathing gently. I drank hot chocolate. I hugged my legs. I thought about tomorrow, and what we'd have to do for Sheila, and for ourselves.

I had known everything before my brother told me, but I didn't want him to know that. Guj Sarwar, currently living on Samarkand, was the only survivor of the battle on the space elevator. He was part of the isolationist faction that had almost destroyed the Ansible. The tigers had climbed up the outside of the elevator at Io Town, with nano-particle scimitars strapped to their backs. They knew the Parliament would send electromagnetic pulses along the outside to stop anyone from climbing up. The fighters had to make their hands sharp claws to grip, even when the pulses tried to throw their hands and feet off. They had to make their bodies capable of surviving the climb into the thermosphere. They had to grow fur, and alter their noses and mouths to seal the flammable oxygen blends against the electo-magnetic defenses. They couldn't count on just goggles. They traded eyes with cave cats. They needed to see in low light to get to the Mesosphere in the dark.

There's only one tiger left after the battle. He's been hiding out on the head of Samarkand for twelve years. Everyone who went after him got sliced to ribbons, or dumped into the wastes. These days, he's just left alone. He can't speak anymore. Tiger mouths don't speak except in growls and roars. He can't type messages into computer terminals, either. His fur interrupts EM radiation too much to get him anywhere near a terminal without shorting it out. His claws are no good at holding a stylus, or a pen. He can only carve burning letters with his deadly scimitar, which isn't an effective method of communication when most things would be burned and eaten into ash by the nanites.

He lives isolated from mankind forever after losing the war; he destroyed himself to fight. Yet, for some reason known only to him, he refuses to turn himself in or commit honorable suicide.

His army of tigers had failed. The Ansible was built. The ships come and go, trading and trading. By the time I was old enough to notice a world outside the ranch, the war that had claimed Guj Sarwar's humanity, and all the brave Isolationists that had become tigers and died on Io Town's space elevator, was already mostly forgotten.

These days, Guj Sarwar was stalking the blood wheat fields in the dark, stealing sausage and chasing down the birds that are native to the thickets on the back of the beast. He left people alone as long as they left him alone.

In the morning, Jiri flipped the heating skin off. We were both sweating. It was better than freezing. We had to wait in our tent and change into dry clothes. If we stepped outside with any damp on us before the sun had burned off all the snow, we might freeze to death.

We drank the last of our chocolate milk. It wasn't going to keep, anyway, when the refrigeration unit would be otherwise in use.

When we were dry, we wrapped ourselves in clean, dry clothes and stepped outside. We had a lot of cutting to do. Sheila's body was trapped under at least two layers of plasteel.

She'd never be the same again, but a clone of her with whatever memories survived would be better than losing her forever. The deep chill of the night would have preserved almost everything. The afternoons got too warm, though. The day's weather would heat up rapidly, melt the snow down into underground aquifers. By mid-afternoon the winds would change and the weather would quickly turn into a harsh chill, snow falling everywhere. We had to get her out before the heat rotted her brain synapses.

That wasn't all we had to do. We were out of water. As soon as noon passed, and the sun turned away from our cliffside, the chill would be back, and we'd have to be prepared in our tent for another long night, waiting for rescue. We needed water to do that, or we'd die of thirst long before we had ever starved.

We were, fortunately, crashed on a cliff that overlooked a mountain stream deep below. The stream was frozen now, but by mid-morning it would flow cold and clean.

As soon as our tent's registered a safe outdoor temperature, we went to Sheila. Jiri had the tools.

"Do you think you can get us some water, Simsa?"

I shook my head. "Sheila."

"I can get Sheila."

"I want to be sure," I said. I choked up.

"Whiny baby... Fine. You do the cutting." He pulled the hand torch from our toolkit. "Be careful, though. Don't heat her body up."

I took the torch. I toggled a couple of the switches. I pulled at the trigger. Nothing happened.

My brother snatched it from my hands. "Don't know how, do you?"

I looked at where we knew Sheila was, under the rubble. "I don't want to leave her."

My brother took a deep breath. "Simsa..."

I started to cry.

"Fine. Just... Try not to get in my way."

He adjusted the nozzles and switches on the little torch. He touched the plasteel. The metal was slow to cut through. It was freezing cold. I watched my brother work.

I looked around the camp for something I could do. We had our tent lashed down tightly. We had a couple boxes of supplies—another toolkit, some emergency rations—lashed down next to the tent. Jiri had the larger toolkit out, with the torch, the anchor and the repel line. The ship's refrigeration unit had ejected, with food and milk, near the top of the pile of rubble, batteries still intact. It was better than emergency rations. When we dug Sheila out, it would keep her head frozen through the warm afternoons.

I wondered if I shouldn't watch for snow lizards, or pterodactyls, or other scavengers after easy blood.

Jiri needed help pulling the first layer off. I took one end, and he took the other. He could barely grip anything with his two missing fingers and the cut up his palm. The stumps started to bleed again. He didn't say anything. He just tightened the bandage until it stopped.

The next layer was going to be harder, because it was the outer shell of the flyer. It was still cold enough below the plasteel, so we knew Sheila would still be frozen.

Jiri took a long drink of our last quart of milk. "Simsa, what else did that poop-for-brains Frankie tell you about the tiger of Samarkand?"

"He told me… I don't know. "

"Well, there were many tigers. Hundreds of them. They knew they would never be able to stop the Ansible, or shut down Io Town's space elevator."

"Why'd they want to do that?" I said. "It's stupid."

"They were idealists—uncompromising. They had to try. They were fools, of course. They killed people. No ideals are worth killing people. They were terrorists. Only idiots are terrorists. If Frankie had been around during that time, he would be just the poop-for-brains that would join them."

"What were they so worried about, anyway? Why do they hate the Ansible and the space elevator?"

"Minerals, carbon, and the planet. You know, our cattle grow here on grass and wheat that we grow on-world. They go to Io Station to be taken off-world, into space, for merchants all over the galaxy."

"Yeah."

"Well, they carry part of the planet with them. Carbon, and vitamins, and little bits and pieces of molecules that we cannot bring back. In exchange, do you know what we get?"

"Money?"

"Plastic. Plasteel. Silicates. Machines made of these things. That refrigerator. This ship. Things that don't make life."

"Frankie doesn't know anything about that."

"Of course not. Anyway, they were being stupid. We can just trade for things later then bring back what we need. It's all stupid."

I knew this already. I had seen the videos. The protests were all over the world for a while, before the Ansible was built, before I was born. I had watched them on Jiri's computer, late at night.

We had to hurry to get through the next layer before the freeze wore off with the direct sun on the plasteel shell. We didn't have much time.

About halfway through the side of the wall, Jiri stopped trying to cut it all. He looked up at the sun. It wasn't mid-morning yet, but it was close to it. He took a deep breath. He started to focus on just one part, near the top, where the hand tool's X-Ray gave a readout of Sheila's head below the plasteel. Jiri cut just there, hurriedly.

"What are you doing?" I said. "You're doing it wrong."

"Simsa, go get water," he said. "I'll be done when you get back."

"I'm not leaving her."

"Simsa, listen, you don't want to be here when I cut through the second wall. It's not going to be pretty."

"I don't care," I said. "I won't leave her."

"It's not that, Simsa," he said. "It's... Look, we're almost out of time. We just need to preserve her head. It's all we can fit in the refrigeration unit, anyway."

"Oh," I said. I closed my eyes. I was crying, again. "Oh."

He was right.

I turned away.

"You know how to do this?" I said. "I mean, you know exactly what you're doing, and you won't hurt her?"

He peeled away a strip of plasteel. "She's going to be fine," he said. "She'll walk funny a few days, then she'll be fine. She'll remember everything but the crash. It'll be like nothing happened. I promise. Go get some water, Simsa. I'll be done when you get back."

"Okay," I said.

I gathered the ropes and canteens. I listened to the sound of the plasteel melting off in strips, tossed aside in a rush.

The rocks were craggy and jagged. I walked down the mountain, and imagined I was climbing down the ridges of a lizard in the wastes. I imagined I was a tiger, sneaking down the neck of Samarkand in the night to steal crops and vandalize the things from off world.

At the bottom of the cliff, the stream was slow and thin. I couldn't easily get water inside the canteens. I used my hands to cup water, and pour it in. Then, I dropped the purifier pills into the full canteens and capped them shut. It took time. I had plenty of time. I didn't want to be on the top of the cliff until my brother was done and had covered up the mess.

A pack of tundra lizards splashed over the rocks in the stream. They were about as big as my father's boots. They only had one, primitive eye. They swayed from side-to-side to single me out against the rocks. I frowned at them. "Go away," I said.

Tongues flicked in the air. These scavengers had smelled the blood on me.

I stood up. I waved my hands around. They backed away. "Go away!" I shouted. My voice echoed up the canyon. The lizards scattered into the porous cliffside at the water's edge.

I gasped and cowered at the walls around me. Had I caused an avalanche?

Tiny rocks dribbled down, nothing more. Jiri would be mad at me for yelling. I should have known better. I was a rancher's son, and this was my planet. I should have thrown stones at the lizards. They're scavengers, hunting for dead pterodactyls and bugs, and never interested in a struggle.

I took my time on the way up, thinking about what I'd say to my brother about my shout. I left the rope pull on its lowest setting. It was safest at a slow setting, up the cliff, especially after that shout.

I hoped my brother had placed some kind of tarp or cloth or bit of abandoned steel over the body. I hoped he wouldn't yell at me for shouting.

Day heat broke. I felt the air bite through my clothes. Snow began to fall. It was going to be another freezing night, and rescue hadn't found our crash site yet. They might not find us for another day or two. Io Town wouldn't notice one ranch flyer out of the five we flew up to the different trading sites. Even our men would empty the cargo trailer and turn home. Our parents would only notice when our flyer didn't come home on schedule. They might try to call and leave a message, but our communicators had been lost in the crash. It might be days before they suspected anything, and even more days until they found us.

The rope pulled me up without any effort. I just walked up the wall of the cliff, slowly and carefully.

Calmness washed over me, as I neared the top. I believed that everything was going to be fine. In a week, we'd all be back home at the ranch, sitting around the kitchen table eating ice cream and nothing would be different.

I crawled over the lip of the cliff and climbed to the top on hands and knees. I looked up, to my brother.

Jiri had collapsed face down on top of the final wall of plasteel. Beetles had found his pooled blood, at his wounded hand, and buzzed around it, slurping it up and feasting on it, laying eggs in the finger stumps.

I vomited.

Then, I stood up. I dropped the canteens. I yanked the rope loose and away from my waist.

I ran to him, and to her.

My brother had slipped in her blood with the lathe in his hand. He had accidentally cut a new part of his wounded hand with it, and that had opened the whole wound where his fingers were missing, up onto his palm. He had cut through most of her head when he had blacked out from blood loss. He was so close to saving her that he hadn't stoped in time to save himself. I pulled him back from the wreckage.

I saw Sheila's face.

Her beautiful face was ruined. It was smashed. It was sticky, partially-frozen blood. It wasn't Sheila. It wasn't the woman who had kissed me twice because I was her favorite, or sung songs while she watched me swimming, or had always pretended to need my help with jars. This face was some other thing—some awful thing, all bloody and mangled and covered in scavenging beetles.

My brother's body was still warm. He wasn't breathing. He had no pulse.

Her head was warming in direct sunlight, losing more synaptic connections every moment spent in the afternoon heat that muddied the bloody ice frost around what was left of her hair.

I grabbed the hand torch. I fumbled with it until I got it to ignite.

I only had the one refrigeration unit.

It was only big enough for one head.

Do I save the lady, or the tiger?

I called my brother a tiger, because I knew he was the one responsible, even then, when I was just a boy. Deep down inside, I knew. I knew all about Guj Sarwar on the back of Samarkand before I'd asked my brother anything. I had read it from my brother's page history on the computer we shared at home. I had read the same tracts and stories and propaganda. I had seen the same videos. My brother didn't know that.

We had been flying cattle to our family holding pens at the foot of the Io Town space elevator to ship off-world, where their minerals and carbons and life-giving things would be lost to this world. The cattle were gone, now.

Sheila had ejected the cattle in their cargo trailer when trouble had started. They weren't awake to scream. They fell. They crashed. Already the lizards and pterodactyls of the high plains would have picked the bones of the cattle clean to the bone.

I had been sitting next to Sheila in the cockpit, strapped in. My brother was behind me. I looked up at her, beautiful and wild, a woman so much older than me, a child, and I loved her terribly. She was terrified. She was shouting and bouncing in her seat and praying and pushing buttons and looking at me and at my brother and back at her dials.

And my brother, I knew, had caused this.

A few cans of condensed air, hidden in the cargo stabilizers, pressurized in flight when the vessel crossed above the troposphere. They exploded, knocking the stabilizers off the side of the cargo container. Guj Sarwar taught that to his followers before they lost their humanity and embraced more violent actions. A good pilot could dump the cargo and fly home safely.

Sheila, the woman I loved, was not a good pilot. She was an adequate pilot. She was only flying cargo because my father, and all his men, were already flying cargo. It was a large shipment. Sheila usually didn't fly. She had asked us to come with her to keep her company. When the stabilizers broke, she didn't dump the cargo fast enough. The destabilized cargo had jackknifed and slammed against her side of the ship. She'd been stunned for a few moments too long before Jiri had shouted at her to dump the cargo. Then we'd been falling, falling, falling…

My brother, the Isolationist. The tiger.

I had the cutting tool in my hand.

My brother, even after what he'd done, had never meant to kill anyone. Even at ten years old, I, too, could sense the romance of the tiger of Samarkand, and the Isolationists. Sheila was just an employee who cleaned our houses, watched over the children, and flew my brother and me to market when we were due for a treat. And, just as importantly, I loved her as only a ten-year-old could love. She was his victim. She never deserved this.

Sheila. My beautiful lady.

I tightened my grip on the hand torch. I could not hesitate. Each moment spent deciding was another memory lost forever.

Did I save the lady or the tiger?

Whom should I have saved?

I am a man, now, with a ranch of my own on Samarkand's back. I will always wonder if I made the right choice.

P.A. CHIC

Tobias Amadon Bengelsdorf

9

The battery is a big one, a nice big red one, enough to run the ceiling fan and the turntable at the same time, as long as the fan is on low. And that's fine. It's enough of a breeze and doesn't kick up too much dust that way. Ash, his wife called it, we're covered in ash. He thought the word lacked a certain creativity.

He listens to One More Kiss, Dear, over and over, while he stares at the bottles in rows on the table. The song has a sadness he feels is appropriate. It's also the only song that plays all the way through without skipping. It's also the only record he has. And thank goodness for that. Even if it still worked, the CD player would be too tacky. He rubs his hand against the side of his head. The bottles are empty, except for two full of water, and three of mold. A thick, dull-green mold. He should clean them, really, for health's sake, but they look so authentic, so desperate.

The fan the battery powers plays its game with daylight and shadow on the wall. The flick-flick of the fan's light, the record's swelling scratch, the empty, moldy jars, everything rotted, everything in its place: a perfect dystopian moment. He sighs a contented sigh. No, wait though, no. It's not a dystopian moment, is it? No, he reminds himself, it's no longer dystopian. There are no more dystopian moments. They've come and gone. That dystopian stuff is old hat. And, come to think of it, those moments weren't like this at all. Those moments, which seemed so bleak at the time, were good, really. As it turns out. All those screams he hated hearing through his closed, curtained, window, the dull thuds and muffled crashes. It was painfully hot with the window closed, stretched on the floor with his wife, both naked, in opposite corners of the room, as far apart as possible, out of each other's heat bubbles. It was hot, but all that crying and screaming—couldn't open the window to that. And the pleading. That was the worst. All that pleading for mercy. He imagined they were on their knees when they begged like that, but he never raised the blinds then, not even an inch, so he was never sure. How he longs to hear them scream again. The screamers were dying, or were about to, but they were alive, and someone else must have been about to do the killing, and that meant at least two people were out there, alive. But he never peeled the curtain, not one light-letting inch; they could have seen him then, and then he'd have been the beggar. No thank you. Dystopia is best viewed from a distance.

What he has now, what he is experiencing now, he reminds himself, drumming the table for emphasis, is a perfect post-apocalyptic moment, not a perfect dystopian moment. It's an important distinction, and he marks down his confusion in his notebook. He's lately been trying to track his mental decline. It's not as visually detectable as his physical decline. He's been tracking that one for a while. It was quicker, and obvious. Lord, but those first blisters were frightening. The mental-state notes are incomplete, but they still show a quick drop, too. Quite a quick drop. There was a day he even forgot his name. (He soon remembered it again and wrote it down as prevention. Tarries.)

The fan and music are holdovers from the dystopian moment, he reminds himself, but the jars of water, the pills, and the sores are part of the p.a. moment; that's what he calls it now, p.a., in lowercase—cool. Stands for postapoc—that's what they called it then. It's what he called it, anyway. Other people, had there been any, would have called it that, too. The postapoc. Could be Indians. The Postapoc Indians, from Postapocaquage, Connecticut. That's funny, so he writes it down.

8

The flinty sun is up again, reheating the bricks. Not that they cooled much in the night. Nice to have the window open, though, now that there are no screams to block out. He closes the window and lowers the blinds, to trap the cool air. Flips on the fan. It plays again with the sliced light, like a train flashing past his window. The same never-ending train. Who could possibly be riding a train? And to where? Then, of course (of course!) he realizes there's no one on it, and it's not going anywhere because he remembers it's not really a train, and he takes his morning pill, which leaves seven. He notes in his log that there's no train. He turns off the fan.

He's already cut back from three pills a day to two, and the sores are worse. And the diarrhea. What a good thing there's no one outside the window. He can't go down to one. There'd be no point in that. It might make them last a little longer, but it wouldn't matter because he'd be too sick to eat. With three he only had sores in his mouth and a little one inside his nose, but with two he's got them on the undersides of his eyelids, the tip of his penis and around his anus. Sitting is a pain in the ass. That's funny, so he writes it down. And he's tired, too. Like there's a tax on every movement, little demons in his muscles siphoning off a bit of go for themselves. He's got food still, sure but, no matter how much he eats, he's tired all the time from reducing the pills. Feels better the less he eats, actually, less to shit out that way, less to irritate those sores.

He wonders why he really got all this stuff together, the water, the batteries, the tuna. He must have known that if it really happened, tuna wouldn't be enough. Did he think he was going to rebuild his town, or go searching for some magical far away place, carefree and un-ionized? He could have bought a boat and caught every last tuna in the sea, bought a canning factory and canned every last tuna in the world until he had a tuna stockpile larger than he could ever eat. Wouldn't have mattered. The pills were the thing. Even adding his wife's to his own didn't give him a large collection, neither did scouring the other apartments. The one time he'd had the nerve to. There was only one apartment he had found that hadn't already been picked over. Mrs. Perchman's. It had a hard-to-find door because it was an illegal apartment. Fighting for space. What nonsense. The whole building was empty now. True p.a. living.

He must have known, somewhere under the surface, that he was doing it for the experience. The experience of sitting here rocking slowly in this chair with the split cushions, listening to this thin recording, watching the dancing train on the ceiling—it's gone—no, he turned the fan off. He must remember these things. These things are the experience, and the experience is the reason, and he's the only one he knows of who is experiencing it. That's a good enough goal isn't it? To be the last one, the last human being hanging out on the planet? The only person who knows how the light looks now, filtering to the old, hum-drum red and yellow and, on special nights, a little purple accent, a little secret brush stroke, just for him. Maybe for someone else, too, but, well, no way to know if that's the case. And on nights like tonight, it casts lavender on the windowsill, a lovely—it's gone. Dark. Must be nighttime. Pill-time. That leaves

Six (Not very many. The end is near. No, nigh. The end is nigh.)

Taking the morning pill leaves five. It jogs his stomach. He washes it down with peaches and tuna and the tiny bit of bread remaining after he slices the mold off. This is all very silly, he thinks. Why bother with the pills? He knows he'll run out. He almost has already. He was the one who said it, of his own plan. He said, "What's the point?" He said, "I have food, a power source, water and water purifiers, the filter kind, the UV kind, iodine tablets, and tablets to remove the taste of iodine, a utility knife, a hunting knife. "But the point of all that stuff, all that fancy stuff, is to help you survive for a little while, just long enough for someone to find you, or for you to find someone. That's it. All the clever gadgets—the water filters, the five strike-anywhere matches, the weather radio—aren't for the long haul, aren't for rebuilding the town, aren't for testing soil or planting crops. So why do it? "Why bother with tuna if the pills will run out?" That's what she asked, and everyone else. "What else could you do?" he asked back. "Get a gun and off yourself as soon as things got uncomfortable?" That's what he said and that's what she did, and wasn't the only one. But he's got them now. He's got them all now. He's here. And where are they? Dead. That's where.

He replays the conversations, as he drools into the sink. It hurts too much to swallow. The sores in the back of his throat are irritated by choking back the pill that's still scraping his stomach. This drooling, really, is the perfect postapoc moment, spitting out the blood that seeps from the sores in his throat and mouth. Not yesterday's rocking in the chair with the fan and record and train-light, that was kid stuff. This bloody drool is the perfection of post-apocalypse chic. Postapoc sounds like an Indian tribe. From Postapoganset, Rhode Island. That's funny. So he writes it down. For posterity.

4

He throws up the morning pill, but fishes out what he can and forces it down again. He could have done what she did, that's what else. That's what else he could have done. The sun doesn't care. It warmed her up so she was rotting when he found her. On the roof. He left the record out last night, and must have slept too long; it sat in the sun. It melted, and warped. It won't play. Just like his wife. Isn't that touching? Ha! He writes it down. He dumps some old, fetid tuna from a bowl into his water jar, and runs it through the filter just for the fun of it. Shame to let such a fancy filter go to waste.

He has an uncommon urge, an urge he hasn't felt in a while: to masturbate. But the first touch coaxes only blood from a sore. Wanting to write a warning to himself, should he ever feel the impulse to try again, he looks for his notebook but can't find it. He sits back in the chair. Dozes for a while, and comes to, coughing, remembering that the book is in the refrigerator, but he can't record the information because he can't find the book. Back to sleep.

1

He holds the last pill in front of him and twirls about the room with it, serenading it, with love songs, promising a golden tomorrow. He won't go to the roof as his wife did. He'll stay inside, make sure the drapes are closed, the sun blocked, sit in the shade, and keep cool. Real cool.

Beyond the Garden Close

Mary Robinette Kowal

Lena rocked back and forth, feet aching from standing so long, as if the metal floors were harder in the auditorium than anywhere else in the ship. The paper bib she wore rustled as she shifted. The waiting that the high-holy put the prospectives through made Lena nervous. Which was part of the point, of course, and Lena tried not to let her nerves show. There were nine prospectives this quarter, standing in a cluster. Lena knew the other women, but maintained the ship-standard illusion of privacy by ignoring them.

She wouldn't be among the prospective child-bearers if Phoebe hadn't wanted a babe so much.

All long-limbs and soft curves, Phoebe had the grace of a goddess, but she'd never be granted child-rights. She had the taint of celiac disease as a hand-me-down from some grand or other and that throwback meant her stock had to be culled from the tree. Even if she made it through the trials today, the high holies would never let her bear a child.

But Lena, now. Lena would pass for sure and certain, only problem was that she didn't want a child. At least not on her own account, but for her love she would do anything. The memory of her fingers trailing around the soft mound of Phoebe's freckled breast as her beloved's nose wrinkled with laughter made Lena want to back out of line, pull Phoebe out of the crowd of watchers and race home. Why change something as perfect as their love? She held her ground. Phoebe wanted a babe.

At the other side of the cluster, the old woman waddled around behind them. She stopped at each girl and put a disk on the base of the skull, where it joined the neck. Lena bent forward to accept hers, sweeping her long hair out of the way.

When the disc touched her skin, the cold sliced through her skull and made the roof of her mouth ache. It would monitor her actions and ensure no cheating occurred. The final trials for the prospective child-bearers differed every time, which didn't stop people from trying to guarantee that their genes were the ones passed down.

Still waiting as the others received their disc, Lena bounced on her toes. The rituals. The endless rituals of ship life touched every act. Sometimes she wondered if an OCD strain had gotten in, all unnoticed, and infected every line. But it was really just a way to pass the time until the next generation took over and then the generation after that, all biding time until they reached Planetfall. Why did Phoebe want to bring a child into a life of endless waiting for a prize that never came?

The old woman slipped into the middle of the cluster, holding a raku pot. She sloshed water back and forth in the vessel, drawing circles in the air. "Strong, quick and smart. That's what you need to be. Which of you says you are better than your grands?"

"Aye!" They shouted as one.

She flung the water ceiling-ward over the group of them. Lena bent back, arching so that her bib faced the ceiling as the water splashed off and spattered back on them. Her bib clung to her skin where the water dampened it. When she righted herself, the girl across and to the right—Marta—had not moved fast enough. Her bib was dry.

Weeping, she was pulled out of the group, leaving only eight. Lena had half a moment of wanting to give Marta her spot, of wanting to admit that she didn't need a child. But Phoebe stood watching and the hope in her eyes staked Lena to the spot.

The old woman bade them all to turn and as dancers, they did. Some girls had spent their whole lives prepping for this moment, and it seemed that their only goal in life was to produce the next generation. If they were near Planetfall, the high holies might have overlooked Phoebe's ailment, but not this far out. Near the front of the crowd, Phoebe had her arms wrapped about herself, chewing on the cupid's bow of her lip the way she did when she was nervous.

Lena tried to smile, to reassure her.

Sorted by the amount of water caught, the prospectives were lined up at the mouth of the labyrinth. Lena stood third in line. The door snicked open, the girl in front stepped through into darkness and vanished before the door snicked closed again. Then the second girl. And then Lena.

The darkness was absolute at first. But as her eyes adjusted, she realized a faint glow came from the bib she wore. The water had a bio-luminescence to it. Lena stripped it off and held it in front of her, blocking her view of the bib itself with her hand so that faint glow did not blind her to the things it illuminated.

A narrow space, not much wider than arm-span, stretched beyond the range of the glow. Lena walked forward as quickly as she dared. Time mattered here. The hall twisted and turned, with no branches, but she kept resolutely forward not letting the turns slacken her pace.

A breeze stopped her. Turning, she felt the walls on either side but there was no crack or hint of an opening. Her hair stirred slightly across her back and Lena lifted her face. Cool air dusted her from above.

Lifting her feeble light, she saw a square in the ceiling, handholds visible, just out of reach. A ladder above them. She studied it, until she felt that she'd gauged the distance, then gripped the bib in her teeth. Blind now to what was above her, Lena jumped.

Palms slapped against the handholds, locking around them reflexively. Her body swung forward, carried by her momentum, and slammed against the edge of the opening. Grunting, Lena pulled herself up.

Hand over hand, she hauled up until her feet gained purchase and then began to climb, still blind.

The ladder curved backward, so she began to hang from it. Her left foot cramped as she flexed the toes trying for some traction on the rung. Between one hand hold and the next, light cut on.

Blinded by white, Lena shut her eyes. Tears leaked from under her lids. Two heartbeats were all she gave herself. Time mattered here. When she reopened her eyes, they stung and burned as they readjusted. Lena hung over a fathomless drop into the bowels of the ship. Ventilation ducts, pipes and service ladders lined the shaft until it reached the glowing core of the engine. The ladder she hung from ended abruptly in a wall.

The drop was impossible.

The grands would have had no reason to build the ship that way, not when every iota of space was needed for the generations. Projection then.

But what lay beneath the projection could be dangerous if she misjudged the jump. Lena wrapped her hand in her hair and pulled free some long strands. Dropping the three hairs, they drifted down to land a body length away, appearing to hover in midair.

Lena released her feet from the ladder and let them drop to touch a floor. She flexed her foot against the floor, which felt as though it were hard metal like the rest of the ship. Without letting go of the rungs Lena walked toward the wall where the ladder disappeared. Then she stopped dead.

Having a labyrinth in the ship made no sense if it was only used occasionally. Not when there were other ways of learning the same things about the women vying for reproduction rights. The disc, for instance, recorded her speed and reactions straight from her brain. If it could receive signals, could it also transmit?

"This whole thing is a projection, isn't it?"Reaching back, Lena pulled the disk off her neck.

The room stuttered and faded around her.

She stood in a storeroom, four of the other girls stood behind her, eyes twitching as if they were deep in REM.

On the far side of the room, a door opened. Light shone in the next chamber. For a moment, Lena wanted to pull the disks off the other girls' necks, but the door started to slide closed as a reminder that time mattered.

She dove through into Classroom A. The shock at finding herself in familiar surroundings almost confused her more than the darkness had. Calling up a mental image of the ship, she could see how the auditorium was only two corridors over from the block of classrooms.

One woman sat, a blank white mask covering her face with crisp neutrality. She held a Personal Screen unrolled in front of her. "Well done. "The mask distorted her voice, stripping it of identity.

"Am I finished?"

"No. Your scores are very good though, so you get the last part of the trial. One question." She tapped the PS. "Why do you want a child?"

Lena stared at her. She did not want a child. Not for herself. She wanted a child for Phoebe. Phoebe who loved her. Phoebe for whom she would give anything to stay with. But that was not the answer they were looking for. "To be part of something larger. I want to contribute to the next generation."

The woman looked down at her screen. "I'm so sorry."

The door to the far side of the room opened, a silent escort. "What? Why not?"

"You hesitated." She shook her head. "You don't want a child, do you?"

Lena's heart thumped. Time matters. "I don't. No. But the woman I love does. Give the child my genes and her love. Please." Her voice broke. "Oh please."

"I'm so sorry." The woman gestured to the door. "But we can't pass on this trait. At Planetfall, a lack of the nurturing instinct would doom us."

Lena stumbled into the hall and leaned against it as the door snicked shut. She rested her back against the wall and slid down to hide her face in her hands. If she hadn't hesitated at the beginning. If she had spoken faster, the woman would have believed her.

The urge for a child, never present before, consumed her. This time, it mattered.

THE BRIDE REPLETE

Mary Robinette Kowal

When the matriarch announced that she was sending the sixteen members of Pimi's small-family across the ocean to settle in Repp-Virja, Pimi thought it the end of her life. For though she had seen only seventeen full years, Pimi considered herself ready to fill her crop and begin the social rounds, seeking a mate. Her mother and the matriarch felt otherwise, though how they could expect her to find a mate in a strange, sideways land like the colonies was beyond Pimi's understanding.

But Pimi packed her luggage and prepared to leave the warm underground rooms of their home. Before her small-family departed, the matriarch held a feast to fill everyone's crop for the voyage. The gas lights gave a gentle glow to the Deep Hall. Four stations with each of the food families, nuts, fruit, dairy, and grain, stood in corners of the room. Like the two fingers on a hand, the nuts and dairy stood at one end of the room; the fruit and grain at the other end represented a hand's two thumbs. Each a distinct group, but vital for grasping life.

Assigned to the fruit dishes, Pimi ate until her crop distended the spotted green and amber skin of her belly like a bride's. She adjusted her tunic to show off her growing roundness.

Pimi's older sister, Ero, hissed in amusement. "Are you readying yourself for a bridegroom?"

Pimi's toes curled and gripped the ground in anger. "No." Perhaps her crop was not so like a bride's as she might wish; she still only rounded out to an adolescent's half-orb, not burgeoning into the sleek sphere for which she longed.

"Good. My turn is next." Ero adjusted the scarf around her head to show off as much of her fine smooth scalp as propriety would allow. The flat bone of her ear plates barely peeked from the edges of the scarf.

She had widened the blue spots above her eyes with paint, enhancing the grace of their pattern. The spots lightened as they continued down her face, past her perfectly round black eyes, until they almost vanished around her nose so that her chin and neck were smooth, pale and nearly white.

Pimi's own amber and green complexion was the more common, a thing of which Ero never failed to remind her. That, combined with her mannishly small stature, made her feel as if she would never find a mate.

Pimi glanced sideways at the engorged belly of their mother. As was natural, Mother would serve as the small-family's replete for the journey. When full, her crop would hold enough to feed them sweetly flavored pap for the half-month voyage. She reclined on a couch accepting food from the hands of their deep-family. Pimi's cousins, aunts, uncles and siblings wore their Fest Day tunics. Red and orange scarves lay over their scalps and fluttered about their shoulders like fire, as they carried dishes to Mother. Her long, slender limbs lay in beautiful contrast to her speckled blue belly, which ballooned onto the floor.

When Pimi became a bride, her crop would be that large.

On the seventh day of Planting Month, Pimi's small-family boarded a Tep-Tep's steamship bound for Repp-Virja. The captain lowered a special winch to bring Mother on board, as it was impossible for her to navigate the narrow plank spanning the gap between the dock and the steamship. On board, the ship's crew ran about preparing the steamer for departure, their flat bellies illustrating the adage, "straight as a sailor's crop." From time to time, they darted into the shade where the vessel's replete fed them lest they faint from hunger. Larger than any replete Pimi had ever seen, veins marbled his green and white skin.

Mother and the other passengers' repletes took their places beside him. Each seemed like a child next to his vastness, though Pimi's mother was quite the most attractive of the lot.

Around her, passengers scurried to stow their belongings. Winged irarad wheeled above the ship, chattering their excitement. Light shown through the thin skin of their wings, turning them into red stained glass. The ocean slapped against the wooden sides of the vessel, but the ship was massive enough that Pimi barely felt the motion. She stood at the railing waving at her deep-family members until long after they had become indistinguishable from the shoreline.

When she left the rail, her mother beckoned her over to the replete's area. There, an attendant rubbed salve over the skin of a passenger's replete. Another dozed, snoring softly.

"Speak, Pimi-min." Mother's crop billowed out into a beautiful blue orb. She held out her arm so Pimi could nestle beside her. "Why are you moping?"

Pimi snuggled against her mother, careful not to touch her crop without permission. "I do not mean to," she said carefully.

"I will not apologize for taking you away from your deep-Family. It is needful for the status of our dynasty— You are needed if we are to establish a new branch of House Kejari in Repp-Virja. You are my natural daughter and I expect you to behave as such." Mother tilted Pimi's head back. "But I am sorry that you are sad."

Pimi ducked her head away and played with the edge of her tunic. "Are there really savages in Repp-Virja?"

"No! Who told you that?"

"I saw them in Opperad's play, The Vessel Laughed."

"Truth, Pimi. You know the difference between fiction and fact." She pulled her arm away. "Don't say anything like that to Matriarch Imji. She'll think the handmaid's blight has got your brain."

"I won't embarrass you."

The waves passed them by and Pimi thought for a moment that her mother would not answer, but she sighed. "No. No, I trust that you will not."

Pimi saluted her and headed below deck, trying to sway with graceful majesty. Someday, her mother would see that for all her small stature, she was not newly-hatched.

As the Tep-Tep's crew tied up the steamer at the dock in Repp-Virja, the sun beat down, trying to set Pimi's red headscarf on fire. Irarad wheeled overhead here, as they had at home. Beyond the gliders and the ocean, everything else had changed.

Pimi stared at the white stone spires of Repp-Virja. In addition to the traditional burrow markers, fully-half of the spires seemed to have structures attached to them as if their homes were not safely below ground. Crowds of people swarmed past the waterfront. Flowing robes, the color of marble, cloaked the passers-by. Their headscarves twined around their heads, wrapping their scalps in snug layers of pale cloth. Pimi's saffron tunic glared beacon-bright against the muted colors of Repp-Virja.

Ero gestured with her chin. "Would you look at that. The entire city is starving."

Only a few of the robes bellied outward and not a single bare crop showed. When the robes swung open, they showed narrow waists, bound tightly with ribbon. Not savages, but strange as a dayfruit in Deep Winter.

Her mother, tall and commanding with blue freckles spattering her skin like rain, crossed in front of Pimi. A light silk truss bound the loose skin of her belly. "Do not gawk. I expect my children to make me proud, not to stare about like uncivilized provincials."

By the time the carriage arrived at the matriarch's cousin's home, Pimi had become convinced that she should have begged the matriarch to let her stay in Arropp-Yraja.

Only the gas lights in Matriarch Imji's home bore any resemblance to what Pimi expected from a Deep House. Tall narrow windows stood open in constant reminder that they were above ground. Sailor-thin servants filled the foyer with pallid silks, almost disappearing against the white walls. All of them had the same tight ribbons binding their waists that Pimi had seen on the streets. She did not see how they could do their work without fainting from hunger.

A woman swooped up the grand ramp, her waist bound so tightly that it curved inward. She dipped her head in a gesture of welcome. "Speak, Matriarch Kejari!"

Mother tilted her head back, indicating that she accepted the hospitality. "We thank you for your welcome, Matriarch Imji."

Stifling a gasp, Pimi looked again at this woman and then around the foyer at the other people. Now she noticed the richness of the fabrics; these were not servants, but members of House Imaji, bound tightly as if they were bragging about their empty crops.

"The pleasure is ours." Matriarch Imji's intricately wound headscarf framed her face, showing off the deep blue spots on her brow and the gentle line of her neck. The speckling continued down her neck and arms. "This must be your family. So… exotic." Her gaze darted down to their bellies, all proudly full to show their prosperity, and her lips twitched.

Pimi wanted to tug the fabric of her tunic over her belly to shield it from Matriarch Imji's disdain, but it was cut to hang open. She tilted her head back in cordial greeting and waited to be bid to speak.

Matriarch Imji turned slightly away and raised her arm. A double-handful of boys and girls came at her call, each with the grotesque bindings constricting their waists. She paired one of Pimi's family with each, until only Pimi, the youngest, was left. Matriarch Imji turned to the blue and amber boy remaining.

"Duurir, will you host Kejaridoti Pimi?"

"It would be my delight, Mother." He inclined his head to Pimi. "Speak, Pimi. May I host you this evening?"

"I thank you for your welcome." Her toes curled. He had called Matriarch Imji "Mother," which meant he was her small-family son. The House of Imarja was reckoned as one of the great Dynasty Houses in Repp-Virja and Matriarch Imji had not passed her off to a mere nephew. She had asked her son, her natural son, to host Pimi.

Duurir scratched his chin. "Mother tells me you are from Aaropp-Yraarja."

As if that were not obvious. Pimi looked down at the floor, the pollen-yellow of her tunic a blazing tribute to her foreign origin. "Yes, we've only just arrived..." Her voice trailed away. What an idiot. Of course they had just arrived.

Duurir drew Pimi to one of the tall windows. "Our deep-family came from Aaropp-Yraarja five generations ago but I have not been farther than the next state. How do you find Repp-Virja so far?"

Strange, disconcerting, too hot. "Beautiful. At home our houses are underground and do not have views as expansive."

"Truth? Parts of our house are underground, in the old style, but few build that way now because the breezes help with Deep Summer heat."

"At home, the snows of Deep Winter were of more concern."

"We only get snow on the mountains." Duurir pushed the curtain aside and leaned out the window. "You can just see the mountains from here."

Through a narrow gap between the tall white buildings, peeked the deep purple of the mountain range to the south of the city. Duurir placed a hand on her back, guiding her to stand before him. "There. See the tall peak?" He was tall for a man and slid an arm over her shoulder so he could point. Her gaze traveled down the muscled length of his arm, past his pointing finger to a blue peak which pushed above the other mountains.

"Yes." Her voice was a whisper.

"I study astronomy at the observatory there."

"I've never met an astronomer before." Pimi winced inside. Such a stupid thing to say. Now he would think her uneducated as well.

"Funny. Most of the fellows I know are astronomers." The warmth of his body radiated through her tunic.

Duurir jumped when Matriarch Imji clapped her hands together four times. "My dear friends, we have prepared a meal to welcome you. Please. Join us."

Pimi followed Duurir and the others into a large, sunny room where more of House Imaji joined them. Instead of small tables with bowls of food around the perimeter of the room, one long empty table spanned the center. Couches circled the table, as if they were expected to dine seated like a replete. Windows let cool breezes waft through like additional guests.

Matriarch Imji moved to one end of the long table. Duurir led Pimi to a pair of couches and, once he was certain of her comfort, seated himself on the couch to her left so that his head faced hers. When everyone was settled, the double doors at the far end of the room opened.

A replete stood in the doorway, his crop so full that it did not seem possible for him to support his own weight. He held two padded mallets in his hands.

Pimi inhaled with recognition; he was a water drummer. She had never seen one outside of a temple before.

Leaning backward so that his back arced like a bow, he took two agonizing steps forward. There he stood until a servant slid a tall stool beneath him. The replete rested on this, raised the mallets and began drumming on his belly. The muted tones seemed to both fill the room and come from elsewhere, evoking the sound of a flock of varamid galloping across the steppe. He began to sing, weaving the sounds of wind and rain into the syncopated rhythm. His breath reflected each mallet strike outward in song.

Pimi leaned forward on her couch, breathless with delight. Around her, Matriarch Imji's family continued their conversations, not recognizing the extraordinariness of the occasion. She glanced at Duurir, anxious to know if she were the only one for whom this was an exceptional event.

He was watching her, eyes half-lidded with pleasure. "May I guess that water-drummers are a rarity in Aaropp-Yraarja?"

The blood left her face in embarrassment; she must look so provincial. "I've never seen one outside the temple."

"I did not mean to embarrass you. It is nice to see someone else enjoy the music." Duurir gestured languidly at the rest of the room, at his family chatting, but did not say another word. They listened to the rest of the water-drummer's song in silence.

The doors behind the water-drummer opened again and a stream of servants flooded past him, each bearing a plate of food. Their tunics belled out from their bodies around the smooth arc of full crops. These were not ostentatiously full, but the gentle swell representative of a day's meal.

Pimi shifted on her couch as she understood: only the servants carried food in their crops here. Her vision lurched, and the beautiful orb of her mother's crop became a grotesque bloating.

In crisp synchronization, the servants set identical plates between each couple. The white porcelain gleamed under the gaslights; skyberries on flatbread. Pimi did not want to eat anything. She was already larger than the servants.

Duurir reached forward, broke off a piece of flatbread and folded it around a cluster of sky berries. He turned to her, holding it out. Around them, the other couples were feeding each other, so she tilted her head back and accepted the food from him.

When she fed Duurir, his lips brushed lightly against her fingertips, kissing the crumbs away. It took her some time to recover her wits enough to carry her end of the conversation. Duurir filled the gaps with talk of the observatory and of all manner of strange phenomena: distant satellites, spots on the sun, strange bodies that traveled through the space around them.

"Now, you have been very patient to listen to my discussion of astronomy. Most of the girls my mother introduces me to find me exceedingly dull."

"But you're not!"

"You are sweet to say so." He accepted a handful of skyberries from her.

"Truth. I am quite possessed of a desire to see a telescope."

Duurir lifted his head from the skyberries and blinked at her once. "I almost think you mean that."

"I do. Quite."

"Well—" he took a berry from her "—that may be arranged. I am returning to the observatory at the end of Small Harvest, but it will surprise me if your Matriarch lets you come up."

"Why?"

His nostrils flared in surprise. "The mountains are our border with Abar. I'm sorry. Of course, things changed during your voyage. You wouldn't know." He waved his hand, gesturing for a servant to clear their plates. "The Abarine High Council had a schism, splitting around Councilor Hadan; he's begun leading border raids into Repp-Virja and our Observatory is close to the pass."

"Oh."

"So you see, while I would love to have you come, I doubt that I will see you there."

"I will petition my mother."

Duurir gave his attention to the next dish, a slice of melon precisely centered on a creamy wedge of cheese.

Fruit and dairy? But they never mixed, not without provoking sour crop. Shocked, Pimi looked across the table to her mother. In the set of her neck, Pimi could see a tension, but her mother seemed to be following the lead of the people around them.

Pimi watched Duurir out of the corner of her eye.

"It must be very different here." He held out a piece of melon topped with a slice of cheese.

"It is." The tang of the cheese burst out of the sweet melon, tingling her palate. Perhaps they did not have to worry about sour crop with such small meals.

"Tell me." His dark eyes were warm with regard. "I want to know everything."

Beyond the windows, someone screamed. The conversation in the room stopped, shocked into sudden silence.

Pimi's toes curled to grip the edge of her couch in the beginning of fear as shouting and the sound of wood splintering became audible. She kept the urge to scream trapped in her throat.

The door slammed open. A flood of men and women dressed in leather armor ran through the doorway. The room overturned in chaos as the guests leaped from their couches, running for the doors on the other side of the room. Her mother stood, staggered and fell to her knees, dragged down by the weight in her crop.

"Mama!" Pimi ran toward her, but Duurir caught her arm and pulled her away, dragging Pimi out the nearest window. On the grounds, she staggered after him, desperate to vomit in her fear, but with no time to stop and disgorge.

Duurir pulled her into a storeroom and closed the door, shutting out the terror for the moment.

"What—"

"Raiders." Duurir's face was grim. "They have not ventured this far across the border before." He held up his hand and leaned his head against the door, listening. With the first flush of fear lighting his face, Duurir turned to her and opened his mouth.

The door slammed open, knocking Duurir back against the wall. A man filled the opening, twin swords held in his hands. The boney scales of his leather armor had inlaid spirals of metal.

Pimi loosed the scream in her throat.

Duurir pushed the door back hard against the raider. The raider stepped aside easily. He raised his sword and swung it at Duurir.

Pimi screamed again, covering her eyes before the sword connected, but she heard the meaty slap of the metal as it struck Duurir.

He grunted. A heavy thud followed.

Pimi jerked her hands away from her eyes. Two strides had the man at her side. He grabbed her by the throat, forcing her to look at him.

Nodding once, he lifted his sword again and brought the pommel down on her head.

The Abarine raiders lived in a series of adobe houses built on the side of a cliff. The land on this side of the mountains was dry and barren compared to the tropical coastline of Repp-Virja.

Pimi waited in a small sandstone alcove off a large hallway, deep under the mountain. A hard muzzle bound her jaws shut and something hard and round filled her mouth. Her headscarf had been lost on the mad ride over the mountains to Abar and her naked scalp almost did more to cow her than the manacle that shackled her to the replete's bench. She could forget the manacles if she stayed still, but the constant play of air across her bare skin touched on her vulnerability with every caress.

She had no idea what had happened to the other people at House Imarja. Though the opening of the unadorned alcove was unobstructed, Pimi could see only the wall opposite her. She could not call to see if others were in earshot, because of the muzzle that bound her mouth.

Wheels squeaked down the hall for longer than winter's Deep Night before a vast replete was wheeled past the opening to her alcove. He sagged against his belly, drooling. His fingerless hands drummed a random tattoo against the tight skin of his crop. Pimi could not stop staring at the empty sockets where his eyes had been. The cart stopped in front of her alcove.

If not for the muzzle Pimi would have emptied herself in terror.

The men and woman accompanying the replete all wore the leather garments that the raiders had worn, though without the spiraling metal inlays of her captor. Underneath the leather, they belled outward in a modest crop, but the weight was worn high, trussed up by their criss-crossing sword belts.

The men went to the side of the cart and unrolled a long hose while the woman approached Pimi. "Now then, I am Maja, Keeper of the repletes. You're frightened, poor chickling, I know. But once we know you are trustworthy you won't have to wear this nasty thing." She stroked Pimi's cheek above the hard line of the muzzle.

Gently, as if Pimi were a varamid chick, Maja unhooked the front of the muzzle. A flow of cool air flowed through the hard thing in Pimi's mouth and she realized that it was a tube. Maja took the long hose from one of the men. On the end, it had a notched collar a hand's span from the tip. She threaded it into Pimi's mouth and twisted, locking the collar to the front of Pimi's muzzle.

"Now then, chickling. Disgorge for me, hmm?"

Pimi's muscles, so ready to vomit before, tightened in fear and locked her closed.

Maja stepped to the side so that Pimi had a clear view of the blind replete. "Do not make me ask you twice or you'll wind up like Blind Irvapp. You'll find me more patient than others, because don't I know how scared you are, hmm? But Councilor Hadan won't brook disobedience. You understand me, chickling, hmm?"

Looking at the mindless fluttering of the vast replete's hands, Pimi opened herself and disgorged in a rush. The hose leaped and throbbed in time with the surges from her crop, flowing down the hose and into the replete, until she was empty.

"There's my sweet chickling." Maja unhooked the hose and opened a jar. She poured three capsules into her hand. Gently, she placed them in Pimi's mouth and connected a different hose. "Make certain these go into your crop, or it will go worse for you. These'll help you stretch, but only if they're in the right place and we've not much time to ready you for Deep Harvest. You'll feel some discomfort, but that is a sign of growth, understand me? Growth is good."

She put the tube deep in Pimi's mouth. "I begin now." Maja twisted the spigot.

Cold vinegar flooded down Pimi's throat. Before she could get the sphincter to her crop open, her cheeks bulged from the influx. No gentle flow here, only the frantic rushing of sour liquid as it pushed into her crop. The cold weight dragged her crop down before it began pushing it out. Unlike the warm thick nectar a replete would have given her, this chilled her as it eddied inside her belly.

When she had been young, she had once swallowed glass after glass of water so that she could play bride with her best friend. Then it had taken only eight glasses to fill her. How many now passed her lips?

Something deep inside shifted and her belly violently expanded. Like three tiny explosions, waves of pressure suddenly pushed against the walls of her skin forcing her to five-day belly.

Maja turned off the spigot, but the pressure did not cease. Pimi's skin tingled and burned as it strained to accommodate the fluid. She arched her back, trying to create more space within her body. As she moved, the vinegar sloshed inside as if she were still half empty.

"That's gas from the capsules keeping you tight, chickling. If you show me that you're a sweet girl, then maybe you won't need to wear this and wouldn't that be nice, hmm?"

Nice? Pimi would do anything to get the hard tube out of her mouth and to stop the pain in her belly.

Maja unhooked the hose and put the front back on the mask, sealing Pimi's mouth closed. She stepped back and studied Pimi. "I can see why Councilor Hadan plucked you for his seraglio… He likes those he can feed from and are pretty enough to fuck."

Pimi clenched her jaw under the muzzle. He'd killed Duurir. She would do whatever it took to get to him and if that meant the seraglio, well, that would not be so different from a social season in Arrop-Yraaja.

Filtering through the screened chambers of the seraglio, giggles and murmured conversations played around Pimi as she lay on her side and let Maja rub salve on her distended crop. The cool gel eased the pricking of the constant stretching, though she really only noticed it in the span after a fresh dosing of soda capsules. The initial rush of gas always hurt, but not so much as that first time. And if she contained it, she grew. Growth meant she was one step closer to Hadan.

"Excited that harvest is coming in, chickling?" Maja peaked over the curve of Pimi's belly, only the top of her head visible from where she knelt.

"I'm sorry I am not bigger." The three months since the raid had only given Pimi time to gain a fourteen-day belly and most of the other girls still dwarfed her. Only the three new girls carried stretching fluid instead of nectar, and Pimi counted her blessings that she was, at least, the largest of them. Keria, a servant girl captured in the same raid as Pimi, was always belching to relieve pressure. These Repp-Virja girls had never aspired to a bride belly like Pimi had. Hadn't they noticed that the larger girls weren't required to wear manacles? "Do you think Councilor Hadan will ever call for me?"

"Don't you worry your pretty head. We'll make sure you've got a right tasty mix in your crop so as no one notices your size."

Pimi nodded, feeling embarrassment steal the color from her scalp.

"Speaking of mix, we had to drain blind Irvapp because one of you lot had dairy mixed into your crop."

Pimi paled further, but Maja was capping the jar of salve and did not notice. "Did he get sour crop?"

"Worst case we've had in years. My fault of course. I should have checked to see what the new repletes were carrying. But who would have mixed like that in the first place?"

Pushing against the replete couch, Pimi levered herself into a sitting position. "I hardly know."

With Maja's help, Pimi stood and leaned way back to balance her belly. With slow, mincing steps, she felt her way across the floor into the main room of the seraglio. Amid the pillowed recesses of the main room, the other girls reclined on their couches. Deep under the mountain, the cool rounded chambers reminded her of home. Rich reds and pollen yellows enhanced every hanging cloth. Her own tunic had a hem densely embroidered with fine gold thread. Should Ero see her, she would think Pimi very fine indeed.

Maja helped Pimi settle on her couch and slid the shackle around her wrist. It was all but unnoticeable among the bangles that graced her arm.

Leaving Pimi, Maja went to one of larger repletes and pressed her hand deep into the soft bell of Dama's crop. "I'm glad to see you've got space."

"Oh, you know Hadan-min. He was hungry both ways when he called for me." She preened, moistening the skin around her mouth. "Said he had to empty me to make space for his manhood."

Laughter filled the seraglio.

Dama lifted her arm over her head and a new bangle rolled back on her forearm, flashing sparks of red light against her fine green skin. No shackle competed with it. "I should say I pleased him on both counts."

When the laughter faded, Maja said, "Well and good, but you've pleased me as well. Harvest is supposed to be a large one this year. We'll need that space."

Not until they reached the Deep Yard, did Maja have the new girls empty themselves. "No point in wasting a moment of stretch, hmm?"

Pimi flushed with water three times before Maja was satisfied that no soda remained in her crop. When she'd finished her last disgorgement, Pimi looked down to her feet. How long had it been since she had seen them? The long grasping toes seemed as if they belonged to someone else. Pimi wiggled each in turn, delighted when they responded. She bent at the waist to touch her feet. The muscles in her back protested before she came near them, but she was able to feel her calves and shins. Across her thighs lay the flaccid skin of her crop, waiting for the harvest.

At the deep end of the yard, near the stables, a small band of pipe and string players tuned their instruments. Snatches of unfamiliar folk tunes skirted around the edges of conversation.

The room filled with other people. Some replete, some Abarine workers, but all ready for the harvesters to bring in the baskets of dayfruit. Sweet, nutritious and delicate, it would rot if not consumed within a day of picking.

The other new repletes were easy to spot, because they too had folds of empty skin hanging across their laps. The ones from the replete caves wore heavy chains. She owed Maja a great debt for picking her for the seraglio. One more day in the replete caves and her face would have been like theirs, slack and dull from isolation in the sandstone alcoves. One man held his face, rocking, as if the sunlight frightened him. Another woman still wore a muzzle—

The woman was Pimi's mother. Dressed in simple muslin, with naked head and shrunken crop she was almost unrecognizable. She stared at nothing, listless save for the tapping of one hand. Her other hand was wrapped in a bandage; only two fingers emerged from the gauze.

Pimi turned and vomited. Great dry heaves shook her shoulders, leaving the sickness still deep in her body. Behind her, Maja walked down the line of girls from the seraglio and put a hand on Pimi's back. "Are you ill?"

Pimi wiped her mouth with the back of her hand. "No. Not at all, I only wanted to be certain that I was truly empty."

"Such a good girl." Maja stroked Pimi's scalp.

Behind her mother's row of repletes, guards paced, checking shackles and muzzle straps. What had her mother done to merit such treatment? A guard connected a web of hoses to each of these repletes' muzzles.

The hoses led back to a pulping machine, its coarse iron gears and blades standing in sharp contrast to the civilized world she had left behind.

The band started to play a bouncing tune that begged its listeners to dance. A slender boy, too young to have more than a child's belly, stepped forward on the stage and raised a megaphone to his lips.

When the irarad saw her mate
With a sigh and a hiss she knew,
Oh—she knew that she'd be late.
And when fate showed me your sweet face
With a sigh and a hiss I knew,
Oh—I knew I'd found my place.

As soon as they had finished with harvest, Pimi would sneak out of the seraglio and find her mother. It could not be so hard. She knew where the isolated alcoves were. Likely, her mother had been next to her and she had never known. Pimi craned her neck, looking around the yard. Perhaps Ero was here too.

Though she saw one man that she thought she recognized as a servant from House Imarja, she did not see any of her family besides her mother.

What if the raiders had dealt with them as they had dealt with Duurir? She had put him out of her mind as a way to survive in this place, but now the thought of him filled her like bittersweet nectar. Her pores pulsed with anguish that she had not known him longer, that one so young and fair should have perished.

The first of the laborers came in with carts of dayfruit. Straining under the load, they deposited baskets in front of each waiting replete. The sweet fruit sent a heady fragrance into the air, of musk and honey, with the warm notes of spice tangled in the midst. Pimi took one in her hand, warm from the sun.

As she bit into it, the juice spurted down her throat. Across the room, a guard dumped a basket into the pulping machine and turned the crank. The pulp and fluid coursed down the hoses to her mother and the other muzzled repletes.

Pimi swallowed. The dayfruit slid down her throat and landed heavily in her crop. Mechanically, she ate another piece, transfixed by the sight of her mother, who swallowed without any seeming awareness of her surroundings.

The bulge in her mother's crop grew faster than Pimi could keep pace. She picked up fruit and shoved it into her mouth, barely taking time to chew. Beside her, Keria picked at the fruit daintily, her crop barely showing any growth.

"Are you afraid they will run out of food, Pimi?" Hissing, Keria looked at her crop. "I'd always wondered why you were so anxious to distort yourself like that. Your family must have been starving all the time."

Shocked, Pimi stopped with a dayfruit halfway to her mouth. "What do you mean?"

"Back in Repp-Virja, it was all we could talk about in the kitchens. As if any of us would demean ourselves to carry food around if we could afford not to. And then your family shows up, pretending to be from a Dynasty House across the sea, but it's clearer than the sky in Deep Summer that you aren't. Carrying great big loads like you're thinking you'll never see another meal."

Keria had never spoken to her this way; their couches were on opposite sides of the room to keep the new girls mixed in with the established repletes.

Maja came down the line, bearing a tray of spices. "Here chicklings, here are some fine things to add special flavor to your nectar."

Covering the gold tray, an embroidered cloth held long seedpods, pale grey-green dried leaves, tiny round seeds and bundles of purple blossoms. She glanced at the uneaten dayfruit Pimi still held. "What's the matter, chickling? Is there a borer in your dayfruit?"

Pimi opened her mouth to answer, but words did not come.

"Pimi spotted the Matriarch of her house." Keria popped a dayfruit in her mouth.

Maja showed her tongue to Pimi. "Matriarch? Don't try to tell me that you are from a Deep House. We never harvest nobles, so I'll not believe that, Pimi."

"But she is. Or they claimed they were." Keria patted her belly, which undulated under her touch. "All of them came to a feast at House Imarji, showing their disdain and repleteful like they were better than Matriarch Imji just because they came from the old country. I was serving. I saw them and they were all bigger than any of us."

"You are from Arropp-Yraarja?"

Pimi inclined her head in agreement, but Keria answered for her. "The lot of them."

"And your matriarch is here?"

"Over there." Keria pointed at Pimi's mother.

Maja almost dropped her tray. "That's your matriarch?"

Pimi nodded and squeezed her eyes tightly shut, not wanting to see or hear anything else.

"Ah, poor thing. I'd not have had you discover her like this." Maja brought the tray over to Pimi. "Still and all, you're a sweet girl. You won't give me cause to doubt you, not like her. Now swallow these down and show me I'm right to be proud of you."

Her gorge rose in her throat, but Pimi swallowed it down. If she had any hope of seeing her mother she had to stay in Maja's good graces. Tilting her head back, she let Maja place the spices in her mouth.

Chewing each took an eternity, though the band played only one song. Pimi continued to eat dayfruit, no longer tasting it. Maja returned to palpate her belly after Pimi had finished the first basket, mixing the spices with the dayfruit.

Except for the muzzled repletes, the sense of celebration was unbroken. No one, save Pimi and the guards, seemed to notice them. Only the music reached into their corner, as Pimi's mother tapped her hands in time with it.

After her third basket of fruit, Pimi shifted to a reclining position to let her crop hang off the couch and rest on the ground. It was harder to watch her mother from this position but between swallows she stole peeks across the yard.

Salina topped off while Pimi was on her fourth basket. When Maja came to lead Salina back to the seraglio, the girl staggered as she stood. Despair bleached her face of color. She waddled without a hint of grace in her movement.

Pimi would not do that. She would show the other girls the graceful sway she had learned from her mother. Maybe, if she could show Maja how much her mother could teach the girls in the seraglio, they would take the muzzle off.

During the seventh basket, Pimi felt herself close to topping off. Her crop was comfortably full and firm to the touch, but without the harsh pressure of the stretching fluid. Her mother was almost twice the size she had been when they had boarded the Tep-Tep steamship to leave home. If Pimi could contrive to leave the Deep Yard at the same time as her mother, she might have a chance to speak to her in the hallways.

Where before she had raced to keep pace with her mother, Pimi slowed down now, trying to delay the moment when she was taken back to the seraglio.

By the eighth basket, Pimi would only eat a piece of dayfruit when Maja looked at her. With each piece she swallowed, she thought that surely she could not hold any more.

And then it was true. Stretched beyond capacity, her belly hurt. The last piece of dayfruit she swallowed lodged in her sphincter, holding it open. She strained, trying to push it in by sheer will.

Maja came down the line and touched her belly. She hissed appreciatively at the hardness. "Well done, Pimi-min. There will be a fine treat for you in the seraglio tonight."

"Let me rest a moment. I would like to finish this basket." Dayfruit still filled half of it and her throat tightened in involuntary protest.

Maja pushed again. The piece of dayfruit caught in Pimi's sphincter rose in her throat. She held down a cough.

"You seem topped off to me."

"But my skin will relax. It always does."

"Truth. Though if you can fit the rest of that basket in, I will be beyond surprised."

With a hand stained blue by the fruit, Pimi picked up a dayfruit and swallowed it, sending it into her primary stomach. "See. I still have space."

"You are a sweet girl, Pimi. Don't hurt yourself trying to make me proud." Maja glanced across the yard at Pimi's mother. "I wish all our repletes were so eager to please. If we'd known she was a matriarch..."

Pimi ate as slowly as she could, but still filled her primary stomach before the bottom of the basket. As she had hoped, her crop relaxed somewhat and she was able to get three more dayfruit into it. The rest sat in her throat, neither in her stomach nor in her crop. Her breath came in shallow gasps; it felt as if her entire body consisted of nothing but dayfruit. The blue of the dayfruit tinted her amber belly green. Maja looked down the line and Pimi swallowed another bite which sat in her throat, itching.

A guard checked Pimi's mother and unhooked the tube from her muzzle.

Pimi struggled to sit. "Maja, I am ready to go now."

From where she palpated Dama's crop, Maja did not look up. "When I finish here."

The guard wheeled Pimi's mother toward the door. Pimi could not wait for Maja or she would miss her chance. Putting her feet on the ground she pushed to stand. The weight of dayfruit in her crop, so much greater than the half-belly of stretching fluid, pulled her forward and down.

As she lost her balance, Pimi's sharp cry fell into a sudden silence between songs, cutting through the harvest crowd. Her distended crop smacked against the packed gravel ground.

The sudden force pushed the overabundance of dayfruit up her throat. She vomited blue juice and pulp down her front.

The girls nearest her shrieked. Baraida screamed, "Pimi's ruptured!"

Her mother raised her head. Horror bleached her features of all color.

Pimi scrabbled, trying to get her feet under her, trying to stand and get away from the mess she had made. Her own body was too heavy for her limbs. She was trapped on the ground as surely as her mother had been when the Abarine raiders had come.

In an instant, Maja was by her side. By the time she had ascertained that nothing beyond overfilling was wrong, the cart bearing Pimi's mother was gone. Pimi had to wait crouched on the gravel until a gurney was fetched to hoist her onto a cart of her own.

"What has happened here?" Councilor Hadan came to stand by Maja. Even at harvest, he wore his distinctive armor; the spirals of inlaid metal swirled across each overlapping horn plate.

"I'm afraid Pimi over-filled herself, Councilor Hadan."

Pimi nearly vomited again as he crouched in front of her. She had not been so close to him since she was captured. Pimi kept her eyes downturned, her stained tunic and belly filling her vision.

"Now why would you do that, little girl?"

Always, her size made people assume she was younger than her true age, but he was very nearly her height. In fact, with his amber and green coloring, Pimi had an impression of what she might have looked like had her mother wanted a boy and placed Pimi's egg in a cool part of the deep-family's hatching cave.

"Speak," he said, giving her permission to respond.

"I wanted to be beautiful for you," she whispered. "So you would pick me instead of Dama."

"And why would making yourself overfull do that?"

Pimi did not know how to answer him—to her, still, it seemed so obvious that a full crop was the most beautiful adornment a person could have. Though, looking at her stained and sorry state, she could not see any glamour in it.

Maja answered for her. "Pimi is from Aaropp-Yraarja."

"Like Kejari?"

"That is in fact, her matriarch."

"Sa-ha!"

"Did you know you'd claimed a Dynasty House in your conquests, Councilor?"

He was silent for a moment and the music twirled around them. "I did not. Well. I hope you are better behaved than your mother. She tried to claw my eyes out when they brought her to me." Hadan tilted her chin up. "You do not look much like her."

Maja hissed. "Were you ever in Aaropp-Yraarja, Councilor?"

"I've not had the pleasure, though I have heard much about their social season."

Maja waved a cart over. "Pimi is the sweetest girl you can imagine."

Hadan straightened. "Well, next time Dama is unavailable, send me Pimi."

Primped and scented and oiled, Pimi held still while Maja broadened her forehead spots with paint. Across the room, Dama writhed and groaned in the grip of sour crop. A doctor oversaw the tortuous task of draining the congealed clumps from her, while the other girls affected not to watch.

Pimi tried not to let the guilt she felt show on her face. Had she not slipped the cheese into Dama's mix, who knew when Hadan would have called for her.

Maja had wondered how Pimi had gotten rug burns on the bottom of her crop. Pimi had feigned ignorance. After all, if they thought a replete's crop was reason enough to not shackle a girl, who was Pimi to let them know that by sliding backwards she could still drag the weight of her belly across the floor.

The outer door of the seraglio opened and two attendants arrived to push Pimi's cart to Councilor Hadan's chambers. Her toes gripped the edge of her couch as if she were not anchored firmly enough.

Ornamented tapestries covered the walls of Hadan's apartment, finer than anything in the seraglio, which Pimi had thought opulent.

As he conferred with his fellow councilors, Hadan's voice carried from a room on the far side of the apartment in uneven waves. At times, it was an indecipherable murmur, at others she would hear words or whole phrases. "...other sorties might..." or "...stay within their borders...." And once, "...from Aaropp-Yraarja in the last raid."

Her toes curled tighter then.

When they broke the meeting and came to her, she kept her eyes downcast and lips parted as Maja had taught. Councilor Hadan ran a hand up her crop, over the crest and across the smooth dip where it belled from her chest. With his hand resting gently on her neck, Hadan said, "This is our newest prize gentlemen. A daughter of one of the

Dynasty Houses of Aaropp-Yraarja."

One woman hissed in amusement. "I see you don't boast of having the mother."

Hadan fondled Pimi's chin. "We broke her before anyone realized that we'd taken a noble." He turned to the man nearest him. "You saw her. All puffed out like a Repp-Virji serving girl."

"Bigger than that." The man hissed. "I trust she's worth it?"

"Shall we find out?" Hadan lowered his head and put his mouth over hers. Pimi opened herself and disgorged in a smooth steady stream. Hadan grunted in satisfaction. He pressed on her crop, swallowing greedily as the flow increased.

He tapped her arm and stood, almost before she could stop disgorging. Bound up as it was, his crop formed a rounded mound at the top of his chest. It could not have held much more than a one-day belly. "Maja's created a fine brew in this one. Please, help yourself."

In all, Pimi fed each of his three companions. Hadan led them back into the inner room of his apartment, but did not call for the attendants to wheel Pimi away.

Left alone on her couch, Pimi shifted with impatience. She had not expected him to have company. Her slackened crop quivered in response to her movement. They must have taken nearly five days out of her. She tried to stand and could almost raise her bulk. She hoped they had not lightened her too much.

As she lay waiting, she listened with half an ear to the conference in the other room. The words and phrases she heard hinted at another raid on Repp-Virja. She could gather no details, only the impression that it must be immanent if they were spending so much time discussing it.

After what seemed hours, the group filed out of Hadan's apartment, leaving her alone with the man. As short as Pimi was, she was almost of a height with Hadan.

Hadan said nothing to her and without his permission, she could not speak. He walked behind her, casually, as though she were a varamid at market. He ran a hand up the nape of her neck and fondled her bare scalp. Pimi shivered as his hands touched the delicate skin above her ear panels.

"Do you like that?" He leaned close, so that his breath tickled her skin.

Pimi nodded. It was expected that she would like anything that he did to her.

Sliding his hands down to her shoulders, Hadan tugged on her tunic, pulling it down her arms. Pimi shifted to let him slide the garment off. Her skin contracted in the cool air of his compartment.

Hadan reached around her and pressed his hands into the soft skin of her crop, leaning against her, so his hard leather armor pressed into her back. He nuzzled her neck. "Well, my exotic beauty. Tell me how they do this in Aaropp-Yraarja. Speak and teach me something new."

Pimi had been through Maja's training for the seraglio, but Hadan would know all those tricks. She prayed that he would find the love scenes from Opperad's play, The Brothel of Intention, exotic. If not, she would have to think of something else. "I would not presume to teach you, Councilor, but it is true that we do approach things differently in Aaropp-Yraarja. If you were my groom, I would want you filled to hardness, and to let the weight of my crop rest on yours as I straddled you." She turned her head and looked out under the edge of her eyelid at him. "I find it strange how skinny everyone here is. A man at home is not considered attractive unless he has at least a five-day belly."

"Sa-ha! Is that so?"Hadan slid his hand between her thighs. "So you find me unattractive?"

"I would not say so, Councilor." She took a breath and then a chance. "But I do think on how fine you would look without your truss."

Hadan nipped her hip gently. "You have succeeded in proposing something I have not tried. You intrigue me."

Pimi reached back to touch a buckle of his armor. He slid across the couch to let her undress him. As she peeled the leather away, his crop sagged. The single day of food made a sad lump in skin that hung to his thighs.

Taking his face in her hands, Pimi lowered her mouth. He opened wide for her and accepted her offering eagerly. The nectar flowed into him until he tapped her arm. She lifted her head and put her hand on his crop, half-expecting him to not allow the intimacy. She pressed and the surface gave slightly. "You can hold more than that, I am certain."

"You do not want me to overfill, do you?" He encircled his crop with his arms, as if amazed at his own girth, meager though it was to Pimi's eyes.

She blanched at the memory of her embarrassment at harvest. "No. That was foolish of me. But I want you to be hard with my gift to you. It is what brides do for their grooms in my country."

He let her push more food into him, until he broke gasping from her embrace. "Hell's frozen gates. I cannot recall ever being this full, not even when setting out on a long campaign."

Pimi slid a hand under his crop to the folds where his genitals were. She pulled the long forks of spiraling flesh out and held them, pulsing, lightly in her palm. Hadan stood to give her easier access, and staggered under his unfamiliar weight. He hissed. "How graceful I am. You see why we do not allow ourselves to be full. It would destroy us in battle."

"But we do not plan to battle, do we Councilor?" She stroked his spirals until they writhed in her grasp. "Lie down for me?"

He gasped and lay down on the floor, then groaned. "The pressure..."

"Do you like it?"Pimi asked.

"I am surprised that I do." He reached for her with a foot and curled his long toes around her ankle. "Show me what else they do in your country."

Pimi let him guide her to stand over him. Her crop, so loose that it hung almost to the ground, required both of them to maneuver it onto him. She could stand, but not walk. As the weight settled and wrapped around Hadan he moaned with pleasure.

Pimi tucked his spirals into the folds of her egg chamber. She would not trigger ovulation for him, but still, she felt his flesh screw into her as if he could line the chamber with fertile seed.

As Maja had taught her and as Pimi had seen at the theater, she stimulated Hadan until he spasmed in ecstasy. At last, spent and sated, he lay on the carpet with his eyes half-closed in drowsy contentment.

Pimi waited until he fell asleep, and then shifted to grip his ankles with her toes. Sliding forward, she pushed her crop in front of her. It slid off the mound of his belly to cover his face.

He woke. Pimi leaned on him as Hadan struggled to free himself. Even half-empty, she still outweighed him and his own unfamiliar bulk fought him. He heaved under her, trying to disgorge.

Warm and sticky, the nectar stung the rug burn on the bottom of her crop. She felt him gag on the pap sealed around him by the skin of her belly.

Pimi held tight to his ankles as she clung to thoughts of her mother, of Duurir, and even of Keria. She leaned on him until he stopped struggling.

Holding as still as a river in Deep Winter, Pimi tried to feel for any sign of life, for any sign that he was not dead, that she had not killed him. Pimi retched at the thought, but held it down. For the moment, until she was certain he was dead, she needed all her weight.

She did not know how long she waited, but at last she was satisfied and released his ankles. Standing, Pimi tried to drag herself off of him. Her posture and weight held her pinned firmly. Panic flared in her lungs before she realized that she could simply disgorge. No one would care if she soiled the carpet.

She leaned as far over as she could, to avoid spattering herself with the nectar she spilled. The carpet was wet and thick with pap before Pimi could pull herself off Hadan.

With the excess skin of her crop bundled up and hidden in the truss of Hadan's armor, Pimi strode with her best approximation of an Abarine warrior. Her legs trembled and cramped from the unaccustomed exercise. She would have to steal a varamid—two, with her mother—if they had any hope of escaping. She rested a hand on the satchel she'd taken from Hadan's room. With luck, the maps would help them find their way home.

In the lower replete chamber, Pimi found her mother in the third alcove she entered. Kejari closed her eyes and turned fear-red as Pimi crossed the room. Moaning, her mother pushed back on her couch as far as her crop would allow her.

"Mother?" Pimi whispered.

Gasping through her muzzle, Pimi's mother opened her eyes wide. Pimi undid the buckles and peeled the fetid leather thing off her mother's face. The skin underneath was pasty and stank like the dead leaves on a watervine.

"Speak, wraith-child. Why do you haunt me?" Her mother touched her thumbs together in the ancient sign to ward off foul spirits. Pimi had not made such a childish sign since she was an adolescent passing under the burial nets.

"I am not a wraith. I am your natural daughter." Pimi grabbed her mother's hand, trying not to flinch at the stubs of thumb and finger. "Truth. Feel the warmth in my bones?"

"But you ruptured."

"No. I over-filled and vomited." The rest would have to wait until they were away. "I need you to disgorge."

"Oh no." Her mother reached for the muzzle with her free hand. "No. It would make Councilor Hadan angry."

Pimi dropped the muzzle on the floor and captured her mother's other hand. "He will not hurt you again. That is truth."

Pimi did not have another set of armor for her mother, though she was able to fashion a truss from a hanging she had brought from Hadan's apartment. Her hope was that her mother would be taken for an Abarine woman, perhaps a Councilor, but the hope was only a small one. In truth, she had thought of how to kill Hadan and find her mother, but the likelihood of her scheme succeeding had seemed so remote that she had been unable to imagine their actual escape from the compound. She knew only that on foot they did not stand a chance.

The sandstone labyrinth of halls threw the sound of every footfall back at Pimi, shattering her nerves with each blow. At her side, her mother followed with the blind trust of an infant.

Pimi stopped outside the pool of gaslight at the intersection of two halls. Behind her lay the replete quarters. The varamid stables were above ground and the hall to her left sloped up. In the absence of other clues, she steered her mother that way.

The light in the intersection blinded her to the dim hall beyond for a few steps. The man coming toward them might have materialized out of the wraithworld for all Pimi could see.

Toes clenching the floor with each stride, Pimi tried to effect the easy swagger of a warrior. Her legs trembled with every step closer and Hadan's swords slapped against her back as if mocking her. What could she do with a sword?

Then they were abreast.

The man inclined his head, as to a superior, but gave no other indication of her passing. For the length of the hall, Pimi listened for some sound that he had realized her deception. Only gradually did it occur to her that perhaps his nocturnal errand was also something he did not want discovered. There was little reason for anyone to be active in the quiet of night. Still, with that encounter past, Pimi felt more secure.

Three more turns, following slopes and breezes led Pimi to an exterior hall. Through the small rounded windows that pierced the wall every arm's span, she could see the fenced paddock of the stables. She slipped through the first door she found onto the Deep Yard fronting the buried city.

Her mother hung back at the door, staring up at the sky. Pimi glanced upward. What constellations would Duurir have seen there? "Mother, we must hurry." It would be hours before anyone visited Hadan's apartment—Dama was regularly gone until late morning on the nights that Hadan took her—but still Pimi did not want to stargaze.

Her mother's tongue flicked out to wet her lips. "You go without me." She still stared upward, backing into the hall.

"No and no. What sort of daughter would I be if I left you here?" The time in the replete caves must have addled her mother's brain. Pimi reached for her hand.

"You would be a living child." Her mother waved her mutilated hand in protest. "I do not want to go back. What is there for me?"

"Your family. Your duty."

"Neither of them saved me here. Why do I owe them?"

"I have saved you." Pimi drew herself up, praying that it was true. She saw though, that her mother had lost her sense of self. She needed a purpose. "And now I need you to save me."

Pimi's mother tore her gaze away from the sky. "Do not think to play my emotions. I have none left."

"I am not playing. Look at me." Pimi held her arms out, so her mother would look at the distinctive inlaid spirals of metal on Hadan's armor. "You took me for Councilor Hadan. I am his match in build and coloring, but not in voice. If you tell the stable clerks that Councilor Hadan requires two varamids, do you think they will dare say no?"

Some of the life came back to her mother's expression as she considered Pimi's words. "Would they not expect you to ask for the steeds?"

Pimi pulled a scroll from her satchel in answer. "Not if I am occupied studying our plans for another raid." The effort of keeping her voice to a whisper made her sound calmer than she felt.

Her mother's face was unreadable in the shadows. "I would not have expected such plans from you, Pimi-min."

"I've had nothing to do but plan and think." Pimi pointed at the stables. "Now, we must go."

The night sounds filled the space between them with the creaking cries of stargliders and the buzz of hairyworms burrowing in the rock cliffs. A varamid's sleepy chirp seemed to break her mother's daze. She adjusted her headscarf and stood straighter to show her full height. "Truth and full. You are truly my Councilor."

With that, she led Pimi across to the stables moving with the magnificent swaying confidence of a matriarch. Pimi stopped at the edge of the paddock, and turned as if to allow the gaslight from within to fall on the scroll she held, but really so that her face was shadow obscured. Her gaze darted from the map to the great yard. The dim gaslights showed but a single guard at the main gate. She supposed that more would be in the gatehouse.

Behind her, the sharp clap of her mother's hands broke the night quiet. "Councilor Hadan needs his varamid. You there, show haste."

"Wha—" A young man's voice, still muzzy with sleep.

"Did I invite you to speak?" The smack of flesh on flesh and the grunt that followed spoke the man's answer for him. "Would you care to speak to the Councilor? Go and bring the steeds for which I asked."

No response then but the man's footfalls as he raced into the stable. Pimi's hands shook the scroll she held, blending the words to a meaningless blur. What if he saw their lie and had gone to raise the alarm? The two swords strapped to her back would give her no aid if her treachery were discovered.

Her mother paced to her side and stood with head bowed over the scroll. "He is bringing them now," she murmured, then pointed at a line on the page... heightened activity in the border... as if they were conferring on some important point of policy.

Pimi grunted, the only sound she trusted herself to make. Unrolling the scroll to another portion she pretended utter absorption while listening to the young man bring out the varamids. One of them squawked in protest.

"Councilor?" Her mother gestured to the waiting varamids. Pimi rolled the scroll, stuffed it back in her satchel and turned to mount. The boy kept his eyes downturned, as she had been taught to do. He never looked at her, but even so, it did not seem possible that she would get away.

Then, she was mounted and her mother rode beside her toward the front gates of the compound. Pimi strained to hear past the sound of her own pulse. The night sounds contained no surprises. The scrape of talons on gravel gave the only indication of their passing. Pimi could not draw breath for fear of destroying the silence.

At the main gate, a single guard waited, leaning against the armored wood, her head tipped down in half slumber. Other guards would be in the guardhouse, no more than seven arm's spans away. Pimi's mother pushed the varamid in front and said, "Sleeping on duty?"

The guard straightened abruptly, her blanch of embarrassment visible even in the dim gas lights. Her face whitened more when she saw Hadan's armor, but she did not speak.

Pimi's mother did. "Open the gate. The councilor and I are going out. I caution you to tell—"

An alarm undulated in a rising wail, echoing off the face of the sandstone cliffs so that it seemed to come from everywhere.

Gas lights flooded the Deep Yard with their bright hiss. In the barracks a clamor arose as warriors raced outside, some still donning their armor.

It had been too much to hope that Hadan's body would stay undiscovered until morning.

As if unwilling to admit defeat now that she had committed herself, Pimi's mother bellowed at the bewildered gatekeeper, "Open by order of Councilor Hadan."

The gatekeeper, isolated and still groggy, slid back the massive steel bar that held the gate shut.

Before she had it fully open, Pimi's mother pushed her varamid forward; its long taloned feet threw the ground behind it with each stride. Behind them, the din of warriors rose as they mounted varamids to chase Pimi and her mother.

Pimi squeezed the flanks of the varamid and leaned forward over its long neck, urging it to speed past the gate and down the twisting canyon road that lead from the mountain city. The road, so simple for the Abarine to defend, gave no easy egress; the first bend lay a scant thirty-four arm's spans past the city gate.

As Pimi's mother rounded the bend, she pulled back on her varamid's reins. Four strides more and Pimi could see around the bend.

An army of men and women filled the pass.

They were trapped as surely as an irarad snared from the sky with a net. Pimi pulled her varamid to a halt, having nowhere else to run. Beside her, Mother half stood on the back of her varamid.

She would not be returned to the seraglio if she was caught. Neither of them would be allowed to live. Pimi reached over her head and fumbled a sword free of its sheath. Holding it aloft, she bellowed as if disgorging all the helplessness she had held inside.

An answering shout rose from the throats of Abarine men and women as they raced forward to pin Pimi and her mother between the two forces. How had she thought this would work?

In that frozen moment, an officer broke from the ranks of the soldiers behind them and brought his varamid beside hers. Not until he was close did she recognize him as Uramikk from Hadan's apartment.

Uramikk kept his attention on the force facing them, watching for some signal. "Councilor. Did you plan to parley?"

She whipped around to face him. He still thought her to be Hadan. Pimi turned back to the front, as her mind caught up with her body.

The troops in front of her must be from Repp-Virja. Flashes of Hadan's conversation crystallized… other sorties might... stay within their borders…. The Abarine had not been chasing fugitives, they had been following their leader into battle.

If Uramikk thought she would parley, then that is what she would do. Pimi grunted, and kicked her varamid into motion. Her mother's varamid followed with the flocking instinct of its kind.

The ranks toward which they rode leveled their weapons at her. Sweet goddess on the mount—the Repp-Virji thought she was attacking them. Pimi pulled up her varmid sharply.

Beyond what she had seen at the theater, she had no idea how someone would signal that they wanted to parley. And she could not say anything without Uramikk realizing that she was not who he thought she was; only the night and the armor hid her identity.

She swung off the varamid.

Uramikk said, "Councilor—"

Pimi held up a hand to stop him, keeping her face turned toward the Repp-Virji. Her legs wobbled as she strode forward four paces. The soldiers kept their weapons aimed at her, but made no move to attack, though surely they would willingly kill her at the slightest signal.

The line of men and women stirred and a group of four tall women stepped out to meet her. They stopped eight paces away. One said, "Speak, Councilor Hadan. I have at my back the combined forces of four of the Deep Houses of Repp-Virja with a warrant for your execution. Will you surrender for the sake of your followers or will you force us to lay open your gates by force?"

Pimi did not speak. Her voice would carry to the man behind her, as clearly as to the women in front. She dropped to her knees with Hadan's sword held out in front of her and tilted her neck so far back in supplication that she stared at the sky. The cold stars glared back at her.

Someone pulled the sword from her grasp. Pimi squeezed her eyes shut, waiting for the sword to come down on her own neck. If they killed her and her mother lived, it would be worth it.

"Wait!" To Pimi's right, her mother said, "I beg you."

Pimi opened her eyes and spun to face her mother. If she told them who Pimi really was, then the entire host of Abarine would fall upon them.

Her mother's neck was tilted back in supplication, with her hands pressed to her crop as if ready to void all for them. Pimi gestured sharply to her mother to kneel. After a moment of hesitation, her mother lowered her eyes in submission and knelt.

Without looking at him, Pimi repeated the gesture at Uramikk. Her toes curled inward as she sought something to grip in her fear. The wind carried the sounds of armor creaking as the Abarines waited with her.

With a muttered curse, Uramikk cast his sword upon the ground. "You are right. We are out-numbered."He knelt beside her and Pimi nearly fell forward to embrace the ground in relief.

Behind them, hard metal rang on the ground as men and women followed suit. She knelt, trembling from anxiety and fatigue until hands hauled her to her feet. As she was dragged forward, past the troops who had the task now of accepting the Abarines' surrender, she wanted to see what happened to her mother, but she kept her head down so none could peer inside her helm. Pimi prayed that with her surrender her mother would not be harmed.

They stopped in front of a cart and roughly turned her. Two of them held her, while a third ripped off her helmet. Pimi fought her instinct to tilt her head back and kept it bowed so her face would not show. The night wind played across her naked scalp, chilling her.

Someone undid the buckles of the armor, peeling it away from her. As they did, the truss loosened and the slack skin of her crop spilled in an empty sack at her feet.

The woman holding her armor gasped and stepped back. "You're not — Where is Councilor Hadan?"

"He's dead. Please." Pimi lifted her head and leaned toward the woman. "The Abarines think I'm him. Don't let them know."

The woman flung Hadan's armor to the ground. "And who are you, little replete?"

"I'm Kejaridoti Pimi from Aaropp-Yraarja." Pimi hurriedly explained everything that had happened since the Abarine took her captive. When she'd finished, she looked around at the assembled troops. "Grateful though I am, I don't understand why you are here."

"The Abarine have only ever taken repletes. Not worth escalating tensions over, you understand. But your mother and yourself... that was quite the affront." The woman who had pulled the helmet from her head came closer and Pimi recognized her as Duurir's mother, Matriarch Imji. "Councilor Hadan would not return you, and we could not let him take such liberties."

A man's familiar voice exclaimed wordlessly. Then Duurir appeared at her side like a manifestation of flame. "Pimi!"

He took her head in his hands and tipped it back, his own bowing in deep welcome. "I had all but given up hope."

Pimi stared at him, nearly falling. His hands cradled her face. The warm rough pads on his thumbs could not belong to a wraith. "But Hadan killed you in the storeroom."

"He knocked me on the head." Duurir lowered his hands as if suddenly conscious that he held her. "Nothing more. "

She kept staring at him, unable to believe that he was there and alive. His face was as she had remembered him; blue spots marching down his brow from his headscarf.

Pimi touched her bare head. Until that moment, she had forgotten that her head was naked. His hands had been on her bare scalp and Pimi hadn't even noticed the intimacy.

"Are you hurt?" Duurir's dark eyes widened.

"No." Pimi looked past him into the night that had once more fallen around them. "Is my mother safe?"

"Thanks to you." His eyes skipped down, resting briefly on the loose skin of her crop.

Pimi drew herself erect. So much had changed since she'd seen him last. "Will you take me to her?"

"Of course." He looked as if he would say more, but Pimi gestured for him to lead the way.

She was her mother's daughter, and no clothes or headscarf or crop could alter that. Later, when she knew her mother was safe, there might be time for courtship.

Dying with Her Cheer Pants On

Seanan McGuire

Bridget ducked behind the remains of a burned-out Impala, crouching low as the zap-zap-zap of blaster fire split the October night. The sound was already familiar enough to turn her stomach. Not just because it meant another survivor had been spotted—because there was nothing she could do to help whoever it was. She huddled against the wheel, making herself as small as possible. She didn't think she'd been seen. She'd know for sure in a few minutes, when the patrol reached her position. There was nothing to do but wait.

It was still hard to believe that aliens were real, not just science-fiction bullshit for the geeks in the computer club to obsess over. Maybe they'd been science-fiction bullshit once, but not anymore. This was real. Some guy on CNN had called them blasters when the aliens first landed, before anybody had a clue how destructive their quaint-looking little ray guns really were. He'd laughed when he said it.

That was sixteen hours ago, nine hours before the start of the homecoming game, and eleven hours before the game's untimely end. Nobody was laughing now, least of all Bridget, who'd been chosen for the unenviable duty of leaving the safety of the gym and crossing the ruins of town to get what Amy was saying the squad would need.

(They'd all put their names into the sacred gym bag, and when Maddy—who was Squad Leader, even though there was barely any squad left—pulled out Bridget's name, she couldn't argue. The gym bag's word was law.)

She wished she'd been allowed to stay in uniform. She would have felt safer that way, more confident, more in-control…more like herself. A Fighting Pumpkin was always a cheerleader on the inside, but there was still an undeniable security in being a cheerleader on the outside, a safety of sorts in their matching orange and green uniforms. Present a united front. Look your best, and you'll be the best. But she would have been too visible if she'd worn the school colors outside; they would have stood out like a floodlight against the scorch marks and gummy ash covering everything in town. Better to blend in. Better to make it back to the gym alive.

The blaster fire tapered off. Bridget managed to huddle down even further as she waited to hear the slithering sound the aliens made when they moved. She didn't want to see them almost as badly as she wanted them not to see her. She'd seen the aliens on the morning news, before the shooting had started, but it hadn't prepared her for the reality of them. The TV couldn't show the way they smelled, or the way their sticky-looking skins seemed to bend the light, as if even it didn't want to touch them.

(Amy had described them best. She'd looked at the pictures being flashed across the emergency broadcasts, sniffed, and said they looked like what you'd get if you let Dr. Frankenstein play with a giant squid, a spider, and a Pomeranian. She then went on to explain that Franken-stein was the doctor, not the monster. As if anybody cared. She would never have made the squad if she weren't the only one who could do a per-fect back-handspring every single time. Plus, it was good to have a brain around, if only because the principal kept refusing to cancel finals.)

Finals were cancelled now, along with Homecoming, cheerleading, and everything else about the world that mattered. The only question left was whether the human race was getting cancelled. Things didn't look good for the home team.

The sound of tentacles slapping against broken pavement drew closer to Bridget's hiding place. She clapped a hand over her mouth to block the sound of her breathing, squeezing her eyes shut. They'd pass or they wouldn't. If they passed, she'd start running. If they didn't...

If they didn't, the sacred gym bag had been wrong. She wasn't the one.

The slapping sounds passed the car, getting softer as the alien pa-trol moved on to search for more survivors. *You missed one*, thought Bridget. She still stayed where she was, counting slowly to a hundred. The sounds didn't resume. Uncurling herself, she rose, her precious burden clutched against her chest.

Bridget ran.

The invasion started at 5:30 a.m. Central Time on the third Saturday in October—Homecoming Weekend for high schools across America. The aliens came in enormous saucer-shaped ships before scattering out in smaller vessels that looked sort of like flying Winnebagos. Those outer space motor homes touched down wherever there were people, opening their doors and spilling dozens of squid-spider things into the streets. Some people panicked. Some people fired guns at them, but the bullets just bounced off their invisible shields. The aliens kept moving, seeming to ignore the people of Earth, no matter what those people did.

The adults promptly went out of their minds, which is basically what adults are for. At least half the squad was under house arrest, but of the fifteen girls on the Fighting Pumpkins Varsity Cheerleading Squad, fourteen were at the locker room on time. Jeanne was fifteen minutes late; her father actually locked her in her bedroom when she said she was going to the game with or without his permission.

("I waited until he went back to the living room and snuck out my bedroom window," bragged Jeanne, after she'd finally shown up. Her pride turned into hysteria when halftime turned into a bloodbath and she realized she'd never see her family again. It was almost a mercy when one of the blasters caught her in the back, reducing her to ash and blackened bones. Almost. Annoying or not, she'd been a Fighting Pumpkin, and Fighting Pumpkins were supposed to take care of their own.)

The entire football team showed up for the game—naturally—and so did enough of the opposing team for the coaches to decide they should go ahead and play. "We'll show those aliens what it means to be American!" said Coach Ackley, and everyone applauded.

It was a good game. It would have been a better one if the aliens hadn't shown up at halftime and opened fire on the crowd. It took them less than five minutes to kill almost a hundred people and send the survivors scattering like quail.

(According to the videos Amy had downloaded to her phone, the aliens actually attacked at the same time all over the world. Bridget really didn't care. She didn't have to smell the entire world getting fried, just the people on the field. So much for the home-team advantage.)

They never even got to finish the game. Funny, the things that stop seeming like the end of the world when the world is really ending.

Bridget pressed herself against the gym wall outside the locker room door, praying she'd managed to get the secret knock right. One missed beat and they might leave her outside, alone, in the dark, with the aliens.

She'd been waiting just long enough to be on the verge of total panic when the door creaked open and Amy whispered, urgently, "Get in here before you're spotted. "

Bridget was only too happy to oblige.

Maddy, Betsy, and Kathryn were waiting in the shower room. The power was out all over town, but they had flashlights, and the screensaver on Amy's laptop gave off a soothing glow. The girls were sitting on a pile of gymnastic mats they'd dragged over from the equipment cage. Bridget blinked back sudden tears as she realized, again, that this was it; this was the squad. This might even be the entire high school. She hadn't seen any survivors in her trek across the town.

Maddy rose as Bridget and Amy approached. Her eyes were only for the bag Bridget clutched against her chest. "Is that it?" she demanded. "Did you get it?"

"Right where Amy said it would be." Bridget held out the bag, opening it to display the contents: a box of dinner candles and a shabby old book in a plastic library dust jacket. The word WITHDRAWN was stamped across the width of the pages in gory red. "I got matches, too."

"Good," said Amy, taking the bag from Bridget's unresisting hands. "We'll need them."

Maddy looked Bridget up and down. "Go get your uniform on. You're going to want to be in your colors for this."

Maddy was the Squad Leader, and she was a senior. Questioning her went against every bone in Bridget's body. She still found the strength, somehow, to ask timidly, "Is this really going to work?"

"It has to." Maddy shrugged. "There's nothing else left to try."

Bridget nodded, accepting Maddy's words as truth. According to what Amy was able to find before the school wireless cut out, the aliens had taken out everything that was thrown at them, including most of the United States Armed Forces, and a Chinese nuclear bomb. They'd been most of the way to conquering the planet when the connection died. Everything had been tried, and everything had failed.

Everything except the impossible. Bridget glanced at the three girls now sitting cross-legged on the shower floor, all of them focused on the book in Amy's hands. It would work. It had to. If it didn't...

Well, if it didn't, it wouldn't be their problem anymore. With that reassuring thought at the front of her mind, Bridget turned to creep back to her locker. If she was going to die, she was going to do it with her cheer pants on.

Five girls in orange and green uniforms stood in a circle in the center of the shower room, their eyes fixed on the gym bag on the floor in front of them. Inside the bag were five slips of Betsy's rose-scented pink notebook paper, each with a girl's name written on it. No one moved. Bridget was barely breathing. For the second time in a single night, and the second time in her entire life, she was afraid of what the sacred bag might ask of her.

"Everybody understands what they need to do?" asked Amy, eyes still fixed on the bag. She'd taken out her contacts, replacing them with the glasses she was only allowed to wear when nobody outside the squad would see her. Aliens didn't count.

Nods from the other girls. Bridget forced herself to nod with them. The bag was going to pick her. She knew the bag was going to pick her. Why were they even bothering?

Because it was tradition, and tradition must be observed, even at the end of the world—maybe especially at the end of the world. "Then it's time," said Maddy. She picked up the bag, giving it a shake. "Who wants to pull the name?" No hands were raised. This wasn't like deciding who was going to go pick up the pizzas, or who had to go tell Coach Ackley the freshmen had been peeping in the girls' locker room again. This was too big.

"You do it, Maddy," said Kathryn. A murmur of agreement ran through the other girls. Maddy was Captain. She'd pick the one the gym bag wanted. That was how the power worked.

"All right." Expression grave, Maddy plunged her hand into the gym bag, rummaged around, and came up with a single slip of paper and the strong smell of roses.

Please, thought Bridget.

"Bridget," read Maddy. As one, the five sighed. "I'm sorry."

"Don't be." Bridget wiped the back of her hand across her eyes, smearing tears and mascara. No one was going to say anything. Not now. "I came to tryouts on my own, remember? I cheered my heart out. That's why I'm here."

"Fighting Pumpkins forever," said Betsy.

It was a good thing to say. "Fighting Pumpkins forever," said Maddy. One by one, they took up the cheer, chanting it in a whisper barely louder than a sigh. Amy passed out the candles and the books of matches, while the other girls dug out their compacts, with their tiny, perfect mirrors. Only Bridget didn't bother. Her mirror was going to be bigger than that.

"It will work," Amy said, folding Bridget's fingers around the matchbook. "Believe it's going to work like you always believed the home team was going to win. Home team advantage."

"Home team advantage," Bridget echoed, and stayed where she was as the others stepped forward, one by one, to hug her and head for the exits. Maddy was the last to go.

"She'll make them pay for this," she said, squeezing Bridget's shoulder, and then was gone.

Not allowing herself to look at the candle in her hand, Bridget turned and walked after the others. She wasn't heading for the exit. She was heading for the bathroom, and the full-length mirror on the bathroom wall.

Everything was silent. Bridget looked at her reflection, wishing she looked braver, or at least less afraid. Portrait of a cheerleader about to die. Maddy was right; she felt better knowing she was going to do it in the school colors. Other schools could laugh about their stupid mascot and garish uniforms, but real school spirit wasn't being badass with a mascot like a Tiger or a Wolf. It was being proud to be a Pumpkin.

Her hands were shaking hard enough that it took three tries to light the candle. The match flared orange, even brighter than her uniform, before dimming into candlelight that bleached her reflection phantompale. She mustered a wavering smile, and waited, still watching her reflection.

The bathroom window was open, just a crack. Enough for her to hear the first handclaps, like gunshots breaking the night, followed by Maddy's well-conditioned voice bellowing, "Ready? Okay!"

That was the signal. Doing her best to tune out the rest of the squad cheering outside the gym, Bridget fixed her eyes on her reflection. Don't look away; Amy's book says you can't look away. If you looked away, it wouldn't work.

("We've all played that stupid game," Kathryn had said before they voted, before the squad agreed to try Amy's crazy suggestion. "It never works. She never comes."

"That was before we knew what the rules were," said Amy.

"What are they?" asked Betsy.

But it was Maddy who answered. Maddy, who'd seen her boyfriend die on the football field; the only Squad Leader in Fighting Pumpkins history to lose a homecoming game and the majority of her squad in a single night. "There aren't any," she said, and that was when Bridget had known they were going to go through with Amy's plan, desperate and strange as it was.)

"Bloody Mary," whispered Bridget. "Bloody Mary, Bloody Mary—" The sound of blaster fire was starting up outside; the aliens were taking the bait, drawn by the irresistible lure of four teenage girls in skimpy pleated skirts cheering their hearts out. It didn't matter what part of the galaxy you were from. No one could resist a cheerleader.

"BLOODY MARY, SHE'S THE ONE!" screamed the Pumpkins outside the gym. "BLOODY MARY, I KILLED YOUR SON!" Each of them would have a compact on the ground in front of her, but they couldn't be sure they'd be able to maintain eye contact long enough to call her name the required thirteen times. That was why one of them had to stay behind, and miss the final cheer. Dying sucked. Dying without your squad around you was worse.

"—Bloody Mary, Bloody Mary, Bloody Mary—" That was six. The blasters were still firing. Betsy wasn't cheering anymore, and neither was Kathryn. It was just Amy and Maddy outside, cheering their hearts out for the last, and least appreciative, audience they would ever have. Was the mirror getting blurry, or was she just crying again?

("See, if you hold a candle and look in the mirror while you say her name thirteen times, she'll come." Amy had been talking nonsense, but they were taking her seriously because after you'd seen your teammates fried by giant alien squid with ray guns, ray guns, for God's sake, nonsense didn't sound so bad. "She'll scratch your eyes out. That's the bad part."

"So what's the good part?" demanded Maddy.

"If you tell her you're the one who killed her son, she'll kill everybody she can get her hands on."

They'd gotten very quiet after that.)

"Bloody Mary." Amy wasn't cheering anymore. It was just Maddy, and the sound of blasters. "Bloody Mary, Bloody Mary, Bloody Mary." That was ten, and Maddy screamed, just once, before the cheering from outside stopped completely. That horrible slithering sound was everywhere, coming from every direction. They were inside the gym. They were inside the gym.

(She was really going to die. No last minute reprieve. No third-act hero. She was going to die with her Fighting Pumpkins cheer pants on, and she wouldn't even get one of those stupid yearbook memorials, because there was no one left to write it.)

"Bloody Mary." Eleven. The mirror was definitely getting blurry, and it definitely wasn't tears. "Bloody Mary." She could almost see the face behind her own, and oh, God, if she was going to stop, it had to be now, but how could she stop, when she'd heard the squad gunned down, and the slithering just kept getting closer? Alien or evil ghost-witch-woman from inside the mirror?

Bloody Mary might be evil. But this was homecoming weekend, and on the Planet Earth, she by-God had the home team advantage.

"BLOODY MARY!" Bridget shouted, abandoning all pretense of quiet. "BLOODY MARY, I KILLED YOUR SON!"

She only saw Mary for an instant as she lunged out of the mirror, hands hooked into claws and descending toward Bridget's eyes. Then came the searing pain, and she was falling, candle wax covering her hand in a spray of burning droplets. Her head slammed against the tile floor hard enough that she heard bone cracking.

"Go Pumpkins," Bridget whispered, as the sound of the blasters started up again. A new sound came with it, dentist's-drill sharp and inhuman. She smiled despite the pain as she realized what it was. The sound of aliens, screaming. "Gimme a 'B'…"

Bridget kept cheering in a whisper as she bled to death on the bath-room floor, not caring that there was no one left to hear her. The sound of Bloody Mary laughing and the screams of the aliens stood in well for the roar of the crowd. She died with her cheer pants on, knowing to the last that she'd done what every cheerleader dreams of.

She'd cheered the home team to victory.

SEAFOAM

Mark Henry

I showed up at the 49th Street Annex prepared to take a verbal beating from Klein and the rest of the Weekday Obsessives—they go after relapses like dogs on dead pheasant. Normally, after I screwed up, it'd take the group a few sessions to figure it out, but this time I couldn't hide what I'd done. There was no way. The thick pads of white gauze and bandages started just beneath my elbows and grew to ridiculous cartoonish mitts where my fists should be, a couple of conversation pieces if there ever was.

"You get into a fight or somethin', Jer?" Klein's pipe reeked of seaweed. The smoke wrapped around his face like an Eskimo's furry hood.

"Nope." I nodded to Fatty, who oddly enough wasn't a member for his clear problem with food, but because he couldn't stop counting. He'd count everything and probably knew how many floorboards were beneath the circle of chairs, definitely how many Oreos were left in their little plastic cells. He shook an extra cigarette from his pack and stuck it between my teeth, lit it.

"Thanks, man," I said.

"So you gonna tell us what happened or what?" Fatty leaned back in his creaking metal chair, his fleshy palpate drifting out from under his shirt and over the front of the seat like an apron. "Inquiring minds wanna know."

"Yeah, Jer." Klein grinned. "What he said."

I took a drag, let the cigarette dangle from my lip and started.

"Remember Beverly?"

Three months ago, Al Graibel, my self-proclaimed P.O. with a P.A. —which is not short for personal assistant, in this case—referred me to this lousy twelve-step group as part of his release maintenance plan. By referred, I mean he threatened me with a revocation if I didn't show up and stare down Dr. Klein and his neuters daily. With no intention of going back to the can simply 'cause Al got a bug up his ass, I went. A week after I started, I had a little relapse that came with a warning from my pierced friend.

A month after that, she showed up.

She sat in the shadows at first, a single leg, green as the sea jutting into the cone of light framing the group in the smoky auditorium. Her high-heeled mule balanced on the pad of her foot like a worm on a hook. She was silent the first two days then, on the third, just as Klein got in gear haranguing me about making a habit of sabotaging my recovery—a habit, like it's a new addiction, trading up, I'm sure he thought—she leaned forward, dark hair falling off her shoulders in waves.

"I'm Beverly." Her voice was crushed velvet, falling off her tongue and up my arms, the lightest fingertips. Gooseflesh rose, something else too, but you don't need to know that.

Everyone knew what she was the minute she left the shadows. The tint of her leg could be explained away as a trick of the light, but the neck scars where her gills used to be stood out like…well, gills.

She was a Beneather. Though they'd started going by 'Neather and that doesn't much matter 'cause she was beautiful, but I'll tell you anyway.

The 'Neathers rose from the trenches and faults under our oceans nearly ten years ago now, showed up on the shores of just about everywhere, a thousand deep and with just as many problems. They used to look more fishlike than they do as though they're mimicking us the longer they're above water. I suppose that's exactly what they're doing. Can't blame them, who doesn't want to fit in?

Took them a couple of years to develop an audible language but after they did, you couldn't shut them up. Not that you could tell it from how quiet Beverly kept.

I never imagined the aliens would show up any other way than in big metal saucers or some shit. The fact that they were here all along and just too deep under the water for us to realize was creepy as hell. And not just to me.

A moment after she introduced herself was the last time we saw Chet the Paper Eater.

"I'm not sharin' secrets with no squid," he said, and stomped out of the room.

Klein started to protest, but then must have thought better and just waved as Chet slammed the auditorium door behind him. I can't say I missed the guy. It was nice to have an intact napkin to set my donut on, or one that wasn't wet with saliva.

Beverly didn't offer up anything that night, but kept coming, each time in a sexy pair of high heels. It got to the point I didn't notice the hue of her flesh, not with her ankle popping.

The most she ever said was, "I have a bit of an addiction problem that I'm working on to the best of my ability."

"Is the group helping any, do you think?" asked Klein.

She nodded.

Right after that session, I was leaving and barreled into her like some clumsy ox, or Fatty or something, which is completely unfair—I have no idea whether Fatty is clumsy, but I certainly was.

"Excuse me, Beverly. I'm so sorry." I held onto her arms till she gathered her balance.

"It's really not a problem, Jerry." She pulled her arms back and hugged her wool coat around her.

"It's Jeremy, actually. Klein calls me by the wrong name on purpose. He knows it bugs me. Said he likes to keep me on edge so I'll be quicker to learn new strategies of coping." I laughed. "It makes absolutely no sense, whatsoever.

"And it's rude." She pursed her lips. "He should be taught a lesson."

"He should," I agreed, I think I even chuckled.

She smiled and bared teeth as shiny and iridescent as Mother of Pearl, an aurora.

"Listen," I said. "Do you want to get some coffee? I meant seaweed tea. Of course, I mean tea."

The 'Neathers were masters of evolution but couldn't stomach certain chemicals, caffeine being one of them. Kind of ironic considering my favorite coffee shop, The Pot Authority, was owned by one of the seafolk, a guy named Bill Sutcliff, serves Cuban coffee in little cups with stirrers shaped like cigars that you select from a wooden box.

I loved that place, still do.

We sat at a table by a sweaty window, a fake flower veiled in dust poked from a Pellegrino bottle and fingerprints dotted the lacquered surface like a pattern. Soft jazz filtered in from ceiling speakers, but the whirring of the blender and hissing of the milk steamer were the real music of the place.

"What did you do, Jeremy?" she asked.

"Huh?" I glanced at her foot—a mere inch from my own—not noticing her eyes had followed mine. I blushed as she arched one feathery brow.

"Klein refers to your issues..." Beverly wrapped the word in air quotes, "Like he would if he meant jail."

I startled a bit. In all those days, listening from the shadows, she'd been paying attention. To me.

"Public indecency. Made the mistake of filling my bladder full of beer nowhere near a bathroom. Cop started yelling at me the second I started to go and didn't let up until long after I'd left a wet line up his state trooper trousers." I chuckled. "Boy was he mad."

I waited.

Then it came. A smile curled on her lips first, then Beverly's hoarse little laugh, somewhere between a whine and sigh, came in curt but pleasant barks.

Then I was calm.

She'd bought the tale, hook, line and sinker. Didn't know a thing about who I really was. I'd practiced that speech a hundred times, complete with the flinching humility and the little nods of acceptance. It sure beat telling her, or anyone, that I was famous.

Or infamous, I guess.

People around here use the story to frighten each other, kids mostly.

"Heard the story of The Licker?" they'd ask.

Everyone has, but you never know which version, so you say, "Nope."

Then they'd go on to tell you about the teenage girl who's home alone with her dog, parents away for the weekend or something. She either gets a phone call, or watches a news story or hears a radio report about an escaped murderer on the loose. She locks her house like a good little girl and goes to call for the dog but he doesn't come, so she leaves the little floppy pet door unlocked and settles into bed to read a book. She drifts off and, later, feels the dog's familiar breath on her feet, its tongue lapping her soles happily, as it always does, alerting her to its return. She pulls away and turns off the light for the night. In the morning, the first thing she sees is the dog's battered and bloody body hung from the door knob, or a nail in the wall or something and on the dresser mirror, or wall, or wherever, written in the dog's blood, or lipstick, depending on who tells it, the words "Humans lick, too. "

That's me.

I'm The Licker.

Only the story is a little exaggerated, like most. For one, I'm no murderer, never even been in a fight. The police were after me on theft, got a little sloppy with the cuffs and I bolted.

Two, I love dogs. I would never hurt one. That girl's pooch was more than happy to gnaw on a raw t-bone while I squeezed through its dog door and locked him out (and, no, it wasn't cold out, so don't even worry about that).

Other than that, it's pretty accurate.

I licked her feet. It's my thing. Doesn't hurt anybody and I'd have been perfectly happy to be up front about it and ask Susan Charlette, the girl, if I could simply clean off her feet with my tongue, if that were an acceptable thing to do in today's society. It's not my fault people have hang ups, now, is it?

Just thinking about it made my mouth fill up with saliva. I swallowed and shot a glance at Beverly's feet.

"That is ridiculous. There's no doubt the officer who cited you has urinated out of doors. Silly." She smiled and sipped at her tea. A bulb of seaweed floating in it like a marshmallow bumped her upper lip, and she giggled sweetly.

"You've got a little sea foam." I pointed to her lip, where it clung.

She blotted it and smiled.

"Why are you attending the Wednesday Obsessives? I mean, if you don't mind me asking."

Beverly set the cup down and looked at her watch. "I guess we have time." She cringed. "I have a bit of a shopping addiction."

"Shopping?" I whistled. "That could get expensive."

"Especially with what I shop for." She smiled and tilted her hips, uncrossing and crossing her legs so that her foot was clearly in view. "Shoes."

"Shoes," I gulped.

"Shoes. I know it's silly, isn't it? Ten years ago I wouldn't have even considered applying a piece of leather to my feet, but now that we 'Neathers are out of the trenches..." Her words trailed off and she reached across the table to touch my hand, fingers brushing across mine. "Oh, it is silly, isn't it?"

I forced myself to look at her eyes, my cup, the couple at the table across the coffee shop, anywhere but those high-heeled shoes and the tiny cleavage of toe above the leather point. "Uh, no. I don't think so."

"Well, it is." She gathered her purse from the floor and stood up, extending her slender green hand. "It was nice talking. We should do it again sometime."

I slipped my hand into hers and felt her tense as if I'd shocked her with static electricity, only I hadn't felt a zap, figured it was a 'Neather thing and let it go.

Her smile blossomed, and a jaundiced flush drifted across her cheeks.

"That was the first night I followed her."

"You followed her?" Dixon slid to the edge of the folding chair, resting his elbows on his knees, mouth still open from the last word. The rail-thin mechanic was always on the verge of a relapse. Hanging around the front windows of department stores ogling mannequins. Most of the mall security guys knew him, called him the doll baby. I don't feel entirely comfortable explaining why.

"You know what I've said about cues, Jerry." Klein tapped a pen against his clipboard. "Your story is full of them, though for the life of me I can't remember a call coming in from you. The steps only work if you work 'em."

The rest of the group nodded their agreement.

"You wanna hear this or not?" I pointed one of my cottony fists in his direction.

"I do," Fatty said, shoving a donut in his mouth.

"Me too," said Rosa the Internet addict from behind her lapful of knitting. I was glad to see her working at the scarf, her nervous pointing and clicking on her thigh bugged the shit out of me. "Go ahead, Jer."

Klein crammed the pen in his maw with a grating scrape and nodded.

I hung back in the alcove of the coffee shop's door, waiting until Beverly turned the corner before darting up the street after her. She was nearly to 23rd when I peeked around the building, and to 24th by the time I slipped behind the column in front of the Venture Bank.

The streets were quiet and few cars spoiled the sound of her heels clicking against the concrete, jumping the shallow puddles of rain with loud clops. Her every movement reminded me of her exquisite feet, the sharp curves of tendons and muscles straining just under the supple flesh, and nails painted and slick, or so I imagined—I couldn't recall ever seeing her toes, just the clefts, those dark mysterious creases. I wiped a bead of drool off on my sleeve.

Beverly lived in a three-storey row house on Winston, a big brick monster with a black door and matching black awnings over the first floor windows. She looked around before she dug in her purse for her keys, jingling them in her fingers before letting herself in and closing the door behind her.

I waited a moment, watching for her to flick on the lights, for those eyes to open onto the street. I watched the first floor windows intently, but it was a window on the third that lit up.

Blood red.

And as soon as it turned on, it was gone. I stayed about twenty minutes longer, sitting on a stoop a few houses down and building a castle of cigarette butts between my feet and a sore, tarred throat.

That was the first time.

"Jesus, Jer. How many times you follow that squid?" Klein asked, jotting notes or doodling or whatever it was he did on that clipboard of his.

"I don't know." I spat the cigarette from my mouth and ground it into the floor with my heel. "Ten. Twelve, maybe."

"That's sick, man." Fatty said, grinding his teeth. "Why not eleven? You couldn't even say it, could you?"

I nodded, didn't want to get Fatty riled, he took his numbers seriously, after all. "Maybe it was eleven times. You could be right."

"One, two, three..." Fatty counted out the numbers to eleven, though his voice fell into mumbles with a mouthful of jelly donut, raspberry dribbling down his chin like gore.

Klein coughed a wad of spit into his fist and stood up. He sauntered across to the refreshment table and snatched a napkin, wiping the phlegm off with a scowl. "Why is it you're telling me this, exactly?"

"Thought we were supposed to be honest here, Klein. You want me to be honest, don't you?"

Klein slouched back into his chair glaring. "Yeah. Honest. Keep goin'."

Two pieces of my puzzle were in place—the feet and the location— only one piece left on the table, I had to figure out how to get in there. I didn't figure Beverly had a dog door. Didn't seem like a dog person, maybe cats, something that didn't require a lot of care. What she did have was an alley.

It took some doing, but I managed to get to the top of a cinderblock wall and scout out the back garden of the townhouse, a little yard and a set of wooden stairs that led to a backdoor with a little curtained window that looked promising.

The next week we went for coffee again.

"Do you like these?" She twisted her foot in the air, the heels on her new shoes were black but the soles were red, almost fuchsia. "Christian Louboutins. Aren't they gorgeous?"

"You don't come to group any more," I said, admiring her foot, the shoe.

"I don't, do I?" She smiled.

"No."

"I think it's sometimes healthier to give in to temptation." She picked up her tea and sniffed it, looked at me through the steam. "Otherwise, Jeremy, what's the point of living at all?"

Klein had told me in that first week of joining the Weekday Obsessives that my issue wasn't that I was obsessed with feet, but that I depersonalized. I could focus on that one part of a woman's anatomy so intently that the rest of her went away, the blood stopped flowing beneath the skin, it turned to art, stone, into an object. I supposed he was right.

I knew he was right.

I went over the wall that night, crossed the garden as quietly as I could and busted the little window out, the whole time hoping it wasn't dead bolted, or if it was, had the key sticking out of the lock like people do when they think they're safe in their own homes.

It wasn't a deadbolt and I was over and in before the glass hit the floor, though that's an exaggeration, obviously.

I stood in the small kitchen and waited. Listening for the sounds of a house asleep, clocks ticking, wood settling in the humidity, refrigerator humming, and air whistling through the vents. Moonlight shone through the windows and caught on row upon row of seaweed bulbs hanging from a rack instead of pans, filling the air with salt and sludge and the faint smell of fish.

Satisfied that Beverly was asleep, I crept through the first floor to the stair hall and took the steps two at a time, always at the edges, never the center where I'd be sure to hit a weak spot and split a creak through the air as loud as a cat screech.

At this point, you're probably figuring that rap the cops had on me back in my Licker days was probably dead on and you'd be right, a thief's a thief and the skills don't go away, they just get used for other purposes.

I listened again at the second floor landing.

This time a slow roll of waves added to the quiet sough. A noise machine, I figured; most of the 'Neathers couldn't sleep without them. Beverly would be no exception. It sounded like it was coming from the back of the third floor. I figured I was right, as I rounded the banister on the third landing and heard those waves crashing louder from the furthest doorway, open as it was. On the opposite side toward the front of the house, another door, the one to the red room, I presumed, was closed and, oddly enough, padlocked.

I looked at the floor, expecting to see a carpet but was met with shiny hardwood. I'm pretty sure I flinched. Hard wood, especially old wood such as Beverly's squeaked something fierce and you never could tell where it would be the worst.

They smelled of orange oil and rubber, but creaked less snaking across them with my whole body. The closer I crouched toward it, the more I imagined the woman's feet padding across it, pressing her essence into the grooves, pivoting, grinding it in.

I pulled myself forward, slipping across the threshold and into Beverly's dark bedroom. Her breathing was soft and faint, a pale whistle of life in an otherwise still space. The ocean sounds were louder there, and in the distance of the recording, seagull caws, undercurrent rolls.

It was quite soothing.

The bed had no footboard and I wondered why I'd imagined one there. It was a cheap metal bed frame, but Beverly had applied care to her decorating, covering the box springs with a coordinating sheet. It was funny what you noticed crawling around on the floor of someone else's home.

I began to rear up, lifting myself off my belly to get a better look, and when I did, like a miracle, Beverly's foot flounced from under the comforter and dangled into the air to the side of the mattress. I had to clamp a hand across my mouth to keep from crying out.

The foot's every curve and hollow was like fine statuary. Important. Its toes, the most perfect semblance of ovals ever assembled. Like five green sweet peas lined up in an open shell. I realized my breath was quickening, heaving, and steeled myself, holding it for a moment to calm down before the excitement bolted through me to my groin and I ended up pole vaulting straight off that floor.

I pushed myself forward until I was inches away and sniffed. The sea. Sweat. Street grime. Something else. Something sweet. My jaw unhinged, my tongue lolled and I began to feel faint. I touched the tip of my tongue to her heel, to her Plantar Fascia to be exact, and tasted everything I'd smelled and more.

Her foot was cold and damp and twitched as I slid the whole of my tongue along its arch, fluttered around the soft pillows of her toes. I surrounded the big toe with my cheeks dragging on it, suckling it like a nipple.

Ecstacy.

Without even realizing I'd passed out, I regained consciousness in a room the color of blood, the carpet was red too, so I figured it was the one I'd passed on the way to Beverly's bedroom, the blood red flicker from the street. It took a moment to realize I'd been restrained while I was passed out, before my eyelids broke free of their crusts. I was stuck to a straight-backed and rather uncomfortable chair by wide military-style belts, double notched and tight, my wrists strapped to the arms with the kind of rubber tubing heroin addicts tie-off with.

"Beverly?" I asked, and immediately heard movement behind me, the back of her hand on my cheek.

"Hello, Jeremy." She walked around to the front of the chair and grinned. "I was hoping that you'd come, but I wasn't sure if it was really you creeping through my house in the middle of the night."

She was talking like she'd set this whole thing up.

"Really? Me? What are you talking about?" I grinned awkwardly, shaking my head from side to side too quickly.

"Oh, Jeremy." Beverly tilted her head and leaned in clutching my jaw and stopping my nervous tic dead. "You're special and you know it. We actually have a lot in common, you and I."

I pulled against the straps. "Are these really necessary, Beverly?"

She ignored the question. "You see, I'm not really a shopping addict." She glanced down at my hands, ran her fingers across my wrists, the straps, tickled the tops of my fingers until the tiny hairs on them stood on end. "I love hands."

I saw her expression, then the drugged haze of her eyelids, the tip of her tongue protruding from between her evergreen lips.

She was in heaven.

My mind traveled back to our first meeting, her foot protruding into the light like a scout, her stories of shoes, her ankle popping, the blatant obviousness of the seduction.

I was the fool.

I was the prey.

"When I heard you shuffling in the hallway, I knew I'd found you and then, when you licked my foot…" Her eyes closed and her mouth spread open in an ecstatic smile. "I thought I couldn't wait. I thought I'd touch you then and there. Put you in my mouth."

"I'm not going to lie to you Klein…" I nodded to the man and looked him square in the eye. "Sitting there tied up and just barely comprehending what the hell was going on, when she said those words I was like instantly aroused. It didn't matter to me that she'd trapped me. For a second, I thought it was the answer. This woman who really got me, 'cause she knew what I went through everyday. She had the same struggles."

"Sounds perfect, except…" he said.

"Yeah," I said. "Except…"

"Go on." Klein's eyes narrowed suspiciously.

Biting the end of one of the bandages, I began to unravel the mitt on my right hand, circling it off with the same motion a carnie employs to collect cotton candy, though there'd be no sweetness at the end of this tale.

None at all.

Beverly crouched in front of me, her eyes level with the tips of my fingers. "You're The Licker. I thought you were an urban legend, one of those stories." Her eyebrow arched. "And then I dug a little deeper. Got the help of some research librarians, newspaper microfiche, the Internet. I was so happy the night we went for coffee. Nearly skipped all the way home. Might have…" she glanced up at my face. "If I didn't suspect you were following me."

"I was," I agreed, nodding. What was the point of lying to someone like Beverly, those green eyes like mirrors of my own.

She touched the tips of my index fingers with hers. "You have lovely fingers, Jeremy. Can you ball them into fists for me, I love the way a fist looks, too." She giggled excitedly.

I clenched them for her into thick solid balls and her head lolled on her shoulder, she sighed.

"You can let me out of this chair, Beverly. I'll let you do whatever you want with my hands. You can touch them, hold them…lick them, even."

I thought I was being enticing, and I'm certain I saw a shiver roll through her at the idea but she stood instead and paced the room. It was then I remembered the feeling of light-headedness that hit me the moment I tasted the sweet sea foam of sweat on her skin.

Drugged.

Beverly was toxic or something. Like one of those Japanese puffer fish that kill an unspecified number of people in sushi restaurants every year. If she licked me wouldn't I pass out again? Maybe die this time?

"Wait a minute, Beverly. You drugged me!" I shouted.

She shrugged sweetly, her face apologetic. "I did. I'm so sorry, Jerry."

"It's Jeremy!" I screamed, panicked.

She was looking at my fingers again, dreamy. She lifted her eyes to mine. "Hmm?"

"You're not sorry." I pulled against the straps, the rubber tubing, bucking in the chair, hoping to unsettle it, bust it apart, get out of there. But it didn't move. Not an inch.

"I'm not?" She asked, rolling up her sleeves. "I'm not sorry?"

Blistered bubbles of milky fluid sat atop her flesh like rows of lime candy dots.

Beverly ran her fingers across the tops of them and a few began to pop, sink in and dribble tiny rivulets of foam down her arms. She moved toward me.

"No. You're not. What are you doing, Beverly?" My heart was beating out of my chest. I was certain she was planning to kill me.

But as I opened my mouth to protest some more, she rushed forward and pressed her arm up to my lips, the fluid burst from her, spraying my face, up inside my nostrils and across my tongue. Filling me with a sour fishiness.

I gagged. Choked on the sea foam in my throat.

She backed away, picked up a towel from a nearby dresser, and rubbed her arms dry. "It's not really a poison, Jeremy. It's more like medicine. It'll just make you sleepy as can be."

Her voice was as sweet and velvety as the first time I heard it.

She crouched in front of me, eying my fingers with what I realized for the first time wasn't lust. It was something else. Against my will, my eyelids started to droop.

Beverly reached up and dabbed a thin bead of drool from the corner of her mouth.

It was hunger.

"I must have passed out because the last thing I remember was her opening her mouth wide, those teeth shimmering and sharp. She hovered a moment and held my ring finger between hers and then snapped down on it, ravenously. "I'd nearly finished unrolling the bandage for the group and when it fell away, followed by the thick pads of gauze pink with blood, the gasps were audible.

"Jesus Christ Jerry," Klein said, face screwed up with disgust.

I held out my fingerless fist to the group, swollen and bruised. Black knots of stitching protruded from each oozing knuckle like spider legs reaching out of the seafoam green infection that settled there.

"I'd show you the other one, but I think you get the idea."

"It's not so bad," a man in a loud bowling shirt said, flinching. Relatively new to the group, Mellon proved himself a compulsive liar in the first minute. "Lots of chicks dig that kind of thing." And a sex addict.

Klein lit his pipe and grimaced. "I'm gonna have to talk to Al about this."

"I'm countin' on it," I said.

"Not bad at all." Fatty agreed, putting his donut back onto his dry napkin and kicking it behind the leg of his chair. I thought I heard him counting the stitches.

"It's definitely fine." Rosa had dropped her knitting into her basket and clicked an imaginary mouse against her thigh.

Dixon's eyes were wide open, fingers up against a store window that wasn't there. He chewed at his lip. "When it heals it'll be as smooth as plastic, you'll see."

"Yeah sure, Dixon." I turned to the group leader, "And, Klein, when you talk to Al..."

The man shook his head, looked away.

"Tell him to put me away for a long time. A very long time."

The Last Stand of the Ant Maker

Paul Jessup

1

When Benjamin was a little boy he painted things. Mostly small things. Like tiny houses. Or dinosaur kits. Or invisible men. He liked using the small brushes. Painting tiny, intricate details.

His hand would cramp up by the end of the day. Painful. Claw shaped. He liked the way this felt. It felt like a good day's work. He would line up his tiny pieces of art and look at them. Hand clawed up. Smiling. His room smelling of paint fumes.

He didn't have any friends. He didn't like to read, watch television, play video games. In school he daydreamed about painting. His teachers thought he was slow. He didn't go near anyone. Could not relate to them.

His mind focused on his hobby. It was all consuming.

2

You would think that an older Benjamin would be different. That he would work, joke around with colleagues. Go to the bar after a hard day at the office. Hit on the waitresses. Make jokes. Get married, even. Have a few kids, even. Forget all about painting.

It actually got worse. His mother died. Cancer. Isn't it always? After that he got the house. All paid off. He only worked when he needed food. And that he bought in cans by the truckload.

He rarely had to work. Instead, he painted. His obsession had gotten more distinct. More of a laser point in the darkness. Ants.

At first he bought model kits through the mail. Ordered them on the internet. That wasn't enough. He began to make his own. Taking apart pieces of his house. Tearing off chunks of wall. Chiseling off chunks of concrete steps. Making little ant bodies, little ant heads. His fingers cramping. Always cramping. As he molded. As he painted.

He would sit in his basement. A can of fruit open on his lap. A spoon resting plainly. Fine and tiny brush pushed into cramped claw fingers. Painting. Intricate designs. War ants. Love ants. Fire ants. Fire-fighter ants. Giant ants. Tiny ants. Shaman ants. God of the ants.

The basement was filled with ants. It was like his own ant farm. Made large.

3

He made highways for them. Byways for them. All the while not noticing that the plants grew outside of his basement window. Not no-ticing the yellow spores covering it. Tapping against it. Like fingers. Rat -tat tapping.

He built ant houses. Ant shrines. Ant cities on an ant hill. Ant bon-fires. Ant beaches. And ant graveyards for those who died during the great ant civil war.

Eventually, he had to go upstairs and find supplies. To make more ants. To make more houses, homes, tunnels. To enhance the life of those he created. He was a good god. A good maker. A benign and loving deity. Whenever an ant died, he wept. They died frequently. Of war, of plague. The ant doctors and the ant scientists tried to stop it. To hold back death.

Not even he could do that. Not even the ant maker could hold off death.

4

There was a girl. Isn't there always? She was eighteen when he first met her. She moved in. Next door. With her husband, Gary. Gary drove a truck. Ate baked beans from a can. She was pregnant. Always preg-nant. Although they never seemed to have any kids.

Benjamin knows he would've noticed kids. Kids are loud. Kids de-stroy. They would've gotten into his house. Gotten to his ants and killed them. Killed them all. He would've had to make a mass grave. One the size of his whole backyard.

Thankfully, they did not have kids.

The girl's name was Emily. She had short black hair. Benjamin thought she was pretty. Every once in a while, she would be bored. Come over and try to talk to him. To make conversation. Benjamin wasn't good at conversation.

All he wanted to do was talk about his ants. She didn't seem to mind. And she was pretty. Benjamin liked her.

5

He didn't like Gary. Her husband drank. A lot. Called Benjamin "That fucking 'tard monkey next door." He would pat his round stomach. Scratch his bearded face. Belch. Laugh.

No, no. Benjamin didn't like him.

6

Benjamin liked lists. Lists and ants and Emily. Lists were perfect. Were cathartic. They helped him organize. He had boxes of lists. Shoved throughout the house.

One list he had was very important. It was a daily list. Each day, marked down. Day, month, year. And beside it was an observation. One that bothered Benjamin.

The plants were growing.

It bothered him so much that he only took notice of it once a day. First thing in the morning. Before the sun came up. When the plants were still sleeping. He would look out the windows. Measure them with his eyes. Mark down their height on his list.

Then he would be back making ants.

7

Emily was a gardener. When she would stop by to talk to Benjamin she would have dirt on her hands. Under her nails. Sweat on her brow. Sometimes, she would bring him food. Garlic. Things of that sort. Grown in the garden.

Benjamin kept a list of what she brought over. Kept a list of the days she dropped by. He checked the list yesterday. It had been two weeks.

That made Benjamin sad. That made Benjamin worry. It didn't last long. He added new notes to the lists. Put them in their shoe boxes. Shelved them away. Began working on the ants.

Something smelled funny in the air. He pulled out a box of allergy masks he kept in the basement. Next to the lists. And the dead ants. Strapped it to his face. Breathed easier.

Back to work.

8

Emily dropped by. But this time it wasn't Emily. But it was. She was very pregnant. Yet she wasn't. Her eyes were full of green fluid. Leaking onto her cheek. Her face was spotted. Cracking. Her hair had vines wrapped up in the blonde curls. When she smiled, Benjamin saw leaves behind her teeth.

They talked like they usually did. About the usual things. Benjamin talked about ants. She talked about gardening. About having a baby. A boy, this time. She was sure of it. Maybe Gary would let this one live? She didn't know. Won't know until afterward.

Benjamin felt like something was off. Something was different about her. She was pretty, still, yes. But she was greener. And smelled of wet earth and mushrooms growing in a cave.

When she left Benjamin was sad. He hadn't been sad since his mom had died. Cancer.

9

The ants weren't coming together. They were falling apart. Each piece, sliding. Damn it. He slammed them. Broke the pieces. This wasn't going right. He took his brush. Walked out of the basement. Upstairs.

This wasn't going right at all. He felt dizzy. His hands shook. A yellow pollen fluttered in the air. Like a mist. In his living room. He looked around. Saw that his living room had changed.

No, no, no. Not today. Why did this have to happen today? He wasn't finished yet. Not yet. Why couldn't this wait until he was finished?

10

He made a list of things wrong with the living room.
The television is dead. Spiders in it.
Vines on the ceiling. Floor.
Plants burst through windows. Bushes.
Red berries on the bushes. Poisonous?
Ceiling covered in bugs.
Yellow spores.
Door is gone. Replaced by wall of roses.
Thorns on roses. Ouch. Blood.
Smells bad.

11

He wore his allergy mask. It helped him breathe better. Now that he could breathe he could work. Still dizzy, just not so much. Made more ants. They needed an ant army. Invaders. Plant invaders. Coming. Attacking.

We need a militia. Seven thousand strong. Will have to recruit civilians. Shamans. Priests. Firefighters. Ant families and ant children. This was a call of duty. A call to honor.

He fell asleep. Paintbrush in hand. Army at the ready.

12

Doorbell. Woke him. Stumbled upstairs. Paint covered hands. Clawed. Allergy mask on. Looked like survivor. Wanted to survive. The pollen was still there. Made walking hard. Like swimming.

He answered the rosebush. Ouch! Thorns. Forgot about those. It was Emily. Beautiful. Skin greenish blue. Eyes no longer leaking. But blossoming. Two flowers for eyes. Leaves sticking out of her hair. When she talked her voice sounded burbly. Like she was underwater. Or lungs full of water. Or drowning. Benjamin did not know which.

"Come outside," she said. "See the sun."

Benjamin looked behind her. There was no sun. Just pollen blotting it out. The world was a haze of yellow. Plants were everywhere. Pushing through concrete. Covering houses. Buildings. Cars.

"No thank you," he said. "I don't like the sun."

She smiled. So pretty.

"Come on, we can play. We can sing, we can dance. You can help me garden. We can catch bees and pollinate ourselves. Doesn't that sound nice?"

Benjamin liked that. Wanted that. But the ants were not finished. The army was not finished. He could not forget about the invasion. It was important. He shook his head. "The army needs me," he said. "My children need me."

She parted her lips. Like plums. "You can kiss me,"s he said. "I know you would like that. Come on, kiss me. Take that mask off. Kiss me. You can even cop a feel if you'd like. Gary wouldn't mind. Just take the mask off. Kiss me."

Benjamin began to pull the mask down. Was leaning in. Almost taken off. When he saw a yellow spider crawl out from between her lips. Scale up her face. Make a web between her two eye flowers.

He kept his mask on. This isn't Emily, he thought. Emily did not have spiders inside of her. Baby, yes. Spiders, no.

"Fine," she said. "I'll send Gary around. Maybe he can talk some sense into you."

Benjamin didn't like that. She slammed the rosebushes in his face. Stormed off. Even though she wasn't Emily he still didn't like making her sad. Or mad. It didn't sit well with him.

Depressed, he went back inside. Went downstairs. Continued to work.

13

There is never an entry for 13. It is unlucky.

14

The ant army was close to being finished. But not just yet. His hand cramped. He needed to hurry. The basement was the only room in the house still safe. Still uninfected. His hand itched as it clawed up. Itch, itch, itch. Felt like something crawling, growing under his skin.

He took some medicine. But the itch did not stop. The pain did not stop. He would have to be done painting for now. Building for now. He couldn't work. Not like this.

15

The rooms in the house infected with the garden:
Living Room
No room to walk anymore
Even the floor is covered in weeds
Insects everywhere
Buzzing.
Kitchen
Stove is now a rhododendron
Lilacs in the Frigidaire
Ceiling fan filled with vines
Second Floor Bedrooms
Beds are trees. Cracking through ceiling.
Floor is moss. Green. Fuzzy.
Bookshelves are moldy.
Books are gone. Eaten by insects.
Attic
No more attic. Just lattice of branches

16

There was a scratching at his basement window. Like a cat wanting to come in. Benjamin looked up. Saw a branch. Scratch, scratch, scratch. The doorbell rang.

Damn it, he thought. Almost finished. If only his hand had stopped itching. Stopped hurting. Stopped moving on its own. And now, now. His arm itched. His eyes itched. His lips and mouth itched.

He scratched, scratched, scratched. Even though it hurt. I don't want to answer the door, he thought. I don't want to prick myself on the rosebushes again.

It rang, it rang. Maybe it was Emily. He would like to see her again. Sigh. Scratch, scratch, scratch. He hoped she was all right.

17

He opened the rosebushes. Gary stood there. His skin was orange. He had flowers in his hair. In his neck. Poking through skin. His fingers were wrapped tightly with vines. His hands tensing. Clenching. Green knuckled. His eyes leaked onto his face. Two buds sticking out. Waiting to blossom.

"Hey, you. Fuckwad. My wife wants you outside. Enjoy the sunlight. Right? Come on. Get out. And take off that fucking mask. It makes you look stupid."

Benjamin looked at him. Gary. Shook his head. "No, no, I don't think so. I like it inside. I like my ants. I need to go and paint some more. Before my hand stops working."

"Come on. Get outside. Fucking idiot."

Hand lashed out, grabbed onto Benjamin's shoulder. Fingers dug deep into shoulder blade. Dragged him outside. Others on the street. Staring. Green skinned. Spider infested. The air wanted to choke him. Even with the allergy mask on.

"Come on, pansy. Take off the fucking mask already. Or do I have to take it off for you?"

Benjamin moved back, shoved Gary's hand off him. Skin was brittle, broke. Bones broke. Smell of rot. Spores flew out from the broken skin. Infecting the air. Little yellow things. Pollen. Dancing.

Beneath his broken skin was vegetation, curled up around bone. Benjamin leaned over. Tried not to vomit. Dry heaved. He looked back up. Gary laughed at him.

"Take off the mask. Or I'll take it off for you."

Benjamin saw a shovel in Gary's hand. Saw it rise up. Going to hit him. Going to hurt him. He moved out of the way. Shovel hit ground. Stuck into it. Gary's skin cracked, broke a little. Vines and leaves peaked out. Pollen spread out.

Benjamin screamed. Ran inside. The others on the street turned. Looked at him. Followed with Gary. Even after Benjamin had slammed the rosebush shut. Even after he had run downstairs. Locked the basement door. Locked himself in.

He had enough canned food to last him a little while. Enough time to make his army. To make a stand against the invasion.

18

Nineteen left to go. Itch, itch. Scratch, scratch. Skin broke. Saw bits of leaves beneath. No, no, he thought. Can't be happening. He kept his mask on. Just in case.

Dizzy. Dizzy. Needed to finish.

A loud bang. On basement window.

He turned. He looked.

No. No. No.

Emily's face. Cold, white, pale. Porcelain. Like a doll. Her teeth parted. Leaves behind them. Leaf tongue. Leaf lips. Leaf uvula. Spiders ran over her face. She was on the ground.

More banging. On the basement door.

No. No. No.

19

Let them come. His army was ready. He was ready. He scratched. Itchity itch itch. It hurt. So much hurt. The army was poised. Ready. Set into fighting formation.

He had a list in his hand. Of all the things he wanted to do before the world died. Kiss a girl. Kiss the sun. Swallow the moon. Go fishing. Become a fish. Not die. Die over and over again. Live. Have something nice for dinner. Have someone nice for to dinner. To breathe again. To be again. Whole again. To raise a family. To raise the dead. To sing one last time. To have a sandwich. To try witchcraft. To burn the world. To be burned. To love. To live. To make something work. Just once. To make it work.

20

Breathe. Breathe. It felt so good to breathe without the mask on. Like breathing underwater. Walking like swimming. He no longer itched. It no longer hurt to paint. To do anything. Pain was distant. A memory. Like his childhood.

He leaned over. Kissed the glass. Where Emily's face was. Smiled. Her head burst. Blood. Pollen. And insects. Inside of her head was a tiny baby. An infant. Made of coiled up vines, and a face that was a flower blossoming. Two tiny eyes stared at him. Was it a boy? Benjamin hoped so. Emily would've been happy if it was a boy.

It crawled up to the window. Placed a hand against it. Benjamin felt connected to it. Wanted to take care of it. Felt something in his own mind. Growing.

He smashed the window. His basement door burst open. Now was the time for war. Now was the time to defend his lists. His sanctuary. His love.

CITY OF REFUGE

Jerry L. Gordon

David watched from behind the crowd, as two men led a young woman up a small set of steps to the hangman's noose. A razor-sharp wire replaced the traditional rope, ensuring a clean decapitation and a bigger spectacle of blood and death. The crowd's palpable sense of anticipation surprised him less than the calm demeanor of the accused. She faced the gallows with such serenity stepping to the noose as if receiving Holy Communion.

The Order's crest pinned to David's putrefying animal hide cloak parted the crowd as effectively as its foul odor. He approached the makeshift structure, sizing up the two men standing on either side of the woman. The tall man in the bowler hat appeared to be in charge, but David focused his steely gaze on the short one with the set jaw. The little man's face erupted with anger at the interruption.

"What can I do you for, Cardinal?" the tall man said, after looking down at the crest pinned to David's rotting coat.

"Bring me the accused."

"What?" the short man exclaimed, stepping forward.

"You heard me, boy."

"She killed my father. I have a right to—"

"Unless you'd like the archbishops cutting off trade to this little haven, you will mind your place." David stroked his unkempt beard, setting his jaw. "Do it. Now."

The man in the bowler hurried the accused forward. On closer inspection, she was more girl than woman. Her tangled black hair and vibrant blue eyes dwarfed her petite nose and mouth. She stood with both hands tied behind her back. Deep bruises marred both sides of her face.

"Are you Jenna, the miller's daughter?"

The girl bowed her head. "Yes, Cardinal."

David produced a handwritten document from a pouch inside his cloak. "You petitioned the archbishops for asylum?"

"Yes, Cardinal."

David handed the document to the short man. "The archbishops have granted Jenna an audience. If her claims are found wanting, she will be returned to you and you can continue," David motioned around, "this exhibition."

"Asylum?" The short man rifled through the document as though he wasn't illiterate like the rest of the peasants. "I've never heard of such a thing."

"It is an unusual request," David admitted, "but one the archbishops have agreed to hear."

"Then I will go with you and speak for my dead father."

"If your testimony is needed, the church will call for you. Until then, there will be no vengeance upon this girl or her family. Understood?"

"Whatever you say, Cardinal," the tall man in the bowler replied, stepping between David and the dead man's son to deliver the girl. "Please give our regards to the archbishops."

David yanked the girl toward him and turned to face the deflated crowd. People looked away, averting their gaze as he brushed past them with his prisoner. Like most havens, this one relied on the church for tools and guns. No one would question the archbishops' judgment.

David's mule grazed on a patch of grass near the front gate, obscured by a cloud of flies. The girl shuddered as she approached the rotting animal skins that covered the beast.

"Will I have to wear a cloak?" she asked, clearly blanching.

"Only if you want to live," David said. "The Fallen may have little interest in this high altitude settlement, but in the lowlands they'll pick your body clean if they think you're alive. Get used to wearing it."

David untied her hands and pulled a long coat of rotting flesh from the mule's saddlebags. The girl vomited twice before she settled into the foul garment. Even then, she retched and gagged uncontrollably. David retied her hands, this time in front of her, and leashed her to the mule with enough slack to allow her to walk.

With a nod to the gatekeeper, the tall wooden doors that protected the enclave parted. David chose to walk at first, leading the mule and his prisoner down a series of treacherous mountain switchbacks.

Here, above the dark clouds, he almost felt safe. As long as the Fallen could sustain themselves in the lowlands, they had no urge to feed in the mountains. For one stray moment he closed his eyes and felt the burn of the sun on his face. One day this will all be gone, he thought. Enjoy it while it lasts.

They reached a small lake halfway down the mountain. David stopped to water the mule and sat down to eat some dried jerky. After a few bites he felt guilty and untied the girl, giving her a small piece of meat.

"Thank you," she said.

David nodded, staring out across the sparkling lake. In his mind, this place could easily double for the Garden of Eden-a place of perfection in a world of death. He rarely entertained religious thoughts, but the lake possessed an untouched quality at odds with the devastation below. It reminded him that there were a few things still unspoiled in this world.

After a long silence, the girl finally spoke. "Aren't you going to ask me what happened?"

"No." David's back popped in three places when he stood. He had the distinct feeling the girl already knew that he did not care. "I'd like to hear more about this city of refuge idea you dreamed up. The archbishops seemed particularly interested in that."

The girl gave him a knowing smile and stood with her arms out, ready to be leashed to the mule. Something about her request had the archbishops up in arms, but they didn't share their thoughts on the matter with him. He buckled the saddlebags and tied her to the beast.

The steep switchback trail opened up, becoming broad and smooth as it descended below the dark clouds. Light rain obscured the twisted remains of a tourist village, nestled in a distant fork of the mountain. From this vantage point it looked deserted, but he knew better.

Giving the old resort town a wide berth, they left the muddy path for a thick canopy of trees. David expected the girl to complain about the never-ending thicket of thorny brambles that scraped, poked, and tore at even the smallest bit of exposed flesh, but she kept her mouth shut. Even the mule seemed mindful of the danger posed by their proximity to the settlement and stayed quiet.

They finally stopped at a dilapidated home in the middle of nowhere. The road leading to the hillside dwelling had lost its battle with the wilderness, and only a small portion of the house refused to yield to the encroaching vegetation. The Fallen had stripped the inside down to its studs, leaving just enough support to keep the house standing.

Almost like they knew exactly what they were doing.

David didn't trouble himself with questions about the Fallen's fascination with the remnants of humanity or the strange cities they built with the material they foraged. Only one thing mattered to him: they seldom returned to gutted buildings. He went from room to room, shotgun ready. With the exception of a few doors and a large, rusting washing machine stored in the back of the basement, the house stood empty. The old Maytag probably weighed too much for the Fallen to have bothered lugging upstairs.

He picked a small room in the damp basement to setup camp. Black mold crept up the back wall, and there was a half-window to contend with, but the room had a solid door he could block with the washing machine. He covered the window with one of his animal skins, lit a small lantern, and went outside to confirm that no light escaped. Satisfied with his handiwork, he fed the mule and stowed it in a windowless bathroom, then he carried the saddlebags downstairs.

The metal appliance mesmerized the girl. She examined every inch of the machine as if it contained some mythical gift from the gods. Whatever the archbishops hoped to get out of her, David sensed she'd disappoint them.

"Do you know what this is?" she asked, running her fingers along the control panel's buttons.

"It's a washing machine. People used them to clean their clothes. We're going to use this one to barricade the door."

She helped him push the old Maytag across the room.

"How old were you at the breaking of the world?" she asked.

"Old enough to wish I hadn't seen it." He shoved the washer one last time before he retired to the concrete floor. "Eleven or twelve."

"That's not very old. How did you survive?"

"My parents were nuts. That's how." He wedged his saddlebags against a corner of the basement and laid his head on the makeshift pillow. Closing his eyes, he hoped the question would die.

"I don't understand."

"Things were different then," David said without opening his eyes. "Not everyone believed in the Catholic Church. You could worship however or whatever you wanted. My parents were part of a group, a cult. They were brainwashed into believing the founder was Christ reborn. They gave up their worldly possessions to help him build a compound and stock it with a ridiculous amount of guns and food. Dad even named me after the son of a bitch."

"I'm sorry."

The saddlebags weren't as comfortable as David hoped. He shifted his weight and opened his eyes. "When the virus started spreading, it was pretty clear our Christ didn't know any more than anyone else. Our group held out longer than most, thanks to our well-armed religious paranoia, but it didn't take long for our fearless leader to decide we all needed to 'walk into God's arms' before the Fallen could take us."

"What did you do?"

"Me? I didn't do anything. I was a scared kid. After my dad watched another family forced into heaven, he tried to get us out of there. Our beloved Christ-on-Earth put a bullet in his back and two in my mom's chest. I'm the only one that got away. I ran...survived."

The girl leaned closer, clutching her dead animal cloak around her. She had adapted to the smell faster than most. "You don't believe in God any more, do you? You're a cardinal. How can you not believe?"

"It doesn't matter what I believe. It only matters that the human race survives. The Catholic Church has managed to keep New Hebron, and a couple other havens, from falling. They saved my life. Who cares if the rest is bullshit? I'm old enough to actually remember the Bible, and I can tell you for a fact it never said anything about the Fallen."

The girl leaned back against the wall. He could see her thinking through his story.

"And this shall be the plague where with the Lord shall strike all nations... the flesh of every one shall consume away while they stand upon their feet, and their eyes shall consume away in their holes, and their tongues shall consume away in their mouth."

"What are you talking about?" he asked.

"Zachariah, chapter fourteen, verse twelve."

"Is that supposed to impress me, some handed-down passage that sounds vaguely biblical? What version of the Bible is that supposed to be from?"

"And he shall snatch on the right hand, and be hungry; and he shall eat on the left hand, and they shall not be satisfied: they shall eat every man the flesh of his own arm." She looked deep into his eyes. "If Isaiah isn't talking about the Fallen, I don't know what he's talking about."

She waited for him to concede the point. When he didn't, she continued, "For since by man came death, by man came also the resurrection of the dead."

David scrambled to his feet. He knew this quote from Corinthians.

"I searched your house and the mill before going to that town square. I didn't find a Bible or any hint of religious material. Who the hell are you?"

"A messenger."

Something about the way she said it shook David to his core. Not because he believed her, but because he had seen the damage brainwashed people could do. He stood over her. "Where did you hide the Bible? Only an archbishop is pure enough to read one."

"There is no Bible." She stood and faced him, unafraid. "My father had something called Asperger's. Said it gave him a photographic memory. He used to have these visions, made me memorize them. He said one day the world would depend on the truth."

David looked for any hint of deception in her face. If it existed, he didn't spot it.

"Your father's supposed to be some kind of prophet then? And what about you? Here to save us all?"

"It's not like that."

"You know what?" David raised his hands in disgust. "I don't care. We've got a long day ahead of us, and I need some sleep. The archbishops can get it out of you." David returned to his saddlebag bed, closed his eyes, and ignored the girl's questions.

That night, he dreamed of the cult leader who shared his name. The false prophet submerged him in a baptismal filled with the blood of his parents. Their dead bodies floated and bumped against the edge of the tank. He pushed and kicked but strong hands held him in their rotting juices. His parents' bodies made a strange sound against the wall of the tank, screeching like metal on concrete. It took him a few seconds to realize the sound didn't belong to his nightmare.

He opened his eyes. The girl had pushed the washing machine away from the old wooden door. He could hear the sound of the Fallen on the other side.

"What are you doing?" he screamed, pulling out his handgun.

"You need proof, and I'm going to give it to you."

"Don't!" He cocked the gun, still not sure he was awake. "Let go of that door, or I'll shoot you dead."

For an instant, David could see fear play across the girl's face. She pulled her hand away from the door but then reached back. He shot her a second too late. The door opened, and in the harsh lantern light, a group of the Fallen stared back at him. With his free hand he reached for the shotgun next to his pack, pumping it on the way back up.

"Don't shoot," the girl yelled, as she clutched her wounded side. "They're not going to hurt you. They're here because I called out to them."

David stood his ground but didn't fire. The Fallen who stood in the doorway looked a little like his grandmother. Dried blood matted her hair, and her face held the slack-jawed appearance of a stroke victim. Something about the old woman lent a sliver of humanity to the maggot-ridden flesh standing behind her.

"Why are they just standing there?"

"Be quiet," she said with some effort while leaning against the doorframe. "I need to concentrate."

A lifetime of silence followed. The Fallen grunted simultaneously, turned their back on the open door, and shuffled their way up the basement steps. David had never seen anything like it. The Fallen didn't let people live.

David closed the door and moved the washing machine back, unable to let go of the ritual. The girl looked to be in bad shape. A dark pool of blood framed her midsection.

"What the hell was that about?" he asked, pulling a shirt out of his saddleback to press against the wound.

"I tried to tell you at the lake…"

Her lips formed the words that would explain, but her voice failed. Somehow, she reached out to him with her mind, giving him a vision of two men stumbling into her and a group of the Fallen by the mountain lake. The older man didn't hold his fire, and she couldn't stop the creatures. Things ended badly for him, but his son managed to escape. The vision faltered as she passed out.

"Welcome back," David said when she opened her eyes again. "I wasn't sure you were going to make it."

He watched her adjust to the new surroundings. It was clear the bunker's electric lights and technology scared her, but she did an admirable job of processing it all.

"The Greenbrier Bunker is the heart of New Hebron. Before the breaking of the world, this place served as a nuclear fallout shelter for Congress." His eyes traced the musty concrete walls. "The infirmary is protected by two feet of solid steel. You are more than safe here."

Her attention shifted back to him. Safely tucked away from the Fallen, he had traded his rotting animal cloak for the deep red vestments of his office as cardinal. Outside of his ceremonial pistol, David looked a far cry from the mountain man who had saved her from the gallows.

"You didn't have to shoot me, you know."

"In my place, would you have done any different?" He reached out to her hand but stopped short of holding it. "As for your injury, I've told the archbishops that we had an accident."

"You didn't tell them the truth?"

"I fear they would take it as a sign you are some kind of devil woman. I may not understand what happened in that basement, but there's no reason to sacrifice you on the altar of misplaced faith. You'll have enough to deal with as it is."

Jenna thought about this for a moment and seemed to come to a decision. She looked around the small infirmary to reconfirm they were alone.

"The things I told you about my father, about his memory of the Bible and his prophecies. He never told me any of it."

"I don't understand."

"My father's visions gave him nightmares. He hid them from me. I looked into his mind to find the truth."

"Is that how you kept them from attacking us?" David asked. "Can you actually talk to them?"

"It's not easy to explain. Their minds are jumbled and cross. There are fragments of desire, glimmers of recognition, but it's all part of a puzzle that doesn't quite fit together. They can communicate with each other but not us. They don't really understand what's happened to them. You've seen the strange cities they're building. They're trying to adapt."

"Why are you telling me this? You know I have a responsibility to take the information to the archbishops." David lowered his voice. "If they find out you're a seer—"

"You will help me because you don't believe." She reached for his sleeve and pulled him closer. "I have written a gospel based on my father's prophesies."

"So you do have a Bible."

"It must not fall into the archbishops' hands, no matter what. You have to promise me you'll keep it safe."

He started to speak, but an image cut his words short. His mind witnessed a tree near a small lake, the same lake they'd stopped at on the first day. Red daises surrounded the exposed roots. The Bible was buried there. The future was buried there. He suddenly felt like he had made a huge mistake bringing Jenna to New Hebron. "I don't understand—"

"Don't understand what?" Archbishop Fletcher asked, as he entered the room.

"How such an innocent girl could be guilty of murder."

"Indeed. That is the question at hand." The archbishop walked to her bedside. "So this is Jenna, the miller's daughter? She doesn't look like a murderer to me. How are you feeling, dear?"

"Better."

Jenna relaxed when the archbishop reached for her hand. His Holiness had a way about him that put people at ease. Far from the traditional aged priest, he was a vibrant man with thick black hair and compelling green eyes. When he smiled, his dark vestments emphasized the effect. In another world, he could have been a movie star.

"The archbishops see occasional requests for leniency, but I must admit we've never received one that quoted actual scripture, much less multiple versions of the Bible." He pulled her request from a vest pocket and cleared his throat. "Whoso killeth his neighbor ignorantly, whom he hated not in time past… he shall flee unto one of those cities and live."

"A city of refuge," she said.

"So I gather." The archbishop leaned closer. "You understand the responsibility that passage places on me?"

"If any man hate his neighbor," she warned, "and rise up against him and smite him mortally… then the elders of the city shall deliver him into the hand of the avenger of blood, that he may die."

"You can quote scripture from memory." The archbishop's eyes widened. "That is truly remarkable. How is it that you have hidden such a miraculous talent?"

"My father had a photographic memory, but he was sick and fearful and hid his gift. He was afraid of what would happen if the church knew the truth."

"And you do not share his fear?"

"I want to live more than I want to keep his secrets."

"Good," the archbishop said. "That shows an evolved understanding of the world. It is true our teachings here sometime diverge from scripture, but we have responsibilities that extend far beyond the old world church. If God's children are to survive, certain deviations from canon are necessary. Don't you agree, Cardinal?"

"I do." David stumbled over the words, his mind catching up with the conversation. He couldn't decide what to make of Jenna's abilities.

He felt compelled to tell the archbishop about the Bible, but something held him back.

"Tell me, child," the archbishop continued, "did your father write down any of his memories?"

"He refused to write them down, but he told me stories every night. Made me memorize them."

"Then we only have you to guide us. With so many denominations lost to the Fallen, a mind like yours is a gift from God. Assuming you are willing to join our fellowship, I feel comfortable speaking for the others. We will grant your request for asylum. Your knowledge is far too important to waste on a question of guilt or innocence."

"You don't need to hear my case?"

"Rest now." The archbishop patted her hand. "Tomorrow we celebrate the Easter Vigil. Before the service, I invite you to join the archbishops for a communion ceremony to cleanse you of the past and prepare you to serve in the Lord's army."

With a smile, the archbishop turned for the door. David couldn't hide his shock. If they were going to offer her communion, she presented a bigger threat than even he imagined. Or did Archbishop Fletcher see it as an opportunity? David wanted more time with Jenna, but Fletcher cleared his throat, reminding him there were preparations to be made.

"Have faith," she whispered. "There are more of us than you know."

Archbishops Thomas and Reynolds stood beside Jenna. The church had provided a white dress for her communion. David waited with the three of them at the roughly hewn entrance to the underground chapel. The level had been added after the archbishops founded New Hebron. He wondered if she had noticed their green eyes. He wondered if she really knew what she was getting herself into.

David had seen what Jenna could do. He wanted to believe in her, but he had seen faith and delusion destroy so many. He went to her in the middle of the night, but she refused to leave. She was determined to see her father's vision through to the end. She talked about a world where humanity could live alongside the Fallen. She talked about her father's certainty there were others with gifts like hers.

A single bell rang out three times, and Archbishop Thomas handed her the Paschal candle. With a deep breath, David moved to the chapel door and opened it. The cavernous space was devoid of any light. Jenna stood with the archbishops on the precipice of the abyss with only a candle to guide her through the rite of Lucernarium.

David watched her walk inside the chapel with the same sense of grace he'd seen when she'd approached the gallows. Her faith was strong enough to bolster some small corner of his own, and for the first time in more years than he could count, he wanted to believe in something greater than himself.

The archbishops accompanied her across the subterranean darkness. They stopped three times on their way to the nave. At each interval, the two men proclaimed, "Christ is the light."

"Deo Gratias," the assembly responded.

David's role was that of gatekeeper. He barricaded the doors and stood guard over the ceremony. If Jenna panicked or tried to run, it was his responsibility to stop her.

As the candlelight approached the sanctuary, David closed his eyes and said a small prayer. When he opened them, he could see her lowering the Paschal candle to the baptismal.

The surface oil ignited, spreading through a series of interconnected channels to illuminate the interior of the chapel. He waited for her to gasp, but she stood her ground, silent. Three full-sized crosses towered over her. One of the Fallen had been nailed to each cross.

Shunts removed infected fluids from the crucified creatures, delivering them to a hidden room behind the nave. How these fluids were processed, David couldn't say. The archbishops did not allow him into that room. The end result, whatever it was, returned to an ornate wooden altar in the form of iridescent green liquid.

Archbishop Fletcher waited for Jenna there, silver chalice in hand. On each side of the altar, a half dozen of his brethren stood, their eyes an identical green. The contaminated liquid had wiped the ravages of age and time away from their perfect bodies, but some profound aspect of humanity had also disappeared with it. They exuded warmth and caring, but David had caught more than a few glimpses of the sociopathic animal lurking just below the surface.

"Life is in the blood," Archbishop Fletcher began, "Jesus gave his mortal life for us, and our drinking of this cup symbolizes our continuous sharing of his restoration."

He filled the cup and brought it around the altar to Jenna. David couldn't see her face, but her body betrayed no fear. As a nonbeliever, he'd nearly wet himself the first time he'd seen the ritual performed. Was it possible she knew what she was doing? Could her lack of surprise denote a plan?

"And Jesus took the cup," the archbishops chanted in unison, "and when he had given thanks, he said, 'Drink of it, all of you: for this is my blood of the covenant which is poured out that you might live forever.'"

She raised the chalice to the three crosses and took a deep drink. David couldn't help himself. He moved closer. He had to know. When she turned to face him, he realized how much he needed to believe in her, in some divine act that could pull humanity out of this twisted abyss.

Jenna's once blue eyes turned a vacant green. He could see that intangible spark disappear as the archbishop's communion coursed through her veins. He suddenly realized her knowledge of the Bible and the Fallen would be used to destroy everything she'd hoped to create. It would be used to hunt down others like her. It would be used to expose him as a co-conspirator and non-believer.

The archbishops converged on Jenna now. They were welcoming her to the world they had carved out between humanity and death. Her father's visions would have told her this was going to happen. Why would she submit herself to the destruction of everything she believed? Why had she trusted him with her vision? She told him she was a messenger. If the message wasn't for the archbishops, then who was it for?

Watching her now, he realized the truth. The message was meant for him.

Before he could question this solemn belief or lose the resolve that came with it, he raised his ceremonial pistol, aimed for her head, and pulled the trigger. Her secrets had to be protected. He turned the gun on the archbishops, not waiting for her to fall to the ground from the fatal head wound. The assembly scattered for the door that he had locked to protect their secret ceremony.

He could feel his future unfold with each pull of the trigger. He would retrieve her gospel. He would travel with it from haven to haven. He would restore the Word of God. He would find others like Jenna and make peace with the Fallen. As the last of the archbishops dropped, he felt certain this had been Jenna's plan all along. She had only been the messenger. It was his responsibility to make her sacrifice mean something.

Moving past the archbishops' bodies, he opened the doors of the underground chapel and took his first steps toward saving the world.

Sol Asleep

Naomi Libicki

Solange looks around nervously, then hoists herself over the metal rim. She wriggles a bit. The coffin is tight. Her eyes point blankly at the ceiling, as she struggles to get her breathing under control. No one is coming in. Marcia promised—Sleepies know Solange has paid her enough. She waits until her breaths come slowly, evenly. She imagines them misting the lid of the coffin, which in reality leans up against the wall, temporarily disabled. Then she closes her eyes. She forces her toes to stop wiggling, her knees to stop jumping. She forces her hands to unclench. Soon she's asleep. She dreams of planets.

It's stupid, but there it is—it's not the pain, or the fear, or the embarrassment of being raped in a tool locker by your younger cousin; it's Mickey's teeth glinting in the low light that Solange can't get out of her mind. So white, she remembers thinking.

She should get back to her dormitory. She's been off-shift for more than an hour. But she's a mess: there's blood at the side of her mouth and down her legs, her smock is torn, and she can't see it but she thinks her face is blotchy with crying. If people see her they'll ask questions, and she doesn't want to have to talk to anyone.

She levers herself to her feet and takes an experimental step. It hurts a bit to walk, but it's not that bad. Looking out the small window in the tool locker door, she can see a woman walking a catwalk above the eucheuma pool and occasionally taking its temperature. Other than that, and a bar of light from Uncle Matt's office, there doesn't seem to be anyone around. Ducking her head, she pushes open the door and heads for the showers.

Solange doesn't know when Mickey got so strong. He hadn't been when they were kids. Marcia could usually give him a good pounding.

Solange had tended to run whenever any of the cousins looked her way when they were in a violent mood. Even when they'd caught her, she'd usually got away again with no more than a bruise or two. But back in the tool locker, she was pinned securely, and no amount of twisting seemed to help.

When she bit the hand covering her mouth, he laughed. His eyes glittered. "Madwoman," he said.

The pain that followed was brief. Solange tasted blood and felt it trickle down the back of her throat, but Mickey seemed absorbed in what he was doing.

Shortly after, he sat back. Manic energy had given way to his usual air of self-satisfaction. Solange drew herself into a crouch and turned away, trying to shield herself from his view. She wasn't quick enough to hide the fact that she was crying.

"It wasn't that bad, Sol," said Mickey.

Solange realizes that she's cold. The water has automatically shut off, and there's nothing left but a pink puddle around her feet. She collects her clothes and does what she can with them—if she ties her smock on the right, the damage isn't so obvious. She can mend it later.

She makes her way back to her dormitory through corridors dimmed for the night, and mostly empty. The few people she does encounter glance at her and then away, uninterested. If the floors and walls suddenly blinked out and there were nothing between them and the stars but space, they probably wouldn't notice that either. Most people never notice anything.

Five cousins sleep in the same room as Solange. Elara and Karen stand in the hallway engrossed in conversation. Hallie works night shift, and Callie is probably asleep. Levana, the new girl who moved in after Marcia moved out, is reading, judging by the light coming from her bed-place. Solange manages to avoid them all and climbs the ladder to her own bed-place, two up on the left. Sleep doesn't come.

After some time staring at the ceiling, she pushes herself out of bed, climbs down the ladder, and lets herself out into the corridor. She walks nowhere in particular. It takes up the time.

It's been two days. For the past two mornings, Solange has arrived at work early for lack of anything better to do with her nervous energy. Her head feels as if it's been in the desiccator, her arms and legs are weak, and she can barely feel her fingers. She's tested the same spot's salinity five times in a row; she's ruined a new plant with clumsy fingers;

she's almost tumbled into the nama pool. Occasionally, a speck of light dances across her field of vision.

After the first day of work, returning to her dormitory more exhausted than she's ever been, she climbed to her bed-place and lowered herself onto the mattress, grateful and expectant. But sleep didn't take, and she no longer expects anything. Instead, when she isn't working, or in the canteen trying to force down a meal of some sort of seaweed that she can't really taste, she walks. After a while, the corridors all start to look the same. She tries to hold distinguishing details in her mind—this pine has a broken lower branch; that door is painted red—only to have them slip away. At one point, she finds herself standing in front of a door, hand hovering over the button, unable to decide whether it leads to her dormitory or not. Solange is no great reader, but a word floats to the surface of her mind, familiar from old stories: lost. So that's what it means, she thinks, and wonders if people who live on worlds bigger than this ship feel like this all the time.

Mickey has been acting a bit nervous around her. Solange supposes he is wondering whether she's going to lodge a complaint against him. But that seems like a lot of work. She can't prove anything, and if she could, Uncle Matt is her boss and not likely to thank her for venting his chance of grandchildren into space. Anyway, what's in it for Solange? She just wants to get some sleep.

Still, she hasn't discussed this with Mickey—he hasn't asked, for one thing—and for the past day and a half he's leapt up like he's suddenly remembered an urgent errand if he found himself so much as working the same pool as Solange. So she's slightly puzzled when she looks up from reeling in a line of mature eucheuma to see Mickey on a catwalk not five meters from her, and looking in her direction.

"Sol," he says, with an impatient edge to his voice, as if Solange has failed to respond the first three times he's said her name. "You should get that looked at."

"What?" says Solange.

With a few quick strides, the catwalk ringing under his feet, Mickey covers the distance between himself and Solange. He grabs her left hand and stretches out her arm, underside up. Then he drops it, quickly. The line she's been hauling on has cut deeply into the flesh just below her elbow, and her forearm and both hands are bloodied. The far side of the line bleeds into the water for a good meter and a half. "Oh," says Solange. She hadn't noticed.

Mickey takes a step backward and holds the hand that touched

Solange's away from his body awkwardly, as if it doesn't belong to him. "Shit, Sol," he says.

After some seconds, he says, "I'll walk you to the hospital." This decision seems to cheer him up immediately. With brisk authority, he takes her by the elbow—the uninjured elbow—and steers her toward the supervisor on duty. Solange can't recall her name, but she's struck by the woman's resemblance to her cousin Elara, who sleeps one bedplace down from Solange. She shakes her head to clear it of the sudden frightening conviction that they are, in fact, the same person.

"I'm taking Sol to the hospital," says Mickey, displaying her injury. "I think she's in shock."

Elara—no, space it, not Elara—winces and flicks her eyes slightly to one side. "Ouch," she says. "I hope that doesn't feel as bad as it looks."

"I don't think she can really hear you," says Mickey.

Solange can hear fine, although there are odd echoes, as if the supervisor is speaking through a metal tube, from a long way off. Still, an excuse not to talk to somebody is an excuse not to talk to somebody. Solange lets herself be led quietly to the hospital.

The medic whom Solange eventually sees makes Mickey go away before starting on her arm. Which is nice. He gives her an anesthetic which is probably useless—she can't feel the needle pierce her skin in the first place—and sews up the cut. Then he tells her to wait in the recovery room for half an hour. "Let me know if you have any problems," he says.

I can't sleep, thinks Solange. If I don't get some sleep I think I'm going to die, I need help...

"Hm?" says the medic. His face is arranged in what is clearly meant to be a friendly expression, but Solange can see the evil underneath. Light glints oddly off of the glass and metal instruments. It must mean something. The medic is Uncle Matt in disguise, looking for an excuse to dock her pay. Solange shrugs and follows the signs to the recovery room.

The walls of the recovery room are a cheerful blue, and there are seats with padding. A knot of women sit talking near the door. A boy with a bandaged foot is playing a game on the wall console, and looks up when Solange walks in. She takes a seat in the far corner, and runs her fingers along her arm, wondering if she can tell where the stitches are by touch alone. She can, with effort. But it's hard to stay interested. Her cousin Marcia is talking to her.

Solange shakes her head. Focus, she thinks. But there really is someone talking to her, and it really is Marcia.

"I saw Mickey and he told me you were here," Marcia is saying. "It's been such a while since we've seen each other, hasn't it? You don't need to wait until you cut yourself open to visit, you know. That looks nasty. How'd it happen?"

"Rope burn," says Solange.

"You look awful," says Marcia. And she begins to talk about herself, and her important job at the freezebox. The way she goes on, you'd think no Sleepy would ever survive to make planetfall without Marcia's personal help. Never mind that Marcia will be long dead by that point. Solange doesn't care, but at least now she barely has to pretend to be listening. Withdrawing her attention is a relief, and it's unpleasant to have it snatched back.

"A coffin?" says Solange, slowly working through what Marcia has been saying. "Like Sleepies sleep in."

"No, dumbass," says Marcia, "an ornamental planter coffin. What do you think?"

"And it's sitting empty?" says Solange.

"Yes!" says Marcia. "So anyway, the temperature was rising, and we were getting ready for the transfer, and we were all so worried that we were going to lose him, and that hasn't happened, you know, for more than eighty years—"

"Can I... see it?" says Solange.

"What? The coffin?" says Marcia. "You're hardly authorized personnel."

Solange forces herself to think. And realizes, with a sort of terror, how difficult it is. "I'll pay," she says.

"I can't do it," says Marcia.

"Thirty dollars," says Solange.

This shuts Marcia up for a few seconds. It looks good on her. "Why?" she eventually says.

"Marcia, I need to. Please," says Solange.

Marcia considers. "It's really, really forbidden," she says. "Okay. Come tomorrow, before your shift starts. Thirty dollars. Up front. No discounts."

After finishing work—light stuff, meter-reading mostly, nothing that needs two fully-functional arms—Solange goes back to her dormitory. Elara is there talking with Karen. Solange doesn't want an audience; doesn't want to talk to Elara at all, really, but restlessness and urgent need soon force her to interrupt.

"Elara, I need a favor," she says.

"Yeah?" says Elara.

"Will you lend me thirty dollars till payday?" says Solange.

Elara snorts. "Pull the other one, Sol."

"No, I'm serious," says Solange. "It's important, I'll pay you back right away, I promise."

"You promised to pay me back right away when I lent you five dollars," says Elara.

"I paid you back," Solange says.

"It was nearly a year," says Elara.

"I mean it this time," says Solange. "I just—"

"No," says Elara, and turns back to her conversation with Karen. And that is that. None of the other cousins is going to feel any differently, even if any of them have thirty dollars, which seems unlikely. There is no point in hanging around here. Solange lets herself out into the corridor and walks.

It will be evening soon, but for now the corridors are still bright. Solange passes people, all of whom—cousin, co-worker, neighbor whose name she can't recall—glare at her under lowered eyelids before looking away. The faces begin to run together. The corridors curve sharply, turning in on themselves; it's no wonder Solange is lost. The bursts of light at the edges of her vision hurt her eyes.

"Sol! Hey, Sol!" says Louis. He's happy to see her. Whether he is real or a trick of her overtired brain, he has grown several centimeters since she's seen him last, all spindly arms and legs.

"Hey, kid," says Solange. "Are the parents in?"

"Yeah," he says, and one of him keys open the door of the homeplace, yelling, "Ma! Dad! Guess who's home!" Another five of him run off in different directions, making the corridor ring with the echoes.

Solange walks into the kitchen. It's full of steam. Ma pops and flickers like an image on a broken screen. "If I had known you were coming, I wouldn't have just made nama soup," she is saying.

"What have you done to your arm?" says Dad. "Doesn't Matt take care of his workers?"

"It's just a rope burn," Solange tries to say. She can't hear her own voice so she's not sure whether she's spoken or not.

"You never come and see us anymore," says Louis. "I have to eat nama soup all the time."

"You know you always fought with Sol when she lived here," says

Ma. "You still fight with her if she stays more than two hours. Maybe if you didn't she'd come home more often."

"I'm not staying for dinner," says Solange, or thinks she does. The kitchen is far too small to pace in. She bumps her elbow on the garbage chutes when she turns around.

"I don't see why flaber ankle vosh," says Dad. "Jimma hoozy lambert skiff?"

Three Louises are running in tight circles around Solange's legs. She can't put her feet down without tripping. They are poking her in the knees with something sharp. "Stop that," she says.

Solange manages to catch herself on the counter before she falls. But the gravity's stopped working; if she lets go she'll float off into space forever. She tightens her grip. "I just need thirty dollars till payday," she says.

"Of course, dear," says Ma.

Solange is sleeping, when a sudden noise floods her nostrils with panic. She leaps out of the coffin and retreats to the opposite corner of the room, as if her distance from the thing will prove she hasn't touched it. She balances defensively on the balls of her feet. It's only Marcia.

"I came to tell you that the techs will be here in five minutes," says Marcia, her eyes widening with innocent bewilderment. "What were you doing?"

Marcia could have told her how much time she had in the first place. She's come to see what Solange is up to. "I was sleeping," says Solange.

"I could see that," says Marcia.

"I was tired," says Solange.

"Tired." Marcia manages to convey with her tone that she knows exactly why Solange has spent a month's wages for half an hour in a room with a malfunctioning coffin. "I'll bet you -were."

Solange can't tell whether she's bluffing or not. Marcia has always been able to play her. But it was good to sleep.

Marcia keys the door, opening it for them, and they step out into the polished corridors of the freezebox. There is sensation in the soles of Solange's feet as she walks.

"You'd better hurry back, anyway," says Marcia. "You want to get some breakfast before your shift starts." Solange is silent. Marcia looks at her penetratingly. "You're not having breakfast, are you?" she says.

"You can't afford it, can you?"

Solange doesn't answer. They turn into a more crowded corridor. Well-scrubbed workers in blue uniforms like Marcia's go about their tasks, and Solange smoothes her stained smock unhappily. "I'll get you something from the canteen here," Marcia offers.

"I should go," says Solange.

Marcia frowns and lets the subject drop. "I'll see you then," she says. They have reached the main hospital, where Solange is perfectly inconspicuous. Marcia turns and keys the door that will let her back into the Sleepy unit. Solange keeps walking the other way.

By the time she arrives at the seaweed farm, her shift is starting. There isn't time for breakfast even if Solange could afford it, which she can't; she's resolved to stick to one meal a day until she's paid Ma and Dad back. She can feel her hunger now, though, and her exhaustion, for the first time in days. She is still on meter-reading, which is good because it requires walking around the pools. If she had to stay in one spot, she'd fall asleep for sure. As it is, she has to bite the inside of her cheek to stay awake.

None of that matters. The important thing is that when her shift is over, she can return to her bed-place, and the dark.

Solange lowers herself onto her mattress and lies back. She closes her eyes and wriggles a bit, imagining metal walls tightly around her. Then she is still. Her breathing is slow and regular. She dreams of planets.

On planets, the sky is so high that ten men, each as tall as Uncle Matt, could stand on each other's shoulders and not reach the top. Masses of water move through it and when they collide, water falls from the sky with crashing noise and flashes of electricity. Strange animals live on planets without any human tending. A person can walk on a planet for days or years without turning, and never reach a wall.

Solange is asleep. In her dream, she will only be awakened on a planet. She will smell the alien, living air, feel the alien earth beneath her feet. She will be awakened reverently by blue-clad people, also aliens, generations distant. Ma, Dad, and Louis; Elara, Marcia, Mickey, and Uncle Matt; the medics and the techs will live, grow old and die, and Solange will sleep through it all. She's different from them. They're warm, but Solange is cold.

Laika's Dream

Holly Hight

I think back to a night on a moonlit beach, the crash of breakers loud in our ears. Mara is beautiful in a floral sundress, her dark hair pulled back into a windblown braid. It's the end of the term, a time for celebration. Situated crookedly in the sand is a bottle of red wine, two glasses, half-empty, perched next to it. We are barefoot and my pants are rolled up to my knees, Mara's sundress riffling against my bare skin as we dance.

She whispers that she loves me, but we are drunk—and careless.

Two weeks later, we've created one of the most stable forms in the universe, a tiny sphere that will one day turn into our beloved Anna. On the ultrasound, Mara's pregnancy is nothing more than a pea-sized shadow. Fluid shows up black while tissue glows white. The amniotic sac isn't much larger than a bean.

"You're due in March," the doctor tells her.

When he leaves, she starts to cry.

I tell her not to worry—but, to my surprise, she looks at me and says fate has dealt her a different hand.

I think of this as it relates to quantum physics. Why didn't I see it coming? In theory, we should remember the future as we remember the past, but something in our mammalian brains prevents us from taking a peek at our fates before they blindside us. I tell myself it makes sense, that a will to live must come from not knowing what happens next.

As an astronomer, I try to answer life's most unfathomable questions. I always thought I wanted to know about such things as supersymmetries and flop transitions. Now my questions, though couched in physics, revolve around what happens to us after we die.

We are always able to go back to the beginning, watching as our blueprints unfold in a cramped darkness, as I once watched Anna's month by month. Only scientists haven't yet been able to see the universe's conception. They know down to a hundredth of a second or so what happened, that first brilliant flash of light, when everything blossomed, but the nanosecond before, the force that ignited the spark, is still man's biggest mystery.

It's no different for the giants than it is for the dwarves. Like each of us, the universe was conceived. All of nature's little spheres, and I call them little because in relative terms they are, the suns and moons, the red and blue giants, the binaries, the dwarf stars, and yes, even the black holes, have parents.

As a professor of astrophysics, I stand before a class of 22, writing my calculations on the board as I share with them the discovery I've made. I haven't told the dean or the head of my department about my hybrid, the connection I've made between the earliest occurring imperfections of genetics and the first moments of the universe, a practical application to the fractal geometry I've applied to M-theory. Everyone else will be skeptical. But I know my students. They are open-minded.

"You forgot something," one woman says, raising her hand.

Turning, I catch a glimpse of tangled blonde hair and troubled grey eyes.

"What about the energy?"

Sheila Porter. Beautiful and sick. It began last term, this degeneration, her illness. She'd been at the top of my class, one of the smartest students I'd ever taught.

She is adamant. "You forget; it thinks."

"Thank you, Sheila." I'm embarrassed for her and she knows it. My gaze bounces around the room; I am desperate for someone, anyone, to speak.

"You don't believe me, but I can prove it."

I clear my throat, the class silent.

"Energy is sentience."

"Ok."

"It's pure consciousness."

"Well, let's—"

"It's God."

"Just—"

"God is everywhere."

Snickering.

Reaching into her pocket, she pulls out a knife. "It's the answer to the horizon problem."

Adrenaline floods through me, white-hot. I stammer. "Just... don't..."

She walks toward me, the knife in her hand. I stand, paralyzed, the class watching, silent. I keep thinking someone will come to my rescue, maybe myself. But I don't move.

She stops directly in front of me, her grin crooked and her grey eyes teasing as she says one word: "Watch."

Quick as light, she shoves the steel blade into a nearby socket, the heat singing the hair on my arm. I lurch backward, a reflexive cry erupting from me. Sparks fly, the smell of ozone heavy in the air. Students leap out of their chairs. I hear the bang of overturned desks, books hitting the floor, the clatter of pencils as they go flying. Hubris. Chaos.

In the fifteen years my daughter lives, stars are born and die. Whole worlds vanish. And Anna? Like space's primordial origins, she begins as a tiny sphere, her neurons dividing at 100,000 per hour. But something else has already happened; she's been given an extra 21st chromosome and that little piece of imperfect genetic material has changed the glorious staircase scientists now call DNA into something it shouldn't be.

Seven and a half months later, she comes too soon, before I can get Mara to the hospital. She's born in the backseat of our station wagon, slippery in my new bride's hands as she lets out her first squall.

"There's something wrong with her," Mara, sweaty and delirious, gasps. "Clark, look at her..."

At the hospital, neither of us speak. The tiny baby that tiny sphere has become has already set our marriage adrift. Mara won't look at her—or at me—knowing somehow that I've caused something irrevocable and that Anna has descended upon us, unwanted. After the baby's whisked away, my wife is wheeled into the Mother-Baby Unit and put into a bed. Nurses check her vitals. Doctors sweep in and out in their white lab coats and all the while I sit in a bedside chair with my head in my hands.

"Mr. and Mrs. Namast?" one of the doctors, a balding 40-ish man, says somberly. "I have some bad news."

Mara looks up, her dark eyes red, anticipation and fear in her gaze.

"Your daughter has Down Syndrome. It occurs in approximately 1 in 800 births." He pauses delicately. "The good news is that, these days, high-functioning individuals can live relatively normal—"

"Normal?" Mara sits up straighter, her face red, fury in her brown eyes. "Did I hear you right? Were you about to say these people live normal lives?"

The doctor takes a step back.

"Does she look normal to you?"

"With all due respect, Mrs. Namast—"

"You want to trade me, then? You got a kid, right? A normal one? How about I trade you my normal kid for your normal kid?"

I jump up, a reflex, a protective father already. "Mara..." I put a hand on her arm. "It's not his fault."

She turns from the stunned doctor, her eyes imploring. "I don't want her, Clark."

Sheila's heart stops four times before paramedics establish a regular heartbeat. She is clinically dead for over two minutes and a walking miracle. Proof, I suppose. And 22 people bore witness.

I visit her in the hospital, wanting to know why. She is haggard, black circles beneath her piercing grey eyes.

"I saw what I needed to see," she says.

"What?"

"God."

I look away.

"You still don't believe me."

"You're sick."

"In this life."

I catch her gaze.

"But not in the other." She smiles.

I swallow a lump, think of Anna.

"I've never been so purely myself."

Anna's brown eyes, her silky blonde hair, and that wonderful dimpled smile run through my mind, attributes unappreciated. My anger erupts. "Do you know how selfish you are?"

"I'm just trying to hang on to who I am," she says. "That's all that matters to me now."

I think of Anna and who she was. Kind and willing to give, but nobody's friend. I realize how alike they are.

"I'll never be smart again—not in the way people want."

Though steeped in the cloud of mental illness, I see her brilliance. "You're still smart, Sheila," I say quietly. "You're still head and shoulders above every other student I've ever—"

"So what?"

I stare at her, dumbfounded.

"You think NASA's going to hire a schizophrenic?"

The words inspire an ache in me, celestial in nature, bone-deep; they are Anna's words.

"I have to think of other ways to make a difference."

"By killing yourself?"

"By proving that there's more to life than what we see."

I want to believe her—desperately. There's got to be more than this. Heartache. Uncertainty. A constant search for truth when the truth we see is never enough or too hard to face.

In the grips of severe postpartum depression a week after Anna's birth, Mara gets up at 4 a.m., slips into a robe and tiptoes into our daughter's bedroom. She peers over the crib railing at our newborn, watching as she sleeps. Tears slip from Mara's eyes as she makes a decision.

"I won't let you suffer," she whispers. For a moment, she thinks about pressing a pillow over the baby's face. It would be painless, easy. It'd look like SIDS. Down's children are prone to crib death.

But she can't bring herself. If she does anything, it has to be abstract, cleanly and comfortably out of view. There has to be some doubt. She has to believe that maybe she didn't succeed, that maybe, just maybe, her daughter might someday be living that normal, productive life the doctor spoke of. So instead, Mara wraps our daughter in a pink receiving blanket, climbs into our beat-up Honda, and drives 40 miles south. All the while, as her cold hands grip the wheel, she shakes and cries. Anna's on the front seat, squalling, hungry and wet, a typical newborn and an anathema.

It's a patchwork morning, grey clouds crumpled over the ocean, cobalt blue in the east. Out on the shore, death is waiting. Mara looks for it there. Some shape of it. A form slipping beneath the waves or around the rocky abutments she sees. Fog clings to the sand, to the water, now calm. She pulls over, closing her eyes as she picks up our newborn, and steps out into a tongue of frigid air.

She tells me all of this later, after driving home, still shaking, horrified at what she almost did—and for fifteen years, I keep her secret.

That newborn turns into a girl of fifteen who likes Star Trek and dreams of going elsewhere. She is high-functioning enough that Mara insists she go to public school. "We're not babying her," she says. "There's more to life than dancing with boys."

I almost believe her, but in the quiet of the night I hear Anna crying, and that's when I realize that there isn't more to life; it is everything to be normal.

Our true heartbreak begins one morning when Anna sits down at the breakfast table, smiling that sweet, dimpled smile and I notice something shining blue on her eyelids.

"Notice anything?" She grins.

I smile back. "You look nice."

She points at her eyes, giggles.

"Anna Grace Namast, you march into the bathroom and wash it off."

I catch Mara's gaze, anger spiking through me. "She's fifteen; she can wear a little—"

"It looks ridiculous on her."

"She looks nice."

"Everybody's going to laugh at her." Mara turns her attention back to Anna. "It's not going to change anything."

I don't remember what Anna did, whether she washed off the makeup. I do remember the look on her face, her fading smile, her brown eyes brimming with tears. And that's when I have to believe in something more, something beyond this, our everyday lives.

At birth, a child's brain has as many neurons as stars in the Milky Way. That's what I thought when I looked at Anna, that she had the whole galaxy in her. And it didn't matter that some small thing went wrong in the beginning; she was still whole, still beautiful. Still a galaxy.

As a scientist, I studied her as such. From the time of her birth, I collected information on Down Syndrome, cataloguing all of the disorder's idiosyncrasies, from the physical (the upturned corners of Anna's doe eyes and her flattened face) to the mental (her "delayed" development, though I tend to think that she simply held onto a child's spirit longer than most), to the genetic (an extra chromosome replicating itself in all of her cells). I wondered who'd caused it. I asked, was it me? Is it my fault she's so unhappy?

Even now I look for the answer doing what I do best. I use numbers and probabilities and I plug them into formulas. I know they can't extrapolate and explain a child's crippled spirit, but maybe they can tell me something.

I write on the board, frenetically, as my students look on. But the principles I apply aren't about cosmic space and time.

"Can anyone tell me what this is?" I point to the numbers, formulas upon formulas. A continuum of inner space, soul.

Silence settles as my glance darts over all of the blank faces. Then I see hers. She knows, smiles, raising her hand. "The human genome," she says.

I swallow a lump. "My daughter's."

"I know." Sheila's eyes sparkle.

"You're applying M-Theory to inner space, to genetics?" another student asks, bewildered.

I nod, my eyes still on Sheila's. "I want to know what happened in the beginning."

I wait for her to come down the stairs, holding the paper up when I see her. "What's this?"

A shadow passes over Anna's face as she pauses at the bottom. "My project."

"What project?"

"It's about what I want to do when I get older."

I gaze at her scrawled handwriting, heartsick. "Anna, this paper's about Laika."

Her smile fades. "I know."

My heart sinks as I stare at the paper about a dog in space, science's first orbital casualty, launched by the Soviets in 1957 and left to die. "What's this got to do with you?"

"I want to be like you; I want to learn about space." She waits, desperate for my approval. "That's the only way I can do it."

A lump catches thickly in my throat; her answer takes my breath away. "That's not true."

"It is true."

"Laika died, Anna."

Her gaze is unflinching. "I know."

I find the letter to NASA a day later, a 6-page offering, Anna's life laid out, her bone-deep pain, her all-encompassing despair and her fierce desire to make up for it by sacrificing herself to science. I don't read much, but I read enough to feel it in the pit of my stomach. Enough that I'll go to my deathbed with the weight of it on my shoulders.

I tear up the letter, viciously, enraged and grief-stricken, breathless as I rip at it with my teeth, the tang of lead on my tongue.

"Clark, what are you doing?"

I turn to see Mara standing in the doorway.

I burst into tears as I let the torn bits of Anna's bequest swirl to the floor. "We're losing her," is all I can manage.

Contrary to the seeming paradox of it, there is such a thing as deterministic chaos. Initial conditions exist. Add time and evolution and you get something else. What appears to be random isn't.

Scientists believe time flows in this way, in one direction. And this fact is often one of life's biggest tragedies; people lay awake at night thinking, if only…never to return to that magical half-second something might've changed an indisputable and heartbreaking truth.

"We lost her years ago," Mara answers.

"You lost her, not me," I shout, my anger spiking. "You were the one who gave up. You were the one who didn't want her."

"Clark Namast!" My wife's voice is full of tears.

Dear God, what have I done? I catch Anna's sweet face peering around the doorway. That angel face, looking at Mara, then at me, disbelieving.

I can't stop her, can't catch her as she runs away from me. Anguish has a strength all its own.

Alone in the classroom, I feel her hand on my arm and I look up to find Sheila's shining grey eyes.

"I want to help you prove your theory," she says. "I want to die again."

I slam down my book. "No way."

"I haven't forgotten what it's like."

Her words stop me, quiet me. I turn to her.

She seems small suddenly, vulnerable, like a child. "Most people forget." She smiles. "It's different than you think."

I look away, a lump in my throat.

Once again, I feel her hand. "It isn't heaven."

I feel sick. Now there is doubt.

"Help me do it."

I shove her hand away. "I can't." I catch her gaze. "I won't."

"What are you afraid of?" Her gaze has hardened. "Don't you want to know what it's really like?"

I jump up and sprint out, papers flying in my wake. I am suddenly, inexplicably, terrified of her.

That night the lights go out sixteen times. My cell phone drops four calls. Seven severe electrical surges fry my TV and DVD player despite the fact that outside, the stars shine. There are no tempests. No sunspots.

Then I get a call from Edric Lind University Hospital.

"She left a note," a doctor tells me. "And your phone number."

I find out that Sheila took fourteen of her Lithium pills, enough to send her into acute renal failure, though doctors were still able to flush her kidneys and save her life.

But I can't face her. Not this time. I turn from the doctor and walk away, realizing at last that I don't really want to know after all.

I return to my office at the University and destroy my research, shredding, deleting, feeling the paper tearing in my adrenaline-drenched hands, all the while recalling a dog lost in space.

Then I see her face in a dream. Anna's dancing brown eyes and her sweet smile. Those dimpled arms poised to embrace me. I awaken with an anguish so bone-deep it chokes me, Sheila's disheartening words flashing through my mind: It isn't heaven.

Then what is it?

She is asleep when I get there, as I stand at the foot of her hospital bed.

Then she opens her eyes, smiles. "That was me."

"Huh?"

"Sorry about your TV."

My breath catches.

"I was trying to tell you no one dies."

I cover my face; I can't let her see me cry.

"I was myself. Pure energy. Electricity. Light. Power. I was with you and I was at the farthest corner of the Universe at the same time. There is no light speed after death. No vast space to traverse." She makes a gesture. "It's all right here."

I swallow a lump, my heart pounding. "What'd you mean when you said it isn't heaven?"

"Heaven's too oversimplified. This can't be defined—or quantified. Everything's here and now. There's no time. No space. It's as though every dimension is unified." She smiles. "It's the answer to the horizon problem."

I nod, drifting. "Death's dimension..." Something I've never considered in my theories or calculations.

"And life's dimension," she adds. "There's a reason there isn't a unified theory. We've never considered the possibility that there was more than one force acting on the point of origin during the big bang."

"A conception?"

She smiles, nods. "Two Gods."

As I offered up Anna's genetic profile as proof, Sheila confirmed what I already knew; that we are all pieces of a whole, the living fractals of an astonishing Union.

I can't stop the flood of memories. The rush into the woods, Anna's footprints through the mud, my strangled voice calling her name. We find her hanging from a tree branch, one of my neckties cinched so tightly around her neck that I cannot find a grip to loosen it.

And then Mara's heart-wrenching screams: "You did this. You killed her. I hate you I hate you I hate you…" Fists on my chest, blows to my heart. Tears on my shirt. A spirit unraveling.

I close my eyes. I can think no more.

"This is your shot," I tell Sheila. "I want you to present our theories at the upcoming Astronomy Conference in Paris."

She gazes at me, puzzled. "But don't you want to—"

"This is yours. You made it happen." I smile. "After the Conference, no one will care about your illness." They are words I wish I could've told Anna.

I close my eyes as I sit at my desk. As I remember her sweet smile. I think of the random fractals that made her up, the same fractals that make up snowflakes, coastlines, and mountain ranges. I recall a night on a moonlit shore and I'm inspired. Two Gods. Maybe love existed long before space and time.

I think of a dog lost in space. A scientific breakthrough. Mankind's step forward. And an unspoken loneliness. I need to find her, to tell her what Sheila told me—though I'm sure she already knows.

ARTIFACT

Peter Atwood

The hover bucked. Davis staggered. The propulsion fans roared. He swore.

He cut power to the fans and looked out the back window of the cabin. The towlines had gone slack and the skimmer tilted, half sunk in the viscous orange lake. "Shit," he said.

Davis had been harvesting for twenty-five years. The lake was too thick for the mollusks to surface in the coldest months, and the summer winds whipped the lake's sludge into a toxic foam, so harvesters like him made the most of the fall and spring.

He pulled his hood over his brow, leaving the mask dan-gling, tugged his gloves up over his sleeves and stepped out onto the rear deck. The hover floated, its impellers turning the lake into a pale orange ring around its air cushion, opaque like pulled taffy. The sun had tugged itself above the horizon, and the air stung his cheeks and eyes.

The skimmer was a basic design: a floating bin with a grilled front. When open, the grill angled down, forming a ramp that rode the mol-lusks up into its bin as the hover pulled it across the lake. He fired up the winch. The torque motor whined as it reeled in the skimmer. Some-thing had fouled it badly.

Davis reached out with the gaff-pole to hook the skimmer. The backwash from the impellers blew up between the vessels, catching him in the face with fumes. He stepped down and ba-lanced his way around the skimmer's rim.

The bin was half-full of sludge. He stirred the orange goop with the end of the gaff. Only a few flat mollusks had been collected so far. Then he saw it: black and round, a fat object, the size of a large buoy, almost submerged. Beads of orange slipped across it, leaving its surface pristine.

An hour after turning back, he saw the headland that marked the eastern end of the span. He had closed the grill, and now the skimmer tugged behind the hover like salvage. The propulsion fans thudded in an interference rhythm.

The radio beeped. Time for the call, he thought. He grabbed the headset from its hook.

"Thanks for doing the dishes," Reeda said.

"No problem, hon." Davis had started cleaning up in the kitchen at the onset of Reeda's morning sickness. Nowadays, it seemed just as important to continue. "Did you sleep okay?" he asked.

"Oh, you know. How's the lake?"

"I'm coming back early. What are you doing?"

"Laundry's on. I'll need to run the generator."

"Could you have a look at the cold-house?" he said. He had forgotten to check it on his way out that morning. "Its cells probably need changing too."

"Sure, I could use the walk," she said.

"Great," Davis said, uncertain. It was rare for Reeda to want to do something so active these days. "I'll be back early afternoon," he told her.

"See you then." She clicked off.

He checked his heading and adjusted the fans. Ahead, a pack of skaters ran across the glistening orange swells, their long lizard tails leaving a fading mesh on the viscous surface.

Davis got his rig onto the wide flats of the shore, a safe distance from the lip of the lake, and deflated the hover's cushions. Behind it, the skimmer was pitched to one side, its back right corner had scored a groove across the packed black sand.

He yanked open the skimmer's chute and stepped back as the sludge drained. He reached in and scooped the ooze along with his gloved hand. When the bin was empty, he climbed up to get a look at the offending object. It sat tilted in a corner and looked like a fat, squashed, oversized child's top. It was unmarked but obviously manufactured.

Goddamn Mirfac, he thought. I am going to sue their corporate ass.

"I've navigated my whole life by the tower out of Bremi," Davis had told Rass the night before. "Hell, I know the shape of every headland along this shore."

"It's not about that!" Rass said. "And you know it."

Their conversation had been working toward this since the two friends had sat down with their tea. Rass sighed, and Davis followed his gaze to the sitting room where Reeda leaned over the coffee table, sketching.

"She's designing her dream home," he explained.

Rass said nothing.

Davis' eyes returned to the kitchen, to the cupboards he had painted himself and the unmatched plates draining beside the sink. "She says she still lives in a bachelor's shack."

"Losing the baby hit her hard," Rass said. He had said this often in the last months.

"I know," Davis said, impatience creeping in. "But she won't get over it obsessing over a house that'll never get built!"

Rass cleared his throat, but Reeda made no sign she had heard.

"Toby saw two fliers over the lake last week," Rass said. "They'll be moving up the span next."

The mollusks Rass and Davis harvested were sold for the blue-white ingots of antimony inside, a by-product of their digestion. Last year, the moon's biggest processor had announced plans to mine the bottom of the lake instead of buying from the harvesters. Mirfac's drones were a common sight now, surveying for antimony concentrations deposited on the lake bottom by decaying mollusks.

The harvesters in Bremi all talked about blocking the company, but no one really expected success. A lawyer had advised them to save the logs from their navigation systems. Laying claim to the patch where you harvested might let you sell your stake for an early retirement.

"Look, Rass, everyone knows my patch. Who's going to dispute it? Not anyone from here to Bremi, least of all some shoe-wearing lawyer from Mirfac."

Reeda came up to the table.

"Rass, would you like some meringues?" she offered. She went to the cupboard.

"Sure," Rass said. He looked at Davis.

"Thanks, hon," Davis said. Her short dark hair was growing out. She had always worn it long, and only now was she starting to look the way he remembered. He missed her. He missed the way she used to smile and tell him not to be so loud when he laughed. "Have a cup of tea," he said.

She had laid the plate of sweets between them and shook her head.

Davis clambered into the bin and kicked the few flat grey mollusks out of the way. He needed to shift the object to right the skimmer. He squatted with a grunt and reached underneath, laying his hands flat against its underside. A tingling sensation danced across his palms. He pulled away. Spots floated in his vision. "God in hell!"

He looked at it again. It was featureless, smooth, black, but giving no reflection. He touched it. Starbursts danced across his eyes.

He stood again. The lights in his eyes—what had first appeared as fireworks—had resolved into geometries. He lay his palm against the black surface and closed his eyes. Circles, triangles, and rectangles—retinal negatives—ordered themselves, searching according to some logic. A pattern of circles and dots hit on a childish outline of a face: a loop enclosing two bright specks and an oval mouth. The mouth flattened and turned up its corners in a smile.

Startled, he lifted his hand and looked out to the lake. A wind was coming off it, and the horizon was pale grey. A squall was building, summer storm.

He squatted again, his suit pinching behind the knees, and positioned himself, wiggling his back against the metal wall of the bin. Reeda would have warned him against what he was about to do. In one sure motion, he got both hands behind it, leaned in, and shoved.

His whole body buzzed—his hands, his chest, his chin where it pressed the top of the object—a chemical feeling. Lights danced under his eyelids. The object was far heavier than it had any right to be. With one gasp, he scraped it across the skimmer's bin. The tingling surged up his arms. The moment the skimmer righted, he let go and stepped back, panting.

He could still see the image that had written itself on his eyes. The childish face had gained detail, strings of light joining, curving, searching their way into a clear portrait of Reeda.

The wind tugged the steering as Davis drove the four-wheeled runabout across the black sand, the device stretch-cabled into the basket behind his seat. He steered past the long, squat cold-house where he stored his harvests, then turned and headed up the rocky crest that marked the limit of the flats. The runabout struggled, its servos whining until he crested. His home stood in the distance across his half-cleared rock-scrabbled lot.

The tingling reached out to him. He felt it behind his ears as if he were clenching his jaws. His skull itched under the skin. Images visited him. He fought them, like a dream he couldn't put aside. He saw the dials on his hover's dash, the lake's undulating horizon, a clattering of mollusks, their fan shapes tumbling into the cold-house's hopper. It was an inventory of his daily life, sorting the pieces. An intelligence was behind it, voracious, collecting every scrap. He saw Reeda bringing him tea. Reeda sitting in the dark when he went to bed.

He parked the runabout at the house, hurried up the back steps, and released the memory he had been refusing to think, fighting to keep it safe. It was Reeda, exhaustion and joy written in her smile, beaming up at him with Sally in her arms. The saddest and happiest memory of his life. He sealed the door behind him and called Reeda's name.

"I'm in here," she answered.

She was in Sally's room. He couldn't help it. The utility closet opened off the back hall, and he stepped to it in his boots. He slid the plastic door open. Wet clothes were clumped unattended in the washing machine.

In the baby's room, Reeda was sitting beside the empty crib.

"The laundry's not done," he said.

"I'm sorry, hon."

"I guess you didn't do the fuel cells either?"

"Please."

His body filled the doorway, his hands on either jamb. Angry. "Reeda..."

"Not here, Davis."

"Where else am I going to tell you? This is where you spend all your time."

"Please, I said." Her voice went quiet.

"I'm fucking tired..." he started, and then relented. His hands fell. "Get the laundry into the dryer. I won't do everything."

She brushed her cheek with the back of her hand. Her eyes were red.

"Look. You can have the runabout tomorrow," he said. "Go see your mom. I'm going to set the generators."

Davis scrubbed down and changed out of his work clothes. In the utility closet, he switched the cells and started the generator. The laundry sat untouched in the washer. He put on a light suit, stepped out the back door and tightened its seals. The house's filters had blown out last summer, and he hadn't got them running again yet. If the season was over now, he'd have to get to that.

The back of the house faced away from the lake, across the rocky plain. Windblown dust smudged the flat horizon. The runabout was parked where he had left it, next to a pile of prefab sections he had bought last winter for an addition he had yet to build. The black object was still cabled behind the runabout's seat.

There was time before dinner, he decided. He was going to walk out to the cold-house. He descended the steps and followed the runabout's worn tracks around the corner of the house.

When he and Reeda had been dating, she had always wanted a stroll after dinner. He had lived in town then, working one of the large harvesters that sailed from the pier. "There's not that much to see in Bremi,"he'd tell her. After you walked the main road and the lake-edge, there wasn't much else. The depot took up most of the shore, and with its cold-houses, hangers, and hovers, it was too industrial to be picturesque.

But Reeda was from Citadel and didn't care. "I like walks," she would say. "And you need to learn what I like." It was kind of a joke.

Whenever anybody asked Davis and Reeda how they met, they always described their second date. On the phone, Davis had joked that he didn't really know her yet, so at the coffee shop, she had pulled out a box of photos. Baby pictures, family holidays, photos from nursing college. "I want you to really know me," she had explained.

He had loved that in her, her fearless openness.

Whenever Davis told the story, Reeda always brought up that the picture he liked best showed her in her high-school uniform. She had played on the slide-ball team, and in the picture her arms were around two teammates in blue shorts and jerseys with large blue numbers. Reeda was number fourteen. "That's the picture he went for straight away," she would tease. "The man cannot resist a girl with a bit of leg."

At the cold-house, he checked the seals on the door and climbed to the roof to check the hopper's seals as well. The wind whipped across the flats and burned his nostrils. He climbed down, rotated the cells in the generator, set the timer, and headed back.

Gusts scoured the ground, and the mounds of cleared rock reached toward him with late afternoon shadows.

He found Reeda in the kitchen chopping apples and liver for dinner.

"What's that thing?" she asked. She scraped the peels and end bits into the compacter.

He sat at the table and stretched his feet. "On the runabout? I don't know," he said. "Some kind of Mirfac probe. Tomorrow I need to check how much it damaged the skimmer." A yellow notepad lay on the table. It showed a floor plan, the windows and doors carefully marked, the rooms labeled. One featured French windows opening to a rock garden. It was marked "Sally's Room. "

"Did you deal with the laundry?" he asked.

She banged her knife and plate in the sink.

"I'm going to call Rass," Davis said, getting up. "I'll get it out of the runabout in the morning. Best not to touch it."

The winds bit viciously. Flecks whisked off the lake, and pellets of foam stung Davis' suit. It was miserable work sorting the skimmer out. One wheel had knifed under and been dragged across the hard mud. He had to take it apart and straighten its hub to get it to roll clean.

Rass had been mystified on the phone the night before. "It's not enough their flyers are scanning the lake," his friend had said. "Now Mirfac's dropping probes to screw up our gear."

Davis had avoided mentioning the visions. They felt like a violation. Wearing gloves had made no difference when he had wrestled the probe from the back of the runabout that morning. A gallery of faces had cascaded before him—Rass, Reeda, his parents and brother, Tam from college, Sally's big hazel eyes—and then somehow, in a single voice, they asked, "You are Davis?"

"No!" He had been surprised by the hollow in his gut, as if he were about to cry. He repeated it in his mind: "No, no, no, no!"

It had seemed lighter. But that wasn't right. It was still obscenely dense, but when he fought to lift it, it had lightened just enough to get over the basket's lip. It dropped and stuck solidly in the ground. He had left it there in the corner by the back steps.

Davis tested the skimmer's wheel, returned his tools to the cold-house, parked the runabout there, and walked back to the hover against the growing wind. The lake was pushing up the flats. A thin, orange tentacle reached into the groove scratched by the skimmer. He winched the skimmer onto the hover's deck, fired up the fans, and drove it up to the cold-house where he closed it down for the season.

When he pulled up at the house in the runabout, Reeda was at the back door, staring at the probe.

"You should leave that alone," he said, unzipping his hood.

Reeda turned and smiled. "It knows me," she said. She kneeled down and rested her hand on the black convex shape.

He moved fast. "Reeda! Don't!" He grabbed her arm and pulled her away. "It's not safe."

"Davis, this can't be from Mirfac. It's something else."

"Doesn't matter. I don't want you touching it."

"It showed me Sally."

"No, Reeda. It's not real. I saw all sorts of things too."

"You don't understand. It's communicating," she said.

"It plays with your mind."

"It… it let me talk to her. It said I can visit her."

Davis held her by the shoulders. "Stop it! Stop it! Sally's gone!"

He saw her eyes measuring his cruelty.

"Come inside," he said. He slid his hands down to her wrists. "I'm going to call Rass to help get rid of it."

"No," she said. She shook her hands free.

"It's not right to obsess. It doesn't help. It hurts me to watch you suffer—"

Her whole physical self burst. "Why don't you suffer!" She slammed his chest. "It makes me hate you. You don't cry. It's not fair. You don't cry."

"Reeda…" He hated this. They were going to fight. He was going to yell. "Reeda, Reeda!" He breathed. "I cried, you know I cried. You were there. I cried—"

"I'm suffering! I'm doing it all!" Her voice broke.

It shocked him—how the anguish inside her was endless. "I am not doing this," he said. "I am not!" He pulled her hands off his chest and went up the steps.

In the morning, Davis woke to the alarm clock's intermit-tent trill. He recalled rolling over and finding Reeda's side of the bed cold. She had come in some time after dark, and he had called out to remind her to seal the doors.

He pulled a T-shirt over his shoulders and walked to the kitchen in his shorts. "Reeda?" he asked.

The room was empty. The kitchen had an outside door that faced the lake. It hung open a crack, and a track of mud led across the floor to the sitting room. "For God's sake," he said.

The baby's room was closed. "How long have you been up, hon?" he asked through the door. "Reeda?" He knocked.

He heard her voice and leaned forward, turning his ear. She was crying. No, it was more coherent than that. Talking.

"Reeda!" he called again. This pushed his patience. He wanted to pound the door open and start yelling.

At the tea maker, he found his pouch from last night and held his mug under the spout. Then he pulled some dishtowels from a bottom drawer. The house was silent except for the wind outside.

Davis got on his knees and started mopping the muddy tracks, working his way from the sitting room to the kitchen door. She needs help, he thought. She needs... he didn't know. He had held her before; he had comforted her once. Those days seemed so far away.

Maybe Rass was right, maybe she needed a doctor. It was so unreasonable—everybody wants to help Reeda because she's not coping, and what help does he get? He gets to crawl on the kitchen floor mopping up dirt. That's what he gets.

He reached the door and pushed the towels up against the metal seal. A foot-wide dent flattened the strips into which fit the door's high-density seal.

"Shit!" He stood and looked back through the kitchen. Reeda had rolled the black object around the house from the back steps to the kitchen door, which was level with the outside. She had pushed it across the threshold, through the kitchen and sitting room, and into the baby's room. He pulled the door shut and turned the seal. It wouldn't go.

He headed back to the baby's room. It must have taken her all night to get the probe in there. "Reeda!" He banged on the bedroom door. There was no answer. "Come on, Reeda." He shook the handle. She had locked it.

Davis stood outside in the growing storm. The lake was an angry orange froth, the horizon lost in swirling clouds of gas. The air tasted of burnt plastic. He hadn't bothered to suit up. Time was short.

The kitchen door was off, and he was pulling apart its outside seal, bolt by bolt. He had left Rass a message to come and help and then found a door section in the pile of prefab sheets behind the house. The wind had caught the flat aluminum, pulling his shoulder. He was going to cannibalize it to replace the kitchen door.

He attacked the next bolt, putting his whole weight on the wrench. It didn't move. He picked up the crowbar and swung his anger at the wrench handle. The bolt jerked loose.

His eyes burned and the wind stung the back of his neck. It would leave scars. He pulled on the wrench, and the nut came loose enough to finish with his fingers. He would have to put on his suit if he wanted to continue.

A pale orange foam was spreading into the house, coating the kitchen floor and pebbling the furniture. Where the froth had melted, rivulets gouged veins in the floor.

Wooziness unsteadied him. He looked at the untouched door section behind him, its ring of sharp clean nuts still in place. There was no way he was going to get this door in place before the storm suffocated them both.

He stepped through the wound in the side of his house and hurried to the closed bedroom. The air in the house was heavy, still. Fumes sank past the back of his throat.

"Reeda," he called, but didn't wait for a response. Holding his elbows, he launched his shoulder against the door. And again. The hollow plastic buckled.

Reeda was on her knees. Her shoulders slumped over the slim mattress of the crib. Resting in her curled arms was the black object. Panic choked him. He linked his hands across her chest and pulled her off, dragging her into the sitting room. He fell, sitting behind her.

He breathed. "Reeda, we have to get out. The house isn't safe."

She looked over her shoulder. "Davis? Your face!"

He stood, grabbing her wrist, and pulled her up. "Come on."

She looked back to the shape on the crib. Her weight shifted forward, and he pulled her around.

"Let me go," she said. "It knows Sally."

"Sally is dead. She died as a baby."

Her eyes snapped into focus. "No, no. It knows her older. She's talking. She drew a picture of a house and a bunny. She told me she wants a bunny."

"Stop!" Davis yelled. "She was a baby. She died in the crib. You got up to feed her. You got up and she was dead!"

"I know! I know!" She turned calm. "Davis, listen. Don't you want it to be true? It makes things from our memory. It's why it came. It told me it can bring her back. It can take us to her. We can live with her."

"You're not making sense."

"You're not listening. You don't know. You closed your-self to it."

"Of course I did! Listen to yourself."

She looked back at the crib. "Why don't you want her back? She's our baby."

He followed her look. The black shape tilted itself upright.

Davis didn't wait. He dragged Reeda through the kitchen. She stumbled against a chair, and then they were outside.

The wind tore at them. He held his collar over his mouth; his chin burned where it touched. Reeda put her sleeve to her face, burying her nose in the crook of her elbow. His eyes watered. The air was orange. At the limit of visibility, gusts curled over the crest down at the flats. The storm would have pushed the lake right up to the cold-house, but even there, in the teeth of the fury, it was their best refuge. Sealed tight.

They passed the prefab door and Davis found the tracks that led out to the cold-house.

He fell to one knee and retched violently. His throat and lungs hurt. She crouched beside him.

"Shallow breaths," he said.

"We won't make it," she said.

"We have to. We're almost… We're halfway there."

He lifted her to her feet, struggling. He stepped forward, but she stayed. "It can help us,she said. "I believe it. We can live with Sally."

Davis looked back. Near the house, the storm warped around the squat black cone, which hovered a foot above the ground. The shape moved through the gale like an equal force of nature.

Reeda saw it too. "See. It can take us away."

"No!" He grabbed her shoulders and turned her into the wind. Her hands went immediately to her face. "Reeda, I need you! You have to get to the cold-house."

She looked at him. He turned her again. "Go!" he said.

Davis turned back. The whine and scrape of the wind filled his ears. The thing moved toward him, the shape of the storm changing around it. He let the wind throw him forward. His hair was slick and burned his neck and forehead.

The dark solid slowed as he neared it.

He felt it touch his mind. "You are Davis," it said. The voice cut out the storm. Reeda's face flashed, just as he had seen it a moment before. Livid and raw, her earlobes half eaten away.

"Leave her alone!" he yelled, and opened his eyes. He didn't realize he had closed them. It floated inches before his thighs.

It tilted as if to go around. He threw himself onto it. It filled his gut; his shoulders fitted around it. He wrapped his arms under, holding desperately. His face, his hands—he could feel nothing but the dizzying vibrations.

"Leave her," he said.

Like a burst dam, he remembered it all. Taking Sally into his arms in the hospital. The sweet sour smell of her skin, the wispy hair on her pink scalp. Reeda's tears of joy. He could still feel Sally's weight in his arms, and his heart ached. "Take me," he cried.

A convulsion grabbed. Every sensation froze. Something flowed in his mind, in his head, dripping, winding like a worm, a coursing voltage.

"Reeda," he gasped. "Go!"

A shock of cold. Like a drain suddenly pulled, everything rushed out. Himself.

My wife, Reeda, will tell you I'm a complainer. She thinks I'm stuck in my ways and can't accept anything new, but my host looks after me, and, honest truth, I don't complain. I've been here… I don't know how long. The house is nice. I like this bright room with the bay window and the rock garden outside. Sally's crib is here.

There's always a meal if I'm hungry. Tonight it was Ree-da's black stew with apples. We take a stroll in the garden after dinner. They ask me to remember. The more I remember, the happier I can be. Some days she's pregnant, sometimes her hair is short. She's young tonight, wearing her uniform—number fourteen.

Reeda was good, you know. She kept playing at college. She didn't go on a scholarship, but she made the team. She was proud of it, you could tell, the way she always perked up when somebody asked her. I tell her I wish—I was going to say, I wished I could have seen her play, but I did, just like in the photo. No, that's not right, if it was in the pho-to, I never saw…

There are things I don't understand. Everything flickers if I turn my head too quickly. Why don't I ever see Sally? I hear her voice in the next room, but she's never there. Some-times I think I died, but then, there's Reeda, just the way I remember.

The other thing I don't understand. I miss her. I miss her so much.

Schrödinger's Pussy

Terra LeMay

I am you, and you are me. We haven't met, but we will, in some months. Then again in a year. More frequently after that for a stretch, though it doesn't last. Or perhaps we never meet. Or just that single time, which was (will be) both meteoric and ephemeral.

Except I remember that weekend and you don't.

I remember them all. All the moments. Even the ones you forgot, and those which never happened. They are all here, in this one place in my mind (in your mind).

Our time together was (will be) catharsis for you, but I will fall in love, like a spaniel. The world cracked open the day we met (or another day, in another place), and we became one. We have always been (will always be) one. We stand in two places at once, two times, two dimensions. We are separate. But I am in your head, in my head.

We grew up on either end of the same street. We both had grapevines growing in our yards. (Have you heard?) Yours in front by the mailbox, ours hidden like a naughty secret next to the fence out back. We only had three blocks between us, go figure, but the road stretched all the way from Antioch to San Juan, spanning a continent, spanning the ocean, spanning a million, million miles. Or only a millimeter.

It took too long for us to find each other. (Sometimes we never do. Sometimes it is too soon.) Once we had, we were inseparable. Except when we fought. Or never meet.

You always walked the difference between our houses, even though the hill between us was almost too steep to climb. I rode horseback (or drove a car) even though going to you is always downhill. Maybe it wasn't laziness. Maybe it was precognitive thought—(Photons in two places at once, two times, two different dimensions, two heads, two minds, two hearts. Twins, inseparable even apart.)—the truth already, so subtle, so soon, so obvious.

Maybe it's only common sense, the knowledge that once I'd gone downhill to find you, I'd have to return the way I'd come, and that hill was always too steep to climb.

Sometimes we met (will meet) in the middle. Halfway up the hill for you, halfway down for me. We'll sit in the gutter next to the mailbox with the ugly plastic flowers zip-tied to its flag. (I stole one of those flowers, sun-yellowed and cracking, once when you were gone. Maybe you never noticed, or maybe the flowers were bright and new when you looked at them. Maybe you stole one, too.)

Did you know, growing up, we went to the same school? I don't think you ever saw me. I watched you in the hallways. We passed each other every day at 11:25 and again in the break between Chorus and Ancient Greek Sexuality. I sat in the back of the class, three seats behind you. Sometimes, if I strained my eyes hard enough, I could just make out what you were writing on your lapscreen.

It usually wasn't notes for class. Sometimes it was porn. Sometimes it was poetry. Or a suicide note.

Once, I came to class stoned on a cocktail of weed and microdots and Corona Extra (with a twist of lime). No one seemed to notice, but you gave me a cock-eyed glance as I shuffled past your desk. I let myself trail fingertips across your papers, and you didn't think I saw you blush. Paper feels like velvet when you're stoned.

One day you will ask me to tell you what it's like to find your future (faith/destiny) in tarot cards or chemicals or the variations of oscillation in ceiling fans. Jesus loves you as much as your light fixture.

Of course, back then neither of us knew what I was seeing (would see/never saw). Neither of us understood. Those were daydreams or flights of fancy. (Nightmares.) Maybe. When everything happens at once, when everything could happen, when everything will happen, everything becomes equal. Potentials are realized. Negated. Equated.

I don't like to think on it too much. Better to dwell on the happy moments, for they are infinitely equal to the unhappy ones. Infinitely better. (Infinitely worse.)

The first time I kissed you, we were in front of our old house. The house at the bottom of the hill. (Uphill in both directions back then. Now. Tomorrow.) I remember tonguing over your braces and worrying that we might get stuck together.

We only kissed. I didn't want to share my bed with you. (Or my head with you.)

Much later (or on some other visit), you made a pallet on the floor beside me and spent the night. I dreamed I caused the apocalypse, gave birth to the antichrist, or learned to split photons with my mind (Option D: All of the above?), and you held me while I told you what I'd seen in those dreams. You said you never dreamed. I tried to open your eyes, but you couldn't put yourself in my place. I wish I could make you understand.

There's so much you don't see (won't ever see/haven't seen yet). How is it that we are the same, but so different? Sometimes we can't even speak the same language.

And yet, we talk for hours when we finally meet, filling up the space with words. You drive us to the lake (the caldera on top of the volcano/the dollar theatre double-feature/your house). Just off the edge of the lake is a small island, hardly more than a sandbar really. The water between the two shores comes halfway up my thighs. I hold my skirt up to keep it dry and you carry my shoes. Your pants are soaked through all the way to the crotch, but you don't complain. There's a wide plank-swing on the island, hanging between two trees. I thought we'd sit on it together to talk but, instead, I sit on it and you push me. We say only two words during the entire night.

"Higher?"

"No. "(Or "Yes.")

We don't kiss that night because I am so intimidated by you. You take me home when it's too dark to see the stars. And then I'm with you two years later (last week). We are making out in your basement. When we come up for air, you take me to look at your paintings, and I accidentally kick over a cup of dirty mineral spirits, ruining the rug. For many years, the stain will look like spilled blood.

Our relationship dissolved after that (except sometimes it fermented, cemented, or otherwise improved). I apologized, but it was too late. By that point, I'd already broken your lamp (knocked it over with my head when I rose up from kissing you) or backed your car into the security-light post in the parking lot at Swif-T-Mart.

"Don't drive when you're high (drunk/splitting photons/in a hypnotic trance). Just don't." I don't drink. I don't do drugs. I'm a straightedge. It's true.

That was the year I discovered how to be everything and nothing. You were the one who showed me how to alter my consciousness. You got me drunk on a bucket of frozen margaritas, then helped me outside when I couldn't stop coughing from all the pot smoke. You showed me transcendental meditation. You showed me the power of prayer.

You showed me how to be in two places at once, two times, two minds. How to be here and there.

You showed me Jesus (Krishna/Buddha/The Invisible Pink Unicorn). You tripped me and I hit my head. Or I tripped you and you hit your head. Or we were both dreaming. (I thought you said you never dreamed.) All our life (lives/past lives) passed in the flash that occurred during the moment right before our death.

One of us looked into a scrying mirror. One of us learned time travel (quantum mechanics/psychomancy/telepathy). One of us learned that photons exist in two places at once, or two times at once, and we learned to split them and share them with you, with me, with each other. One of us fell into a black hole.

Do you remember? So much happened between us in no time at all. Time did not exist for us. It's overwhelming.

I say, "I think I'm going to throw up."

"That's okay. You're in the bathtub. It'll wash down the drain."

It didn't.

"You'll see," you said, "Chemicals don't change people." (Or maybe you said, "Time travel is impossible." Or "I can control your mind with my psychic powers.")

But it wasn't true.

Chemicals changed you. We both had psychic powers. You invented a time machine, and I used it.

In school I sat beside you, one row closer to the door. You smelled like watermelon lip gloss. We were fifteen and sixteen, and I still wanted to kiss you but wasn't brave enough. Besides, you had a boyfriend who wore heavy metal T-shirts and smoked cigarettes.

The second time I kissed you (the first time) we were at Caitlín's pool party just after we'd graduated from high school (elementary school/rehab). My very first kiss with anyone, ever. You had a different boyfriend every week, back then. Someone discovered how easy it was to play Spin the Bottle in a swimming pool with a plastic two-liter bottle half-filled with water. We held our breath and kissed where no one could see us.

When I am everywhere and nowhere, I revisit that moment. I hold you under the water. My eyes were open; yours are closed. Air bubbles cling to your lashes, and you put your hand on my breast. I taste your wintergreen breath-spray and the chlorine in the pool.

I once tried to tell you about that kiss. A hundred million times I've tried to tell you about that kiss in the pool, but you never remember, and you never believe me. I don't know why I keep trying to remind you.

It's okay. I remember. I remember you rescuing me. I remember calling you to come over to my apartment and sit with me when I couldn't stand reality. How many times did you let me stay with you when I had no other place to go? (Where can you run to when you are everywhere and nowhere?)

When you moved away, I thought my heart would break forever. I never wrote you letters, but you wrote back anyway. You wrote me replies to questions I never asked you. When the Internet was invented we had secret liaisons on GEnie. You sent me poetry.

Once, you showed me my letters. I did not remember writing them. Once, I showed you a poem you sent me. You said you'd never seen it, hadn't sent it. Both were only echoes, slipping across reality.

Sometimes, we never met at all. Sometimes we meet while you are away at college. I fly out to see you. We make love in the airport, and the world ignites in apocalypse while we bring each other to orgasm in a bathroom stall. We are frantic, as if we know with certainty that we only have a few moments left together.

"I love you," I whisper. It echoes off the bathroom walls, and old women powdering their noses can hear us in the stall. I can smell their rosewater perfume even over the cleaning chemicals and urine.

"I love you more," you say. "I love you a hundred times more."

"That's impossible. I love you to infinity."

We are silent, both pondering the possibilities inherent in that statement. ("I hate you."/"Don't know you.")

You ask the impossible question, the question that begins and ends everything.

"What does that mean? What is love to the infinite power?"

"I think it's like a wave function. An uncollapsed wave function," I say, but I don't even know what that means, really. I was never any good at theoretical physics. (In another instance/timeline/universe, I don't reply.)

"You don't love me at all."

"Don't you believe in God? (Allah?/Zeus?/The Flying Spaghetti Monster?)" I say. I'm crouched with my feet up on the commode, in case airport security comes through. Men can be arrested for sharing a bathroom stall in an airport. "God is infinite. God is in everything, even a ceiling fan. God loves you." (Or maybe, I talked about physics, instead—and the practical applications of the infinite.)

"I don't believe in God. I'm an existentialist. I am God." (Or maybe, we discuss alchemy, or paradoxes.)

"Then I am you," I say, "and you are me, and I love you infinitely."

"And you do not love me at all."

I couldn't argue.

What is infinity? Surely it is more than nothing? Isn't it? I rest my cheek on your cheek. You kiss me again for the first time, and there is paper (a pill/a microchip) on your tongue (or a love note in your hand), but now it is on my tongue (in my hand).

I love you, like a puppy, and you don't love me at all. But you are me, and I am you. We love each other just enough, and not too much. We are strangers, and we are the same person. We are crazy more than we are sane. Again and again, or only once, (or never) we make the wrong choice/the right choice. When every moment in our life is singular, there is no choice.

We are Love, infinite.

BIOGRAPHIES

GLENN LEWIS GILLETTE has a storied publishing record reaching back to the early 1970s when two of his stories appeared in *Analog*. More recently, his worked has appeared in *The Edge of Propinquity*, *The Jewish Spectator*, and the anthology *Mystic Signals 2*. Mr. Gillette passed away in November, 2010, and this anthology is dedicated to his memory.

JENNIFER PELLAND lives in the Boston area with an Andy, three cats, and an impractical number of books. Her short story collection *Unwelcome Bodies* was released by Apex in 2008, and contains her Nebula-nominated story "Captive Girl." In 2011, Apex published her debut novel, *Machine*, to much acclaim. She's been published in the *Solaris Book of New Science Fiction, Volume Three*, and she has a story coming out in the debut issue of *Shock Totem* later this summer. In her so-called copious spare time, she studies belly dance in a futile attempt to be graceful before she completely loses her knees. Her web site, which includes a link to her blog, is at jenniferpelland.com.

Although **BRAD BECRAFT** currently resides near Carrollton in northern Kentucky, he is originally from Mudlick, a tiny spot on the map in the eastern part of the state. He taught high school Physics and Math before moving into the private sector, where he now works in the Science and Technology division of a Carrollton area manufacturer.

Brad shares his home in the country with his wife, Gail, their three children; Jon, Jacob and Jordan along with their assorted horses, dogs, cats, chickens, gerbils, and fish.

Brad's been writing for a number of years, but this is his first sale.

MAURICE BROADDUS is the author of the *Knights of Breton Court* series as well as the novellas *Orgy of Souls* (co-written with Wrath James White) and *Devil's Marionette*. He has been published in numerous magazines and anthologies, from *Weird Tales* to the *Dark Dreams* series to *Apex Magazine*. Visit him on the web at www.mauricebroaddus.com.

EKATERINA SEDIA resides in the Pinelands of New Jersey. Her critically acclaimed novels, *The Secret History of Moscow* and *The Alchemy of Stone* were published by Prime Books. Her next one, *The House of Discard Dreams*, is coming out in 2010. Her short stories have sold to *Analog, Baen's Universe, Dark Wisdom* and *Clarkesworld*, as well as *Haunted*

Legends and *Magic in the Mirrorstone* anthologies. Visit her online home at www.ekaterinasedia.com.

KEFFY R.M. KEHRLI lives in western Washington and is therefore typically disoriented by non-rainy days. His work has previously appeared in *Sybil's Garage* and will be appearing in *Talebones*. He attended Clarion in 2008 and can be found online at www.keffy.com.

ALETHEA KONTIS is the New York Times bestselling author of Sherrilyn Kenyon's *Dark-Hunter Companion*, as well as the *AlphaOops* series of picture books. She has done multiple collaborations with artist Janet Lee including *A is for Alice*, *The Umbrella of Fun*, and the illustrated Twitter serial *Diary of a Mad Scientist Garden Gnome*. Alethea's most recent work can be found in the Apex Publications anthologies *Harlan County Horrors* and *Dark Faith*.

For more information, visit aletheakontis.com.

PETER M. BALL is a writer from Brisbane, Australia, whose work has previously appeared in *Fantasy Magazine*, *Strange Horizons* and *Apex Magazine*. His unicorn-noir novella, Horn, was published earlier this year by Twelfth Planet Press. He can be found online at peterball.com.

ALIETTE DE BODARD lives in Paris and has been publishing stories steadily since 2006, several of which take place in the world of this story. She won the Writers of the Future competition in 2007, and is currently working on more stories and a novel. She was a 2008 nominee for the Campbell Award.

NIR YANIV is an Israeli writer, editor and musician. His first short story collection, *Ktov Ke'shed Mi'shachat (Write Like a Devil)*, came out in 2006, and he is the co-author (with Lavie Tidhar) of the short novel *The Tel Aviv Dossier*. He served as editor of the Israeli SF Society's website and later edited the magazine *Chalomot Be'aspamia*. He lives in Tel Aviv.

ROCHITA LOENEN-RUIZ is a Filipina writer living in The Netherlands. A graduate of the Clarion West Writing Workshop and recipient of the Octavia Butler Scholarship for 2009, her work has appeared in a variety of online and print publications including *Weird Tales, Fantasy Magazine, The Philippine Speculative Fiction* anthology and the upcoming *Ruin and Resolve* anthology.

Visit her online at rcloenen-ruiz.livejournal.com

JAMES LAFOND SUTTER is the Fiction Editor for Paizo Publishing, publisher of *Pathfinder* and *Planet Stories*. His short fiction has appeared in such venues as *Catastrophia* (PS Publishing), *Machine of Death*, and *Aberrant Dreams*, and his forthcoming anthology, *Before They Were Giants*, pairs the first published short stories of speculative fiction greats from Ben Bova and Larry Niven to China Miéville and William Gibson with anecdotes and instructional critiques by the authors themselves. In addition to fiction, he has published dozens of role-playing game products and over a hundred journalistic articles. He lives in a crooked house in Seattle with seven to twelve roommates, and more information on his fiction, game design and hardcore metal band can be found at www.jameslsutter.com.

GENEVIEVE VALENTINE'S fiction has appeared in *Clarkesworld*, *Strange Horizons*, *Fantasy*, *Federations*, and more. She is a columnist at Tor.com and *Fantasy Magazine*. Her first novel, *Mechanique: A Tale of the Circus Tresaulti*, was released by Prime Books in 2011.

Her appetite for bad movies is insatiable, a tragedy she tracks on her blog glvalentine.livejournal.com.

JAMES F. REILLY'S writings have appeared in several magazines, including *Horror Garage*, *Apex Digest*, *City Slab*, and *Tales of World War Z*, as well as the anthologies *Gratia Placenti*, *Undead*, *Read by Dawn Vol.1*, *Vermin*, and *Dark Futures* from Dark Quest Books. James currently lives in Massachusetts, where he divides his time between feather-dusting his collection of Mandrill skulls and participating in Boer War reenactments. James has a wife and son. Pray for them.

Reilly also runs the popular Horrorview.com website.

TOBIAS AMADON BENGELSDORF'S first story collection, *An Implausibility of Gnus*, was published in 2009 by Another New Calligraphy. His fiction has appeared in *elimae*, *Pure Francis*, and as a FeatherProof Minibook. He is the editor of *Fiction at Work*, and the *Quickies! Mascot*. He lives in Chicago.

J.M. McDERMOTT'S *Last Dragon*, his first novel, was shortlisted for a Crawford Prize, and was #6 on Amazon.com's Year's Best SF/F of 2008. It's currently available from Apex Book Publishing as an inexpensive eBook or in print. In 2012, Apex released his collection of weird fantasy and horror, *Disintegration Visions*. Visit J.M.'s blog: jmmcdermott.blogspot.com

Mary Robinette Kowal is the 2008 recipient of the Campbell Award for Best New Writer. Her short fiction has appeared in *Strange Horizons*, *Cosmos*, and *Asimov's*. Mary, a professional puppeteer and voice actor, lives in Chicago, IL with her husband Rob and eight manual typewriters. She has earned three Hugo Award-nominations.

She has performed for *LazyTown* (CBS), the Center for Puppetry Arts, Jim Henson Pictures and founded Other Hand Productions. Her design work has garnered two UNIMA-USA Citations of Excellence, the highest award an American puppeteer can achieve.

Seanan McGuire was born and largely raised in Northern California, which explains her love of rattlesnakes and deep fear of weather. (California doesn't have weather. California has climate.) Seanan is often described as a vortex of the surreal, and many of her personal anecdotes end with things like "and then we got the anti-venom" or "but it's okay, because it turned out the water wasn't all that deep."

Seanan's first novel, *Rosemary and Rue*, was published by DAW Books in 2009. The sequel, *A Local Habitation*, followed in 2010, with three more already on the way. Because this wasn't time-consuming enough, Seanan also decided to masquerade as her own evil twin, Mira Grant, author of the Newsflesh Trilogy (published by Orbit/Orbit UK). The latest of this Trilogy earned a Hugo Award-nomination.

Mark Henry traded a career in the helping profession to scar minds with his short stories and novels. He blames his crazy ideas on premature exposure to horror movies, and/or witnessing adult cocktail parties in the '70s. But surviving earthquakes, typhoons, and two volcanic eruptions might have had something to do with his nihilist fantasies. Despite being disaster prone, he somehow continues to live and breathe, residing in the oft maligned, yet not nearly as soggy as you'd think, Pacific Northwest, with his wife and four furry monsters that think they're children and have a complete and utter disregard for carpet.

When not twittering or wasting time on Facebook, Mark somehow conjures up irreverent urban fantasy comedy about zombies who swig cocktails and vampires in bullet bras who drag race. He also writes young adult fantasy about Purgatory's angsty teen ghosts under the pseudonym Daniel Marks.

Paul Jessup is a critically acclaimed writer of fantastical fiction. He's been published in many magazines, both offline and on, with two books published in 2009 (short novel *Open Your Eyes* and the short story collection *Glass Coffin Girls*) and a third to come out in 2010 (the illustrated book *Werewolves*). You can contact Paul Jessup via email at paul.jessup@gmail.com

JERRY GORDON is leading at least one life too many. As a full-time author, grad student, web programmer, and editor, he lacks the time to write a witty bio, but assures you that if you keep drinking, he'll get funnier. In addition to co-editing *Dark Faith* and *Last Rites*, he's published stories with *Apex Magazine, Indie Review,* and the *Midnight Diner.* He recently finished his first novel, *Severed Dreams,* and can be found blurring genre lines at www.jerrygordon.net.

HOLLY HIGHT majored in Criminology and Political Science, working in government before deciding to quit her job and write full-time. She got her start writing nonfiction in 2008 and has since sold stories to *Running Times, Competitor Northwest, Cosmos Magazine,* and *Analog.* She lives in Oregon with her husband and son.

NAOMI LIBICKI grew up in Columbus, Ohio, and moved to Israel at age 16, where she still lives with her husband, son, garden, and approximately 2000 books. She makes a mean apple strudel.

PETER ATWOOD is a writer and editor who lives and works in Ottawa, Canada, where he once grew up and to where he returned after living in Toronto, Seoul, and Cairo. He is an alumni of the Clarion Science Fiction & Fantasy Writers' Workshop, and his story "All In" (*Weird Tales,* 2008) was nominated for an Aurora (Canada's SF awards).

TERRA LeMAY was born on top of a volcano (in Hawaii) and since then has crammed a lot of unusual experiences into a relatively short number of years. She tamed a wild mustang before she turned sixteen. Before twenty-five, she traveled throughout the U.S. and to parts of Europe and Mexico. She has also held some unusual jobs, like training llamas and modeling high-heeled shoes (though not at the same time!) At her current day job she pokes holes in people for a small fee, in a tattoo studio north of Atlanta.

"Shrödinger's Pussy" is her first published short story. You can find her online at www.terralemay.com.

Jason B. Sizemore is best known as the Editor-in-Chief of Apex Publications. A small press begun in 2005 with the first issue of *Apex Science Fiction and Horror Digest*, Apex Publishing now puts out approximately twelve books per year from award-winning authors and both established and new voices in the speculative fiction genre.

As a quarterly print magazine, *Apex Digest* earned critical acclaim and positive reviews over the course of three years and twelve issues. With the move to digital in 2008, *Apex Magazine* was able to raise its author pay rates to SFWA professional level, allowing it to be declared a SFWA qualifying market in July 2009. By then, the magazine was only one small part of the Apex Publishing oeuvre. The book division of Apex allowed Sizemore to feature longer collections from rising stars within the genre such as Black Quill Award winner and Bram Stoker Award nominee Fran Friel, reader favorite Lavie Tidhar, and multiple Hugo Award nominee Michael A. Burstein. A series of novellas and anthologies from Apex have also earned critical and fan acclaim, including a recent *Publisher's Weekly* starred review for Gene O'Neill's *Taste of the Tenderloin.*

In 2011, Sizemore earned his first Hugo Award-nomination for co-editing Apex Magazine with Catherynne M. Valente and Lynne M. Thomas.

Acknowledgments

Jason would like to thank the following people for all the hard work and dedication that make such a thing as *The Book of Apex* possible: Deb Taber, Jennifer Brozek, Mari Adkins, Catherynne M. Valente, Ferrett Steinmetz, George Galuschak, Patrick Tomlinson, Zakarya Anwar, Lillian Cohen-Moore, Sarah Olson, Laura Jones, Justin Stewart, Tommy Delk, Katherine Khorey, Deanna Knippling, Sarah Peduzzi, Samantha Hendrix, Lynn M. Thomas, and Maggie Jamison.

"These voices
deserved to
be heard."
Frederik Pohl

Featuring
S.P. Somtow
Zoran Živković
Mélanie Fazi
Kaaron Warren
Jamil Nasir
Aliette de Bodard
Jetse de Vries
Anil Menon
and others

NEW FROM APEX PUBLICATIONS
The Apex Book of World SF
edited by Lavie Tidhar

"This literary window into the international world of
imaginative fiction, the first in a new series,
is sure to appeal to adventurous sf fans and readers
of fiction in translation"
Library Journal, August 2009

ISBN: 978-0982159637
APEXBOOKCOMPANY.COM